I0831369

THROUGH THE NIGHT

Tales of Shades and Shadows

THROUGH THE NIGHT

Tales of Shades and Shadows

MRS G. LINNÆUS BANKS

Edited and with an introduction by

Gina R. Collia

Published by Nezu Press
Queensgate House,
48 Queen Street,
Exeter, Devon,
EX4 3SR,
United Kingdom.

This edition published 2023

Through the Night: Tales of Shades and Shadows first published by Abel Heywood & Son (Manchester) and Simkin, Marshall & Co. (London) 1882.

ISBN-13: 978-1-7393921-3-0

Due to the historical nature of the text, some language used within this collection of short stories has the potential to cause offence to the modern reader. However, in the interest of preserving the original text, it has not been altered. The punctuation and spelling of the original have been maintained, and the original formatting has been used wherever possible. Only very minor publisher errors in the original text have been corrected.

Footnotes contained within this volume have been compiled by the editor, Gina R. Collia, aside from the small number marked with an asterisk, which were made by Mrs Banks in the first edition.

CONTENTS

Mrs G. Linnæus Banks
The Lancashire Antiquarian
by Gina R. Collia

Isabella Varley was born 'in a thirteen-weeks' frost' at 10 Oldham Street, in the middle of Manchester, on 25 March 1821,[1] the daughter of James and Amelia Varley (née Daniels). She was the oldest of five children: John Daniels Varley was born in 1823, Elizabeth Ann in 1828, James Edward in 1831, and Frederick Elihu in 1836. Her paternal grandfather, James Varley, was a chemist and the discoverer of bleaching by chloride of lime.[2] He was present at the storming of the Bastille, 'spoke fourteen languages, and had travelled all over Europe on foot at the time when such an undertaking was adventurous.'[3] Isabella's father, also a chemist, operated as a drysalter until, due to ill-health, his business ran into trouble, at which point the house in Oldham Street was converted into a one-windowed shop to enable Mrs Varley to open a haberdashery.[4]

Isabella's parents were quite well-known watercolourists and theatre people, and they had a wide circle of creative friends, including writers, poets, actors and artists, to whom Isabella was introduced at a young age. She was a naturally inquisitive child, quick to learn, always questioning, always observant, and her parents were keen that she should receive a good education. They were also politically active and encouraged their children to take an interest in political and public affairs. Isabella grew up in a nurturing environment, encouraged to take an interest in the world around her and free from the constraints usually put upon young girls at the time to restrict their interests to those considered suitable to the fairer sex.

Young Isabella was called a 'chatterbox' and 'Miss Inquisitive',[5] traits which served her well in later life; 'I owe to my habits of free speech and observation much of the material out of which my novels have been constructed'.[6] Being a delicate child, she spent much time indoors, usually reading by the fire; when she was not 'boring her eyes out' reading, she questioned her Aunt Jane, who was twenty years her mother's senior, 'about the doings, and dresses, and manners of people in her young days', and 'was carried back far into the last century.'[7]

Isabella's early schooling took place at a small but reputable establishment run by Miss Hannah Spray at 55 Dale Street, not far from her home on Oldham Street, 'three doors from the "Haunch of Venison".'[8] It was during her time at Miss Spray's academy that she began designing fancywork;[9] she was an accomplished needlewoman and knitter and produced original patterns every month for the next forty-five years.[10] She was also a born antiquarian and began to hoard relics of all varieties before she was eight years old. Over the years, she accumulated a large store of relics, including 'tesselæ, scraps from coffins and tombs from Thebes or St. Helena, from the garments of Wyclif or Queen Victoria'.[11] She possessed an excellent collection of shells, some rare, kept 'according to classes and fully named'.[12] And, much later in life, she exhibited her collection of tiles and other relics from the 1849 John Richard Walbran excavations at Fountains Abbey, North Yorkshire, to the Lancashire and Cheshire Antiquarian Society on 10 April 1896.[13]

In 1833, when Isabella was twelve years old, the Varleys left Oldham Street and moved to 9 Stanley Street, Cheetham.[14] Around the same time, Isabella moved from Miss Spray's school to that of Rev. John Wheeldon in George Street, where she finished her formal education, which had been 'largely supplemented by home influence, a good library and the intelligent literary, theatrical and artistic friends who thronged her father's house.'[15] She was already writing short stories and composing poetry at that time, the former for the enjoyment of her siblings, and her first published work, the poem 'The Dying Girl to Her Mother', appeared in the *Manchester Guardian* on 12 April 1837, when she was only sixteen years old. One year later, at the age of seventeen, she took over an established 'school for young ladies in Stanley Street, Cheetham, Manchester,'[16] which she ran for the next eight years.

Her mind always active, Isabella continued to educate herself. She joined the Mechanics Institute in Cooper Street,[17] and with membership she gained access to a library of six thousand books, industrial exhibitions and regular, high quality lectures. She also continued to take an active interest in politics and the world around her; she joined the Anti-Corn Law League in 1842, which held the first anti-corn law bazaar in Manchester in the February of that year, raising almost £10,000.[18] She was a skilled researcher and a talented teacher, and by the time her father died, in 1842, Isabella, then twenty-one years of age, was an established and successful school mistress.

On 5 October 1843, Charles Dickens, a champion of education, gave a speech at a fundraising soirée at the Manchester Athenæum, an institution founded in 1835 to provide a place of education and recreation for the working class men and women of the town. It was a cause close to Isabella's heart, and she and her sister were present. Looking back on the occasion, she wrote in the *Manchester City News* in 1896:[19]

> '… my sister and I waited for the appearance of my brother to escort us home (when) Charles Dickens, leaning on the arms of someone else, came down the big empty room, brushing the skirts of our limp dresses as he passed—I think I can see him

now, his long, light hair… At that time I thought it much even to have seen him so closely, little dreaming that I should ever be introduced or have occasion to correspond with the author of *The Christmas Carol*.'

The following year, Isabella's first collection of poetry was published; *Ivy Leaves: A collection of Poems* was issued by Simpkin, Marshall & Co. in December 1844 and was sold by Mrs Varley from the family shop in Market Street. Following the collection's publication Isabella gained 'quite a local reputation'.[20] However, the *Dublin Evening Post* wrote, 'many passages in her book are indicative of good sense. She would best succeed, we think, in the moral essay. Verse requires a force and finish, in which she is not yet proficient.'[21]

Isabella's teaching career came to an end following her marriage to George Linnæus Banks at the Collegiate Church, Manchester, on 27 December 1846. George Banks was born in Birmingham on 2 March 1921,[22] the son of John and Sarah Banks. His father was a seedsman and florist; he was also a devout Methodist who disapproved of any books that were not religious—he once threw a copy of *Robinson Crusoe*, that his son had borrowed, into the fire.[23] While still a young boy, George had been sent to work for an engraver, but his eyesight, which had been damaged at a young age, made him unsuitable for the work. Next, he had been sent to work for a modeller, and he worked on some of the capitals in Birmingham Town Hall, but his health was affected and he had to quit that job too. He was then apprenticed to a cabinet maker, but his master's failure put an end to his career. Finally, having shown some promise as a writer from a young age, he turned his attention to writing for newspapers and magazines.

Whilst Isabella's days as a schoolmistress were at an end, her days as a writer and poet were not. In the summer of 1847, *The*

Lace Knitter's Intelligible Guide was published as a shilling book by Hutton & Co., this time issued from the pen of Mrs. G. Linnæus Banks, the name she went by for all but her poetry following her marriage. The book received positive reviews; the designs in the book were considered pretty, with the instructions for making them 'clearly pointed out by the painstaking authoress.'[24]

Immediately following their marriage, Isabella and her husband set up home in St. Thomas's Place, and less than a year later, on 3 October 1847, their first children, twins Linnæus Nelson and Elihu Lover, were born.[25] Sadly, Linnæaus died at the beginning of the following year.[26] A short while later, little more than a year after her marriage and in a state of mourning, Isabella moved to Harrogate, where George edited the *Harrogate Advertiser* until 1852; she left Manchester—her family and friends and everything she knew and loved—for good, returning only rarely during the next five decades, and then only for brief visits. It was the first of many upheavals, as she was required to relocate each time George moved on to a new newspaper; as the *Manchester Courier* commented in 1887:

> '… he sowed seeds here and there, removed from sphere to sphere, as it were, in the intellectual life, seeking distinction in many paths, and was altogether too restless and too impatient for results to become specially identified with a practical success in literature.' [27]

They had been in Harrogate only a short while when, in January 1849, the second of their twins died; he was just fifteen months old.[28] The following year, the couple's first daughter, Josephine, was born on 17 Jul 1850.[29] Another move, this time to Birmingham, followed in 1851, and a second daughter, Frederica, joined the little family the following year on 5 May 1852.[30] By then, George was the editor for the *Birmingham Mercury*, and the family had moved to his mother's house at 3 Vaughton Terrace, Aston. The following year, little Josephine died,[31] and by the summer of 1854 Frederica was also dead.[32] In deep mourning, and heavily pregnant with her third son, Isabella was once again required to pack up the family's belongings and relocate, this time to Ireland.

George Banks was appointed editor of the *Dublin Daily Express* in the summer of 1854, and his family remained in Ireland for four years, living at 1 Whitehall-terrace, South Circular Road, Dublin.[33] The couple's third son, Arthur Caxton, was born not long after their arrival, and two years later, on 16 sep 1856, George Collingwood was born.[34] Throughout the early years of her marriage, Isabella continued writing and contributed to various journals, but her time was spent, for the most part, taking care of her family; she 'stitched, taught, contrived, cooked and led the hard-working, self-denying life in which all aspirations of literary success are stifled at the call of duty by so many wives and mothers who might, under other circumstances, have gained fame and money.'[35]

In 1858, George became the editor of the *Durham Chronicle*. and the family moved again, this time to the Grey Tower on North Road, Durham, which had a reputation for being haunted. Less than a year later, at the beginning of 1859, the couple's third daughter, Agnes Josepha, was born,[36] their son Arthur died,[37] and the family was on the move again. In 1860, after a very brief period at the *Brighton Excursionist*,[38] George took on the role of editor at the *Sussex Mercury*, a position which lasted less than a year. Then, in 1861, the family moved yet again, this time to 16 Adelaide square, in New Windsor, Berkshire,[39] where, in the summer of that year, their daughter Esther Isabella was born.[40]

Without wishing to indulge in too much conjecture, the obvious question arises: why did George Linnæus Banks flit about from one job to another, never staying in one place for very long and forcing his wife, often in a state of mourning, to pack up and move on at the drop of a hat? There are a few clues scattered about here and there. There is no doubting the fact that he was a hard-working man, but according to the Scottish poet and novelist Isabella Fyvie Mayo, George Banks 'had the spark of genius' but 'lacked every high quality that [Isabella] possessed.'[41] He had a marvellous ability to win confidences, but used this talent to persuade admirers to lend him money. And it appears that monies once handed over to him were difficult to recover; George was involved in a court case in 1861 in which one of the witnesses, in response to a question, replied, 'I thought you knew enough of Bankes [sic] not to lend him money.'[42] Isabella, each time she discovered that her husband was in debt again, felt it was her duty to 'discharge his obligations and save the innocent from suffering by him'.[43] Perhaps for George the constant flitting was less about seeking new intellectual challenges and more about outrunning his creditors.

In January 1861, George founded the *Windsor Royal Standard* and hired Isabella's youngest brother, Frederick Elihu Varley, as a reporter, the engagement terminable on three months' notice. On 4 February, Messrs Sullivan and Terrell joined the partnership and, shortly after that, expelled George and sacked Frederick without paying the latter his quarter's salary in lieu of notice. Varley sued, and George was back in court, along with Sullivan and Terrell; Varley won and was awarded £19 10s and costs.[44] A few months later, in February 1862, George, Sullivan and Terrell were back before a judge again, this time in an action for libel.[45] Ultimately, 'the great pecuniary loss experienced in connection with that paper went a long way to hinder his subsequent efforts.'[46] He later founded the financial paper *The Exchange*, and that also left him 'a heavy loser'.[47]

There was, for obvious reasons, a change in the fortunes of the Banks family during the following years, by which time, having moved to London, they were living at 33 Cloudesley Square, Islington.[48] Though George was still active—he was ever a busy man—he and his family were suffering the financial consequences of his erratic career as a newspaper editor. After years of focusing on her role as wife and mother, and always putting her husband's career first, Isabella returned to writing; though, 'it was rather because her circumstances compelled her to try to help find food and education for her brood than because she desired literary position.'[48] Of a delicate disposition since childhood, she was plagued by ill health 'of an almost incessant character', and that, coupled with the pain and sorrow associated with losing five of her eight children, 'had worn on her spirits, but left a deep residuum of feeling and thought on which to draw for her writings.'[49]

In June 1865, *Daisies in the Grass: A Collection of Songs and Poems*, written jointly by Isabella and her husband, was published by Robert Hardwicke, and it was generally well received. The most important publication of that year, however, was Isabella's *God's Providence House: A Story of 1791*, a 'wonderfully readable' story of 'love, trial, scheming, and superstition' set in Chester, published by Richard Bentley.[50] The novel established Isabella's reputation; 'her first novel was a success beyond the usual fate of first novels, and her vocation for the future was found.'[51] The *Sunday Times* wrote, 'This title is entitled to rank as one of the most genuinely interesting and meritorious novels of the season. Mrs. Banks has great power of framing characters that are at once interesting and true to nature.'[52]

God's Providence House was followed by *Stung to the Quick: A North Country Story*, published by Charles W. Wood in 1867. Set in

Durham and County Durham, the novel was described as 'a very superior one of the sensational class,'[53] in which Isabella exhibited a 'remarkable aptitude in dealing with the manners and idioms of a people, the outlines of whose character are rugged, and broad, and deep.'[54] *The London Daily Chronicle* wrote, 'We commend the work heartily, as one destined to hold its place in the literature of the day, and add fresh laurels to the brow of the authoress.'[55]

Whilst Isabella contributed short stories to various periodicals during the following few years, her next novel wasn't published until 1875; *The Manchester Man* appeared in eleven instalments, with illustrations by Charles Green, in *Cassell's Family Magazine* before being published in three volumes by Hurst & Blackett in 1876. A rags to riches tale, it tells the story of the hero Jabez Clegg's rise from foundling babe to wealthy businessman, set against a chronicle of Manchester's great transformation, written 'with much graphic power',[56] from the time of the Napoleonic Wars to the period of the Great Reform Act of 1832. It was, and still is, 'the most memorable and most popular work of her life'.[57]

The next few years saw the publication of the novels *Glory: A Wiltshire Story* (1877), *Caleb Booth's Clerk: A Lancashire Story* (1778), and *Wooers and Winners*: *Or, Under the Scars, A Yorkshire Story* (1880), all published by Hurst & Blackett. A short novel, *Geoffrey Olivant's Folly*, was issued by J. W. Allingham in 1877, and *Ripples and Breakers*, a volume of poetry, was published the following year by C. Kegan Paul & Co. Also, from 1878 Isabella became a regular contributor to the *Manchester City News*. From 1880 she contributed a number of stories to *The Girl's Own Paper*, and her work appeared in many other leading journals of the day, including *All the Year Round*, *The Argosy*, *Cassell's Family Magazine*, and *Belgravia*.

In March 1879, Isabella contributed to a pamphlet on women's suffrage, of which she was a supporter. In it she wrote, 'I owe a shipwrecked brother's life to the exercise of the female right to vote amongst a tribe of cannibals in the Oriental archipelago, and I have, therefore, reason to uphold the principle.'[58] The brother referred to was James Edward Varley, whose story Isabella recounted in her novel *Caleb Booth's Clerk*. In the novel, she renamed her brother Fred, but beyond that minor alteration the story of the shipwreck, including the 'Australasian cannibal women' who 'in advance of civilisation' had the vote,[59] is apparently 'true in all its peculiar details'.[60]

By the beginning of 1880, Isabella had moved home three more times within London. While writing *Glory*, she lived at 40 Frances Terrace, Victoria Park, and 82 Greenwood Road, Dalston.[61] In January 1880, she and her family were living at 'Ivy Bank', Navarino Road, Dalston. By that time, she had been the primary wage earner for several years, her health was failing, and George, who had cancer, was drinking heavily and repeatedly threatening to kill himself, having attempted to do so one time already;[62] 'Infinite trial and endurance were faced and borne by this cultured and admirable woman, whose frame was as fragile as her heart was dauntless.'[63]

In January 1881, George underwent two painful surgeries. Four months later, on 3 May, he died;[64] there is little doubt that, at the end of his life, 'mental infirmity was mingled with moral aberrations.'[65] But despite all that had happened, all that she had suffered, Isabella's 'cheerfulness remained indomitable, and her industry unflagging.'[66] And, as her friend Isabella Fyvie Mayo wrote, 'there is reason to believe that she thoroughly enjoyed all her labours.'[67]

During the year prior to George's death, Isabella had been trying to persuade various publishers to issue cheap editions of her previously published books. From August 1881, a series of cheap, uniform volumes was issued by Abel Heywood & Son, Manchester, and Simpkin, Marshall & Co., London, beginning with *The Manchester Man* and including all of Isabella's novels that had been published to that date, aside from *God's Providence House.* Works previously unpublished in book form were added to the series in 1882, including the novel *More than Coronets* and two collections of short stories, *Through the Night: Tales of Shades and Shadows* and *The Watchmaker's Daughter, and Other Tales*; a third collection of tales, *Sybilla, and Other Stories,* was added in 1885.

Almost from the outset, Isabella added an appendix to her books to 'indicate the source of [her] inspiration' in writing them.[68] She was known for her historical accuracy and meticulous attention to detail, and she amassed a large library of 'books on antiquarian subjects, old maps (a particular hobby of hers), dialect works, and books dealing with places, and especially with their history, legends, folk-lore and traditions'.[69] As a reporter for the *Yorkshire Gazette* wrote in 1895, 'her thoroughness in collecting and narrating an infinite number of the details which go to make up provincial life give her works a unique value to the historian and the student'.[70] Her appendix to *Through the Night* provided invaluable information which, aside from being fascinating, made researching her stories and writing the following possible. I warn you, though, that a number of details from the stories are included in the next several paragraphs, so you might want to put off reading them until you have read the tales themselves.

Through the Night contains fourteen tales, the first of which is 'A World Between'. The story concerns Charles Beckton, whose father has just died, leaving him master of Tarnbeck, the guardian of his half-sister, Amy, and the keeper of her inheritance. The latter is kept within the family's secret depository, known as the 'Palmer's Scrip', and when the contents of the scrip go missing, a supernatural event uncovers their whereabouts. Unfortunately, too little information is given in the appendix to find out anything more about the origins of this tale.

'The Pride of the Corbyns' is likely to cause some discomfort to modern readers. Though, as Isabella explains, such a thing 'can scarcely be understood at this time, and in England', the cause of the haunting, the placement of multiracial dead in a family vault, was a matter of concern to those living in Barbados during the first half of the nineteenth century. The story is based on the legend of the Chase Vault and events which took place there from 1912 to 1920. Between 1807 and 1812, three coffins were placed within the vault. When it was opened again, at the end of 1812, those three coffins were found to have been tossed about the place. From that time on, every time the vault was opened to take a new inhabitant, the existing ones were found to have been flung about. Eventually the vault was sealed, as nobody dared deposit another body inside it.[71]

In 'Wraith-Haunted', Mrs Carson is recalled from Bristol to her family home in Manchester by a visitation from her mother's ghost. From that time forward, she is cursed with visions of the dead just prior to their dying. Mrs Carson certainly was a real person, and the story of her husband's death and burial within a week of their marriage is also true. Mary Ann Daniels, Isabella's maternal aunt, married William Carson on 22 January 1816, and he was buried just seven days later, at the age of thirty, on 29 January.[72]

'The Piper's Ghost' is the tale of Dugald Macpherson, a Jacobite piper who follows his chieftain into battle in the name of Charles Edward Stuart and is wounded in a skirmish near Penrith. He seeks shelter in the home of the kindly farmer Joe Hodgson and his young daughter Hannah, but he is forced to flee for his life on a snowy

Christmas Eve and ends up almost drowning in the river at Elvet Bridge, Durham. This story is based on a legend attached to the Old Gaol on Elvet Bridge. It was said to be haunted by the unsettled spirit of an old piper who was washed down the river during a flood. Once recovered from almost drowning, he became an inmate of the gaol, dying there a few years later. As the story goes, after his death the sound of bagpipes being played could still be heard by anyone crossing Elvet Bridge at midnight.[73]

In 'St. Cuthbert's Cup', stern, dark-browed William De Turp, 'a man soured by disappointments', makes a pact with the Devil to gain power and riches. The vessel given to De Turp to drink from is described as being made of:

> '...greenish blue glass, curiously constructed and ornamented. It narrowed bottle-wise at the neck, but round it ranged two rows of trumped-shaped tubes, their slender tips closed, their wider ends opening like gaping mouths within.'

The cup or vase referred to is in fact the Castle Eden Claw Beaker, an early Anglo-Saxon glass claw beaker found at Castle Eden, County Durham.[74] It was dug up during work to a hedge in 1775, and when discovered 'the mouth of the vase was applied to the skull of a human figure'; it was full of earth and when emptied 'appeared to have a subtle aromatic smell.'[75] William de Turp (fl . 1150-90) did exist; he donated land to the church of Durham.[76] And the Hell-Kettles referred to in the story are deep pools, the result of a 'convulsion of the earth' in 1178-79.[77] They are located in Darlington; there are two in existence now, the third was filled in during the 1950s.

'In the south transept of the large and venerable church of Houghton-le-Spring may be seen the mutilated effigy of an armed knight'; so begins 'The Fairies Cradle', before going on to explain how the effigy came to be there and how the wicked Sir John-le-

Spring was murdered in the arms of his mistress in the bower at Houghton-le-Spring. Sir John did exist, and he was murdered in 1312 by Robert Lascelles of Yorkshire; he was in the arms of his mistress at the time.[78] There is a stone monument to Sir John in Houghton Church, and his armour was indeed torn down and carried off by Ralph, lord Neville, who was excommunicated by Bishop Kellaw for doing so.[79] It is said that unearthly footsteps are heard around the monument on the anniversary of Sir John's assassination.[80] The 'Fairies' Cradle' of the story, a tumulus 'consisting of field stones gathered together', is located 'in a field on the right-hand side of the road from Heppleton to Hetton'; it was said that fairies led their moonlight circles atop it.[81]

In 'My Will', Gilbert Leslie, being extremely ill and under the impression that the end may well be nigh, has his will drawn up by his old friend Matthew Sharp. He is then plagued by visions in which he is warned to 'Look to your will!'.

> 'I seemed to stand in front of our red-brick house in Cheyne Walk, yet not I myself, in the flesh, but in the spirit; and, gazing on it, beheld Anna and Bertie, both in deep mourning, at an upper window. As I looked I saw the dark building shudder, totter, and fall with a terrible crash, burying wife and son both in the ruins, despite my own frantic efforts to save them.'

He receives no peace until he does as he is told. There is too little information given by Isabella in the appendix to uncover any further details about this story.

'Judgment Deferred' is one of the best stories in the collection. In it, the Begum is found drifting at sea with all on board dead, save one man: Alfred Stanhope. According to Stanhope, he is heir to a fortune and was sailing to England from India with his private secretary, Oliver Craven, to claim that fortune when the crew of the ship mutinied and murdered all who stood against them, including Stanhope's dog, Selim. But Stanhope is not all he claims to be, and all bad deeds must be punished eventually. As Isabella states in the appendix, this tale is 'wholly imaginative', but with reference to hydrophobia—the historic name for rabies—the incubation period can indeed last for a year, and madness doesn't occur until the late stages of the disease.

'A Dour Weird' tells the sad story of Susan Gray, whose 'dour weird' (hard fate) is foreseen by the renowned Scottish fortune-teller Margery Grant. Susan is thrown out of her family home when she chooses to marry a Scottish soldier, loses husband and sons at the Battle of Carunna during the Peninsular War, then ends up penniless in her old age, 'left to drift, one of England's many martyrs to martial glory.' The story is based on that of 'Auld Susan' in 'The Soldier's Widow', which appeared in *Chambers's Miscellany* in 1845.[82] In real life, Margery Grant was not a part of Susan's tale, but she was a real person and a renowned Scottish witch. She died on 23 February 1866 at Mill of Ribrae, in the parish of Forglen, at the age of sixty nine, and a number of newspapers carried her obituary.[83] She believed that she was sometimes 'changed by evil-disposed persons into a pony or a hare, and rode for great distances, or [was] hunted by dogs, as the case might be."[84]

In 'The White Woman of Slaith', a fierce storm drives a ship to its doom against the Neb at Slaith, lighting flashes revealing 'the white figure of a woman lashed to the broken mainmast, and hapless sailors clinging to the bowsprit and rigging.' The inhabitants of Slaith, all hoping to reap the spoils of a wreck, are eager to see every soul perish. All but Maggy Blackburn, who attempts to save the white lady when she is washed up on the beach. And for that act of kindness, she is spared the white lady's wrath. For, a year after the wreck, to the day, the inhabitants of Slaith 'beheld the shadowy form of the dead and buried woman, but tall as a ship's mast, glide over the sands, shake a threatening hand at the village, and touch the stern and sails of every foredoomed boat'.

Slaith is based on the pretty North Yorkshire fishing village of Staithes, and 'the Neb' is 'Old Nab', a tall rock formation between Staithes and Port Mulgrave. In 1767, during the first week of January, 'One third Part of the Inhabitants of Staiths [were] ruined, having lost their Boats, Cobles, Fishing Nets, and a great many their Houses and Furniture.'[85] The 'white woman' is a form of apparition common to the folklore of many different countries. In Britain, white ladies are generally seen in rural locations and are commonly associated with water.

The information given by Isabella in the appendix for the final few stories is quite general, so it has not been possible to find more detail concerning their origins. There is no entry at all for 'The Fate of the Fosbrookes' in the appendix. This must surely have been an error on the part of the publisher; Isabella was too fastidious to omit an explanation for one of her stories from her book.

'Larry's Apprenticeship' is set in Ireland. Larry M'Cann is on his way to take a cow to market when he encounters fairies in need of a coffin; only mortals can make a fairy coffin, so they teach Larry carpentry to enable him to make one.

In 'The Fate of the Fosbrookes', Rupert Fosbrooke is meant for the army but determined to be an artist. Following an argument, in which Rupert declares 'I will *not* lay down my paint brush for a sword', his father throws him out of the house and renounces him in his will. Years later, Rupert's mother, Dame Barbara, lies dying and calls out for her lost son, but his brother, Reginald, conspires to keep him away. On Dame Barbara's deathbed she promises 'if there be treachery, let those who kept thee back answer it, for never shall a Fosbrooke die in his bed till the lost be recalled, and younger and elder join hands in love and friendship under the old roof-tree.'

In 'A New Leaf', elderly Mrs Lane has two granddaughters: obedient, mild-mannered Ruth and wilful Jessie. The latter, though engaged to another, has fallen in love with Alfred Lawrence, Squire Appleton's secretary and a thoroughly bad sort. Jessie has agreed to marry Lawrence, much against her grandmother's wishes. However, she is temporarily deterred when she sees the ghost of her dead grandmother; 'Behind her sister's chair, with her warm shawl pulled awry, her plain black satin bonnet crushed, its white lining and primly-quilled cap speckled with blood, stood her grandmother with pale face and finger up, as if she said, "Beware!"

'The Plainbury Mystery' is the final tale of the collection. The Earl of Plainbury is dead, and his wife, Lady Matilda, a gambler and a drunk, intends to get her hands on his money, regardless of the fact that it is her son, Lionel, who is named as heir to the dead earl's estate. She is aided by the mysterious Doctor Mendoza, whose 'long thin fingers terminated in long-pointed nails, like talons', and his niece, the alluring Mizpah.

Following the publication of *Through the Night*, Isabella wrote eight more novels. F. V. White & Co. published *Forbidden to Marry* (1883) and *In His Own Hand* (1887). *Miss Pringle's Pearls* was published by Hutchinson & Co. in 1890, and *From the Same Nest: A Homely Tale* was published by the Church Monthly Office in 1891. *A Rough Road: Or, How the Boy Made a Man of Himself* was published in 1892 by Blackie & Son Ltd., and in 1893 Griffith Farran & Co. published *The Slowly Grinding Mills* and *Bond Slaves: The Story of a Struggle.* Isabella's final novel, *The Bridge of Beauty: A Fiction Based on Fact*, was published in 1894 by the Sunday School Union.

By the end of the 1880s, Isabella was in very delicate health and living in far from prosperous circumstances. Those who knew and admired her felt that she should be offered a Civil List Pension, and in 1889 Mrs Arthur Stannard (who wrote under the pseudonym John Strange Winter) prepared and presented a petition, supported by many leading authors, to achieve that end. Unfortunately, the Civil List Pensions had already been decided for that year, so the petition failed, but Isabella was given a grant of £200 from the Royal Bounty Fund.[86] It was necessary to wait three years before submitting another application, so the petition was renewed again in 1892, and again no pension was forthcoming, though a grant was given. Mrs Stannard tried again in 1895; once more, the petition failed and a grant, this time of £150, was given.[87]

Isabella died at the age of seventy-six on 4 May 1897 and was buried three days later in Abney Park Cemetery in Stoke Newington.[88] In the end, her death came as a shock; she had been ill for so long, but those around her had had no reason to expect her imminent passing. By that time, her popularity amongst readers had waned, but she was much loved and sorely missed by those around her. I will leave you with the closing paragraph of one of her many obituaries, written two months after her death by her friend Isabella Fyvie Mayo.[89]

> 'Her end was as her life. So long infirm as to be much confined to her room, her actual last illness was very short. One who was present at the last days says, "I never before realised what the end of a good woman could be. He intellect was as clear as possible, and she took everything so naturally: unto the last thinking of the welfare of others, and, as she said 'Not afraid to face her work in the life beyond.' " '

Notes

1 Isabella added a handwritten note to her copy of the *Annals of Manchester* for 1821: 'I was born in Oldham Street, March 25th, Sunday, daughter of James and Amelia Varley: baptised by Joshua Brookes at the Collegiate Church, Isabella: became in due time the wife of George Linnæus Banks and the authoress of *The Manchester Man*, etc., I. B.' In the same volume, alongside the notice for the death of Joshua Brookes on 11 November 1821, Isabella wrote, 'I was born March 25th in a thirteen-weeks' frost and Joshua Brookes baptised me—little guessing that I was to be his future chronicler.' Quoted by E. L. Burney in *Mrs G. Linnæus Banks: Author of* The Manchester Man *etc.* Manchester: E. J. Morten, 1969, p. 9.

2 Charles Tennant of Glasgow claimed to have discovered chloride of lime and took out a patent, having received the information of its discovery from a disgruntled employee of James Varley. He then prosecuted Mr Varley for infringement of patent. The case went before Lord Ellenborough, Chief Justice of England, in 1802 and Mr Varley won the case, but it cost him £10,000. Isabella provided details of the case in 'Notes and Queries', *Manchester City News*, 27 October, 1883, p. 154.

3 Mrs. Fenwick Miller, 'Mrs. Linnæus Banks: The Lancashire Novelist', *The Woman's Signal*, 22 October, 1896, p. 1.

4 Ibid., p. 2.

5 Ibid.

6 Ibid.

7 Ibid.

8 Burney, op. cit., p. 24.

9 Ornamental needlework, such as embroidery.

10 Sidney Lee (editor), the 1901 Supplement to the *Dictionary of National Biography, 1885-1900*, p. 123.

11 Burney, op. cit., p. 22.

12 Miller, op. cit., p. 2.

13 Lancashire and Cheshire Antiquarian Society, *Transactions of the Lancashire and Cheshire Antiquarian Society*, Volume 14, 1897, pp. 156-7.

14 *The London Gazette for the Year 1840*, Volume 1, p.406.

15 William Andrews (editor), *North Country Poets: Poems and Biographies*, London: Simpkin, Marshall & Co., 1888, p. 1.

16 Ibid.

17 Miller, op. cit., p. 2.

18 *Who's Who* for 1897.

18 A. C. Howe, 'Anti-Corn Law League' in the *Oxford Dictionary of National Biography*, published online 24 May 2008: https://doi.org/10.1093/ref:odnb/42282

19 *Manchester City News*, 25 January, 1896. Isabella believed that this event had in fact taken place in 1845, not 1843, but she was an elderly woman looking back from 1896 at the time.

20 Miller, op. cit., p. 2.

21 *Dublin Evening Post*, 25 March 1845, p. 3.

22 *England, Select Births and Christenings, 1538-1975.*

23 Burney, op. cit., p. 74.

24 *Birmingham Journal*, 14 August 1847, p. 3.

25 *Lancashire, England, Church of England Births and Baptisms, 1813-1911*, Manchester 1840-1849.

26 *England & Wales, Civil Registration Death Index, 1837-1915.*

27 Thomas Gibbons, 'Life-Tales Retold: No. V, George Linnæus Banks', *Manchester Courier*, 7 May 1887, p. 10.

28 *North Yorkshire, England, Church of England Deaths and Burials, 1813-1995*, Giggleswick 1839-1850.

29 *Lancashire, England, Church of England Births and Baptisms, 1813-1911*, Bishop´s Transcripts, Manchester, 1850-1859.

30 *England, Select Births and Christenings, 1538-1975.*

31 *England & Wales, Civil Registration Death Index, 1837-1915.*

32 *England & Wales, Civil Registration Death Index, 1837-1915.*

33 *The Evening Freeman*, 17 September 1856, p. 4.

34 Ibid.

35 Miller, op. cit., p. 2.

36 *England & Wales, Civil Registration Birth Index, 1837-1915.*

37 *England & Wales, Civil Registration Death Index, 1837-1915.*

38 Gibbons, op. cit., p. 10.

39 *1861 England Census.*

40 *England & Wales, Civil Registration Birth Index, 1837-1915.*

41 Isabella Fyvie Mayo, 'The Late Mrs. George Linnæus Banks', *The Argosy*, July 1897, pp. 21-25.

42 *Brighton Gazette*, 21 March 1861, p. 6. In relation to the sensational cases surrounding the South Coast Steam Printing Company, owned by Alfred Hawkins. Edward Kriens, a teacher, was charged with forging a bill of exchange with intent to defraud Hawkins; Hawkins claimed that Kriens had forged his signature. At the same time, there was the connected case of George Morgan v. Alfred Hawkins in which Morgan sued Hawkins to recover the sum of £21 15s on said bill; Morgan won. Then, Dr Muir, the headmaster of a grammar school, who was involved in the other two cases, was accused of trying to bribe a witness, Henry Crowhurst, to suppress evidence. The latter was the one who made the statement in court about George and the danger of lending him money. Finally, there was the case of Kriens v. Hawkins, in which the former sued the latter for damages and was awarded £300. George received the bill in payment of a debt, and he gave evidence during the case against Edward Kriens; Isabella's brother Frederick, who was employed as a reporter at the company, also gave evidence.

43 Mayo, op. cit., p. 23.

44 *Windsor and Eton Express*, 12 October 1861, p. 4.

45 *Sheffield Independent*, 26 February 1862, p. 4. Turner v. Sullivan and others. Turner was a solicitor accused, by Elizabeth Geraldine Stokes, of sexual assault. When the case was reported in the *Windsor Royal Standard*, Turner believed the story to be libellous. George didn't contest the case,

but Sullivan and Terrell pleaded not guilty. The jury found in favour of the newspaper, but George, as a result of allowing the judgment to go by default, had to pay damages of one farthing.

46 *Manchester Courier*, 7 May 1887, p. 10.

47 Charles Henry Poole (editor), *Warwickshire Poets*. London: N. Ling & Co., 1914.

48 Burney, op. cit., p. 84.

48 Miller, op. cit., p. 2.

49 Ibid.

50 *Morning Post*, 26 July 1865, p. 2.

51 Miller, op. cit., p. 2.

52 Quoted in the *London Evening Standard*, August 1865, p. 7.

53 *York Herald*, December 1867, p. 10.

54 *London Daily Chronicle*, 21 December 1867, p. 2.

55 Ibid.

56 *Manchester Evening News*, 5 May 1897, p. 4.

57 Ibid.

58 *Sheffield Daily Telegraph*, 17 March 1879, p. 3.

59 *Caleb Booth's Clerk* (Uniform Series, 1882), p. 273.

60 Ibid., p. 295.

61 Burney, op. cit., p. 95.

62 Ibid.

63 Mayo, op. cit., p. 22.

64 *England & Wales, Civil Registration Death Index, 1837-1915*.

65 Mayo, op. cit., p. 22.

66 Ibid. p. 24.

67 Ibid.

68 See p. 422 of the current volume.

69 Miller, op. cit., p. 1.

70 *Yorkshire Gazette*, 31 August 1895, p. 3.

71 *Folk-lore: A Quarterly Review*. Volume 18, 1907, pp. 379-382

72 *Lancashire, England, Church of England Marriages and Banns, 1754-1936*

and *Manchester, England, Deaths and Burials, 1813-1866 (Cathedral).*

73 William Hone, *The Table Book of Daily Recreation and Information: Concerning Remarkable Men, Manners, Times, Seasons, Solemnities, Merry-Makings, Antiquities and Novelties, Forming a Complete History of the Year*, London: Hunt and Clarke, 1827, p. 208.

74 British Museum, item no. 1947,1009.1.

75 *Sunderland Daily Echo and Shipping Gazette*, 24 October 1947, p. 2.

76 William Fordyce, *The History and Antiquities of the County Palatine of Durham; Comprising a Condensed Account of its Natural, Civil, and Ecclesiastical History*, Vol. II. London and Edinburgh: A. Fullerton & Co., p. 366.

77 *The Monthly Chronicle of North-Country Lore and Legend*, October 1887. London: W. Scott, p. 353.

78 William Whellan & Co., *History, Topography, and Directory of the County Palatine of Durham*. London: Whittaker & Co., 1856, p. 388.

79 Ibid.

80 William Sidney Gibson, *Descriptive and Historical Notices of Some Remarkable Northumbrian Castles, Churches, and Antiquities*. London: William Pickering, 1848, p. 100.

81 Robert Surtees, *The History and Antiquities of the County Palatine of Durham*, Hartlepool Section. Sunderland: Hills and Company, p. 210.

82 *Chambers's Miscellany of Useful and Entertaining Tracts*, Volume III, issue 26, p.30-32. Edinburgh: William and Robert Chambers, 1845.

83 *Banffshire Journal*, 6 March 1866, p. 5.

84 Charles Hardwick, *Traditions, Superstitions and Folk-lore (Chiefly Lancashire and the North of England:) Their affinity to others in widely-distributed localities; Their Eastern Origin and Mythical Significance*. London: Simpkin, Marshall & Co., 1872, p. 235.

85 *Derby Mercury*, 23 January 1767, p. 2.

86 *Northern Daily Telegraph*, 25 July 1889, p. 2.

87 *Yorkshire Gazette*, 31 August 1895, p. 3.

88 *UK and Ireland, Find a Grave® Index, 1300s-Current.*

89 Mayo, op. cit., p. 25.

PREFATORY

It is the fashion now-a-days with one section of the community to decry all allusions to the supernatural as remnants of bygone superstition; another section, rushing to the opposite extreme, professes power as potent as the wand of Prospero to commune with the spirit-world, and summon the long-departed back to be heard, and seen, and felt, through the night of the dark séance; a third, and much larger proportion—in which may be included the writer—holds a midway position, admitting the possibility that disembodied spirits *may* haunt certain places and certain people, but that it is by no means an assured fact.

Science, which has driven so many a beautiful myth from our nurseries, and driven the childhood out of our children at the same time, has done much to depopulate Fairyland. The elf and the hobgoblin only linger in green nooks untrodden by the proverbial schoolmaster; and he has shaken his rod at the wraith and the banshee. It is an age of scepticism; men—aye, and women too—walk abroad and with faces unabashed avow their disbelief even in Deity. Can we wonder that the same scepticism mocks at ghosts, and all that a belief in them implies?

Is it not, therefore, an anomaly that the era of hard science and scoffing unbelief should have given so many mystic and ghost-stories to our literature?

Can all these be wholly imaginative? Nothing of the kind. Some scrap of family history, some waif of confidential communication there may have been, which crystallized into a story, vivid with life, and form, and colour, at the point of the author's pen. And not a few of these may have been given to the world by professing cynics, who laugh lightly at their own work, lest a shadow of suspicion of belief should expose them to society's ridicule.

Not so the Author of this book, who, in the course of her long life, has come in contact with so many persons both of credibility and culture who have assured her that either they or their friends have been visited by apparitions, that in spite of a rebellious will, and what is called common sense, she has been forced to the conclusion of Hamlet—

> There are more things in Heaven and earth, Horatio,
> Than are dreamed of in our philosophy;

and it is upon such personal narratives that these stories of shadows flitting through the night have been founded. She excerpts, of course, the old North-country traditions, and the fairy lore, with one or two others which are wholly fiction; and in the Appendix at the close of this volume may be found her authority, oral or otherwise, for aught which may seem incredible.

It may be objected that such shadows flit only *through the night* of superstition, but she holds a theory that disembodied spirits are around us everywhere, the messengers and ministers of Almighty God, and that it is possible He may either, in His love and wrath, for reasons inscrutable to us, permit certain eyes to be opened to behold that which is dark to others. But that such revelation is common, or that the spirits of the dead can be summoned up for vulgar exhibition is too monstrous for credence.

In George Cruikshank's amusing brochure on ghosts, he makes merry over the *ghosts of garments*, the "ghost of a stocking," and so on, but *if* spirit does take a visible shape at all, why not take the shape of a cloak or a stocking, or a suit of armour, as readily as of the discarded body?

And so long as those mysterious affinities exist between kindred souls, which herald the coming foot, the coming letter, or awaken simultaneous thought, so long as the thousand-and-one premonitions and coincidences of our daily life remain inexplicable, so long as the historian and biographer chronicle visitations from the world of shadows, the self-sufficiency of utter incredulity is inadmissible. And so the Author trusts no apology is needed for these stories of fays, and wraiths, and phantoms, who are said to have come as messengers of good or ill, whether in the gloaming, or through the night, the night which surrounds the living and breathing world; or for her title, since elves and spirits, tricksy and solemn, shun the garish day, and, like the stars, be only visible *Through the Night.*

A WORLD BETWEEN

CHAPTER I

MY father's will had left me master of Tarnbeck, and sole guardian of my half-sister Amy, the child of a second marriage; a light, laughing, fairy-like creature, all song and sunshine.

Fashion did find her way to Tarnbeck occasionally in the train of Lady Clevedale and others, and had trifled with skirts and bonnets; but never dared Fashion lay a ruthless hand on Amy Beckton's glorious flaxen hair. So it rippled in light curls to her waist at nineteen freely as when the buoyant school-girl of nine chased butterflies in the green lanes, with her tresses floating on the wind.

The Becktons of Tarnbeck had held their own when a strong arm, a strong will, and a strong hold were the three requisites either for the acquisition of power or its maintenance.

Alas for the degenerate scions of those warlike ancestors, whose armour shared with antlers and other trophies of the hunting-field the honour of decorating the entrance-hall! Sword and halberd, gun and pistol, hunting-horn and hound, had given way before the followers of William Caxton.[1] The cannon on the battlements could not be trusted to fire a birthday salute, the strong-room was the library, and for three generations the owner had been a confirmed bookworm.

The castellated mansion was peculiarly situated. It was built of coarse grit-stone, on an elevated knoll, at the junction of two rapid

---

[1] William Caxton (c.1422–1492) was the person who introduced the technology of printing to England.

streams fresh from the hills, which, on their marriage a hundred yards or so away down the valley, assumed the dignity of a river. In wet seasons, when the becks,[2] swollen by heavy rains or melting snows, overflowed their banks, the water crept upwards like an insidious enemy on all sides, until the house stood isolated on a raised island, calmly defiant above the threatening waters, which never passed the vanguard of firs, however close and angry might be their advance. An array of medieval windows, and the Gothic entrance with its nail-studded door, opened northwards, towards the hills and recesses of Clevedale, where the tumbling becks supplied water-power for one or two woollen mills; the cottages of the operatives looking like flocks of dingy sheep on the distant hill-sides. This was the original front of the buildings; but Amy preferred the modernised back with its southern aspect of green pasture lands, straggling plantations, and the impetuous streams which chafed and fretted before they blent and rolled away placidly under willows and sedges, a respectable river. A fierce semi-circular-fronted tower, having two unequal wings, pierced with loopholes for defence, had Tarnbeck been in its fighting days, before the ivy crept over it, and the baron's hall in the central tower had been converted into a spacious drawing-room, with three lofty windows at the embayed end. Over this was the library, our room of rooms, triply lit in correspondence with the apartment beneath, but teeming with well-bound, well-bought volumes on shelves which occupied every available space.

Amy had had full liberty with lace and muslin, gorgeous satin and damask, to brighten up the dark nooks of Tarnbeck, so long as she left the entrance-hall and the library as our good father had

---

2 Northern English, beck: small stream.

bequeathed them to us. So the thick old Turkey carpet still preserved silence beneath the foot; dark and cumbrous ancestral chairs and tables served as depositories for tomes as cumbrous; the summer sun shot his rays through heavy crimson velvet drapery, and fell with a ruddy glory on the large, elaborately-carved, old oak cabinet, which, black as ebony, had faced the windows and defied the sunbeams to pierce its secrets for many generations.

There is no doubt I am a bookworm, as my father was, but I have not reached the age of mustiness: perhaps Amy's friends have helped to preserve some of youth's freshness in the student whom she twitted with old bachelorhood at thirty.[3]

Yes, Amy's friends, all Amy's. The laughter from the croquet lawn, the music from the drawing-room, the whiffs of cigar from the terrace, all indicate the friends of my beautiful, lovable little sister; the pet of Clevedale society, the fiancée of Frank Fairclough, whose father is head partner of the firm owning the chief mill in Clevedale. Have I no more than a brotherly interest in her friends? Ah! well, we shall see.

I suppose I am naturally too shy and reserved to cultivate friendships. At all events, I have never had more than one *friend*, Oscar Bergheim; and he went away—to place a world between us.

Oscar was the son of a Swedish merchant, sent to England for education; and we met when mere boys at a public school, both boarding with the same master. There are few animals more cruel than the untrained school-boy; and this native savagery drew together Oscar and myself, in spite of our utter dissimilarity. I was a pale, slight boy, more inclined to pore over a book in a corner than to join in rough games in the playground; I was soon dubbed

---

3 Twit: to tease, to make fun of.

"Miss Charlotte," and marked out for persecution. Oscar, though three years my junior, was stout, muscular, dark-browed, fiery-eyed, impulsive, with a capacity for loving and hating rare amongst men. His ignorance of English, his foreign accent and manners, made him also a butt for the bullets of ridicule and practical joking; but he went in for a tussle with one of the bullies, and gave the ruffian a grip which served for the whole squad. Still in speech they had him at a disadvantage, until I (who from my father had picked up a smattering of many strong tongues) became interpreter for him, and he became champion for me. "Damon and Pythias," "Orestes and Pylades" were among the wordy brickbats hurled at us; but they fell like feathers, and our friendship grew with our years.

There were no home-goings for Oscar; he was too far away. It saddened me at vacation time to see his efforts to hide his home-sickness, his longings for Sweden's streams and mountains. At my earnest entreaty he was invited to spend his holidays at Tarnbeck; and his rapturous admiration of the picturesque old place won my father's heart at once. Then Oscar had a store of genuine Norse rhymes and ballads, which made him free of that tabooed chamber, the library, and set my good father corresponding with half of the antiquaries in England.

Amy was then a blue-eyed, flaxen-haired child, with speech as imperfect as her slave Oscar's. She was the veriest tyrant to him. Putting her sash for a bridle in his mouth, she would mount his shoulders and drive him on all-fours as inexorably over the hard gravel as over the smooth lawn; throw ball or hat into almost inaccessible places, and demand their recovery, and would go to sleep in no arms but Oscar's. One vacation he fished her out of the beck into which she had fallen; another, caught her runaway pony; and finally pounded Frank Fairclough (then home on the holidays) almost to a jelly for throwing duck-weed on her new muslin frock and calling her contemptuously "a wax doll."

When, at seventeen, Oscar Bergheim was hurriedly recalled to Carlscrona, with no leisure for leavetaking, the nine-year-old damsel wept bitterly, and she was scarcely consoled by the large box of Swedish toys sent over as a souvenir to his "little sweetheart."

At nine we weep with the eyes. At twenty we begin to weep with the heart. And so I wept my one friend Oscar's removal. He had been my sole companion and confidant, and, despite my seniority, my patron and protector. I never got into a scrape he did not champion me through, though it occurs to me now that but for his leadership I might never have got into the scrapes at all.

Letters and summer visits to Carlscrona bridged over the sea. My father's death changed everything.

I was appointed sole guardian of Amy, who was in her seventeenth year. Then I had the conditions of my father's will to carry out. The entailed property was unencumbered, but the personal was weighted with so many legacies as to embarrass me considerably. I was, moreover, charged with my sister's care and maintenance until her marriage or majority, when I was enjoined to deliver up the title-deeds of certain properties, her own mother's jewels, and securities for moneys in bank and Funds to the value of £15,000. All of which were lying, and were to lie, in the family depository known as the "Palmer's Scrip."

This was one of those receptacles so ingeniously contrived within the recesses of the old carved cabinet as to defy suspicion or search, and doubtless dread secrets had been consigned to the Palmer's Scrip in times gone by. The knowledge of it was held as a sacred trust, only to be passed from sire to son in the hour of extreme peril, and the master-key was only permitted to drop from the owner's dying hand into that of his successor.

My father, who had no mysteries of his own, had been wont to leave the outer doors of the cabinet open for convenience; and, having full trust in me, had initiated me into the secrets of slides and springs ere I was five-and-twenty. Yet it was with no little awe that I approached the cabinet the week after his funeral, holder of the little key and all which it represented. There were two entrances to the library, one on each side of the cabinet which filled the space between; I not only locked the one, but tried the lock of the other door, which, leading principally to guest chambers, was kept fastened and rarely used. Noiselessly and reverently I cleared from the table the books and papers which had been my father's latest studies. There was a solemn hush in the house; my footsteps made no sound; and yet as I put the curious little key into the ornamental key-holes, I felt as if the room were peopled with shadows of dead and buried Becktons, all striving to prevent intrusion on their dead-and-buried secrets. As the doors flew open I thought, too, of the now cold hand which had last opened those leaves; and, overpowered with emotion, sank on a chair unable to proceed. The cabinet had three outer doors; within were several smaller ones closing on pigeon-holes and drawers. There were also two carved figures in niches, but only one affects my narrative. It was a Palmer, with hat and staff and scallop-shells and scrip complete.[4] The scrip, notwithstanding the will, was an innocent immovable bit of wood-carving, but on pressing the least prominent button of his "sandalled shoon," when the outer doors were unlocked, the entire figure

---

[4] Palmer: a pilgrim. Scrip: a small bag or wallet, a kind of satchel, with tassels at each bottom corner. The staff and scallop shells are a symbol of religious pilgrimage.

revolved, and displayed a cavity behind, at least a foot deep, divided by three shelves—on each of which lay papers yellow with age. But it was not until the lowest shelf was pulled forward that the true scrip was revealed by the retirement of the adjoining nest of drawers. When these moved back a lid held down by them flew open, and the box it covered was the Palmer's Scrip.

The title-deeds, the money securities, and an old case of trinkets were there. The chief of the latter were a set of sapphires, another of emeralds, and one of garnets, by no means so antique as the casket.

Closing the cabinet on replaced notes and parchments, I stepped downstairs to the drawing-room, casket in hand, hoping by the display of her mother's jewellery to divert the current of Amy's thoughts, and so for a time lighten the sorrow which seemed to press so heavily on her fair young head.

My entrance was arrested by a strange voice, low, grave, and musical, a voice which thrilled me as nought had ever done before. By nature somewhat reserved and shy, I hesitated, with the door in my hand, whether to face the enemy or beat a retreat. Amy's prompt "Come in, Charlie. I want to present you to Miss Proctor," decided the question for me. And decided a much more momentous question at the same time.

There was nothing in the serene eyes or the calm gravity of the young lady to whom I was introduced to daunt any man; yet my embarrassment was painful. I coloured to the roots of my hair, and it was not until Lucy Fairclough smilingly put her hand in mine, saying, "What have I done to be overlooked this morning?" that I recovered my self-possession.

Lucy Fairclough was an average specimen of northern England's womanhood; but the daughter of Mr. Fairclough's partner was something more. She was scarcely above the middle height; there was nothing marvellous in her brown hair or mild hazel eyes; her features were not chiselled to absolute proportion; yet there was such an air of fitness and harmony in face and figure, so much that was womanly in her manner, so much reposeful grace in every movement, that I was hopelessly fascinated on the spot. Not even in her garb was there a tint to startle us in contrast with Amy's sombre crape. Both she and Miss Fairclough were dressed in complimentary mourning, the effect of which was more soothing than gloomy.

"What curious specimen of antiquity have you there?" asked Amy, to break the first pause.

At the mention of the talismanic word "jewels," three pairs of eyes sparkled simultaneously; but I saw a quiet smile gather on Miss Proctor's face at the eager persistence of her friends to have the casket opened.

Conquering a strange foreboding of evil, I yielded to their entreats; and we clustered round a small table near the middle window for their inspection. This brought me into close proximity with Miss Proctor; and as, case by case, the sparkling gems were displayed, and as I compared her calm appreciation of their beauty with the demonstrative admiration of Amy and Lucy, the ice of shyness thawed rapidly.

I was in no haste to retreat with my charge, but joined Amy in her solicitations that the young ladies should remain at Tarnbeck and dine with us. On my volunteering to send a messenger to Fairclough House, and to be their escort should Mr. Frank not be at liberty to join us, Amy looked amazed; but they consented, and I retired to fulfil the first part of my promise, and to replace the casket, little dreaming how bitterly I should regret their exhibition in the future.

Frank Fairclough responded to the invitation with an alacrity I neither comprehended nor appreciated at the time; and notwithstanding our recent bereavement, which, of course, had a subduing influence, the hours flew by so rapidly and satisfactorily that Lucy's frequent reminders of their flight and the propriety of moving homewards seemed to fall on deaf ears.

That was but the precursor of many social evenings, to which, as our sorrow wore away, other guests were admitted; but I never left my beloved books so readily as for our pleasant quintett parties, of which Miss Proctor made one. All happiness has an end. Mine terminated when Miss Proctor went back to Leeds at the expiration of a three-months' visit.

Other friends came and went; notably the Faircloughs, but I shut myself up in the library, rarely quitting my shell, whilst Amy visited and received visits alone; until Lady Clevedale read me a sharp lecture on the impropriety thereof, and suggested a companion or chaperone for my pretty half-sister.

Frank Fairclough (who had long been forgiven his contempt for "wax dolls") frowned, and Amy pouted, at the proposition; but Aunt Lydia had not been at Tarnbeck two days before Amy danced round her, declaring she was "a dear old darling," and clenched the assertion with a hug and a kiss which the genial old lady reciprocated.

Aunt Lydia was certainly an acquisition. She relieved me of much anxiety and responsibility in the care of my sister; then she guided the reins of household management without taking them from Amy's hands, and was to the blithe little beauty just the companion, confidante, and wise counsellor the motherless girl needed.

When Amy was eighteen, Lady Clevedale carried her off to London in triumph, not without many misgivings on my part, and expostulations from Frank Fairclough, whose interference I felt at first inclined to resent.

Yet his warmth and vehemence took me somewhat by surprise, and his manly earnestness impressed me more in his favour than years of previous intimacy.

It was my first glimpse into his heart, where I clearly saw Amy enthroned, though never a word said he of an interest in her welfare deeper than that of a true friend. And he might have shaken my resolution but that my promise to Lady Clevedale was already given.

During her absence my solitude was broken in upon, to my great content, by the unexpected arrival of Oscar Bergheim, whom I had not seem for more than two years. He, like myself, had lost a father in that interval, and having no taste for mercantile pursuits, was about, so he said, to retire from the firm. Business connected therewith had brought him over.

His stay was short, and I half fancied Amy's absence had something to do with it. We talked over old times, visited old haunts, played chess together of an evening; but he had evidently outlived our quiet life, and I felt as if an imperceptible, impalpable film was spreading between us and our old friendship. To bear him company, I smoked and drank more than was my wont. It occurred to me that Frank Fairclough, from his larger intercourse with the world, might assimilate better with him—but lo! I brought a lighted match to gunpowder. There was an explosion, and Oscar Bergheim departed from Tarnbeck the next morning.

He did not leave England, however, so soon as I expected. Amy's artless letters to Lucy and myself told of meeting him in society, then of his frequent visits at Lady Clevedale's, and his brotherly attention to herself.

The day following the receipt of this last communication Frank Fairclough was summoned to London on unexpected business.

More than a year had flown. The woods were dressed in their fullest robes of green; the sombre firs put forth pale fingers with which the sunbeams toyed; hill and dale and garden were glorious with summer's crown of flowers; the air came up the valley from the south, and through the open windows filled the rooms with the sweet scent of new hay from the meadows. Soon the sun turned towards his western couch, the starlings flew home to their nests on the battlements, and twittered their vespers ere they tucked their heads under their wings, while the grasshopper and nightingale, on the alert, answered from below.

I was imbued with the fullest sense of all this sweetness, but I felt rather than saw or heard these country time-keepers. I sat, from habit, by the fireless grate (which a fluffy haze of some fibrous material veiled), studying neither nature nor books, but human hearts.

Alicia Proctor was again at Fairclough House. Aunt Lydia and Amy had driven up the dale to greet her. I, who had been longing for a sight of her as a parched Arab for a desert spring, had not dared to join them. And there I sat, taking myself to task for my timidity, asking myself over and over again what there was in the pale shy bookworm of thirty to attract so perfect a sample of fresh womanhood as Alicia.

I had nursed my love in solitude and silence until it had grown almost too big for my heart, yet the "dear Alicia" of my dreams was only "Miss Proctor" when we met; and I had small reason to hope she had penetrated my secret.

A sharp rap at the room door put to flight my cogitations. My "Come in!" was followed by the entrance of Amy, in an airy azure robe and jaunty hat trimmed to match, with a flush on her face as if fresh from her drive. She was accompanied by Frank Fairclough, whose arm (or I was mistaken in the twilight) encircled her as they passed through the doorway.

I was not left long in doubt.

I usually sat with the side of my chair inclined towards the windows, so that the light should fall on my book or paper; it fell now on the faces of the pair as they came together round by the cabinet, and Amy, kneeling on the footstool at my feet, threw her arms round my neck, and whispered, "You love me very much, do you not, Charlie dear?"

"You know I do, Amy," I answered, smoothing her radiant aureole of curls with my disengaged hand, as the other held her close.

"And you would like to make me happy?"

"Are you not happy, Amy?"

"Ah, yes; but very much happier, I mean, Charlie."

I glanced up at Fairclough's manly face before I replied. It wore a look of anxious expectation.

"I would lay down my life, Amy, to secure your happiness."

A moment's hesitation; a tug at a tiny glove; then, in lower and more tremulous tones, as a sparkling ring was revealed: "Frank has placed this on my finger, Charlie. May I wear it?"

Frank, who had been silent hitherto, interposed.

"Charlie, may your sister be permitted to wear that ring as a token of betrothal until I replace it with a plainer one?"

Amy clung to me, and Frank looked out of his clear grey eyes, alike entreatingly. An overwhelming sense of responsibility overpowered my utterance. I paused to reflect. I think the form of Oscar floated before my eyes, obscuring my vision.

Frank was the first to break the painful silence.

"Charles Beckton, you *must* have seen that I have loved your sister for many years. My father, though fully approving my choice, imposed silence upon me. But for that I should have declared myself last year, when I trembled for my hopes, and for my love, consigned to Lady Clevedale's fashionable coterie. My business in town was solely to watch over our darling. I felt that my presence was needed, Charles." (He did not say why.) "Our firm takes me into partnership this week, and that change in my position sets my tongue at liberty. You see I use my freedom to forge fresh fetters. I have Amy's promise. Surely, old fellow, you will not withhold yours?"

I had risen, and buried my head in my arms against the carved old mantelpiece. From time to time vague suspicions of this had flashed across my mind, to be as instantly dismissed. I had regarded Amy as a child, and had other views for her maturity. The crisis had come all too soon, and my day-dreams were dispelled. I felt Amy's hand creeping to my shoulder, and a plaintive murmur in my ear.

"Charlie, are you sorry for this? I thought you knew that I loved Frank, and would be glad to give me to one you knew so well—so good a man."

She touched me there. I did know him for a good and true man, firm and self-reliant, the very one to guard and guide my darling. I was not so sure of Oscar's principles; yet had I, without warranty, built up an aerial castle in which he and Amy were to reign blissfully together.

I was roused by Frank's voice—somewhat husky in its tone.

"Come, come, old fellow, I did not expect this! Amy and I have been picturing a pleasant surprise, a cheery welcome. You should not have left us so much together had you not looked forward to this with satisfaction. Was not love inevitable?"

I turned round.

"Yes, yes, Frank; you are both right. It is only I who have been blind. Now kiss your bachelor brother, Amy, and go to Frank, with my best blessing. I believe you have chosen better for yourself than I should have done for you. Frank, give me your hand."

CHAPTER II

Frank was in Leeds when, a week later, Oscar Bergheim took us by surprise as before. Ours was a quiet household, and, except now and then a quaint old antiquary, we had few male visitors staying with us. His sudden advent would have put Aunt Lydia in a flutter, had it not been a whim of mine to keep Oscar's room (in which no other friend was ever lodged) always aired and in readiness. He, too, was the only one to whom the library door was unreservedly open. It had been so in my father's days; it was not likely to be otherwise in mine.

How tall and handsome he looked as he grasped my hand in the ancient entrance-hall with all the heartiness of bygone times! How courteously he acknowledged Aunt Lydia's old-fashioned curtsey, and how eloquent were his soft dark eyes as he held Amy's small hand in a tenacious clasp, and said, "I trust my little sweetheart is glad to see me again!"

I saw the colour mount to her face, and so did he; but we put different constructions upon it. I sighed to think that he might, like myself, have indulged hopes not to be realized; and, observing her continued embarrassment, was gad that Miss Proctor and Lucy Fairclough were spending the day at Tarnbeck.

How much more at ease was he than I! I envied his graceful self-possession as he took Amy in to dinner, whilst my arm trembled under the light touch of Alicia. So charming was his manner, so fluent and sparkling the conversation with which he enlivened the repast, that my own awkwardness impressed me painfully in the contrast. It was never so with Oscar Bergheim.

And so it was throughout his stay. He shone conspicuously, and I, nowise loth, sank into the shade. We had, all unconsciously, fallen into our old positions. I admitted his superiority by my tacit acquiescence in all he proposed; in fact, I bowed down to the hero I had created.

He had a fine voice, well cultivated. He opened the piano, and we revelled in song and music for a space. He longed to breathe the fresh air, and we were straightway strolling under the firs, or among the flower-beds, and, like children, pelting each other with young fir cones and roses, or plucking blooms for general presentation. He proposed cards, and Aunt Lydia responded on the instant, produced the cards, and helped him to arrange the table. But he appointed the game, and we novices were duly initiated.

He expressed his desire to renew his acquaintance with the neighbourhood, and immediately we found ourselves arranging boating-parties, croquet-parties, sketching-parties, pic-nics, rides and drives, with a zest unknown to Tarnbeck.

Lucy Fairclough, Aunt Lydia, and I were alike carried away by his impetuosity and enthusiasm; but I noticed that Alicia was graver than her wont, and that Amy shrank from his pointed attentions.

I observed also, with a thrill of delight, that when he pressed forward to hand the ladies to their carriage, Alicia calmly placed her hand in mine, quietly ignoring his proffered assistance.

His presence created quite a revolution in Tarnbeck. The magnet drew other friends into the circle, and one pleasure-party succeeded another in rapid succession. But, whether at home or abroad, Oscar always attached himself to Amy with a kind of protecting devotion which she could not resent, and which gave me pain to witness under the circumstances.

I resolved at length, out of my great love for both, to acquaint him with the fact of Amy's engagement; but the task was not left to me.

In the mountain limestone, about seven miles up the dale, was a natural cavern, known as the Hermitage. It was screened from observation by larches, pine, and mountain-ash, and only accessible by a narrow zig-zag footpath cut in the steep face of the rock. This terminated at a green plateau in front of the cavern, close by the side of which gushed a stream of the purest water. It had worn a runnel for itself across the platform, and fell in foam over the crag to be lost in hazel bushes, brambles, and bracken at the foot of the hill. This was a favourite resort for gipsy-parties; and Oscar, remembering the spot, had pitched upon it for our pic-nic.

Out party numbered just a dozen, including the vicar's two unmarried daughters, the Rev. John Smiles, the curate, Dr. Halgarth's son James, in all the flush of newly-acquired honours as M. R. C. S., his sister, and a student friend, who kept very close to Miss Halgarth. The rendezvous was Fairclough House.

Amy and Lucy, being capital horsewomen, were mounted. So were Miss Halgarth, her brother's friend, and Oscar.

I, being an indifferent rider, presented myself as Jehu of our basket phaeton,[5] containing my bosom's secret idol and Aunt Lydia, whose youthful heart and spinsterhood were voted sufficient qualifications for our party. The vicar's carriage, thrown open, held his stately daughters, the curate, and James Halgarth.

[5] Jehu (c. 842–815 BC), commander of chariots for the king of Israel. Phaeton: an open carriage, drawn by one or two horses.

Jock, our groom and ferryman, was in attendance. Hampers had been sent on by servants in advance.

The drive proved delightful. The morning air was fresh and exhilarating; the September sun shone, if not with a scorching glare, at least with sufficient warmth to brighten up the grey stone houses of the overgrown village, and to gild the spire of the ivy-coloured old church.

In my supreme content, I neither observed the equestrians before us nor heard the sound of hoofs rapidly advancing from behind, until Aunt Lydia, in the seat at our back, exclaimed:

"I declare, Charles, here is Mr. Frank Fairclough!—I understood you would not be able to leave Leeds for a fortnight?"

This latter was an interrogative addressed to that individual, who checked his horse to shake hands with us all.

"So I thought," was his prompt reply. "But you see there is an all-powerful magnet to draw me hither."

"And I thought," murmured Alicia, in a tone meant only for his ear, "there was no magnet potent enough to draw Mr. Frank Fairclough from duty to pleasure."

"Thanks for your good opinion, Miss Proctor. I am drawn to duty and pleasure both on this occasion," was the response, given with more emphasis that I saw any reason for at the time.

He raised his hat from his wavy brown har, urged his glossy chestnut horse forward, and in less than two minutes was by Amy's side.

We were near enough to perceive that his appearance in our midst was unwelcome by one of our party. Oscar Bergheim's palpable start, as Frank saluted Amy, caused his horse, a frisky bay, to swerve and plunge, to the additional annoyance of the rider, who, unused to the saddle, had not too firm a seat.

The episode was soon over, and we drove on, little recking how dangerously Oscar chafed at the want of self-command which he had exhibited before Amy and his cooler rival, and which the sudden exhilaration of the fair lady's spirits did not tend to subdue.

I was assisting Miss Proctor and Aunt Lydia to alight when they dismounted, or I might have trembled as Amy did on seeing Oscar's black brows come down over his flashing eyes, when, with a smiling "Come on Frank!" she put her arm through her lover's as a matter of course, to be helped up the rough pathway, so long, at least, as it would hold two abreast. The vindictive look sobered lively Amy in an instant. Would that I had had the same warning!

The ride and the fresh air had sharpened us for luncheon. The three equestrian Graces came forward, in their closely-fitting jaunty jackets, to help Frank and myself to unpack delicate comestibles with which only feminine hands could deal. Oscar, Halgarth, and his friend Jackson ran to and fro between the hampers in the cave and the tablecloth on the grassy plateau, where Aunt Lydia presided over the arrangements.

Gradually we fell into our places, with little confusion but much laughter. There was a popping of corks, a plopping of wine into glasses, a rattle of cutlery and crockery, small talk and badinage, and all went merrily.

Oscar, who sat between Miss Halgarth and Amy, was apparently more than usually buoyant and agreeable; but he drank an unusual quantity of wine, and I, sitting opposite, by the side of Alicia, observed that he visibly winced whenever Amy addressed Frank, whose place on the grass was in close proximity.

Luncheon over, Aunt Lydia retired to the cave for a nap on a pile of carriage cushions; baskets, satchels, and hooked sticks for pulling branches within reach were appropriated, and the party, in straggling pairs, strayed down the path to the copse below, ostensibly in quest of hazel-nuts and blackberries.

A natural affinity seemed to draw Alicia and myself together. I was carefully guarding her down the rocky path, when the voices of Oscar and Frank in loud altercation above painfully arrested our steps.

"Resign the lady, sir!" thundered Oscar Bergheim.

"Not to any man; certainly not to *you*," was Frank's emphatic reply, in which evidently lurked a covert sarcasm.

"I have the prior claim——"

"And I have the authorized right."

There was the sound of a blow, followed by a scream from Amy.

The nature of the path had retarded our return. We reached the platform to see Aunt Lydia (roused from her nap) and Amy, white as snow, wringing their hands, and the two men struggling as for life or death on that limited arena.

Jock and his fellows, apparently benumbed, were afraid to interfere.

They were locked together, swaying to and fro perilously near the cliff.

Once before, in bygone years, those two had fought, and Oscar had won an easy victory. Now they were better matched. What Oscar had in size and weight, Frank had in agility and nerve.

They held each other in a vice-like grip, regardless alike of Amy's piteous appeals or my entreaties. Backwards and forwards they swayed, when to our horror the treacherous earth gave way under Oscar's feet, and he fell, crashing through the light branches of a giant elm (which towered above the copse, and swept the face of the cliff) dragging Frank with him, and scaring a pair of crows from their rugged nest.

There was a moment's awful stillness. Amy had fainted. Lucy

was speechless with terror in the copse below, whence distant voices answered ours.

"Thank God! They have not fallen to the foot of the crag!"

I ventured to look over. A jutting shelf of rock, overgrown with rank vegetation, had providentially broken their descent midway; and there they lay motionless, Frank uppermost.

Were they dead?

Whilst we on the platform above were consulting how to reach them, Alicia, with the help of Jock, had loosened the cords from our hampers, and knotted them into a stout rope; but it was not sufficient to peril another life upon. To scale the precipitous rock was still more hazardous.

I was slight and lithe of limb, and, though unskilled in athletic games, could climb a tree or scale a cliff with any man. I saw that the large boughs of the grand tree through which the foes had crashed still overhung the rocky ledge.

It is a marvel I kept my footing as I flew down the unequal path to gain the tree below. In an instant coat and hat lay on the ground, and my limbs clasped the great bole of the tree. It was a tough ascent, but I mounted steadily to a strong arm above the level of the ledge. Along this I crept as far as it would bear, then grasped it with both hands, and with a swing landed by the side of my prostrate friends.

My example was infectious. I had barely ascertained that both were living than I was thankful to find Halgarth at my elbow.

"Fairclough is reviving," said he. "The sprinkling of that tiny cascade has done the poor fellow a service. Your friend Bergheim's case is more serious. I wish we had some brandy."

Brandy, thanks to Alicia's forethought, was being lowered from the cliff. The stimulant restored Frank to consciousness; but on

Oscar neither water, brandy, nor the removal of Frank's pressure had any visible effect.

A welcome emissary from below in the person of Jock. He bore one end of a thin line by which we hauled up a stronger one, then cart sheets and blankets (from a farm close by) already formed into hammock litters. Into the first of these we placed Frank, whose ascertained injuries were a broken wrist and a sprained ankle; and, by using the giant bough as a crane, we contrived to lower him to the anxious group beneath.

We had a much more arduous and hazardous task with Oscar, from his weight and utter helplessness, placed as we were on a ledge where there was barely room for the three to stoop or stir. A groan, as we lifted him into the second litter, was the only token of sensibility he gave.

How different was the slow, sad procession homewards from that which had left Clevedale in the morning! My agony is not to be described. We were bearing back my guest, perchance to die beneath my roof; my sister's lover lamed and injured; my tender-hearted Amy scarcely in full consciousness; and I seemed to hold in my breast the pain of all.

CHAPTER III

Oscar did not die, though for very many days he was delirious, and life trembled in the balance. Above all his injuries there was concussion of the brain. And no wonder: he had gone down with all the force of Fairclough's superadded weight; and, but for the mosses and weeds which covered the providential rock like a cushion, he must have fractured his skull. As it was he had escaped by little less than a miracle.

We had hired a nurse from the village, and Jock and Thomas shared alternately with me my constant watch by Oscar's bedside during his delirium. Aunt Lydia also was the best of good nurses. Yet, as the fright had thrown our darling Amy also on a sick pillow, I was glad when Alicia Proctor said, "You will be worn out with your double duty. You must suffer me to relieve you occasionally. Between Mrs. Fairclough and Lucy, Mr. Frank is likely to be spoiled with over-nursing."

I know not whether she did more good to our patients or to myself. Her presence to Amy was more than medicine. Her sweet voice, her gentle tone and manner, acted on the girl's shattered nerves as a soothing charm; and before the week was out her remaining languor gave way before a drive to Fairclough House.

Frank's sprained ankle was a much more tedious affair than had been prognosticated; and before he was able to reach Tarnbeck his rival was gone. It had been well for him that he was himself invalided, or Amy's pity for Oscar, who in his delirium raved constantly of her, might have changed the destiny of three lives.

It was early in October when Dr. Halgarth first permitted his patient to take possession of a small sitting-room which adjoined his chamber in the west wing, and was almost on a level with the library. He was soon able to sit up and walk about the room, and to propose cards and other games as a relief to the tedium of the hours.

One afternoon I was called downstairs to a tenant whose premises had been considerably damaged by high winds the previous night. I left Amy playing chess with Oscar in this sitting-room. She wore a dress of dark blue silk, relieved at the wrists and throat with lace, and as I glanced back I thought she had never looked more lovely.

Perhaps Oscar felt so too. I had barely closed the door, when he, oblivious of the game, laid his wasted hands on hers and looked steadfastly in her face. Possibly the ring on her finger, sparkling as she moved the pieces, arrested his attention, and was more significant to him than it had been to me.

"Amy," said he, with forced composure, detaining the hand she would have withdrawn, "I have a question to ask you: Did Fairclough speak truth? Have you promised to marry him?"

Amy trembled. A flush rose to her forehead, but she answered unhesitatingly, "Yes."

His brow contracted as if with pain. After a pause he asked, in a low impressive voice, "Do you *love* him?"

His manner quite precluded evasion. She felt constrained to speak truthfully and openly. "Mr. Bergheim" (she had ceased to call him Oscar), "you should not ask me that. But since you have done so, I will answer you. I love Mr. Fairclough with my whole heart."

"Incredible!" he muttered between his teeth, as if to himself. Then taking her other hand in his to keep her on her seat, for she was rising, he resumed, impassionately: "Amy, that whole heart was mine for years. True, you were then a child; but I had hoped to find it mine still; and mine it shall be, in spite of that mercenary wretch, who seeks not you but your dower."

Amy rose indignantly.

"Nay," he urged, "you know how devotedly I love you; you see to what that mad passion has reduced me. Have you no pity?"

"Oh! Mr. Bergheim, you forget yourself. I gave you my answer in London. It is not honourable to speak to me now in this way. I cannot listen——"

"Not honourable! Talk of honour to men consumed by love and jealousy!" he hissed. "But if I may not love, I can hate; and my revenge shall touch your lover where he is most sensitive!"

I met Amy flying along the gallery in a passion of tears. Alarmed, I drew her into the library, and after a time succeeded in calming her, and learning the cause of her emotion.

At once I sought Oscar, whom I found in so dangerous a state of excitement that I was compelled to postpone my remonstrance.

Reaction left him so prostrate that he had once more to be carried to bed; and three more days elapsed before Dr. Halgarth permitted him to return to the little sitting-room. After that he seemed to doze away the hours, and want no company.

Feeling at liberty I walked to Clevedale to inspect the injured premises, and give orders for rebuilding the shattered chimney-stack, repairing the roof, &c., and on my return went to the library to put the builder's estimate with other papers.

As I opened the door I thought I heard a rustle, followed by the click of a lock, and a draught of wind upon my face. There was no one in the room; the windows were closed, the cabinet doors open, as I usually kept them. So impressed was I that I even tried the door beyond the cabinet. It was, as usual, locked.

Not convinced, I stirred the fire, which had gone down through inattention, left the room, relocking the only door I had opened, and hastened along the gallery to Bergheim's apartment. I found him lying in a doze on the sofa, as I had left him two hours before. Inquiry did not solve the mystery, and I was compelled, reluctantly, to ascribe to a freak of the imagination the supposed closing of the door. How my senses could have deceived me was perplexing.

On the following Tuesday, as we sat by the drawing-room fire, with the lamps lit and the amber curtains drawn, Oscar, who had not regained his composure, but followed Amy's movements with moody eyes, announced his intention to leave us. Aunt Lydia put up her hands in surprise. Amy pursued her tatting in silence.[6] I remonstrated, on the ground that he was unfit to travel.

He met my objection with the plea that he should regain vigour neither of mind nor body at Tarnbeck; that the atmosphere of the place was unwelcome to him. His glance sought Amy as he spoke.

What could I say? I was loth to lose my friend, unwilling to let him travel until he was thoroughly restored; but I felt that the man whose passions could so transform him was not the Oscar Bergheim I had clung to; and my heart ached as it acquiesced in his decision that it was best he should go.

I drove him myself to the little station some four miles away, packed him snugly in a first-class carriage, extorted a promise that he would travel by easy stages, and would write when he reached London. But I drove back brooding over his renewed insinuations that Frank Fairclough was mercenary, and only sought Lucy to prop a failing business with her money. I felt that the imputation was false; but for the life of me I could not shake off the fear of the possibilities it engendered.

In less than a week the following letter came to hand:—

"Liverpool, Oct. 19, 186—.

"DEAR CHARLIE,—I have consulted a physician, who advises a sea voyage, change of scene and climate, as my only chance for either brain or heart. The chain which drew me to these shores has been rudely snapped: I sail for Australia this afternoon. When next you hear from me there will be a world between us. A word from Amy might recall me. She will never speak it, and I have a presentiment we shall never meet again in this life. I know I leave

---

[6] Making a kind of knotted lace with a small shuttle.

an enemy at your elbow; but neither time, distance, distraction—nay, not even *death*— should sever a friendship such as that which has existed between Charles Beckton and his old schoolfellow,

"OSCAR BERGHEIM."

"Thank heaven, the scoundrel has gone without doing more mischief!" exclaimed Frank, glancing from his arm in the sling to the bandaged foot lying on a cushion before him, when I called at the hall to report. "I shall not regret the price I have paid to be so well rid of him, though I am tied by the leg at a most unfortunate crisis. There are damaging rumours afloat respecting the stability of our firm (whence originating no one knows); but the consequences may be serious, and I ought to be up and doing."

My mind misgave me somehow, as I attempted the defence of Bergheim. I think the remembrance of Oscar's conversation on the way to the station somewhat tempered the warmth of my manner, as I replied: "Frank, I cannot listen to such an epithet as 'scoundrel' applied to my old friend. It is true he made a savage attack on you; but the successful lover should make some allowance for one with an impulsive temperament, whose jealousy at the sudden overthrow of life's hopes overpowered his reason."

Frank had cause for chagrin at his lameness. The report that the firm of Fairclough, Proctor, and Fairclough was "shaky," running through the commercial world, seriously affected its credit and stability; and, had not its available resources been equal to the demand, the old house would have gone. The first use Frank made of his restored power of locomotion was to trace the rumour, if possible, to its fountain-head.

He spent the evening prior to his departure at Tarnbeck. I had discreetly left the lovers to themselves, and was busy poring over

"Cary's County Atlas," with "Grose's Antiquities" by my side, when Amy's light tap at the door heralded her entrance. Her flaxen curls contrasted well with her purple dress; and I thought she looked bewitching as she came coaxingly towards me and put her arm round my neck, as was her winning way when she had a request to prefer.

"Charlie, would you mind letting Frank have just a peep at my mother's jewels? I do so want to let him see how I shall look in them."

I pretended to be grave and solemn, and put on my studying cap before I answered:

"Well, well, my love! go back to Frank, and I'll see presently, I'm busy just at the moment."

The business was a fiction. No sooner did the door revolve on its hinges, than I left my books, and turning to the open cabinet, touched the button on the Palmer's sandal. The figure duly turned, exposing the three shelves. I pulled the lowest. Back went the adjoining drawers, and up flew the released lid of the secret Palmer's scrip. My hand went down for the casket.

The casket was gone! Gone, too, bank-book, securities, and the title-deeds of Amy's property!

I stood aghast, paralysed, incapable of speech or motion. I could not even think.

I have no remembrance of closing the rifled receptacle, or of sitting down; yet I must have done both; for when Amy, impatient of delay, again tapped at the door, I was seated on a chair by the fire, with my head in my hands bowed down to me knees. She tapped several times before I was roused to consciousness. My own voice, as I bade her come in, startled me. No wonder that Amy, as she beheld my crushed figure and haggard face, stood for a moment in blank alarm, before she rushed towards me with a faint cry.

"Charlie, what is the matter with you? Are you ill?"

She had supplied me with a plea—I *was* ill, and I answered feebly, "Yes."

"Shall I send for Dr. Halgarth?" she asked anxiously.

"No, no! I shall be better presently. A sudden dizziness seized me, that is all. It will soon pass. Go back to Frank, that is a dear girl, and take no notice."

She obeyed me in part. She went back to Frank (jewels forgotten), but only to communicate her alarm, and bring him and Aunt Lydia to the library. I endeavoured to rally, but in vain. The shock had been too severe and sudden. It must have marked its impress strongly upon me, for, notwithstanding my remonstrance, Jock was despatched in all haste for Dr. Halgarth.

The old doctor could only shake his large head, look wise, talk of some shock to the nervous system, and prescribe doses of medicine.

My malady was as great a mystery to him as the empty Palmer's scrip was a mystery and terror to me. I had no disease, only the shadow of a dark cloud over me. I sat alone more persistently than ever, but I never read; or, if I took a book, my mind wandered from the page to brood over the abstraction of the jewels, the title-deeds, and other securities.

It was not the mere loss of so much property that troubled me, although that was considerable. Had it been my own I could have borne its loss like a man. But it was a *trust* confided to me. My sister's dower, which I was bound to produce and surrender on her marriage morning. The nature and values of the several money securities were duly set forth in my father's will; the jewels I had prematurely exhibited; and there was no replacing them by substitution, any more than the old parchments. Then the bare fact of the theft proved that the guarded secret of the Palmer's scrip was known. But to *whom*? Few entered the library save those near and dear to me. Strangers were rarely left alone in it. Never with the cabinet open.

Brooding over the matter brought me no nearer to its solution. I sought our family lawyer and confided in him. His perplexity equalled mine, but he suggested that which I had shrunk from—application to the police. I took the next train to London. When I spoke of the pillage of a secret receptacle, which I could not lay bare, to a detective even, an incredulous smile stole over the official's face, as if there was either a doubt of the tangibility of the property, or of the robbery. Nevertheless, the machinery of Scotland Yard was well oiled and set in motion. Bankers were privately communicated with, pawnbrokers' searched for the missing jewels. As well might we have dredged for them in the Red Sea. I returned home more dispirited than I went, only to isolate myself as before, and brood over the impenetrable mystery, which daily assumed more formidable proportions.

Amy's wedding was fixed for the fifth of January. December stepped onwards with brisk strides, and the tower was as blithe with preparations for the trousseau as the master's melancholy would permit. As I sat day by day looking into the fire, until the flames went down, and the red died out disregarded, all that Bergheim had said of Frank's mercenary disposition flashed across my mind and took unfair possession of it.

I had a keen presentiment of Frank's incredulity—he knowing how religiously the secrets of the cabinet had been preserved from generation to generation. I felt that the odium of the robbery would attach to myself, and I should stand condemned as a treacherous custodian who sought to deprive his half-sister of her lawful inheritance. As residuary legatee the law compelled me to make good all trusts, and this I was willing to do to the utmost of my means. But this would not save my good name. There was no second key to the cabinet; none had the secret of its springs but myself.

One gleam of thankfulness shone through the gloom. For the first time I was thankful that my deep love for Alicia was unspoken, and, as I imagined, unsuspected. I must be content to bury my hopes among my books, and let the name of Beckton die out in my old bachelorhood. Once my library had been peopled with intellectual companions; now I sat solitary. Authors no longer spoke to me through their works. The very skies wept in torrents, as if in pity for my misery. The swollen becks rushed on; the river rose higher and higher, until it encircled the knoll, and Tarnbeck was as isolated as its master. Yet wedding preparations went on merrily downstairs, Alicia and Lucy, who were to be bridesmaids, braving the rough ferry in coming and going, to confer on knotty points of feminine adornment.

There was a servants' ball at Fairclough House on Christmas Eve, to be followed by a family party the next day. All our domestics, except Thomas and Hetty, had gone thither in glorious array for the occasion. Frank had borne off Amy to share the general festivities, after vainly endeavouring to "drag the hermit from his cell," as Amy phrased it.

I had a pleasant fire, closely-drawn curtains, and a well-lighted room. No outward accessory to comfort was wanting, yet I sat there gloomy in the midst of light and warmth, my eyes fixed on the old cabinet, racking my brains how to discover the thief and the missing valuables, tormented by suspicions of those around me, and by the penetration of a stranger into the family arcana.

I had declined supper, and had sat with my head on my hands for hours. The antique Nuremburg clock above the mantelpiece roused me to the flight of time by striking twelve in quick vibrations. The last wave of sound yet lingered in the air, when a loud pistol-shot, and the whiz of a bullet past my ear, caused me to start from my seat and rush to the curtained window whence came the sound.

No one was there concealed. The glass was uncracked! The bright Christmas moon lit up a wide waste of waters, and the wintry grounds, where no assassin could lurk in concealment. I turned to the other windows with like result.

I examined the cabinet against which the bullet had apparently struck. There was neither mark nor indentation!

Amazed and perplexed beyond measure, I examined the scant household. I found Aunt Lydia toasting her toes on the fender-stool in the cosy parlour, and trying her eyes over the *Leeds Mercury*. Though that apartment so closely adjoined the library, and had the same outlook, she had heard neither shot nor footstep.

"You have been dreaming, Charles. My ears are good, and I have not heard even a leaf rustle in the ivy, all is so still." So said my aunt. But I denied the dreaming.

Downstairs in the kitchen I found Hetty concocting egg-flip for Thomas, who sat with his limbs stretched out, his pipe in his mouth, the very impersonation of calm enjoyment, by the hot fire, where a great yule-log, lit from last year's brand, was sputtering and blazing cheerily. The cat had made a cushion of Jock's favourite terrier, and both were dozing comfortably on the hearth. It was evident they had heard nothing.

"Shot, measter? I heerd noa shot. And whoa could get anigh Tarnbeck ta fire oather gun or pistol, wi' th' watters out, an' th' boats a' on this side?"

"Thomas is right," assented Aunt Lydia, who had followed at my heels. "Nothing but a kelpie could approach the Tower through this flood without a boat, and kelpies are not supposed to carry firearms. My dear Charles, you sit alone until you grow morbid and fanciful. Who should seek to injure *you?* Besides, no shot could reach you from outside in the middle of a room so elevated."

"But I *heard* it, Aunt, and felt it stir my hair."

"Now, do be sensible, Charles, and don't look so absurdly obstinate. Suppose," she added, "to satisfy yourself, you and Thomas take a survey of the grounds. Hetty and I will go over the house."

There was no one hiding—there was nowhere to hide—the bushes were bare, and the evergreen wall half under water for the first time within memory.

A small looking-glass hung by the kitchen dresser, and as I passed through, burdened with a second mystery (for I was unconvinced), I saw reflected within it Thomas, behind my back, tapping his forehead significantly with his forefinger, and nodding towards me, as if to intimate to Hetty that my wits were wandering.

CHAPTER IV

Without giving offence I could not absent myself from Fairclough House on that special Christmas Day. But if I was present in body I certainly was absent in mind. Not even the gentle voice of Alicia could restore my old self. I joined in games and dances, but I felt as if I were a marked man.

The glare of lamps, the music, the laughter of children, the very life and motion, distracted me. I crept away into the billiard-room, now deserted, and began to knock the balls about as vacantly as I had taken up the cue. I cannot tell how long I had been playing there alone, when a light step, crossing the tessellated hall, stopped at the door, causing my pulse to quicken and my face to flush. A mist came before my eyes, and I struck my ball unsteadily, as, after a moment's hesitation, Alicia came forward and slightly touched me on the sleeve.

The subdued intonation of her voice, no less than a touch, thrilled through me, as she asked, with real concern in her face:

"Mr. Beckton, why do you desert your friends? Has anything annoyed you?"

"No. But like Dr. Johnson, I am not a gregarious animal. I feel myself out of place in a crowd," was my evasive answer.

"I know you only as a cheerful and intellectual companion," she returned. "To-night you seem gloomy and abstracted. The free comments I have heard respecting your absence have given me pain; therefore I have come to seek you, and carry you back. Unless," she added, after a fluttering pause, "I myself have incurred your displeasure."

"You! Alicia—Miss Proctor! *You* displease me! Good Heavens! If you—I beg your pardon—I am out of sorts. Pray excuse me. I am not fit company to-night."

"Will Mr. Beckton forgive me if I use the freedom of a sincere friend?" Her delicate hand again fell lightly on my sleeve, and her serene eyes met mine with an eloquent look of entreaty as she continued:

"Your friends fear you are not fit for your own company; that some secret is preying upon you which you are afraid to divulge. And, oh, Mr. Beckton, all the whisperers are *not* friends; there are slanderous suppositions abroad."

I felt that the bolt had fallen before its time, yet I could not speak a word. She went on earnestly: "I myself know you to be the soul of honour and chivalry. If there be a weight on your mind, it is from some outer cause. That you had had a shock I heard from Dr. Halgarth. If you have a painful secret, can you—will you—entrust me with it? It is true I am but a woman, and my counsel may be of little worth, but I have sympathy, and even that may help to chase some clouds from your sky."

Overpowered, I had fallen into my solitary attitude, and buried my face in my hands, leaning with my elbows on the billiard-table. If ever angel spoke to mortal, Alicia was one that night to me. I loosened the fetters on my tongue, and threw the burden off my soul in confidence to her. Though not at liberty to lay bare the arcana of the cabinet, I told her how mysteriously Amy's dower had disappeared from the thrice-guarded depository—of my inability to trace the thief, or to replace either documents, book, or jewels in their integrity, even if I made monetary restitution, which I was preparing to do through the medium of a mortgage on a portion of the Tarnbeck estate.

Alicia followed my narration with marked and sympathetic attention, only interrupting with an exclamation of surprise, or a question here and there. But when, in answer to her natural query, "Why did you not at once make the theft known?" I told of my hesitation lest I myself should be branded with their abstraction, and Frank Fairclough should reject the hand of my darling sister, she drew herself up in noble defence of our friend.

"What grounds have you for suspecting Mr. Frank of such baseness? He could not possibly doubt your integrity, notwithstanding the mystery of the case, and he is too upright and honourable to break off his engagement to your sister, even had there been a leaven of Mammon in his choice, which there is not. Someone must have poisoned your mind against him."

In fealty to my boyhood's friend I said nothing of Oscar's insinuations, but, deferring to Alicia's unbiased judgment, resolved to throw myself upon Frank's generosity on the morrow. Engrossed in the subject, neither of us had heard how often Time had flapped his wings, nor yet the closing of the door, which someone, conceiving ours a tender interview, must have shut quietly.

The inference was natural but mistaken. No word of love had been spoken; yet when Amy tripped in with the sportive exclamation, "What are you two arch conspirators plotting, whilst a disconsolate sire is waiting his missing daughter?" both started and blushed with self-consciousness; and we left the billiard-room to take our places in "Sir Roger de Coverley,"[7] sensible of a new link between us, with hearts that beat in unison, and hands that thrilled to each other's touch.

Mr. Proctor went back to Leeds by the first morning train, and Frank drove Alicia over to Tarnbeck in the afternoon to remain with Amy until the marriage.

After dinner I bore Frank off to the library, and, though not without considerable nervous hesitation, laid the whole facts before him. He listened most attentively, and questioned minutely, but I could see that from first to last no doubt of my integrity crossed his mind, and he was cooler than I had expected.

"It was a stupid trick of your governor to consign so much valuable property to the keeping of a private cabinet, however well guarded by secret springs. Woodwork is proof neither against fire nor crowbars, and might well tempt burglars." After a pause for cogitation he resumed: "You say you are bound by oath not to disclose the secrets of the escritoire. Should you feel equally bound to prohibit

[7] The name of a country dance.

my unassisted examination. Someone must have penetrated it, and why not I?"

I gave my assent willingly, and thereupon Frank began to pull and push the carvings wherever a prominence caught his eye. He made one or two unimportant discoveries, but the insignificant little button escaped detection. Still he persevered. Suddenly a bright thought struck him, and he sat down in the chair opposite to me.

"Beckton, were you ever a somnambulist?"

I saw the drift of his conjecture, and answered readily, "Not to my knowledge."

"Nor any of your family?"

"Nor any of the family."

"Well, this is altogether unaccountable. Depend upon it, someone else has had access to this room, with ample leisure to try the cabinet, as I mean to do before I give it up." He rose as he spoke, and turned again to his task, over which he had spent two hours, just as the clock was on the stroke of midnight.

As it struck, a cry burst from my lips. Oscar Bergheim stood by his side at the cabinet, with a pale face, and a red spot on his broad shirt-front. At my cry Frank turned round.

"What ails you, Beckton? You look as scared as if you saw a spectre!"

"Oscar," I cried rising with outstretched hand. "Oscar, my dear friend!"

There was no response. The figure passed to the unused door and was gone, the door remaining closed. I saw Frank watching me in amazement. No doubt I looked bewildered.

"Frank, did you not see Oscar Bergheim standing there?"

His eyes followed my pointing finger.

"Oscar Bergheim? Nonsense! He is in Australia by this time.

I saw nothing and no one."

I shook my head. "But I did!"

"My good fellow, the fact is you have brooded over this unfortunate theft until your brain is teeming with morbid fancies. You had better go to bed and get a good night's rest. And make your mind easy. I want Amy herself—neither her jewels nor her money. Her real property will not run away, and there is little fear of a claimant coming forward whilst bricks and mortar hold together. And now I must be off; there will be black looks when I get home for keeping the servants up so late—or, rather, early."

Frank came again in the evening, after the mill was closed and dinner over; and, dismissing the groom, announced his intention to remain the night, as he said, for the pleasure of a long chat, but as I suspected, in reality to watch over me.

Under the pretext of a headache, which music increased, I stole away to my retreat soon after his arrival. After a long gossip with the ladies he came to the library as if to say "good night." But he lingered; again sounded the dumb cabinet—the Palmer never opened his scrip. But precisely at twelve Oscar Bergheim stood there again, with the red spot on his breast, to disappear as before, unseen by my companion.

This time my terror was palpable. Perspiration gathered on my brow, and a tremor shook every limb. I feared some accident had befallen the friend of my youth. Frank laid his cool fingers on my pulse in evident perturbation, sought Aunt Lydia for a sedative to still my nerves, and would not leave until he saw me in bed and asleep.

I found him with Alicia and Aunt Lydia in full conclave the next morning. The conversation broke off abruptly on my entrance, and after ordinary salutations we sat down to breakfast.

It was not until afterwards that I ascertained that Frank and Aunt Lydia had exchanged mutual confidences respecting my declarations—the alleged shot on Christmas Eve, Oscar Bergheim's appearance on the 26th and 27th, and, finally, the missing treasure. The two came to the conclusion that study had turned my brain, and that even the loss of the dower was a delusion. Only Alicia maintained a belief in my sanity.

That night Alicia claimed my assistance in a troublesome translation. How every fibre quivered as she sat by my side at the table, and occasionally our fingers met as we turned over the leaves! Amy came dancing in and out, until an arrival below found her more agreeable occupation, and we were left in quiet—quiet so profound that I heard our hearts keep time with the ticking clock. Still we plodded through the book; but I have no remembrance what we translated. All at once—I know not and care not how—in turning a leaf my hand closed upon hers. I flung my arm around her, and strained her to me with a passionate clasp, only to release her instantly, and sob, rather than say, "Heaven forgive me, Alicia; I could not help it. I love you more than my life."

"And I love you, Charles," was the quiet, unexpected answer, which, at the same moment, stilled my nerves and set my heart aflame. All my prudent calculations, all dread of the paternal Proctor, vanished as I held her in my arms unrebuked, and laid my kisses on her brow and lips.

In the unlooked for excitement Alicia lost sight of the purpose with which she had come to the library (I need scarcely say the translation was a fiction). The striking clock broke in upon our dream of bliss. Simultaneously we turned expectant.

The cabinet doors flew open, and there stood the semi-transparent figure of Oscar Bergheim in his summer suit of grey tweed, with his finger on the button of the Palmer's scrip. Then he glided to the door, looking back, as if inviting us to follow. For a moment he lingered, a yearning look in his eyes.

"Let us follow," whispered Alicia, clinging to me. It was evident the apparition was visible to her also. She had more nerve than I. Lifting a small reading lamp, she advanced, still holding fast my arm. I had to open the door through which the figure had passed. It was standing in the archway of the west wing as if awaiting us. It moved onwards towards Oscar Bergheim's chamber, the door of which stood open. We followed in silence, the palpitation of our hearts being audible in the stillness. Our lamp barely dispelled the gloom around us, yet Oscar's form stood clearly outlined as it stopped at the wide fireplace (closed and fitted with a modern stove) and laid one hand on the central medallion richly carved in wood above it, the other over the red spot on his heart.

Ere we could advance another step Oscar's semblance was gone, and with it a sense of light and companionship, however dread.

As if by mutual agreement, yet without a word, we hurried together from the west wing along the dim corridor and staircase to the lighted drawing-room below.

Aunt Lydia was nodding on one side of the fire; Frank, lounging on an amber satin settee, with Amy on a low stool by his side, was toying with her silken ringlets.

The light of another world must have lingered on our faces, the pair started up so appalled. Aunt Lydia was aroused. Alicia was the first to tell what we had both seen. Frank looked incredulous, but there was no more thought of my insanity, Alicia, at least, was not a dreamer.

Poor Amy's teeth chattered with fright. Frank threw his protecting arm around her, and, remembering she had been kindly kept in ignorance, told her, with all the brevity of a business man, of the mysterious events which had made my life miserable. Long before he had concluded she left Frank's arm to put both her arms round my neck, and lay her bright head on my breast, reiterating the words, "Charlie, Charlie! as if I cared so much for money or trinkets!"

Alicia suggested that there must be some connection between the apparition and the missing valuables, and proposed that an instant search should be made in Oscar's chamber. All agreed to the general proposition, but Amy and Aunt Lydia demurred to its immediate attempt. "Why not leave it until daylight?" they both cried in a breath.

"I think the sooner your brother's mind is relieved the better," put in the thoughtful Alicia, and I thanked her with a pressure of the hand which no one saw.

"I think so too," assented Frank, with decision, but Amy, who had gone back to her lover, looked up beseechingly in his face, and he wavered. We had been standing grouped around the fire. Aunt Lydia resumed her seat, and one by one the rest sat down also. There was no thought of going to bed. Amy would not hear of Frank leaving us.

The fire was replenished, the lamps retrimmed. Jock, who was sitting up to ferry Mr. Frank and his horse over, was sent to his repose. In a body we made a raid upon the larder for refreshment, even Alicia not caring to visit the dark and unknown regions alone. Frank and I brought wine from the dining-room, and we prepared to wait for the slow daylight, in a sort of shuddering, anxious expectancy, somewhat allayed on my part, by the new happiness I had found in Alicia's love. We sat next to each other, and I think my arm stole along the back of her chair. Once I caught a surprised glance from Frank's eye, followed by a merry twinkle, and a demure expansion of his closed lips, as if well satisfied.

Conversation was carried on in whispers, and when general was of a weird and ghostly character.

With morning came courage, which baths and breakfast strengthened. What the domestics thought of our sitting up I did not inquire.

About ten o'clock we went together to Oscar Bergheim's room. The light streamed in through the Gothic windows, and fell on the bed where he had tossed so wildly in his delirium. Frank was for raising the stones of the hearth. Alicia would try the medallion where the shadowy hand had rested. For some time it baffled our efforts, but at length the whole panel slid downwards, and there, in a deep recess, lay Amy's dower—casket, bank-book, parchments, etc.

Who shall tell the deep thankfulness of my heart at that moment? What had I not recovered besides! An avalanche seemed to slip from my life and leave me sound and free. I could now look up to Alicia unimpoverished, unsuspected. I was too happy to do more than wonder what had befallen Oscar, and why he had been permitted to return for my behoof.

Amy's wedding was an event in Clevedale annals. The vicar officiated, and Mr. Smiles assisted. The bridal dress, of white silk and lace, looped here and there with orange blossoms and jessamine, was the gift of Lady Clevedale, who herself shone graciously upon the occasion, and the wondrous loveliness of the bride was the theme of all the strangers present.

But the revelation made after the breakfast, when I resigned my trust and surrendered Amy's dower, furnished a topic of after conversation for miles around.

When I had given Amy a parting kiss, and wrung the hand of Frank, as he stepped beaming into the carriage which bore them to the station, I invited the awful Mr. Proctor into the library. When he left I was accepted as his son-in-law.

The bridal tour was over; the young couple were fairly installed in one of Amy's own houses, four miles up the dale, which old Mr. Fairclough had furnished for them handsomely; Hetty and Aunt Lydia were turning the Tarnbeck Penates upside down in anticipation of another wedding, when the mail from Australia brought the following letter with its enclosure:—

"Melbourne, December 26, 186—.

"Sir,—It is with pain I convey to you the melancholy tidings of our passenger Mr. Bergheim's death, the more so that he died by his own hand. His manner throughout the whole voyage had been peculiar—at times hilarious, at others moody. Yesterday (Christmas Day) we sighted Melbourne at mid-day. The sun was glaring hot, and its rays pouring down melted the pith on the steamer's sides. Mr. Bergheim paced the deck with his head uncovered. I warned him of the risk of sunstroke; a passenger remonstrated with him, but he only laughed. In about an hour he went down to his cabin. An hour and a half later (precisely at 2.30 p.m.) the sharp report of a pistol-shot rang through the vessel. Your friend Mr. Bergheim had shot himself through the heart. The enclosed lay on the desk before him. As we were almost in port, the remains were carried ashore for interment. His papers supplied your address.

"I am, Sir, yours respectfully,

"JAMES STEVENS, Commander of S. S. 'Naiad.' "

If I read this with emotion, supernaturally prepared as I had been, how much more was I moved by the terrible enclosure!

"Steamship 'Naiad.'

"MY DEAR CHARLES,—I dare not call you friend; you will reject the title when you know all. Yet I must unburden my conscience before I go mad outright. Charles, you know how much I loved your sister, even from her infancy. Not until my father's death was I free to marry. Then I sought Tarnbeck. Amy was in London. Without a word to you, I followed. I found ready entrance into Lady Clevedale's circle. Amy had grown into a lovely woman—lovelier than my dreams; but she did not recognise me. I followed her everywhere, but my attentions annoyed her. I avowed my love, and she rejected me—gently, but firmly. Still I did not despair, until Fairclough came between us. I saw her smile on him, and it maddened me. Wheresoever she went, there was he as her shield—quiet, unobtrusive—but there. And, looking back, I know that he loving her well, was justified. I had disgraced my father's name, and Fairclough knew it. I was going headlong to the deuce, and he knew that too. I was not worthy to marry your pure sister, and he knew that, and told me so to my face. Baffled, but not despairing, I presented myself at Tarnbeck when Fairclough's business should have kept him away. Fool that I was, I thought that I had your sanction, and so set up a claim to her. He came between us again at that accursed pic-nic; and, in my unspeakable agony, I struck him. You know what followed. To me there was a blank, and then the torment of the lost Amy's gentleness led me to tempt my fate again. Good heavens! it was only to hear her avowal of love for Fairclough! Then the demon of jealousy fired my soul with revenge. Charles, do not wholly hate and despise me. During the last vacation I spent in my youth at Tarnbeck I sat alone in one of the library windows. The heavy curtains hid me. Your father entered. He unlocked the cabinet; I watched him touch a spring and pull a shelf, and saw the result. The shelf and figure went back to their places. When he left the room the cabinet door stood open. I stole from my lurking-place and tried the spring, and I had mastered the Beckton secret. You have only one key to both the library doors. There were two. I abstracted the one. Your father—unsuspicious soul!—never, to my knowledge, observed its loss. You will ask why I took it. I cannot tell; unless from a desire for power and mastery. My principles were at a low ebb even then. You will have missed all that your father left secure for Amy. I took them—I, your trusted friend. Not for their value—they were useless to me—but for revenge. I was mad. I thought that Fairclough would abandon a portionless girl, and leave me a future chance. He may have done so—I know not. I had not taken them an hour but I was stung with remorse, and remorse fought with revenge. I was a thief. I parleyed with my conscience, and quitting the Tower, left the things behind me, where no Fairclough can ever find them. My torment was not over. If I hugged myself with revenge at first, I have suffered tortures since. Not till we were fairly at sea did the consequences of my act to you, my more than brother, dawn upon me. Oh, that I could undo the past. It cannot be. I have blighted all I loved. I can only atone with my own blood. There is a world between us as I write—there will be another world between us when you read.——Farewell—forgive me if you can.

"You will find the accursed things hidden behind——My—I cannot—Fairclough would——"

Jealousy and revenge had clearly overpowered remorse. A red splash was the only signature to the incomplete letter. But the fatal shot had carried its message instantaneously to me, though a world lay between us; and who knows but repentance came even as the spirit fled, and hence the apparition we had seen.

We kept all knowledge of Bergheim's fate from Amy. She would never have worn her jewels without pain had she known what they had cost. But I showed the letters to Alicia and Frank. It was not until then that he told me he had traced the false reports, which had shaken their firm, to my friend Oscar. He had been only silent lest he should grieve me. And I did grieve. But when my dear Alicia came to rule at Tarnbeck, we closed Oscar's room with all its memories, though we never saw his remorseful spirit again after Amy's dower was recovered.

THE PRIDE OF THE CORBYNS

CHAPTER I

THE LAST OF THE CORBYNS

DEATH stood knocking at Archibald Corbyn's door—not at the door of Corbyn Hall, but at the door of the Corbyn heart; and when that had ceased to beat, one of the oldest, wealthiest, proudest, and most aristocratic families in Barbadoes would be extinct.

It was a boast of Archibald that the highland district in the north-west, of which Mount Hillaby is the centre, owed its name of Scotland to the loyalty of the first Corbyn, who, settling beneath the shadow of those conical hills, first cleared away dense forests of the bearded fig for the better cultivation of cotton.

He was one of those nine British merchants who, in the reign of Charles I, landed and built Bridgetown as a commercial depot, each having a grant of a thousand acres, contingent on the payment of forty pounds of cotton annually to Sir William Courteen, the original founder of the colony. Tracing down the family history, Archibald would tell with a glow how another Corbyn had introduced the sugar-cane into the island, in spite of troublous times, and how he erected the first primitive windmill to crush out the sap, when he had only open-air boilers in which to crystallize that sap into golden sugar and golden coin.

Riding home from St. Andrew's church on one of these occasions, with his old friend and shipping agent, Matthias Walcot, by his side, he pointed to a mound, below which two streams, rushing right and left of Corbyn Hall from the mountains, there met at a sharp angle, and ran on to join Church River until that ended in a lakelet known as Long Pond, partially barred by sand and vegetable wash from the sea.

"There, Matthias," he said, "the first Corbyn roof-tree stood just where that group of courida-trees now casts a shadow over the grass. It was but a rude wooden shed with palm-leaf thatch—old Cuffy has a better now—but young colonists have to rough it, and if a man has pith in him, what matter?"

As they turned from the white mountain road into the long avenue of sandbox and cocoa-nut trees, and neared his handsome two-floored, square, stone mansion, with pillared piazzas and overhanging balconies on three sides, overgrown with creepers and standing picturesquely against a background of white clay-tipped, rugged, dark brown rocks, variegated with waving cane fields, he told how he owed the substantial abode before them to the spirit of desolation which, riding on the wings of devastating hurricanes, had in two successive centuries swept homesteads and plantation into one indiscriminate wreck.

"That was in 1780, when Jamie Corbyn, my grandfather, was the owner. *He* was a man with pith in him, was Jamie; and when he saw his plank walls flying about like so many palm-leaves, he just made up his mind to build under a sheltering nook of the hills; and since stone came almost as handy as wood, he built a house that should stand during his lifetime and his son's after him."

"Well, Mr. Corbyn, it is an ill wind that blows no one good," Mr. Walcot put in. "It blew the Corbyns a house that will last."

Archibald's mood changed; he sighed heavily. "Ay, friend Matthias; it did blow the Corbyns a home to last—a home sacred from intrusion. Our dead were washed out of their graves, and my grandfather, horrified, planned and built yon solid half-sunken mausoleum at the extremity of the wood to receive the ancestors the hurricane had unearthed. And there he too lies, with his sons and daughters in niches by his side; and there I in time shall be laid, with no child nor relative to mourn or follow me. My dear brother Charles lies under the sea, and I am the last of the Corbyns," with another sigh. "He built a home for the living and a home for the dead, to serve for many generations to come; but I am the last of my uncontaminated race, and when the mausoleum doors close upon me they will close for ever."

Uncontaminated! Ah, there the full pride of the Corbyns spoke out. No drop of Indian or negro blood flowed in Corbyn veins. He was pure white as his first English ancestor; could stand the test of any hotel in the United States, and draw his fingers through his hair without showing a tinge of blue in his oval nails, or the slightest "kink" in his flowing locks—a grand distinction this in Barbadoes, where so few even of the wealthy planters but had a taint of the creole in their composition, however infinitesimal. And no West Indian could more fully appreciate the value of the vaunt than Matthias Walcot.

But Death knocking at Archibald Corbyn's door was growing clamorous, and black blood or white would be all as one within the hour.

Dr. Hawley and Matthias Walcot stood by his bedside, and Dinah, his old negro nurse, readjusted his disordered pillow or wiped the heavy dew from his clammy forehead with gentle, sympathetic hands, and watched his wasted fingers pick the counterpane with sad forebodings.

With quick intelligence she caught the meaning of a glance from the doctor to Mr. Walcot, and escaping from the chamber by the open window, with her big black hands before her face, she leaned over the edge of the balcony to sob out of sight and hearing.

Yet her own ears were alert for any sound from the sick-room, and presently the feint voice of her dying master attracted her attention. True to negro instinct, curiosity arrested grief. She crept to the open window.

He was saying, in feeble gasps, "Will in my desk—I've left you—sole executor, Matthias. I know I can trust you. Use my slaves well, and—no whipping, Matt!"

There was a pause. The doctor administered a stimulant; Archibald evidently revived.

"And, Matthias—I—charge you—leave no stone unturned—find a Corbyn to inherit—Charlie's dead body never found—may be after all—I—not—last of the Corbyns. Mausoleum close for ever—Corbyns extinct—pure race—"

The voice was lost in indistinct murmurs. There was silence.

"He's gone!" whispered Mr. Walcot; "hush!"

The doctor placed a finger on his lips, and with the other hand checked Dinah's impulsive return to the room.

"Matthias—England—advertise—I have—last Corb—"

Close the jalousies:[8] exclude the light. The master of Corbyn hall can neither see the sunshine nor hear the universal wail that from every corner of that wide estate follows his soul to the gates of heaven and pleads for its admission. Archibald Corbyn, too proud of birth to do aught unworthy to his pure blood, has been a master without peer!

There was a small grating in the thick door of the mausoleum, which was reached by a descent of four or five steps. This entrance, which fronted a bye-road, was bricked up. The mausoleum itself was a solid stone structure, with little or no attempt at ornament;

[8] Slatted blinds or shutters.

externally about fourteen yards square, with a domed roof rising not more than four feet above the level of the road; the ground on all four sides sloping downwards towards the building. It was consequently in a deep hollow, and was further sheltered from high winds by the hills which rose steeply above the road on the other side, and by the wood of manchineel and sandbox trees, which had marched up to its three sides like a protecting army of giants. Here and there might be seen rotten stumps of coca-nut trees, destroyed by a general blight long before Jamie Corbyn made his Machpelah among them and brought the dead to the dead.[9]

Though they were clothed with parasitic verdure, they had a weird aspect on a moonlight night, these ghostly skeletons of forgotten forest-palms.

It was mid-day. The ripe pendulous pods of the thorny sandbox trees burst one after another, and scattering their seed-rings to earth with sharp reports, as if a platoon of distant musketry proclaimed the fall of each. But another ripe seed was ready to be "sown in corruption," and a louder report proclaimed that.

It was the inevitable gun fired through the unbricked grating, to dissipate noxious gases generated within, lest the opening of the vault for the dead should let out pestilence on the living.

A night had passed. Intelligence had flown swift-winged over the little island. The vault was purified; the door stood open. From all parts of Barbadoes planters and others had assembled to show their respect for the dead. Rising and falling with the undulations of the hills, a long procession of carriages and pedestrians marked the white road with a line of black for half a line or more. Slaves

---

[9] Machpelah: from the Bible, a field and cave bought by Abraham as a burying-place.

and friends, bonded and free, white, creole, quadroon, mulatto, and black, were there with sable suits and white head-gear; but of all those hundreds, not one relative to hold the pall or shed a tear over the silver-mounted black coffin as it was borne to its niche in the sepulchre with solemn funeral rites; and the door was closed on hospitable Archibald, the "last of the Corbyns."

"Brick it up close, Dan," said centenarian Cuffy to the labourer at work; "nebber be opened no more. Massa nebber rest in him grave if a drop of nigger blood be berried with him. An' I'm 'fraid, Dan, there be no real white massa to come after good ole massa."

" 'Fraid not, Cuffy?" questioned Dan ruefully—for Cuffy was the oracle of the plantation—adding, "Ah, him proud gemp'lman, but him berry good to black man. Wonder who be massa now?"

A momentous question this to a slave!

Cuffy extended his withered arm to an opening between the distant foliage, where a glimpse of the shining Atlantic might be seen three miles away.

"Ib dat hungry sea swallow up young Massa Charles, I much 'fraid, Dan, Massa Walcot will be. *He* got a splash ob colour in *him*, but his heart no so warm as our poor massa'a for all dat;" and old Cuffy turned away mournfully, shaking his head.

Corbyn Hall had got a new master. The will which made Matthias Walcot sole executor made him virtually proprietor.

All that stood between him and absolute ownership was the very improbable chance that Archibald's younger brother, Charles, had escaped when the Mermaid, in which he had sailed from Bristol seven years before, foundered off the Irish coast, and not a soul was known to be saved. There was also the remote possibility of his having left a legitimate heir on dry land; but as no echo of wedding-bells had ever wafted to the brother in Barbadoes, this was as improbable.

The brothers had parted in anger; and Archibald had never been his own man after the Mermaid went down. He was only forty-eight when he died; and his will was full of mournful regret. Matthias was enjoined to spare no cost, neglect no means to find a rightful heir; but if within ten years no claimant could be discovered, then—and not till then—Matthias Walcot and his heirs were to possess the Corbyn estate, with all its living brood, in perpetuity.

Matthias Walcot passed as an honourable man amongst men; had been esteemed and trusted by the dead; would have resented the charge of dishonesty. But the temptation was great, and *he* was *not*.

Prompt to take possession, he was not prompt in measures which *might* eventually oust himself and his. He made languid official inquiries at first; sent occasional advertisements to an English newspaper; and persuaded himself, and tried to persuade D. Hawley, that he had been very active.

CHAPTER II
THE WALCOTS AT HOME

I said Corbyn Hall had a new master; I should have said a mistress and three masters, a younger lady being thrown in. There was Mrs. Walcot, dominant, of large dimensions and lofty pretensions; there was Miss Walcot, slight, languid, listless, and intensely fashionable; and there were two sons, William and Stephen, the most bumptious of all bumptious Barbadians.

What a revolution their advent created in that hospitable, free-and-easy bachelor household! The will interdicted unnecessary change until heirship was determined. But Mrs. Walcot was disposed to read its provisions liberally. She did not sell or destroy plain old-fashioned fittings: they were simply huddled into a lumber room out of her way, and replaced with the very brightest and newest importations from Europe, before even the dogs and horses had well learned to recognize the new mastership.

Matthias himself forgot he was only executor. He turned his shipping agency and his stifling office on the wharf over to his tall sons, and settled down comfortably at Corbyn Hall as proprietor and planter. But Mrs. Walcot was fond of society, and was not content to dwell for ever ten miles from town and two or three from their nearest neighbours; so their old house at the Folly was retained, ostensibly for the convenience of William and Stephen, and the lady rejoiced in a town-house and a country-house, and became a very grand personage indeed. She oscillated between the two houses, paid and received visits, went shopping, and ransacked the heterogenous stores of every dealer in Broad-street, to the intense disgust of Scipio, her mulatto charioteer, whose lazy life was at an end.

Nor was Scipio the only grumbler on the estate. Flippant lady's-maids invaded the sanctity if Chloe's kitchen and Cassy's laundry. Will and Steve in house or stable were as ready to use their riding-whips on the shoulders of valet or groom as on the flanks of their steeds. There were sharp overseers in the boiling-sheds, on the rocky slopes amongst the waving yellow canes and the changeful fields of Indian corn, and among the bursting cotton-pods. The change sank into the negro heart, and from Chloe in her kitchen to Cuffy in his distant hut, there were sunken spirits and low-voiced murmurings. If a "boy" carried his dish of cuckoo to window or door sill, or squatted on mat or ground outside to eat his dinner at ease, he was sure to become the centre of a group no longer shaking their fat sides with laughter, but shaking their woolly heads mysteriously, and comparing the present *régime* with the past.

Dinah—or aunt Dinah, as she was called—who had nursed the infant, sick, and dying Corbyns for two generations, and ruled supreme in Archibald's time, had been deposed, and the poor old thing fretted much, as might any other prime minister in disgrace.

It was none of Mr. Walcot's doing. Had he been consulted, he might have remembered her presence in the planter's death-chamber, and from motives of policy left her to govern her coloured brood as of yore.

Yet even he knew not what she had heard, nor how it had worked in her brain. As it was, she brooded over her dying master's words, and felt their import greater than reality.

Old Cuffy—still the nominal head-gardener—she made the depository of her knowledge, and the pair held frequent and solemn conference. From these twain, no doubt, the first faint murmurings against Walcot rule went out like a breath, as soft and unsuspected. And now aunt Dinah was troubled with ominous dreams, and Cuffy grew portentously prophetic.

Meanwhile Mrs. Walcot, blessedly obtuse, prepared to give a grand ball before the rainy season should set in, with one match-making eye for Laura and another for William, who had set both his on a lovely orphan heiress, then the ward of Rev. John Fulton.

Vainly Matthias, with due regard to appearances, urged that it was "too soon." Madam was wilful, and issued her invitations to the cream of Barbadian society, with a select few of her former Bridgetown friends, whom she hoped to overpower with her grandeur.

Mourning was all but discarded: a gauzy black scarf for herself, a black sash for Miss Walcot, were all that memory could spare for the late master of the mansion whose family diamonds they wore. The coloured attendants were arrayed in the gayest of tints: brilliant turbans, kerchiefs, and petticoats, flashing striped trousers and light jackets, fluttered everywhere, like swarms of black-bodied butterflies, to which every guest-bringing phaeton added its quota, either in driver or lackey.

Odour of fruits and flowers and wines, flash of glass and gilding, wax-lights and mirrors, sparkle of eyes and jewellery, flutter of satins, gauzes, and hearts, patter of feet and tongues, melody of piano, guitar, and song within.

Banjo and beating feet, the rollicking song and the dance, a babel of laughter and gabble without; and Cuffy and Dinah sullenly aloof in the shadow of a manchineel-tree—the only two to whom Mrs. Walcot's magnificent ball had brought neither pleasure nor occupation. The hooting owls in the sandbox trees were scarcely such birds of ill-omen to the Walcots as were these two, brooding over that festival as being an indignity to the memory of their dead master.

Song, and dance, and rippling laughter, flushing cheeks and fluttering fans! A shrill scream, like that of the Shunammite's son[10]—"My head, my head!"—and with one hand spasmodically raised to her brow, Laura Walcot fell back into the arms of her partner in the quadrille, speechless and gasping!

In vain ladies proffered scent bottles and vinaigrettes, and gentlemen darting through open casements brought back clusters of soft sandbox leaves to bind on her throbbing forehead, as antidotes to pain. The dark green but served to show how deathly was her

[10] In the Bible (2 Kings 4:18-37), the Shunammite's son was restored to life by Elisha the prophet.

pallor; and Dr. Hawley, brushing in through the crowd from the card-room, could do little more than shake his head gravely, and say "No use, no use! Too much excitement!"

Mrs. Walcot shrieked in hysterics; Matthias sat with bowed head like one stupefied; the haughty brows of William and Stephen lowered in presence of the grim intruder—Death.

Startled visitors departed, or remained for the ceremonial of the morrow. An awful hush fell over and around the mansion. The negroes, strangely unlike themselves, indulged in no noisy demonstrations of grief. They were silent, save when whispers of "Doom" and "Judgment" passed from mouth to mouth in stifled undertones.

As the white coffin of the maiden was being carried into the house, Cuffy, standing under the piazza, heard William Walcot give Dan instructions for the opening of the Corbyn mausoleum.

Uplifting his head and his bony hands in superstitious horror, he clasped them as they dropped before him, and ejaculated: "There! Berry young Missy Walcot in Corbyn grabe! Nebber. Old massa's flesh creep in him shroud if dat blue-nailed missy laid inside there!"

The tall old man, venerable with the grayness of his hundred years, drew a long breath, then stalked unbidden into the presence of Matthias and Dr. Hawley, and stood before them erect, with fiery eyes, much as Elijah must have stood before usurping Ahab.[11]

"Massa Walcot better not berry him dead with the Corbyn dead. Sure's you live, Massa Arch'bald nebber 'low it!"

"Not allow it, Cuffy! What do you mean?" said Mr. Walcot testily, looking up amazed and annoyed.

---

[11] 1 Kings 18:16-45: Elijah challenges Ahab to a demonstration of his deity's power versus the God of Elijah at Mount Carmel.

"Massa Corbyn leave him hall, leave him plantation, leave him money to him friend; but him keep de Corbyn maus'leum for de Corbyn *only*. IF"—and undaunted Cuffy laid special emphasis on the "if"—"IF no heir, an Massa Arch'bald *be* last ob de Corbyns, den dat maus'leum be closed till Judgment'day!"

"Cuffy, you presume on your gray hairs. I shall lay my poor child where I think fit. I do not suffer my slaves to dictate to me. Your mind is wandering. Quit the room; this is no season for intrusion."

Dr. Hawley listened in silence. Cuffy still maintained his ground.

"Massa Walcot, de 'mighty God above send Cuffy to warn you. Dere am *doom* on dis house till Corbyn heir be found, and de first thun'erbolt fell last night. For own sake, Massa Walcot" (Cuffy never said "*massa*" only), "berry pretty missy in de churchyard!"

A similar scene was enacted upstairs.

Dinah, arranging the folds of the fine muslin shroud, and the fan-shaped face cover to stand stiffly up until the last moment, made way for the bereaved mother to kiss the pallid lips ere it was folded down. She ventured to ask the place of interment.

Being told, she bent her aged knees, and implored her mistress to change her plans, or evil would be sure to come of it.

Mr. and Mrs. Walcot were alike obdurate and indignant. Cuffy and Dinah were declared crazy and superstitious, and cautioned to make less free in future.

But though they laid their daughter's corpse in the Corbyn mausoleum, in spite of premonition, for some innate reason they did not place it in any one of the unfilled niches; it was left on the floor in the centre of the sepulchre.

And then the Corbyn vault closed for the first time on one of another name and another caste.

CHAPTER III
THE MYSTERY OF THE MAUSOLEUM

It is not customary for Barbadians to court the heavy noxious dews and the bloodthirsty mosquitoes by being abroad after nightfall; but the unwonted events of ball and burial on two consecutive days had brought to that lonely plantation a concourse of people, some of whom were determined by the claims of friendship, others of business, to a late hour.

It was close upon midnight when Dr. Hawley and another friend shook hands with Mr. Walcot under the portico of the Corbyn mansion; and stepping into his light cane phaeton, he bade his black Jehu "Tear away home."

Once clear of the sombre avenue, where accommodating fireflies hung out their tiny lamps, the white marly road shone like a streak of silver in the bright moonlight. They spun along rapidly, to the drowsy music of their own wheels, in concert with the droning trumpet of obsequious mosquitoes, and the thin metallic pipe of an occasional cicada, to which their pony's hoof beat time. Otherwise the stillness was unbroken, save by Sambo's involuntary ejaculations to the steed.

As they neared the point where the road branched off to the sea-coast, passing the mausoleum on its way through Corbyn Hall Wood, a shrill scream was borne up the bye-road on the clear midnight air.

The pony stopped involuntarily, quivering in every limb.

"Golla, massa! what am dat?" cried Sambo in a fright.

Before Dr. Hawley or his friend could reply, a second scream, louder and more piercing, smote upon the ear, and was followed by a succession of unearthly yells.

"Quick, Sambo! Turn to the left. There is some foul play going on down this road. Quick! or we may be too late to prevent a tragedy."

But Sambo's white teeth chattered, all the more because the pony obstinately refused to obey the rein—willing to bolt down the road home, but determined not to turn to the left for either man or master. As he snorted, reared, and plunged, threatening the slight vehicle with destruction, and the shrieks still continued, the doctor and his companion leapt out, and ran at full speed down the road, athwart which sparsely set palmetto, or cocoa-nut trees cast spectral shadows.

A faint sea-breeze met them, laden with the mingled perfumes of fruit and flower, but with it came more hideously the strange discordant noise. Then two or three wild dogs darted past them, howling as they went. Then with garments flying loose and eyeballs glaring, a negro woman, blind with terror, ran against the doctor. A man, little less excited, was close at her heels.

"Hallo! what is the meaning of this outcry?" demanded the doctor, grasping the man by the arm, under the impression the negress was escaping from ill-usage.

The man—who proved to be the undertaker's foreman—could only gasp between his chattering teeth, "Dre'ful! Dre'ful, doctor; dre'ful!"

The woman—a seamstress whom the foreman was gallantly escorting home—had continued her flight.

"You black scoundrel, what have you been doing?" cried the doctor, giving him a shake.

The man's protest was drowned by a fresh outbreak of the same appalling cries.

Dr. Hawley, exclaiming, "Again! What is that?" released his arm, convinced that he at least was not the peace breaker.

"O! doctor, dre'ful, dre'ful down dere! Dead man's fight."

"Pish!" "Rubbish!" from the doctor and his friend; and they rushed forward, drawing reluctant Cicero back with them.

But they too stood aghast as they approached the mausoleum. The noise—a demoniac compound of blows, groans, shrieks, and howls—evidently *issued from the bricked-up sepulchre!*

It seemed, indeed, as though a desperate combat raged within the closed-up tomb; and the blood of the spectators curdled as they listened.

They were not the only auditors. A neighbouring planter and a sturdy sea-captain, named Hudson, on their way inland, had been arrested on their journey likewise, and seemed rooted to the spot with a mysterious dread.

Could anyone imagine a scene more terrible! The mausoleum, worn with age and weather, overgrown with moss and lichens, sentinelled by sandbox trees and blighted coca palms, whose shroud-like drapery of creepers gave them the aspect of ghosts of dead trees keeping watch for ghosts of dead men; and scared by the unearthly din, owls and monkeys screeched and chattered, to make if possible a greater pandemonium.

"I have seen the ocean in its fury, heard the winds break loose, and the artillery of heaven rattle, but never did I hear anything so terrible as this. It makes my very flesh creep," said the captain, addressing Dr. Hawley. "Can you, sir, offer any solution of this mystery?"

What Dr. Hawley might have said was interrupted by a final burst of triumphant yells, followed by a peal of still more discordant laughter, which died away in feeble cachinnations, till silence scarcely less awful fell on all around.

A harmless snake then uncoiled itself on the mausoleum steps and dragged itself across the road, a pair of green lizards crawled over the dome of the mausoleum to bask in the moonlight; and the unaccountable noises having ceased entirely, the party drawn together so singularly moved away in a body.

As a natural sequence, conversation turned on the place they had just quitted, Archibald Corbyn's funeral, and that of Laura Walcot; and so much was Captain Hudson interested, that when they shook hands and separated at the fork of the roads, he had promised to call on Dr. Hawley at his house near Kissing Bridge before sailing for England.

Seven persons (including Sambo) went their several ways surcharged with the story of a horrible mystery.

What wonder that the succeeding midnight brought a crowd to the spot, to test, verify, or ridicule, as might be? Notwithstanding the previous shock to his nerves, Dr. Hawley made one. With him was Stephen Walcot, much concerned by this commotion over his sister's grave; and on the extreme verge of the assembly they saw a group of old Corbyn servants huddled together like a flock of timid sheep, with Cuffy and aunt Dinah at their head.

The doctor had lost no time in making Mr. Walcot acquainted with his nocturnal experience. Matthias had only curled his lip, shrugged his shoulders, and said, "Were I you, doctor, I would not repeat this nonsense. Your patients will not care to consult a medico who takes too much wine." He had spoken to the sons. William laughed outright. Steve, subdued by his sister's loss, gave their informant a more respectful hearing, and, in spite of his brother's banter, volunteered to watch the tomb that night with the doctor, little surmising how many would share that watch.

Twelve by Dr. Hawley's repeater! The silent expectant crowd shrank back with affright as, without one moment's premonition, the air was rent with a volley of shrieks and yells, which wakened the echoes of the hills, and a chorus from owls and monkeys drove the racoon from his bed, the pigeons from their nests, and sent batwings from the shadows to flutter in the moonlight.

For one whole hour the noises were unceasing. If superstition drew the crowd together, fear dispersed it. Only the most daring of the auditors remained, and amongst these were Cuffy and Dinah, who stood apart with hands upraised, as if invoking unseen protection.

Bearing Cuffy's adjuration and previsions in mind, Dr. Hawley —well acquainted with negro subtlety, and anxious to find a natural solution for the phenomena—drew the centenarian apart, and, with Stephen by his side, subjected him to a fire of cross-questions.

"Know nuffink 'bout it, doctor; 'cept Massa Corbyn not rest. Him angry; all him dead family angry," was all they could elicit.

Yet, in spite of his genuine trepidation—for every nerve seemed to quiver—there appeared some reservation, of which the doctor took a mental note for question at a fitter time.

Mrs. Walcot was frantic. Sorrow for her daughter's loss was reduplicated by this scandal over her very grave. Mr. Walcot and William repudiated all notion of the supernatural, and ascribed the strange phenomena to a plot between Cuffy and his colleagues. Stringent orders were left with the overseers that no slave should quit the plantation after sundown, or approach within a given distance of the mausoleum, under penalty of a flogging.

But that did not quell the nocturnal riot. Matthias brought his own eyes and ears to the test, had the place examined by day, placed a cordon of military around, but all to no purpose.

For five nights the supernatural warfare continued. Trafalgar Square and the Bridgetown ice-houses were thronged with thirsty gossips, and Barbadoes throbbed with superstitious fear to its very finger-tips.

Then it ceased. The excitement gradually died out, business resumed its sway, the Walcots were condoled with, and the dead reposed in peace.

Still superstition held the haunted mausoleum in dread; and urgent must be the business and hardy must be the man that should travel that road by night.

Even over the Corbyn mansion crept a sort of eerie atmosphere. There was less laughter, and more whispering in secret corners. Every figure in mourning robes seemed to cast a shadow of death on the hearth. A cloud deeper than that of grief rested on the brows of Matthias and his wife; and the infection spread to the white tenantry on the estate.

CHAPTER IV
OBEAH!

A fortnight later Dr. Hawley rode out to the Hall. It was purely a friendly visit, so he said; but ere he went away he asked his host how he was progressing in his search for a legitimate heir, adding that a friend of his, a Captain Hudson, of the barque Adelaide, would readily undertake any commission in furtherance of that end in the mother country.

Mrs. Walcot bridled up, and Matthias, reddening, answered stiffly, "Thank you, doctor, but I can manage my own business without the intervention of strangers. I need no reminder of my duty. A sea captain is scarcely the person to institute inquiries of this nature."

"Perhaps not," assented the doctor dryly, with a peculiar smile, as he took his departure, much like one who has done half his errand.

Had their voices wafted to Cuffy through the open casement, that he should quit the jasmine he was pruning by the portico to hurry to the avenue? Whether or not, he stopped the pony under the shadow of the large trees, and whispered earnestly and mysteriously:

"Dr. Hawley, you good man; you lub ole massa. Him spirit angry; all de Corbyn spirits angry. Last night Dinah dream—dream of Massa Charlie. He wet an' white upon the steps; he ask to come in, and Massa Walcot shut the door—an' Death come in instead! Doctor, dere be nudder Corbyn somewhere, an Massa Walcot no try to find him; an' spirits *berry* angry. Cuffy work Obeah charm to-night, to keep de evil doom from de black boys and girls dat lub ole Massa Corbyn!"

"I would advise you to have nothing to do with Obeah, Cuffy. It may breed ill-feeling and do mischief," said the doctor, as Cuffy loosened his hold of the reins, and Sambo cracked his whip.

In Corbyn Hall Wood, remote from the Hall itself, close by a mountain streamlet which ran down to join the river, was a bubbling boiling spring. The spot was lonely and sequestered, shadowed by the palmetto and the manchineel. Gourds and squashes trailed along the ground and hid the iguana, the green lizard, and the spotted toad. No pine-apple or banana grew beside it; no seaside grape spread its branches low to the ground, hanging thick and ruddy clusters under every branch, glossy with leaves of green; but all that was dark or rank grew there.

It was a dismal spot. Yet hither dusky forms came stealthily in the middle of the night to watch and share with Cuffy in the dread rites of Obeah incantation. To his fellows he was known as a Mandingo priest, and the hold he had on their superstitious souls was strong and terrible. His hut was near at hand, and in this weird corner of the plantation had he been wont to concoct healing balms, philtres, and the yet more potent Obeah, whose spell, wrought in secret, was supposed to work in secret, and set human skill and precaution at defiance.

Dinah was there—a fitting priestess of these mysteries—and Dan and Scipio, and Chloe and Cassy, with others whose names are unrecorded.

There was a fissure in the ground close to the boiling spring. To this Cuffy applied a light, and instantly a jet of flame shot up, and the poor dupes bowed down to the fire-spirit. From a hollow tree was produced an iron pot. Half filling this from the boiling spring, it was suspended on a triangle of sticks over the natural naphtha flame, and the weird rites began.

There was a low monotonous chant in a strange tongue, a dance around the seething pot, which in the lurid light was half demonaic; and Cuffy, swaying to and fro, muttered words unknown even to his confederates, as one by one he threw into the pot snake-wood from the trumpet-tree, sap from the deadly manchineel, a snake cucumber, the poisonous sandbox leaves and rings, a living lizard and a toad, a turtle's egg, the root of a cat's-blood plant, a bat, a young owlet, a dead man's hair, pernicious scum from Long Pond, and other venomous ingredients with and without a name.

It was a horrible compound—a deadly poison; and as it bubbled in the pot, white teeth and eyes gleamed out from midnight faces, hideous from their own imaginings.

The charm wrought out, the mixture poured into a calabash bottle and closely stopped, the refuse buried in the ground, the pot restored to the hollow tree, the magic flame extinguished with wet sand, Cuffy dismissed his impish brood to their huts, and bore away his revolting decoction, to be buried the ensuing night under the threshold of the Hall. The doom hanging over Corbyn would then fall upon the fated mortals who should step across it first; and thus, Obeah satisfied, his followers would be protected.

Be sure there were early risers among the initiated, and sharp eyes to watch the threshold under ban, and warn off unwary footsteps.

Mr. William Walcot was the first to leave the house; but months went by, and still he came and went healthily and haughtily, in spite of Obeah; and he was more frequently at the Hall than either his father or Stephen liked, the Folly being his home proper. The father considered that Will interfered too much on the plantation, to the neglect and detriment of his shipping agency; while Steve, aware of the comparative proximity of the Hall to the Parsonage, regarded him as a dangerous rival.

The fact was that the elder of the twain had determined most fraternally to "cut his brother out" of the favour of Miss Wolferstone, if the clergyman's rich and lovely ward had any leaning in that direction, and altogether comported himself as if he were his father's natural and certain successor on the estate.

But Mrs. Walcot sickened: an inexplicable disease, which caused her lower limbs to swell painfully, marred her enjoyment, and made her splendid mansion little better than a prison, although stately Augusta Wolferstone and lively Mary Fulton came like sunbeams now and again to brighten it up. Then Matthias grew anguish and shivery. Finally, Steve, diverging from the wood-path on his way from the Parsonage one Sunday at the hour when sun and moon looked each other in the face, fell over a fern-covered boulder and broke his leg.

Cuffy and Scipio, out after dark on some occult errand, directed by his groans, found him lying amidst the rank vegetation, just over the spot where the Obeah refuse lay buried. "A coincidence," the old man observed to his companion; with the addendum, "Sorry Massa Steve hurt: him best cane of bundle."

Cuffy moreover showed his sincerity by binding cooling herbs on the broken limb whilst Scipio ran for a litter, and by setting the said limb skilfully as a surgeon, long before Dr. Hawley could be found.

Superstition regarded these untoward circumstances as so many visitations of warning and admonition. Indeed, so freely did Barbadian society discuss the Walcot succession to the Corbyn property by the light of Walcot ill-luck, that Matthias found his bed of roses invaded by gnats stinging worse than mosquitoes, to say nothing of the private thorns planted by conscience under the rose leaves.

From the morning when Dr. Hawley entered his office like a spirit of evil, to tell how his dead child's rest was disturbed, his own rest had been disturbed by nightmare memories of Archibald's death-bed. The dying man had trusted him. He had ill-deserved that trust. He had not meant to defraud the heir, if there was one; he had only been lukewarm in his efforts to find him. But was there one? He thought not; and so advertising was only waste of good money. Besides, it might tempt some knave to worry him with fictitious claims. However, some day he would send Will or Steve to England to make inquiries; and there was time enough.

And so he tried to salve the conscience that would not be salved; especially as Dr. Hawley now and then gave it an unexpected prick, and Cuffy and Dinah looked unutterable thorns.

The rainy season had almost passed. Steve's leg was nearly well; he could move about by the help of crutches; and Scipio had more than once driven him, very gently, over to the Parsonage, to be especially petted, both by Miss Wolferstone and Mary Fulton, the English parson's English daughter.

It was Will's turn to be jealous. He "could not see why a broken leg and a pale face should be so devilish attractive to a woman. They didn't attract him!" It went to his heart to see Augusta Wolferstone place the easiest cane chair in the verandah ready for his brother, and adjust the softest cushions to his special need. He was exasperated, too, that business should keep him so much at the wharf, and an accident clear the way for Steve to woo the girl in his absence.

So persistent were his grumblings that Mr. Walcot, for the sake of peace, went back to his old office to lighten Will's labour and give him an occasional holiday. On one of these days, William, who slept chiefly at the Folly during the wet season, rode from Bridgetown to St. Andrew's, calling in to see his mother on the way. He there learned that Stephen, taking advantage of a fine day, had gone before him, and was then at St. Andrew's Parsonage.

This roused his domineering temper; and with scarcely a civil word to his ailing and querulous mother, and a very uncivil cut with his riding-whip to the creole groom who held his horse, he set off neck-or-nothing, resolved to try whether he or Steve had the best of it before the day was out. So vicious was he in his brotherly love that he cut at his horse as if it had been Stephen's self, and dismounted in front of the Parsonage, little improved by seeing Steve on a couch under the verandah holding a skein of purse-twist for Augusta, whilst Mary read aloud to both.

His first remark was a sneer at his disabled brother's womanish occupation, his next a rude retort to Augusta's defence of Stephen. A bad beginning this; and his consciousness that it was bad only paved the way for further discomfiture.

Later in the day, he demanded, rather than solicited, a *tête-à-tête* conversation with Miss Wolferstone, and with little delicacy and less tact urged his suit as one whose claims were imperial—urged it as Steve's elder brother, and heir to the Corbyn estate.

Whatever claim he might have had on the young lady's regard he lost in that interview. His rudeness and unbrotherly feeling were so palpable, she felt impelled to resent both.

"I have no desire, sir, to marry the heir to the Corbyn or any other estate; but I do choose to marry a gentleman. I must therefore decline the honour of your alliance;" and she swept from the library as she spoke, without giving him a chance for another syllable.

Without a word of adieu to the ladies he darted from the house, almost too impatient to wait for the saddling of his horse; certainly too much irritated to accept the genial invitation of Mr. Fulton to remain the night, even though the weather had changed, and the rain was the rain of the tropics.

A sane man would have remembered that previous rains had flooded lowlands, had swelled mountain runnels to rivers, and rivers to torrents, and, so remembering, have taken the safer high-road by which he came, however circuitous.

But he, blinded by passion, disappointment, and jealousy (had he not left his silken brother behind him?) dashed homewards the near way, across Church River and through the wood.

Over the bridge he went safely enough; but when he reached the Corbyn rivulet, fed by Haggart's spring, he found his way stopped by a formidable stream rushing tumultuously on towards Long Pond. In no mood to hesitate, he madly urged his reluctant animal to attempt the perilous crossing.

He must have either missed the ford, or the horse lost its footing, and been carried down by the force of the water. His body was found the following day at the entrance to Long pond, blue, swollen, and swathed in a shroud of the poisonous green scum of the pond.

CHAPTER V
ON THE WINGS OF THE WIND

Once more orders were given to open the Corbyn receptacle for the dead.

The preparatory gun was fired into the vault; the brickwork was removed, the door opened for ventilation, then for preparation; and lo, the place was strewn with coffins and wrecks of coffins, skeletons and fragments of skeletons; and old Archibald's black coffin lay across Laure Walcot's white one, which was itself dinged and battered as if with heavy blows.

Scared out of his senses, Dan ran, as the crow flies, with his strange tale to the mourners at the Hall.

Incredulity faded before the fact. Matthias was staggered and terror-stricken, The air was sultry, even for sultry Barbadoes, and that left no time for fresh arrangements. The solemn ceremonial *must* proceed.

The hearse had reached the mausoleum before the disordered coffins could be replaced, or the *debris* collected and cleared into a vacant niche.

Then, with many misgivings and intensified anguish, Matthias saw the white coffin of the unmarried young man deposited by the side of his sister's, and the creaking door closed upon both.

And as he and Steve, now his only son, were driven back to

the Hall, he saw how great a horror had fallen on the funeral guests one and all.

Nor did the horror end there.

Again scuffling, wild yells, and shrieks made darkness terrible for five successive midnights; and then the haunted mausoleum sank to silence like a common grave.

And now there was a lull. The calamitous storms of fate and the season seemed alike to have spent their fury. The earth was green, the sky was bright, and Matthias steadfastly put the past behind him, refusing to look back. Like Pharaoh of old, he hardened his heart, unwilling to "let go" his hold of Corbyn.

Not so Stephen. His bumptious front had lowered when his sister was stricken down in the very midst of festivity. Old Cuffy's prophetic warnings had not fallen on deaf ears. He appealed to his father to remove the remains of sister and brother from the Corbyn mausoleum, and to take prompt steps to find a living heir, if such existed. Matthias was obstinate; so was he, and a *little* more conscientious.

He conferred with Dr. Hawley. Judge his surprise to find that the Captain Hudson, whose services his father had rejected with so much asperity, had eight years before picked up at sea a woman lashed to a spar, who supposed herself the sole survivor of the Mermaid, in which husband and son had both gone down. The Mermaid's destination had been Barbadoes, and the woman's name was Corbyn. Shortly after, happening to hail a passing schooner, the Boyne from Cork to Bristol, he transferred the rescued lady to that vessel, his own barque being outward bound.

"And, my young friend, as you appear anxious to see justice done," added the Doctor, "I may tell you I have already guaranteed Captain Hudson his expenses in the prosecution of a search for that lady."

A hearty hand-shake at parting sealed a cordial agreement between the twain, and Steve set off for the Parsonage with a lighter heart than had been his for many a day.

The season rounded, bringing with it a prospect of Steve's marriage with Miss Wolferstone when their term of mourning expired.

Long before that, fresh sables were called for.

Mrs. Walcot's unaccountable disease, aggravated by grief and her exclusion from society, had terminated fatally.

An altercation again arose between father and son respecting the place of sepulchre. It ended in orders for the opening of the mausoleum under Mr. Walcot's own eye.

The sight he beheld was enough to chill the blood; but it never turned him from his purpose. Scientific men discussing the phenomena had talked of gaseous forces; but he spoke only of conspiracy amongst his black slaves to bend his will to theirs.

Again the battered and broken coffins were replaced, and the fragments hid out of sight; again he laid his dead among the Corbyn dead.

Again the Corbyn dead arose at midnight to protest against intrusion; again the night was hideous with discordant cries; and, as if the free spirits of the air were leagued with the captives in that tomb, the rising wind howled and shrieked in unison.

Fiery Barbadoes could not remember more oppressive weather. The louring clouds, the stifling heat, the sultry heavy atmosphere had boded tempest, and at midnight came down the rain in sheets, driven by a breeze from the north-east which grew and strengthened to a tremendous gale. Then there was a treacherous calm, and then suddenly the winds ran riot; and from three to five o'clock mad hurricane swept the island from end to end, flashing lightnings forth to trace destruction by.

Daylight broke on August 11th, 1831, upon ruin and desolation. Houses and huts were blown down, fields laid waste, trees uprooted, valleys inundated. Wreck strewed the coast. The Government House was unroofed, the Custom House blown down, churches were damaged; the verdant paradise was a wilderness.

Amidst the general wreck, Corbyn had not escaped; yet the Hall itself stood firm, though the windmill sails and cap were torn to shivers. But the Walcot House at the Folly had disappeared, and with it much valuable property.

The coast had its black chronicles. A ship had been driven on the rocks in Long Bay, and only one of her crew was washed ashore. He was the second mate, a fine young man with light wavy hair, straight nose, ample forehead, and blue eyes. He had been borne on the crest of a wave, and cast on a rock with just strength left to scramble a few yards beyond the range of the swooping billows, and to thank God for his miraculous preservation.

He was bruised, ragged, and destitute; yet in the universal ruin his wants were all but disregarded. A compassionate negress gave him a draught of rum and a piece of corn-cake, but her own hut was dismantled, and shelter was far to seek.

On all sides he saw desolation and trouble. Dispirited, he turned to the highway, in hopes of gaining a shelter before nightfall. Some unseen hand led him in his helpless friendlessness to take the road William Walcot had traversed in his frenzy. Now, as then, the little stream was swollen to a great one; but the sailor was a good swimmer, and having daylight to his task crossed in safety where the other lost his life. The path through Corbyn Wood was blocked in places by fallen trees, which made his progress slow and perilous. There was no lack of scattered cocoa-nuts and other fruit to stay his hunger, but night fell as he slept the sleep of exhaustion on an uptorn tree-trunk.

He was awakened by loud shrieks. Following the sound, he emerged from the plantation on to the open road, and soon reached a low windowless building, across which a large sandbox tree had fallen. As he neared it the shrieks were overpowered by loud hurrahs, which somehow made his chilled blood tingle with a sensation akin to a shudder.

People like himself, cast adrift by the hurricane, were on the else avoided road. In answer to his questions, he was told that the nearest habitation was Corbyn Hall, and that low-domed edifice, the haunted mausoleum of the Corbyns.

"Corbyn?" echoed the sailor; "did you say Corbyn? My name is Corbyn, and I have an uncle Corbyn living in Barbadoes!"

"Was your uncle's name Archibald?" asked a passing gentleman on horseback.

"Yes; and my name is Archibald. My father's name was Charles."

"Is not your father living?"

"Alas! no. He was drowned in the wreck of the Mermaid, on his way to Barbadoes, when I was only twelve years old."

"H'm! And where were you at the time, young man?"

"Shipwrecked too, sir, and my mother also. I clung to a hen-coop, and was picked up half-dead by the skipper of the Boyne."

"And your mother?"

"She too was mercifully saved, as I have been this day; but as Providence willed it, the captain who had picked her up sent her aboard to us, his own vessel being bound on a long voyage; and we had reason to be thankful for it, or we might never have met again in this world. But"—impulsively—"are you my uncle, sir? You ask so many questions."

"No; Archibald Corbyn has lain for eighteen months in yonder tomb. But I knew him well. I see you are in a sad plight, and in no condition to walk a long distance; so I recommend you to present yourself at Corbyn Hall—no matter the hour at this awful crisis. I do not suppose you will be a very welcome visitor to Mr. Walcot. Executors seldom like to disgorge; and if you can prove your identity as old Archibald's nephew, you are heir to this estate, and my gentleman will have to turn out. In any case, should he treat you as an impostor—as is not unlikely—any of the old negroes will give you food and shelter, if they have it. Your name will ensure *that*."

"I thank you, sir," was all that Archie in his weakness and bewildering whirl of emotions could utter, as he bowed and turned as directed towards Corbyn Hall.

"Stay!" cried the stranger, wheeling his horse round. "I am a clergyman and a magistrate—the Rev. John Fulton, of St. Andrew's. There is my card. Show it. Should Mr. Walcot reject you, call upon me to-morrow; or upon Dr. Hawley, of Kissing Bridge, Bridgetown. We will see you are not wronged. My business is urgent, or I would accompany you now.

Bareheaded, barefooted, ragged, sea-stained, weary, footsore, and bleeding from sharp stones and sharper thorns, the famished, shipwrecked heir dragged himself slowly to Corbyn Hall, to sink exhausted on the very threshold.

There he was found by ever-wakeful Dinah, whose screams, "A ghost, a ghost!" roused the whole tribe of woolly heads from the mats on which they slept—and blown-down huts had filled house and piazza to overflowing.

"Massa Charlie's ghost!" from a chorus of tongues reached the chamber where Matthias lay shivering with ague. Watchful Stephen leaned over the balcony to seek the reason of the uproar.

Quick as thought he was in their midst, supporting the fainting youth in his strong arms. Little need to ask his name: the likeness to a picture in the house told it without voice.

Archie Corbyn was carried within; and while Scipio was despatched post-haste for Dr. Hawley, he was restored, refreshed, and tended with an assiduity no Walcot had ever been able to command. The previous day's hurricane had not created a greater commotion than the finding of the fainting sailor it had blown amongst them.

Matthias Walcot, however, was not disposed to receive Archie Corbyn on the strength of a likeness and his own *ipse dixit*.[12] He put upon him the onus of proof, in the secret hope (hardly confessed to himself) that difficulties might arise and his own position continue intact. At all events he would remain master in the interim; and—but that he feared a rising amongst his slaves, headed by his own son—so much were his principles demoralized that, in the face of conviction, he would have compelled Archie Corbyn to seek other quarters until his rights were indisputably established.

Steve stood by the heir gallantly, though his coming did close the prospect of succession to a fine domain. So did Dr. Hawley and the Rev. John Fulton, his first advisor. Cuffy and Dinah worshipped him. But he had no warmer champions than Mary Fulton and Augusta Wolferstone, with whom, no doubt, it was more a matter of feeling than of legal right.

Dr. Hawley and Steve had opened their purses to him, and once provided with means, he dressed, and looked the gentleman he was.

Archie's first care had been to write to his mother, begging her to leave England for Barbadoes without loss of time, armed with all necessary credentials.

---

[12] An assertion without proof.

Scarcely three weeks after the despatch of this letter, Dr. Hawley sought Stephen Walcot at the wharf.

In less than an hour Sambo was driving a party of four in the doctor's phaeton as fast as the unrepaired roads would permit.

They alighted at Corbyn Hall.

Archie Corbyn was at the Parsonage.

Steve was always glad of an excuse for a visit there. Resuming his seat, he was whirled thither, carried off Archie without a word of explanation, and left the young ladies excited and curious.

In the drawing-room of Corbyn Hall Archie found, to his joy and amazement, his mother. With her was Captain Hudson, to whom he was indebted for her appearance on the scene before his own missive was half-way over the ocean. The sea-captain had proved too good a seeker for Matthias Walcot, who sat there nervous and fidgety, with one arm resting on a side table, on which he kept up a spasmodic tattoo with his long finger-nails.

What further credentials were wanted than certificates of birth and marriage, and magisterial attestations, and Captain Hudson's testimony?

Corbyn Hall was once more in the hands of a Corbyn, and from Cuffy the news spread like an electric flame.

Archie Corbyn was magnanimous. Setting Stephen's heartiness against his father's tardiness (he called it by no worse name), he offered both a home until their own house at the Folly could be rebuilt; and he did not call on his executor to refund the moneys so lavishly expended out of Corbyn coffers.

Yet Matthias had another bitter draught to swallow before he returned to his shipping agency and to the Folly.

The midnight outcry at the mausoleum had never ceased since Mrs. Walcot was laid therein. The hurricane had torn away the newly-plastered brickwork, and now it sounded as if heavy hands were beating down the door.

Dinah took care that Mrs. Corbyn should not remain uninformed; and ancient Cuffy gave to Archie his version of the mystery with fervid impressiveness.

"It Cuffy's 'pinion, massa, dat Massa Arch'bald nebber rest till dem Walcots be cleared out. Him berry proud ob him pure white blood, an' dem Walcots hab got berry mixed blood under dere white skins."

Archie took counsel with his friends, Steve amongst the rest. The result was the removal of the Walcot coffins to a vault in St. Andrew's churchyard. They were found, strange to relate, wedged together close to the door by the coffins of Archibald and Jamie Corbyn.

Quiet fell on the mausoleum after that—a quiet in nowise disturbed when, after the lapse of some three or four years, the elder Mrs. Corbyn was placed there reverently by her son.

In saying the elder Mrs. Corbyn, it must be understood that when, proud of her generous lover, Augusta Wolferstone gave herself and her money to Steve Walcot, Archie Corbyn took to wife without a fortune the fair English girl, Mary Fulton, whose heart he had won as a poor shipwrecked sailor before it was proved that old Archibald was not the last of the Corbyns.

Cuffy and Dinah lived to see slavery abolished in the West Indies, and to watch the toddling feet of more than one young Corbyn, into whose undeveloped minds they did their best to infuse the old Corbyn pride of race and pure blood.

WRAITH-HAUNTED

"YES, Helen?"

The speaker, a tall, elegant woman, in whose every lineament beauty yet lingered, as if loth to accept from Time his seventy years' notice to quit, looked up interrogatively at her niece, a blooming matron, busy writing invitations for a juvenile party.

"I did not speak, aunt."

"Did you not? Nor you, Mr. Birley?"

Mr. Birley, engrossed in his evening paper, looked up somewhat vaguely.

"Eh, what?"

"Did you call me?

"What, I? Certainly not."

"Strange!" murmured Mrs. Carson, involuntarily glancing at the ormolu timepiece ere her eyes bent down once more on her interrupted sewing. The fingers pointed to ten minutes before nine.

Click, click, went her needle steadily through the seam; Mrs. Birley's pen made a faint sound as it traced the pink paper; and Mr. Birley studied the "share-list" and "markets" with more than ordinary assiduity. A spaniel coiled up on the hearth dozed in a dog's paradise, in the glow of a ruddy fire, which lit up every corner of the crimson room, and was reflected cheerfully by glass, gilding, and polished furniture.

Presently, Mrs. Carson's head was raised again.

"Well?" said she, glancing alternately from niece to nephew.

"What?" questioned both in a breath.

"One of you spoke this time—I heard my name distinctly."

"Indeed, Aunt Marianne, I have not uttered a syllable; I have not lifted my eyes from my desk since you addressed me last."

"Nor I from my newspaper. Mrs. Carson," continued the gentleman, "Dash is snoring most melodiously; possibly you mistook his utterance for mine. Not very complimentary if you did, I must say."

"Indeed I did *not*," returned she, with more emphasis than the occasion seemed to warrant. "I certainly heard myself called by my Christian name."

"Nonsense, aunt; I am sure no one spoke. You must be dreaming."

Again Mrs. Carson's eyes sought the timepiece on the mantel-shelf: the index had advanced five minutes.

"May be so; old people do dream sometimes," replied she quietly, resuming work with a sigh as if to dismiss the subject.

With a light laugh Mrs. Birley dipped her pen into the ink, and Mr. Birley sought his lost paragraph.

Had either husband or wife cared to listen, there might have been heard a beating heart keeping time with the sharp click of the needle and the steady tick of the timepiece. But there was only one listener, and she, seemingly occupied with her needlework, sat with lips apart and head bent in mute expectancy.

The hall-clock gave warning. With a first stroke of *nine* her work dropped; she grasped the arms of her chair and rose. Her face was blanched and rigid, her brown eyes were wild and wandering. For some moments she stood thus, then with a groan sank nerveless in her seat.

Her companions, alarmed, were by her side in an instant.

"My dear aunt, what is the matter?"

"Are you ill, Mrs. Carson?" and Mr. Birley as he spoke made a movement towards the bell.

The old lady, recovering, arrested his hand, "Are you sure neither of you spoke to me?"

"Quite sure," was the simultaneous reply.

"Do you think any of the children called me?"

"Why, Aunt Marianne, what *are* you thinking of?—the children have been in bed two hours."

"Did neither of you hear anything?"

"I heard nothing."

"Nor I, save the scratching of my own pen and the rustle of James's paper."

Mrs. Carson looked from one to the other as if incredulity struggled with a foregone conclusion; then in answer to their inquiries, said seriously, "I distinctly heard my own name, 'Marianne,' called thrice, with an interval of five minutes between each call, although *I saw nothing!*"

"Saw nothing! Why, what did you expect to see?" asked Helen, much perplexed.

"Bosh!" muttered Mr. Birley between his teeth as he resumed his seat and study.

"*What* I expected to see is not easy to say; but I heard a voice I have not heard for thirty-five years. It is a solemn warning."

"Of what, aunt?"

"Of *death!*" was the low and measured response.

Mr. Birley laughed outright; his wife fidgeted nervously.

"James," said the old lady, "I know you think me a superstitious old fool, and are laughing in your sleeve at my supernatural forebodings; but if you have patience to listen to an old woman's story first, I will then tell you what I believe is foreshadowed now—you can laugh afterwards, if so inclined."

Mr. Birley yawned and compared his watch with the clock; but there was a grave dignity in the speaker's manner which awed him into something like attention. His wife's curiosity was already aroused; she drew her chair to the fire, and with a gesture and grimace meant to call her spouse to order, said—

"Well, aunt, we are listening."

"Well, Helen, I suppose you know, if James does not, that when your grandfather Denton was in business he was for many years his own traveller; and as there were no railroads, few stagecoaches, and those only on main roads, he used to travel with a horse and gig. On one of his journeys he met at a roadside inn a Mr. Lavery, from Bristol, likewise travelling on his own account, although in a different line.

"The two had met before on the road, but on that occasion he found Mr. Lavery not only invalided but crippled by rheumatism. The women of those days were a different type from the present generation, and your grandmother was not only an excellent nurse but possessed a valuable specific for rheumatism; so being a man of impulse, without even a letter to announce his return—for a letter would have been longer on the road than himself—my father brought Mr. Lavery, wrapped up in blankets, to his own house, and placed him under my mother's care. For months the patient remained an invalid guest, tended by my mother, his wife being sent for after a while.

"Out of these services rendered and accepted grew a very warm friendship, one token of which was Mrs Lavery's declared inability to dispense with the society of one or other of the Misses Denton. I, however, was the favourite, my visits generally extending over many months.

"I was about two-and-twenty when my last visit to Bristol was made, and—I may say so now without vanity—I was known as the beautiful Miss Denton; perhaps one reason why Mrs. Lavery was so proud to have me with her. Fond of dress and company herself, she was glad to have an attractive companion, and introduced me into much gayer society than my own mother had thought well for her daughters.

"I had been in Bristol nearly nine months, when the first of those peculiar occurrences which have marked my life stamped its indelible impress on my soul and memory.

"Mr. Lavery was away. Mrs. Lavery and myself had been to a card-party, which, as was customary in those days, broke up about ten o'clock. There had been music as well as cards, and I having then a very fine voice——"

"*Then!* You had a fine voice when I knew you first, twelve years ago," interrupted Mr. Birley.

"Well, James, perhaps so; but I *had* a good voice *then*, and naturally was pressed to exercise it. One of the guests, Mr. Carson, whom I saw that night for the first time, apparently had neither ears nor eyes for anyone else; he seemed literally entranced by my singing, and whispered as much to me as he handed me to my sedan-chair when we left.

"Neither admiration nor adulation was new to me, yet at the one compliment of this young Scotchman I flushed with a strange pleasure such as no flattery had ever called up before. The words lingered in my ears all the while I was carried home; even his peculiar intonation had an unwonted fascination for me; and indeed, when I retired to rest, I found myself still dwelling upon those incidents of the evening in which the handsome Mr. Carson had the most prominent place. I'm afraid I answered Mrs. Lavery's remarks somewhat at random, and went to bed with this stranger's parting words floating through my mind as I fell asleep.

"I mention this, my dears, merely to show that there was no possible link of connection between my thoughts and that which followed.

"The bed assigned to me was an old-fashioned four-post, with heavy moreen curtains and full valances,[13] the curtains suspended from brass rings which ran upon iron rods. Mrs. Lavery, in her husband's absence, always slept with me.

"I had been asleep some time, when I suddenly awakened with a start, hearing myself called. I sat up in the bed affrighted. The curtains at the foot were slowly undrawn, the rings jingling as they slipped over the iron rods, and there, in the aperture, distinctly visible in the frosty moonlight, stood the form of *my mother* in her night robes. She was thin, and ghastly white; but a smile of ineffable sweetness parted her wan lips, from which issued slowly the words 'Marianne, Marianne, Marianne!' Raising her hand as if in benediction, she melted away, as it were, into the moonbeams.

"Terror for a moment held me fast. When I recovered my self-possession I roused my bedfellow. She had seen nothing, heard nothing, and was therefore sceptical. In vain she strove, like you, to persuade me I had been dreaming; the still open curtains refuted that, for she recollected closing them with her own hand as she got into bed. She then suggested that the maid had played me a trick; but we found the door locked, with the key inside, as we had left it.

"Oh, Mrs. Lavery," I moaned in an agony of apprehension, "something is wrong at home—my mother is either ill or in trouble, perhaps dying, and wants me. Oh, that I had never left her!"

---

[13] Strong, ribbed cotton fabric.

" 'Now do, my dear child, go to sleep; you have had a nightmare, that is all. It is not much more than a week since you heard from home; all was well then,' said Mrs. Lavery, trying to soothe my distress.

" 'Oh, that was ten days ago,' I argued. 'It is a fortnight since the letter was written. What may have happened since then! I must go home at once.'

"There was no response from my friend; sleep had overpowered her sympathy. Neither my terror nor distress had fully roused her.

"For me there was no more sleep that night. I sat up shivering in bed until the piercing cold compelled me to lie down. I watched the still open curtains and the retreating moonbeams as they marked on the wall the passage of the silent hours; but although my mother's pale face and languid voice haunted my memory, the actual presence came no more.

"Night shadows linger long in December, and I was afraid to rise until daylight, but the first streak of dawn found me astir collecting my scattered possessions; and by the time Mrs. Lavery had got up I had almost completed my packing, for I had determined to go home, and knew that the "Royal Mail" coach would start that very day for Manchester, and, if I missed it, I must wait three days for another.

"Mrs. Lavery's astonishment is not describable; the episode of the night had left no impression on her sleep-bound faculties. She tried raillery, banter, persuasion, to induce me to abandon a 'foolish whim, the off-spring of a dream.'

"She changed her tone when the sluggish postman called out to the deaf servant 'a letter for Miss Denton, and a shilling to pay!' in a voice which penetrated to the breakfast-table, and my trembling fingers almost refused to unclasp my purse or break the seal, which, however, was *not* black.

"Well I remember the tenor of that letter. It told that during my father's absence from home some rollicking fellow with that in his head which was *not wit* had knocked loudly at our door in the middle of the night when all were asleep, and then run off. My mother, always a light sleeper, had started up under the impression that your grandfather had returned unexpectedly, and in her hurry to reach the door before he, in his irritable impatience, should knock a second time, caught her foot in the coverlet and fell heavily against a carved oak coffer. There she was found in the morning with her collar-bone broken. The fracture was reduced, but she never fairly rallied, and I was summoned home, her symptoms being alarming.

"We were yet discussing these sad tidings when Mr. Carson was announced. He called, he said, not only to inquire after our health, but to offer his services in conveying either message or package to my friends in Manchester, whither he was then bound. (You need not smile, Helen; it was a common practice at that time to burden travellers with friendly letters and parcels, until their delivery at the journey's end became quite a tax.)

" 'You have come quite opportunely, Mr. Carson,' Mrs. Lavery answered briskly; 'you will relieve me from a sore dilemma. Miss Denton's mother having met with a severe injury, our young friend is summoned home hastily. She has never travelled alone in her life, and I was debating how I could trust her so far without a guardian. Will you undertake the charge? I know I can rely upon your care.'

"I saw a flush of pleasure light up his clear eye and handsome face as he answered earnestly, 'If Miss Denton will graciously accept my humble services, I shall only be too proud of the trust.'

"In my eagerness to depart I had lost sight of the dangers and discomforts of the long journey to an unprotected girl, but the picture drawn by Mrs. Lavery to deter me from quitting Bristol, as she then thought, needlessly, had made the prospect something formidable. There was no disguising my satisfaction when a protector offered himself so unexpectedly; and if I thanked him quietly, I know it was sufficiently.

"Mr. Carson's place had been booked the day before—outside. He hastened to the coach-office to secure an inside seat for me, and to transfer his own. A fruitless errand; every inside place was already secured. There only remained the hope that some male passenger would surrender his inside seat in favour of a lady.

"A vain hope. The 'insides' were all long-distance passengers, and to a man resented any infringement on the right of 'number one,' expressing their personal opinions more freely than courteously.

" 'Mr. Carson,' I whispered, 'do not let there be any altercation on my account' (he was waxing warm). 'I should dread being penned up with those coarse men for two days; I would much rather sit outside with you.'

"An incautious speech, but the grateful look which answered it sent my blood tingling with very shame to my finger-ends. He answered soberly, 'I do prefer the outside in all seasons; but, then, I am hardy. You are not fitted to brave the inclemency of a midwinter frost. Only the urgency of life and death should tempt you to make the experiment.'

" 'It *is* the urgency of life and death,' I answered. 'But I am not afraid of a little cold; my pelisse is warm, and my fur tippet protects my chest.'[14]

"I bade my weeping friend 'good-bye.' Without another word Mr. Carson assisted me to mount the movable ladder to a seat at the

---

14 Pelisse: long, fitted coat. Tippet: scarflike garment worn around the neck.

back which held two, and fronted the guard's solitary post. Just then a messenger, despatched by Mrs. Lavery, came up laden with a rug and shawl.

"With much care Mr. Carson placed the rug beneath my feet, and adjusted the shawl around my knees. I felt at once that I was in good hands, though in my ignorance I considered the precaution unnecessary.

"The leaders' heads were released, the coachman cracked his lone whip, the guard blew his horn, a final 'adieu' was said, and I had started on the most momentous journey of my life.

"Rightly judging that my emotions were not less deep because they did no more than well-up into my eyes, my new protector entered into a conversation with the guard to divert his attention, and left me to my meditations. Sombre enough they were. I could not quit my friend without regret; but what weighed heaviest on my heart was the presentiment that my mother was *dead*, and that I had seen her *passing spirit.* More sorrowful and gloomy became my thoughts as one by one the milestones were left behind on the turnpike-road, and notwithstanding my wrappings I began to feel a little chilly.

"I need not weary you with the details of that long and miserable journey, only rendered endurable by the unremitting attention of my protector, for such in truth he was. Not only the scenery, but the weather and temperature varied with the districts through which we rode. From hard black frost we passed to a region where snow lay thick on the distant hills, like a shroud on a dead giant, and in light patches here and there by the roadside or on the trees, which tossed their skeleton arms in the breeze and played at snow-ball with us as the coach swept past. From falling snow we made an advance under a canopy of weeping clouds—first a drizzle, then rain, soaking, persistent, pitiless rain, rain without intermission, rain which would have penetrated a plank.

"No wonder, then, that notwithstanding the plaid which Mr. Carson had stripped from himself to fold round me during the chill of the first evening (using as a substitute, when too late, a horse-rug obtained from an ostler at a fabulous price)—no wonder, I say, that several hours before we reached our destination I was drenched to the skin, and utterly worn out both in body and mind.

"When the steaming horses drew the miry coach up before the Bridgewater Arms, I had lain for some time in a state of insensibility on Mr. Carson's shoulder, utterly unconscious of his supporting arm, or of the anathemas vented by the sympathising guard on the stolid "insides," whose victim he clearly considered me to be.

"Uncle Bancroft was fortunately in waiting, for I had to be lifted from the coach-top, and my generous friend was himself too cramped and benumbed to render further assistance. Brandy was poured down my throat, and as soon as a hackney-coach could be found I was conveyed, not to my father's house, but to my uncle's, Mr. Carson never leaving me until I was safe under the roof of my friends and showed some signs of returning animation.

"My shoes, stockings, and upper garments, sodden and saturated, had to be cut from my swollen limbs; but of this I knew nothing, for a fever had supervened and blotted out everything.

"Evasive answers were given to my first inquiries for my mother, as I was too weak to hear the ruth; but when I approached convalescence, I was told everything. *She was dead when I commenced my journey—had died on the 23rd of December, close upon midnight.* Her last inquiry had been *for me.* Glancing feebly around from one weeping relative to another, she had said: '*All here! All! all except Marianne. Marianne, Marianne, Marianne!*' "

"Helen, there could be no question that my mother's parting spirit had visited my bedside. The impression made was thenceforth ineffaceable."

"The coincidence was certainly remarkable," said Mr. Birley; "still, I incline to think the whole a dream."

"There was something very awful about it, even if it was a dream; you must own that, James," put in his wife.

"It was *no* dream; but my next revelation took place in broad daylight—*that* could be no dream," said Mrs. Carson sadly. "I have called my journey momentous, and justly. It influenced my life. My friend in his care for me had sacrificed himself. Hardy as he was, inflammation laid its hot hand upon his chest, held him down, and only let him rise with a spot marked like a target for the shaft of death. Gratitude and pity rose to heart and lips when I first saw his altered face. That journey had indeed fused two souls into one. Whatever impressions our first meeting had made, my sufferings and his self-sacrifice had confirmed. What I had found him during our long and miserable ride I found him ever, and loved him as such large-hearted, self-denying men should be loved. There was no talk of marriage between us for at least eighteen months; but there was no doubt whither we were drifting. Every moment he could spare from business was spent with me; and I think it was principally on my account that he induced his uncle in Glasgow, a muslin manufacturer, to engage a traveller and give him a permanent agency in Manchester, opening a ware-room for the sale of their goods.

"Shortly after that I became his wife, with the full approbation of friends, and with every prospect of happiness. He had furnished for me, simply but well, a house in Hanover-street, then a thorough Scotch colony, and my father's house being in Cannon-street, I was not more than a quarter of a mile from home. As was then the custom, we were married on Sunday, it being likewise my birthday, the 21st of December, and at once took possession of our new abode.

"The twenty-third was signalled by one of the fiercest conflagrations Manchester had known for years.. A cotton-mill at Ancoats had taken fire whilst the hands were being dismissed. Some were in the upper-stories at the time; the narrow staircase was crowded, and many lives were in danger. Attracted by the glare, Mr. Carson was quickly on the spot, forgetful of all but the duty before him, and to his heroic efforts three girls at least owed their lives. They came to thank him a week later. Alas! where was he? His hair was singed, and so was his coat, from which the tails were dangling loose; he had been wetted through alike with perspiration and water from the engine, but he waited until all danger to others was over, and when he reached home his clothes were apparently dry. He kissed me, apologised for keeping me waiting tea, and sat down to describe the incidents of the fire. Of his own exploits he said little; but on the plea of fatigue excused his sitting down to tea in the plight he then was. After the meal, he dozed off, which I attributed to his recent exertions and the heat of our own fire. It was only on going to rouse him that I discovered his clothes had been wetted, and I was too inexperienced to calculate the consequences.

"The following day I had promised to spend with my father and sisters. William was to join me on closing the warehouse. Being a bride, I was, of course, an object of special attention, made more of by my relations than at any other period of my life. I found there a perfect levée of aunts and cousins, discussing the bride's cake and future prospects with equal freedom. In the midst of out lively chat time fled past. There came a sharp rat-tat-tat at the street-door.

"Why, that is William's knock; what brings him from the warehouse so early?" exclaimed I, running to anticipate the servant in opening the door. Without another word than 'Marianne,' strangely spoken, he passed me by, never stopping to kiss me, as was his wont.

"I confess he had spoiled me. I pouted, petulant tears welled to my eyes, and I lingered with the fastening of the door before I turned round.

" 'Marianne!'

"He was calling me from behind. I dropped the latch and followed him, as I thought, into the room I had just quitted.

" 'Where is William?' I asked, looking round but not seeing him.

" 'He has not come in here.'

" 'Marianne!'

"The voice seemed to come from the room on the opposite side the hall. I ran thither, anticipating the loving embrace he was too reserved to give before strangers.

"He was not there.

" 'William, dear, where are you? don't hide from me!'

"There was no answer. I ran into the back parlours—upstairs—downstairs, calling his name. *He was nowhere to be seen.*

"By this time the house was in commotion. Sisters and cousins alike had heard the knock, but no one had seen my husband or heard his voice.

"As they looked from me to one another for an explanation of that which is inexplicable, I having protested that Mr. Carson had passed and spoken to me in the hall, a sudden light flashed over and appalled me. I remembered *seeing the hall-panelling through his figure!* With a startling shriek, I rushed bareheaded from the house, tore across Cannon-street, along Sugar Lane, and up Shude Hill, like a mad woman, nor paused till my grasp was on the handle of my own door.

"That was ajar. A bad omen. I found my beloved husband extended on our bed, a doctor by his side vainly trying to bleed him —*the blood would not flow.*

"Inflammation—the result, no doubt, of his over-night's wetting and fatigue—had seized him suddenly.

"On his way home he had called on his doctor, who never left him again in life.

"Before night fell on the earth, the night of Death had fallen on my idolised husband, and my soul was in eclipse.

"Maid, wife, widow in a week, a widow all unconscious of her widowhood. A dumb, dreamy, statuesque automaton. I lived and moved, but that was all.

"I was taken home. When the funeral was over, the house in Hanover-street was given up. I was incapable of managing it.

"In this state I remained until my boy was born. Then the ice at my heart thawed, and tears came to my relief. The babe lived, and I lived for him.

"How I idolised that boy! I watched him night and day with more than a mother's care. He grew up a fine strong youth, the image of his dead father, whose name he bore. His father's uncle would have taken the entire charge of him; but I would not part from Willie, so we were summoned to Glasgow together, and there lived until the death of old Mr. Carson, when Willie was sixteen. The old gentleman left considerable property behind him, much of which was bequeathed to my son.

"Having no ties to Scotland, I came back to the old home, from which two of my sisters had gone away to homes of their own.

"Between myself and his grandfather, Willie stood a fair chance of being spoiled. He grew a tall, athletic man, not overfond of business or study, but much given to all manly sports and pastimes; in which he was encouraged by his grandfather. As for me, I saw no harm in his pursuits, and never dreamed of danger.

"Willie had a friend close by with whom he often put on the gloves, or practised fencing and single-stick.[15]

"One day, towards the close of the year—my sorrows have always come in the midst of other's rejoicing—I sat reading by the fire; my father was playing his favourite game of backgammon with my sister Sarah; you, then a child of three years, sat nursing a kitten at your mother's feet; she had brought you to spend Christmas with us.

"My father, I must tell you, had then given up business, and our garret was filled with old lumber from the warehouse, several open baskets or 'wiskets' containing waste 'cops,' spindles, and other refuse amongst the rest.

"Our quiet was broken, and the rattling dice drowned by a loud clash and clatter upstairs.

" 'Someone has left that garret-window open again, and the cats are making fine havoc with those cops, I know; hark how they rattle!'

" 'Go upstairs, Sally, and shut the window,' said my father, pausing in his game.

"Sarah went. All was still.

" 'The window is fast enough, and I saw no cats,' said she, as she sat down again to the board.

"Again the clash and clatter, as of metal, clear and distinct.

" 'Helen, do go up. Take my stick, and rout the intruders out; I'd swear the cats are there.'

---

15 Fencing with a wooden stick held in one hand.

"Your mother went, and came back with the same report—nothing there; all silent.

"Again the self-same clash and clatter, louder than before. I, haunted by old memories, felt my heart sink.

" 'Here, Marianne, lass, lend me thy arm; thou and I'll go up and see what all this din's about; but don't thou look so scared.'

"We mounted the first flight, he leaning on my arm. All at once the clatter ceased.

" 'Mother, mother, mother!' came floating like a breath down the stairway, and while we paused to listen—for my father heard it also—the figure of Willie brushed past us, with one hand pressed upon his heart.

"I trembled and grew faint. *I had seen the balustrades through the form.*

"My father chuckled outright. 'Ah, the young dog, so it was Willie playing tricks upon us, after all.'

"I said nothing until I reached the parlour. As I rightly conjectured, no Willie was there.

" 'Father,' said I, clasping my hands in anguish, 'that was not Willie, it was his wraith. I have been *wraith-haunted* all my life.'

"My father looked dazed; my sisters, perhaps with a good motive, rallied me on my Scottish superstition, much as you have done; but ere their laughter had well subsided, there was an imperative knock at the street-door.

"We were summoned to our neighbour, Mr. Neale's; an accident had befallen my son.

"He lay on a couch pale and bleeding, wounded in the chest, the room in disorder, foils upon the floor. He had barely strength left to press my hand, and say 'Mother, do not weep; Tom could not help it—the button came off his foil. Mother, forgive—' and I was childless.

"I was spared all the agony of the inquest, for there was another blank in my memory; and during my mental oblivion your grandfather died, borne down by the double sorrow.

"You see, I have good reason for saying I am wraith-haunted, and for knowing that the voice I heard to-night is a call from the spirit-world to me."

Mr. Birley and his wife both looked perplexed and serious.

"I do remember something about a ghost in grandfather's garret when I was a very little girl. But how is it I was never told of the 'warnings' you think you have had?"

"They were hushed up lest my grief should be re-awakened. And now let us go to bed—it is late. The issues of life and death are in higher hands than ours."

The morning broke—clear, sparkling, exhilarating. Mrs. Carson made her appearance in her ordinary health, a little paler it might be, but that was all.

Mrs. Birley had hesitated whether to issue her invitations, but finally resolved not to disappoint the children, and so they were sent.

The nursery-doors were thrown open, and all hands, big and little, summoned to the task of decoration with evergreens and holly.

In the midst of it all a carrier brought a large box, inscribed, "Aunt Carson's Gift," The old lady had made her purchases the day before. There was a general rush to wrench open the lid, and make a raid on the contents. Books, dolls, workboxes, a desk, toys noisy and noiseless, were there, each labelled with the fortunate recipient's name. Flushed and elated, the youngsters rushed hither and thither displaying their prizes. Frocks and pinafores filled to repletion dropped their contents, until the little ones might be tracked by straggling Shems and Noahs, cups and saucers, whistles and drumsticks.

The box had been removed, the litter cleared away, the stray waifs collected, when Mrs. Carson descended the stairs after her customary nap. A wee round toy, the colour of the stair-carpet, had been overlooked; she stepped on it and fell from top to bottom, striking her head against the balustrades.

There was a rush through the house to where she lay stunned on the oilcloth. Reverently and sadly she was carried into the nearest room—the one occupied over-night. A messenger was sent on horseback for a surgeon and for Mr. Birley.

Shocked beyond measure, the latter gentleman hastened home in time to hear the fiat pronounced.[16]

"An injured spine—concussion of the brain—no hope whatever."

A physician summoned hastily confirmed the surgeon's decision.

The weeping children were huddled from the room.

"How long may she linger?" was Mr. Birley's question.

"She may go off any moment, the shock to her system is so great; she *may* last two or three hours."

"Do you think she is conscious?"

"I am afraid not."

Mrs. Birley, sobbing, whispered to her husband, "James, do you think aunt did hear anything supernatural last night."

Two days before he would have said, "All bosh!" now he answered, "God only knows! It is most mysterious."

"If she did she will not die until nine o'clock."

"At nine!" murmured the dying woman; "at nine."

She was evidently conscious, and something more she said, but the words were inaudible. Husband and wife watched the clock as intensely as Mrs. Carson had watched it the night before.

---

16 Fiat: decree, authoritative determination.

Ten minutes to nine! The retreating pulse quickened under the doctor's touch. The lips moved.

"William!" was faintly audible to the bent ear.

Five minutes to nine! The "change" was perceptible.

"Yes, William!"

There was another pause—a burr—the clock's note of warning. There was a rattle in the throat of the dying woman.

"Coming, William!" was gasped out audibly.

NINE!

A last leap of the pulse—a last flicker of the eyelids—the "call" was obeyed.

Mrs. Carson, wraith-haunted, spirit-summoned, was of the dead!

THE PIPER'S GHOST:
A LEGEND OF ELVET BRIDGE, DURHAM
CHAPTER I

IN the red annals of war few more romantic passages occur than those which recount the story of Charles Edward Stuart, the Young Pretender. It is a story of blind infatuation, alike in leader and adherents.

On the five-and-twentieth day of the hot month of July, 1745, with heart burning as the month, the sanguine man of five-and-twenty summers landed near Moidart, with little money and few men, in the vain hope to drive out the Guelph, and replace the Stuart on the throne of England. Round the standard raised at Glenfinnan rallied Scotland's rebellious chieftains with their clansmen; others joining on the southward march. Victories were gained, towns taken, and further success might have followed prompt action; but the Prince wasted precious time in idle ceremonies, giving his enemies a chance to collect and concentrate forces. From Manchester, which he entered Nov. 29th, he departed with a reinforcement of 300 men on December 1st, to return on the 8th of the same month worn and dispirited: a council held at Derby having peremptorily insisted on retreat.

Thence dates a story of disaster which we need follow no farther than Clifton, a village a short distance of Penrith, where a sharp skirmish took place in the effort to cover the retreat of the cavalry over Clifton Bridge. This was done successfully, the troops advancing under the Duke of Cumberland being repulsed with loss.

When the sharp contest was over it was too dark to distinguish the slain who filled the surrounding ditches; whilst the retreat towards

Calisle was pressed on with such haste that the dead were left unburied, the wounded unattended, in the bitterest of bitter weather.

Amongst the latter was a piper named Dugald Macpherson, who had followed his chieftain with the blind devotion so characteristic of the old Scottish clansman; and in whose breast the gallant young Prince stood second only to the "Macpherson."

Sounding the pibroch of the tribe,[17] he was struck down almost at the outset, but not before he had seen one of his stalwart sons fighting by his side cleft through the brain by the same sabre that was next turned against himself.

Scarcely could he have seen the elder brother's flashing claymore deal vengeance on the destroying horseman, than trampling hoofs beat out his own sense of pain or anguish.

Rain was falling heavily when Dugald, recovering consciousness, found himself lying in one of the many pools of water which the bad weather and worse roads had provided, providentially, as it were, for the stanching of open wounds. He was stiff and sore, as much from the bruising hoofs which had passed over his prostrate body, as from the sabre-cut in his shoulder, the haemorrhage from which had long ceased. It was too dark to distinguish more than shadowy outlines, and only the moans of dying men broke the stillness.

Where were the skirling bagpipes of the Scots' army? How was it their shrill music was inaudible? What sounds could pierce the silence like the blast of the warlike pipes? Had his clansmen been defeated, that he was left to die like a dog?

"It maun e'en be sae, foul fa' the red-coated Southrons! Gin Lord George had keepit the grund,[18] the chief was ne'er hae left his

---

[17] The classical music of the Scottish bagpipe.

[18] Lord George Murray, who headed the Macphersons in this skirmish.

auld piper Dugald in siccan a plight as this! They maun be miles awa e'en noo, or I wad catch the skirl o'the muckle pipes in ilka sough o' the wind. But whar be her ain pipes?"[19]

As he thus muttered, rather than spoke, he made a circuit with his right arm on the miry earth, and found his treasured bagpipes within his grasp.

He clutched the bag as a prize; but his sudden exclamation of delight was checked, for in that wide sweep of his arm his fingers had grasped a kilt and philibeg,[20] and like a lightning flash came the recollection of seeing his youngest born struck down like a log by his side; and the glad ejaculation terminated in a groan.

With an effort he raised himself into a sitting posture, his left arm being too painful to use, and drew himself closer to the dead Highlander.

Once again he put forth his hand into the darkness, but it was to feel anxiously and carefully over his garb and accoutrements, and then to grasp nervously the cold hand, which something more akin to instinct than recognition had told him was that of his son, his brave Allan.

"My bairn, my braw Allan! Eh, but this will be a waefu' tale for thy mither at hame. Oh, that sic an auld worn-out stump as mysel should be left, and the tough green sapling be cut down in its prime. Yet wherefore should I lament? Hasna' he fallen whar a Macpherson should fa', in the thick o' the fight, wi' his face to

---

19 *Meaning*: 'It must even be so, ill befall the red-coated Southerners! If Lord George had kept the ground, the chief would never have left his old piper Dugald in such a plight as this! They must be miles away even now, or I would catch the cry of the great pipes in every sigh of the wind. But where be her own pipes?'

20 Philibeg: féileadh beag, short kilt.

the foe! Shame on ye, Dugald, for a doited auld body, lamenting when ye should be proud that ye'r ain bairn shed his blood for his chief an' his prince, the bonnie Prince Charlie!"[21]

The poor piper drew his sleeve across his eyes, and set his face with stern resolution to exult in his son's glory. But it would not do; the father overpowered the warrior, and big drops rolled down his weatherbeaten, blood-stained cheeks, across one of which was an ugly gash.

Grey dawn was creeping up the east, raw and chilly as dawn ever is (whatever poets may sing to the contrary), and with the dawn came the instinct of self-preservation. But the old man's first care was for the ghastly remains beside which he knelt.

"What can be dune; I canna gang awa' an' leave my fair-haired bairn to the corbies and hoodie craws!"[22]

He had already arranged the young soldier's plaid around the head as a decent covering; and now—for he was a stout, brawny man, in spite of his sixty years and aching wounds—he strove to draw the body from the roadway to a hollow in the broken ground close by, which he might deepen with his claymore, and cover with mould and stones.

Bloodshed was no new thing to Dugald; but had it been, the

---

[21] *Meaning*: 'My child, my fine Allan! Eh, but this will be a sorrowful tale for your mother at home. Oh, that a sick and old worn-out stump as myself should be left, and the tough green sapling be cut down in its prime. Yet wherefore should I lament? Hasn't he fallen where a Macpherson should fall, in the thick of the fight, with his face to the foe! Shame on you, Dugald, for a stupid old body, lamenting when you should be proud that your own child shed his blood for his chief and his prince, the bonnie Prince Charlie!'

[22] *Meaning*: 'What can be done; I can't walk away and leave my fair-haired child to the ravens and hooded crows!'

fate of his son would have closed his ears and eyes to the sounds and sights of that limited battle-field. He saw only his dying boy! He had found a sheltered nook between two boulders, had hollowed out a cavity to receive the corpse, and, with infinite pain to himself, had drawn it almost to its resting-place, when a labourer from the village drew near.

There was no need to ask help. The rude but kindly peasant, seeing how he was employed, and how unfit for his pious task, came to his assistance. He had a spade over his shoulder, and with that soon deepened the shallow grave, and covered the dead from sight.

Dugald proffered his son's dirk and sporran as remembrancers; but the man thought he offered payment, and shook his head, sturdily declining the gift.

"Nay, nay, aw canna tak pay for only doin' ma duty. Besides, aw moight get into trouble wi' them things. Who knows!"[23]

In the pre-occupation of his hand and mind the sound of rapidly advancing cavalry had not arrested Dugald's ear, but now the well-known sounds of martial music were borne on the wind—not the familiar drone of the pipe, but the whistle of the fife, the roll of the drum, the breath of the bugle, all telling him of enemies at hand.

The friendly labourer thrust a lump of cheese and an oat-cake into the piper's hand (he had previously bound up the wounded shoulder with the laced neck-cloth of a dead officer), and decamped hastily, lest his very friendliness should be his own death-warrant.

Dugald was thus left to shift for himself.

---

23 *Meaning*: 'No, no, I can't take pay for only doing my duty. Besides, I might get into trouble with them things. Who knows!'

But, first, he must secure his bagpipes, dear to him almost as his own life. He gathered the instrument in his arms like a living thing. Nearer came the troops. Whither should he flee?

In danger, thought is rapid. Stealthily as a cat, and as swiftly as his condition would permit, he bent his steps to the river side, keeping close to the thick-set hedge.

As the first horseman came in sight, his head disappeared below the level of the bank, and he lay crouched beneath the shadow of the sheltering arch long before they gained the scene of the last night's conflict.

What cared the stern Duke of Cumberland for dead or dying not of his own army? But these *were* his soldiers with a few exceptions, and Dugald heard hasty orders given for the interment of the dead, the removal of the wounded to the village, and for the custody of some ten or twelve wounded prisoners.

Dugald's heart beat quicker. What if Sandy, his firstborn, was among these? Better he lay in the bloody grave with Allan than fall into the merciless hands of the English commander!

No fear, Dugald, thy son is already marching towards Carlisle! And yet there is an English officer wounded nigh unto death, who remembers well the face of him whose vengeful claymore left him but one hand. A hand to hold the reins, but never a one to wield again a sabre, which had cut down father and brother before your Sandy's eyes!

Colonel Philip has a memory, but no conscience. Pray God, old man, that thy surviving son fall not into that man's hands hereafter!

Though a company of men had been told off to clear the ground of dead and wounded, and though the former were buried with scant ceremony, it was a work of time; and every moment seemed trebled to the piper, who was liable to discovery at any instant. Besides, his wounds were painful, and, hardy as was his nature, he was not made of cast-iron.

Long after the last footstep had crossed the bridge, Dugald hesitated to leave his place of concealment lest some straggler should confront him. At length he crept out, and, keeping behind the tall hedge which skirted the road, soon left the village in the rear, at once widening the distance between himself and friends or foes alike.

Avoiding the high roads, he struggled on until almost nightfall, when, faint with hunger and pain, he stopped at a poor cottage in a bye-lane. Children were playing in front, and a woman sat knitting on the doorstep. He was a ghastly object—the blood unwashed from his face, the bright hues of the tartan disguised with mud, his very gait betokening his unfitness to proceed.

The woman rose as he advanced. Though his speech was almost unintelligible, his condition was not.

At the hasty summons "Grandfather," an old man came forward, helped him into the cottage, and into the seat in the chimney corner which he had just quitted.

Oat-cake and a bowl of milk were set before him, and then there was some whispering. One of the children was despatched somewhere, to Dugald's alarm.

He, however, had no cause for fear. The child speedily returned with his father, a sturdy, good-natured looking man, coarsely habited.

Fresh whispers! "Some poor Jacobite body; do you think Dr. Kendal would come and dress his wounds if ye went and told him?" and "Mayhap he would!" was their sum and substance; and then the husband departed.

The hospitable woman, whom her husband had called Nanny, moving about quickly, brought water and washed the gore and mud from poor Dugald's face with as much gentleness as if she had been a practised nurse, and he a one hour's child.

Soon the husband returned, and with him Dr. Kendal from the neighbouring borough of Kirkland, a man who stood well in his profession, but was more than suspected of strong Jacobite proclivities.

At all events he came readily, dressed and bound up the piper's wounds as readily, although he suspected payment was altogether out of the question. But no, Dugald Macpherson was not a poor man, he tendered a gold piece in return for the service rendered; which Dr. Kendal refused as steadily as the peasant had refused the gifts offered in the morning. All the doctor would take in fee was news of Prince Charlie and his movements; for posts were few and newspapers still fewer at that time than the present. Humble as was the accommodation of the cottage, a bed was found for the stranger.

Refreshed by the night's rest and a breakfast of milk and porridge, Dugald quitted the hospitable roof at an early hour, after depositing the rejected gold coin in the grandfather's snuff-box.

To have remained longer would have endangered the safety of all concerned. To harbour a Jacobite was no slight offence.

He sought to return to Scotland; but the route was unknown, and soldiers were everywhere.

Travelling by unfrequented roads, stopping at farms or hovels, he found himself in the heart of Weardale, and once amongst the hills seemed to breathe more freely.

Amongst the dalesmen hospitality seemed the law. At West Gate a farmer opened his doors to him; and again near Stanhope a bluff yeoman named Hodgson sheltered him for some days.

Christmas was fast approaching, snow lay thick on hill and dale, travelling was next to impossible, even to men acquainted with the intricacies of the fells. But the yeoman and his daughter Hannah, whose Christianity was practical, treated the wandering piper as an honourable guest, not as a poor refugee. He was pressed to remain, and Hannah ventured to hope his shoulder would be well enough by Christmas Eve for him to pipe for the dancers at their yearly gathering.

"Naething wad gie me mair pleasure, my bonnie lassie, but I fear the poor piper maun gang awa, lest nae guid come o' his biding sea lang we' ye."[24]

"Hout, man! King George will ne'er send into the dale after a solitary piper; at all events, not while the snow lasts," quoth Farmer Hodgson heartily, "so make your mind easy, friend, and be ready to pipe away when Hannah and the lasses are ready to foot it with their sweethearts."

But rosy Hannah, a plump damsel of nineteen, had more sweethearts than one. That is, she had one whom she avowed, Luke Raby, the son of a neighbour, a frank hearty fellow of two or three and twenty; and one other whom she discountenanced.

The latter, Simeon Crawlaw, was an ill-conditioned, pettifogging lawyer, who had wriggled himself into the good graces of the local landed proprietors, so far as to become their agent and collector. In this capacity he stood between the Rabys and their landlord, a very thorn in Luke's side.

Joe Hodgson's farm was his own; had come to him from a long line of ancestors, and Simeon Crawlaw coveted his broad pasture lands and well-stocked byres quite as much as he coveted possession of the hazel-eyed, ruddy-lipped maiden to whom they would descend.

---

24 *Meaning*: 'Nothing would give me more pleasure, my pretty girl, but I fear the poor piper must go away, lest no good come of his biding so long with you.'

As may be expected, there was not much love lost between the two suitors. Luke Raby, as the successful candidate, could well afford to be magnanimous to his rival, whom in his heart he thoroughly despised; but that Hannah's rejection had stirred up malice that lay, like an evil sediment, at the bottom of the lawyer's heart, and he retaliated her refusal upon the elder Ruby in a series of petty annoyances, which irritated the young man almost to exasperation.

Joe Hodgson, whose massive frame was a fit casket for the large heart within, had declared for "a fair field and no favour." "You see, Lawyer Crawlaw, Hannah has no mother, and is all the child I have; I don't thwart her inclinations in little matters, and I'll be hanged if I do it in a great one. And the choice of a woman's husband is a great one, I take it."

"But, Mr. Hodgson, Miss Hannah is so devoted to you, so ready to fall in with your plans, so obedient to your wishes, that a word from you, I'm sure——"

"Hout! hout, man!" interrupted the farmer hastily, "no word of mine shall bar the bairn's free choice. I should be a scoundrel if I made my girl's love for me a reason to break her heart. At the same time I've no objection to your trying your luck, and may the best man win."

The best man *had* won, and Simeon Crawlaw was yet smarting under his recent discomfiture, when news spread through Weardale that the Pretender had abandoned his design of marching on London, and that the Duke of Cumberland and General Wade were rapidly advancing from different points to cut off his retreat to Scotland.

In no period of great political excitement did party feeling run higher than during what is now known as the Jacobite rebellion. Into remote districts rumour spread like thistledown upon the very winds; oral intelligence, quite as reliable as the printed broadsides, circulated by pedlars and chapmen, the travelling stationers of the time.

Discussions, dissensions, and heart-burnings followed every accession of news; but as any open demonstration in favour of the Pretender was sure to be succeeded by imprisonment and fine, if nothing worse, discretion became the better part of valour, and men communicated by signs or spoke in *equivoque*.[25] Informers flourished, and prisons were gorged. Knowing the aptitude of both Joseph Hodgson and his presumptive son-in-law to speak freely and from the heart, Mr. Crawlaw held it wise to dissemble, and hide his humiliation under a show of patient resignation, the better to scrutinize their movements, and lie in wait like a beast of prey until some incautious word or act should lay either open to suspicion, and so feed his revenge.

Not that either the yeoman or Hannah's lover had a taint of Jacobinism, but they had both a tendency to take the weaker side; and on this characteristic he hoped to trade.

No news of the occupation of Penrith or the skirmish at Clifton had reached Hope House, when Dugald Macpherson, faint with cold and hunger, sought shelter and food at that door whence never poor supplicant was sent uncheered.

It was not necessary to ask if he belonged to the proscribed Jacobites. His dress, his tongue, his wounds declared him a fugitive from the rebel army. He had lodged in the outhouses of people who dared not admit him within their good stone walls. But for his wounds, this would have been little privation to the hardy Highlander. But straying out of the track, now regaining it, every mile had been

[25] Verbal ambiguity, double meaning.

lengthened into three or more. Once or twice he had plunged into snow-drifts, from which he only escaped as by a miracle, and altogether these hardships had told upon the old man.

Joseph encountered the wet and haggard piper on the threshold, and without a question asked or story told, bade him "Come in for God's sake," brought him into the glowing kitchen, seated him in the ingle nook, ordered the maids to get bread, cheese, and ale before the famished wanderer, and bade him "fall to with a will!"

Hannah's charity was as active as her father's. She hunted up some of his disused clothes, in which the old piper might attire himself whilst his own were dried and cleaned, and laughed heartily at the figure he cut in garments unfitted to him in every way.

She doctored his wounds too with some skill; but, indeed, Dr. Kendal's dressing had left little to be done, and when the farmer begged the piper to remain, they were healing rapidly.

Thankful for their hospitality, but unwilling to bring his host into danger, he hesitated; but when Joseph Hodgson made light of the risk, and Hannah seconded his invitation, with so winning a smile, what could the old man do but remain, in spite of his prescience of evil to result?

And there he might have remained in shelter and security undisturbed but for the prowling habits and keen scent of Simeon Crawlaw.

Few stand on the ceremony of knocking at the door of a farmhouse—or did, in those unsophisticated days; so when the lawyer walked unannounced and uninvited into the farmer's kitchen, which Hannah and two able assistants were transforming into a Christmas bower with holly and evergreens, no one was surprised save the sly fox himself.

For the presence of Luke Raby he was prepared; but who was this kilted stranger, who stood as erect as if he were an earl?

The plastered face told of recent conflict; the pipes on the side-table told his calling; but the port and bearing of this man as plainly told he was no common strolling piper, picking up pence at fairs, or wakes, or wayside inns. He was evidently the piper to some distinguished tribe or clan; and if so, a man of sufficient mark amongst them to be worth hunting down, and his entertainers with him.

Here was a rare chance!

His greeting was, however, as oily as if he would fain smooth the lives of all present.

"Ah! Miss Hannah, how do you do? I vow you are always employed for the good or pleasure of your friends, and you look as fresh and bright as the holly in your hand."

"You should have said the ivy, Mr. Crawlaw. Holly is sharp and prickly to handle, its berries are poison; the clinging yet supporting ivy, verdurous in summer as winter, best portrays Hannah to my thinking," said her lover, with a glance of mingled tenderness and admiration.

"We speak as we find, Mr. Ruby," retorted the lawyer, with marked emphasis. "The ivy may have clung round you. I, though wounded by the holly, can admire its beauty, while confessing it dangerous."

"I hope you don't think *me* dangerous, Mr. Crawley," said Hannah, with flushed cheeks, as she leapt lightly from the oak settle on which she had been mounted.

"Dangerous to a man's peace of mind, Miss Hodgson," replied he, in an undertone meant for her ears only.

Hannah looked distressed. "What can the old rascal be saying now?" muttered Luke between his teeth, hammering at a nail as if he wished his rival's head in its place, and coming down the ladder without more ado.

Mr. Crawlaw changed the subject. "You have not introduced me to your Scotch friend."

"Oh, Mr. Macpherson—I forgot!" She repaired the omission. Mr. Crawlaw struck up a conversation with the piper, intending to draw him out; but the canny Scot was as wary as his interlocutor, and he made no new discoveries.

He, however, did his best to seem friendly, assisted the trio to festoon the whitewashed walls, and would fain have helped to adjust the huge mistletoe bush, had not Luke Raby entered a protest, as a breach of privilege.

But he only remained long enough to set them at ease. When they adjourned to decorate the panels of the best parlour, he took his departure, on the plea that he had business with a near neighbour; promising, however, to make one of the festive party on Christmas Eve, a promise he meant religiously to fulfil.

"I wish, hinny, you had not asked that man," said Luke, when he was out of hearing. "He will be a sad spoil-sport."

"It was not I who asked him; it was father," answered Hannah. "I would as soon have a toad hopping about the floor. But, Luke, dear, is it not best to be civil to him?"

Luke, with some reservation, admitted it was.

"Yon's a fause loon, lassie, or my auld e'en deceive me; there's muckle mischief under that gleg tongue,"[26] suggested Dugald.

"What, Lawyer Crawlaw!" exclaimed Hodgson, entering the room. He had parted from him at the gate, and coming in overheard

---

26 *Meaning*: 'That one's a false rogue, lassie, or my old eyes deceive me; there's great mischief under that sharp-witted tongue.'

the last remark. "Nay, the man doesn't show at his best here; Hannah knows why; and if he does bear an indifferent name elsewhere, that's the fault of his calling, I reckon."

"Aweel, it's nae business o'mine; but it's dootless aye best to beware o'uncanny folk,"[27] replied the cautious piper, with a sideway nod, as expressive as his words.

CHAPTER II

Christmas Eve had come. So had the guests, for a rapid thaw had cleared byeways and made open roads passable if not pleasant, and Christmas gatherings at Hope House were no means to be despised.

Long tables were literally loaded with good things in all the ponderous prodigality of old-fashioned hospitality; and their preparation had kept the house in a bustle for a week or more. Game laws were stringent, but keepers were friendly; so hare and pheasant made as goodly a show on the board as goose and turkey. Huge joints of beef and mutton, flanked by brawn and Yorkshire pie, were matched with corresponding piles of vegetables, with stoups of home-brewed ale to wash all down. Then followed plum-pudding and plum-porridge, mince-pies and tartlets, creams and syllabubs, apples, pears, nuts, such dried fruits as were accessible, home-made wines, and other dainties.

Appetite and mirth honoured the welcome and graced the feast.

The piper, in his picturesque costume, sat at the board an

---

27 Meaning: 'Well, it's no business of mine, but it's doubtless always best to beware of mischievous folk.'

honourable and honoured guest; but indeed, the whole scene had made a study for a painter, sparkling and glowing with light and colour. Dark-haired Hannah, dispensing smiles and hospitalities so bountifully, shone in her ample dress of richly-flowered taffeta and jaunty cap, but as one rose in a blooming parterre; whilst the young men of the party rivalled the feminine portion in their display of lace on ruffles and neckcloths, of Bristol-stones in buckles for shoe or knee, and full tints in the deep-flapped vests and long wide-skirted coats they wore, even if their elders toned down the whole with more subdued drab and brown. Polished silver and pewter flickered with faint reflections from candles in tin sconces on the embowered walls, or in the extemporised chandelier suspended from the huge beams o'erhead; but they twinkled feebly in the warmer glow of the fire on the open hearth, where the Yule log, blazing on a bed of pit coal, sent out showers of bright sparkles, and lit up every beaming face, every cleft and cranny of the ample "house."

But even feasting has an end. A clearance being made, the elders retired to the quiet parlour to play cards and backgammon, or discuss dangerous politics in whispers; whilst Dugald, primed with a stiff dose of whisky-punch from a mammoth punch-bowl, gathered his pipes into his arms once more, and struck up a reel that brought the dancers to their feet in all haste.

In the good-humoured contest for places, couples came incontinently under the mistletoe bough, and coy damsels submitted to be kissed, in deference to indefeasible right; though the grace with which the concession was made depended much on special caprices and individual likings.

Up to a late hour Mr. Crawlaw had not put in an appearance; to the great relief of young Raby and Hannah, both of whom expressed as much in a confidential moment.

Dance followed dance. Not tame quadrilles, through which the staid dancers glide without an effort, but dances which required good limbs, good breath, and strong flooring.

In the midst, Mr. Hartley, an elderly man, a partner in a Weardale mine, who had only just arrived, called the beaming host aside, and asked several questions in quick succession; questions of import in the sequel. "Hodgson, did you not expect Lawyer Crawlaw here?"

"Certainly," was the answer.

"When was he here *last?*"

"On Monday evening."

"Monday! Hm! Quite two days. How long may our friend the martial piper have been with you?"

"About a week."

"And Crawlaw saw him?"

"Yes! But why put me through this catechism? You do not do it idly, I am sure!"

"Idly! No, by heavens! Friend Hodgson, there has been an encounter between Cumberland's advance and Charles Edward's rear; and this Scotch piper is a fugitive. Your liberty is endangered by your harbouring a rebel."

"Hout, man, common charity—" interjected the blunt farmer, to be in turn interrupted.

"Yes, yes! I know all that, as so, no doubt, does that knave Crawlaw. But what does the Government or its tools care for common charity? Common charity will hardly save us from the common hangman in these ticklish times. You must get the piper out of the house with all speed, not less for his safety than your own."

"But why this haste, Hartley?" interrogated the yeoman, as in a mist.

"Well, I met the lawyer on his way to Durham with exultant mischief in his winking eyes; and from a word he dropped I feel assured he has gone to turn informer. He has never forgiven your daughter's preference of a younger and better man. Faugh! I hate the sneak!"

Loth as Joe Hodgson was to turn the piper forth on Christmas Eve, a hunted man, he felt the absolute necessity of giving him a chance of escape ere the hounds of the law were on his track.

No time was to be lost. Mr. Hartley returned to the glowing kitchen, where blind-man's buff had superseded dancing. A hint sent Hannah to her father, Luke Raby quickly followed, as by inspiration.

Another hint, and Dugald left the merrymakers, taking his cherished pipes along with him. He was warned that he was in peril and must escape. Fortunately, the snow was almost gone, and footsteps could not be tracked in the thaw. Luke Raby volunteered to be his guide through the mazes of the dale. Once beyond, he must assume the character of an ordinary wandering piper, so as to lessen suspicion.

"Dinna greet, my bonnie lassie," said Dugald, as tears sprang into Hannah's eyes. "Dinna greet on Christmas Eve. I wad rather hae streekit my auld limbs under the mouls wi' my ain Allan, than hae brought trouble and sorrow to hearts sae kind and leal. An' I fear the warst is not ower."[28]

A hasty parting, and Dugald, with sad forebodings in his heart, left Hope House with his young friend. The square stone building looked darker, from the contrasting light which streamed from

---

[28] *Meaning*: 'Don't cry, my pretty girl… Don't cry on Christmas Eve. I would rather have laid out my old limbs under the earth with my own Allan, than have brought trouble and sorrow to hearts so kind and loyal. And I fear the worst is not over.'

doors and windows, and the sounds of laughter fell sadly on the ears of both.

To Luke Raby every winding of the dale was familiar. Keeping near the high road, yet away from it, he led the piper steadily on, though over-ways only passable by a mountaineer. As they left Wolsingham in the rear, the distinct beat of hoofs was audible: then followed the murmur of voices. Raby drew the piper into the shadow of a dense planting by the road-side, whilst the horseman passed.

Voice and figure betrayed one to be Simeon Crawlaw, whilst the conversation of all three, carried on in the loud tones of semi-intoxication, assured them that his companions were constables, and that Mr. Hartley's friendly warning had come not one moment too soon.

Hitherto they had proceeded with caution, lest a sudden turn of the road might bring them in contact with the suspected informer and his coadjutors. Now they pushed on.

Two miles farther the highway to Hexham crossed the path they had trod.

"Here we part, good Dugald," said Luke, kindly; "I must return in haste, lest I should be missed. Keep to the road straight before you; it leads direct to the North. In two hours you will be out of the jurisdiction of Durham, and may cross the borders ere pursuit be possible; even if it be thought worth while to pursue, which I much doubt."

Dugald gave his proffered hand a hearty grip.

"Fare ye weel," said he, "and tak wi' ye an auld man's blessing, for yersel and yon winsome lassie. Ye'll wed ere it be lang, and then may yer bairns grow up as guid as yersels! I can wish ye nae better, I'm thinking. God bie wi' us a'. Should Prince Charlie win his ain, Dugald Macpherson may hae it in his pooer to requite his freends."[29]

How strangely is the web of life mingled! These men parted, never expecting to meet again. How little the most far-seeing can tell whither his next step will lead!

Let us, however, follow Dugald, as he strode along through the mire, the mist, and the darkness.

His heart was heavy as the road he travelled, where the half-melted snow yet lay in knee-deep ruts, in which one leg would dip with sudden jerk that might have dislocated looser joints. But Dugald lived before the days of Macadam, and took the bad roads as matters of course.

Pondering on the fate of Scotland and his sons, he reached a point where the road was crossed at an acute angle. Hesitating, he turned to the right, where he saw signs of habitation. It was Gorecock Hall, and he had turned when he should have gone forward. Yet he walked on with long strides. Roads again crossed, still he kept to the right, and went wrong. When he hoped to have reached Northumberland, he was passing Neville's Cross, nearing the city from which he should have fled.

And now he met drunken men, who had not slept off the night's carouse, some who wished him a merry Christmas, others who, when asked the road, jeered at his strange garb, or spoke morosely. All, however, eyed him strangely.

At length he found himself in the heart of Durham when its

---

[29] *Meaning*: 'Farewell... and take with you an old man's blessing, for yourself and that winsome girl. You'll wed before long, and then may your children grow up as good as yourselves! I can wish you no better, I'm thinking. God be with us all. Should Prince Charlie win his own, Dugald Macpherson may have it in his power to requite his friends.'

inhabitants were casting off the dreams of night.

That was no safe abiding place. Crossing the Market Place quickly as he could, he stepped boldly through Claypath Gates, and on up Gilliesgate.

A city watchman, armed with a formidable billhook, going to report himself after his last round, perceived him, and summoned him to "Stop in the King's name."

To stop was to be taken! An alley offered an escape. He darted into its dim obscurity. The watchman gave chase, shouting as he ran.

Dugald dashed headlong forward—the way led to the river—there was a sound of rushing waters—the river was a flood—the path covered and crumbling—the stream lapping the foundations of the houses—another unconsidered step—the man was in the swollen stream, struggling for his life.

As he rose to the surface, he struck out. But the swirling waters bore him on. The most powerful swimmer could not have stemmed that torrent. How, then, could an aged man, whose shoulder yet was stiff with a recent would, hope to escape?

Instinctively he had clung to his bagpipes. They fettered his right arm, but they also helped to buoy him up. He floated, drifting with the stream.

Fortunately every available spot was lined with people striving to recover from flood such household goods as had been washed from other homes.

Elvet steps were filled with excited men (and women too), provided with poles and ropes.

As the whirling eddies swung the piper round, still washing him onwards towards Bishop Pudsey's many-arched bridge, a simultaneous shout arose from the occupants of the steps—"A man in the river!"

Just then a mass of drift-wood struck him on the head. It stunned but saved him. Another instant he would have been under the arch, and lost.

It drove him nearer to the steps, a noosed rope was flung round his body, and he was drawn to land.

Senseless and apparently dead he was carried up Elvet steps, by rough-looking but tender-hearted men.

"Poor fellow, he's getten a drop ower much ower night at sum Kirsmas feast, and stumbled ower inter the river,"[30] surmised one.

"He'll not get fu' agen in a hurry when he gets ower this bout,"[31] remarked another.

"Tak care o' the man's bagpipes," bawled a woman. "He'll want em gin he does come round."[32]

Where should he be carried?

By this time the city watchman, whose sudden chase had had so disastrous a result, came upon the scene. "Carry him to the gaol, the governor will best know what's to be done with him," said he of the billhook, with a voice of authority not to be questioned.

The gaol was then the North Gate of the city, defended by sallyport and portcullis, the latter rusting in its grooves from disuse. It had been rebuilt by Bishop Langley about 1417, and was a fine specimen of the strong architecture of the period. It divided Saddler Street from the North Bailey. The portcullis, which had been raised quite a century, fell suddenly, during some alterations in 1778,

---

30 *Meaning*: 'Poor fellow, he's had a drop too much over night at some Christmas feast, and stumbled over into the river.'

31 *Meaning*: 'He'll not get drunk again in a hurry when he gets over this bout.'

32 *Meaning*: 'Take care of the man's bagpipes… He'll want them if he does come round.'

stopping the road until workmen with saws and axes cut it to pieces. The gaol itself was not destroyed until 1820, when a more modern building was erected on its site.

When the watchman, therefore, ordered Dugald Macpherson to be carried to the gaol, he suggested the most accessible place, and when the bearers hurried with their senseless and dripping burden along Elvet Bridge (which, of course, extends far beyond the actual stream) and up the Maudlin or Magdalen steps (so called from a Magdalen chapel which once stood there) into Saddler Street, they took the nearest route to the gaol.

The governor was a man of some humanity for his vocation; and so, notwithstanding Dugald's questionable guise, all then known appliances were used for his restoration.

The blow he had received in the water had, more than his immersion, given a shock to the system, following as it did months of hardship, excitement, and pain.

He recovered, it is true, even whilst the Christmas bells were ringing; but brain fever supervened, and there was but rough tendance in the gaol.

Leaving him, therefore, to rave wildly of his Allan and Sandy, of Bonnie Prince Charlie and his chief; of bagpipes and bloodshed, condemning himself and others in his delirium; let us return to Hope House, and see how all things fared with the good yeoman on that Christmas Day.

Though Luke Raby retraced his steps with the vigour and activity of early manhood, leaping over impediments which would have daunted a less resolute man, he found that Crawlaw and his myrmidons had reached the farm before him.

They were armed with warrants for the arrest of a Scotch piper called Dugald Macpherson, suspected of being in open rebellion against the reigning sovereign; and of Joseph Hodgson, yeoman, for knowingly harbouring the same.

But the piper was nowhere to be found, and, as may be supposed, no one knew more of him than that he was an itinerant piper earning a precarious living by attendance at dances and places of entertainment. His departure was accounted for on the plea that he was anxious to be in readiness for another merry-making the following day at Bishop Auckland, and as that was a goodish step he had asked permission to retire early.

In the absence of proof the constables were forced to retire, their search-warrant having resulted in nothing but discomfiture to themselves and their leader, Mr. Simeon Crawlaw, who had endeavoured to hide his share in the transaction by entering the house alone to reconnoitre, leaving his followers at some distance from the gate with instructions not to advance for some time. He walked into the midst of the mirthful party with assumed ease and affability, greeting Hannah and her father with apparent cordiality as of old.

But forewarned is forearmed. Mr. Crawlaw was questioned as to the cause of his late arrival; but no word or look betrayed their knowledge that his excuses were fictions. They were equally on their guard when the constables presented themselves.

Of course their entrance and errand spread dismay and confusion, so genuine that suspicion was disarmed. Mr. Crawlaw became suddenly fussy, as if desirous to justify his friends, dexterously cross-questioning the domestics in his apparent officious zeal to prove non-complicity. And he did prove more than he desired.

All he elicited was, that a poor piper, half-famished, and wet with floundering through snowdrifts, who had been hurt in a drunken brawl on his way from St. John's Chapel, had been taken in by the master, and kept out of charity, because he would not have turned a dog out into the snow; and that when the snow was going he stayed to play for the dancers, there having been no chance to get a fiddler.

The men insisted on a rigid search of house and outhouses; and finding nothing, went away swearing at their want of success.

Joe Hodgson could not, however, be churlish to anyone on Christmas Eve, and as the men buttoned their long, heavy overcoats to depart, he called them into the lesser kitchen, and regaled them with cake, cheese, and hot ale.

"Better luck next time," said one of the men, as he raised the wooden bicker to his lips, a toast the discomfited Lawyer echoed in his heart.

Luke Raby had returned in the height of the search, and having taken the precaution to change his muddy boots for the shoes previously worn, was seen helping Hannah to allay the fears of her friends as if he had never been absent.

So far, so well.

Such visitors as lived at a distance from Stanhope remained the night, and Christmas Day passed cheerily enough. The yeoman's heart was too generous to harbour suspicion of Crawlaw; and concluding that the arrival of the officers so closely upon the lawyer's heels was a mere coincidence, he decided that Mr. Hartley's unconcealed dislike of the agent had led him to draw false conclusions, and so dismissed the matter from his mind, with a hope that the piper was fairly out of reach. He was consequently as jolly as if no warrants and prisons ever existed, and made fun for the young people with all the zest of thorough enjoyment.

Luke Raby, however, had a deeper insight into his defeated rival's heart. He had too often felt through his father what the man's petty malice could effect, and how he never lost an opportunity to goad or wound those who chanced to offend him, to question the verity of Mr. Hartley's statement; even supposing he had not seen and overheard the agent and officers of justice on the road. Not wishing to disturb Hannah, whom he loved dearly, he kept his fears to himself, and strove to appear as gay as the rest.

His father's farm lay on the other side of Stanhope, two long miles from Hope House; and when, at a late hour, he took leave, promising to see her again on the Sunday, he lingered as lovers do, but uneasily, and embraced her with a fervour so unusual that the girl rebuked him laughingly, saying,

"Why, Luke, you might be parting with me for ever."

"My darling, I trust not; but these are strange times, and God only knows!"

"Well, I shall expect you on Sunday; so mind you are here. Good night." So, extricating herself from his clasp, she tripped into the house, and he strode homewards, vainly striving to cast off despondency.

He was not at church on Sunday morning, and Hannah returned home alone, more pettish than anxious, having no knowledge of impending evil. As she drew near home she met Tibby, her old nurse, wringing her hands in sore distress.

Pettishness gave place to bitter anguish. Father and lover, both were on their way as prisoners to Durham Gaol!

CHAPTER III

Simeon Crawlaw's suspicions had been lulled, not stifled. His sharp, blinking eyes had noticed Luke's hat and cloak, hastily thrown down on a chair in a back room at Hope House when the search was over, and close by his long riding boots, not merely wet with mud, but thickly flecked with *unmelted* snow. They had been evidently used very recently, and on untrodden roads.

Bearing this in mind, and forgetting the "good-will to men," which every steeple rang out that Christmas Day, he once more betook himself to Durham Gaol. But the governor, after giving his orders concerning the resuscitated Dugald, had gone to spend the day with friends in a livelier and more odorous locality; and would not be back until the following day. So Mr. Simeon had to bridle his impatience and wait until the morrow.

Meanwhile he repaired to the Half Moon, at the corner of Elvet, to refresh himself after the manner of men; and found the pathway obstructed, and the rooms filled with people talking volubly about the flood, and—the Highland piper who had been rescued at Elvet steps just as he was being carried away by the stream.

Here was news! He listened, questioned carelessly, and came to the conclusion that Mr. Macpherson was the man; and if so had dropped as it were into his very grasp. At all events *he* was snug in prison; that was something gained.

After an interview with the governor and an identification of delirious Dugald, once more he trotted to the Mayor to make another deposition, and obtain an extra warrant for the arrest of Luke Raby, with what success we know.

The blow fell heavily. In those days prisons were little better than graves, so few escaped who once entered their noxious precincts, loathsome to the senses, loathsome to the soul; and for suspected Jacobites there was more law than justice.

Still Joseph Hodgson had a brave heart, and seeing Luke Raby wince as they passed under the North Gate to the strong door of the gaol, followed by a noisy crown, he said—

"Hout, lad, never be cast down! They can prove nought against thee, and charity's no crime. Keep up thy heart! We shall be blithe at home again by New Year's Day."

"Amen!" responded Luke, with a fervour which expressed his doubts.

They were not at home on New Year's Day. Delays occurred before they could be brought before the chief magistrate, and then they were hauled back to prison to await their trial at the next gaol delivery; Joseph Hodgson for harbouring, Luke Raby for aiding and abetting, the escape of a known rebel.

There was no concealing the animus of Crawlaw, informer and accuser, now; indeed, so transparent was it, that the Mayor checked his protestations of loyalty, and declared that had the guilt of the prisoners rested on his unsupported testimony, he should have dismissed them at once. But the gaoler who had listened to the ravings of the piper rescued from the river had given evidence which compelled their detention. Then first the yeoman and Luke Raby learned the extent of their own and Dugald's misfortune.

In spite of the magistrate's stern rebuke, Simeon Crawlaw returned home exultant. "Mistress Hannah would have leisure to repent her hasty choice *now!*"

But Hannah did *not* repent. She loathed the mean wretch more intensely than ever; whilst the misfortunes of father and lover increased her devotion to them seven-fold.

Mr. Hartley was a true friend to her in her distress; not only giving wordy solace, but active assistance. He engaged a good legal firm in their behalf, and bespoke able counsel. Moreover, he overlooked the accounts of the farm-bailiff, and gave such general supervision as kept things in order at home.

She, poor girl, spent much of her time with old Mrs. Raby, who, like her husband, refused to be comforted for the loss of her son.

Time went by, sorrow in the farms—sadness in the gaol!

Even Joe Hodgson's brave heart sunk under the influence of his confinement. There was little or no separation of untried prisoners, and their days were spent among criminals of the worst description.

In about a month the piper was brought into their midst sorely changed by fever. His shaggy locks had been cut or shaven away, and a thick grisled stubble was rising on his poll like a beard a fortnight old.

There was little light in that cramped and stifling prison room. At first the piper saw only a number of strangers; but his eye lighting on Mr. Hodgson and Luke Raby, who advanced to greet him, his start of recognition was accompanied by a quick spasm of pain over his bronzed face.

"Wha wad hae thocht o' meeting ya in siccan a place as this? It canna be for gieing food and rest to a sinking auld man that ye hae been brought hither. Guid guide us! I had better hae died wi my Allan than lived to see saw sad a day. Wae's me! wae's me!"[33]

He had begged for his pipes, and brought them with him. At once he began a wild lament that filled the prison walls, seeming to gather consolation from his strain.

As the days went by, his old spirit came back to him. He played lilts and strathspeys,[34] and the more reckless prisoners, clearing a space, danced roughly to his music.

---

[33] *Meaning*: 'Who would have thought of meeting you in such a place as this? It can't be for giving food and rest to a sinking old man that you have been brought hither. God guide us! I had better have died with my Allan than lived to see so sad a day. Woe's me! woe's me!'

[34] A type of dance tune.

At times he vented his feelings in "Charlie is my darling," "Blue bonnets over the Borders," "Wha wadna fecht for Charlie,"[35] and other equally patriotic airs. At first the gaolers stopped his Jacobite tunes with threats to take away his pipes; but after a time they ceased to trouble themselves, being probably glad to have the cheerless monotony of their own prison-life broken by the inspiring melodies.

His pipes had a good effect in rousing the prisoners sinking beneath their own individual sorrows, or lapsing into moodiness from lack of occupation. The very prison walls, cut and carved with rude devices of ships and flowers and animals, told plainly how time lagged even with men whose days were numbered. Dugald therefore was to such men as a beneficent spirit, and many were the blessings he received from lips which were more apt to curse than to bless.

At long intervals Hannah was permitted to visit her father. These were painful interviews. There was no privacy. Even her presence could not restrain loose tongues and coarse jests; and both Luke and he shrank from her introduction into such a den. Mr. Hartley was ever her kind attendant, but even he was unwilling to prolong her stay.

The day of trial at last. The court was crowded; for both the prisoners had many friends; whilst the lawyer had a still larger number of "good haters," open and secret.

We have no space to report the trial, we can only give results.

Joseph Hodgson was found guilty of harbouring the rebel Dugald Macpherson, and Luke Raby of aiding and abetting his escape; but as no proof of "guilty knowledge" was forthcoming, and as they had already suffered some months' incarceration, and

---

[35] *Meaning*: 'Who Wouldn't Fight for Charlie.'

were known for loyal subjects, their punishment was remitted to a fine, heavy, it is true—but still a fine, and within their means.

Dugald Macpherson was not likely to escape so readily. His course had been traced from Clifton Bridge, and there was little doubt but the gallows would be his doom.

In the course of the proceedings it transpired that he had lost a son in the skirmish near Penrith; and had a second in the Pretender's army.

On the mention of his sons, Dugald became very excited, spoke vehemently, and could not be restrained. Thereupon one of the counsel present rose and said, "Then, my lord, it would be this prisoner's other son, Sandy Macpherson, whom I saw hanged at Carlisle with a number of like rebels, when the Duke of Cumberland re-took the town. I recognize the resemblance between father and son."

Dugald clutched at the rail before him, his face and throat worked convulsively. "What! Sandy, my Sandy, Sandy Macpherson hangit like a dog!" he shrieked more than spoke, and dropped down in a fit.

He was removed insensible, and sentence was deferred.

Judge and jury alike pitied the old man, whose last hope was so rudely snapped.

When an hour later he was brought back for judgment, he looked round vacantly, seemingly unconscious of his situation.

He was condemned—not to the gallows, but to be imprisoned for life, a sentence by many thought far too lenient for a *rebel*, and there were undertoned mutterings of Jacobite tendencies in the presiding judge.

He was simply a man and a father, and could feel for the Scotch piper in his misery.

Dugald was taken back to his prison-cell, but henceforth he became inane and imbecile. He would have occasional flashes of reason, but rarely. His sole delight was to finger his pipes, and to play martial or melancholy music as his moods alternated.

Dugald's sad condition tempered the rejoicings at Hope House on the release of Mr. Hodgson and Luke, the close intercourse in prison having created a strong feeling of attachment to the piper, who bore up so bravely under his own misfortunes, and was ever so ready to lighten the load of others.

Simeon Crawlaw had little reason to rejoice in his revenge. He was openly hooted at as an "informer," his clients left him, his agencies were taken from him; he removed to a distant county, but odium followed him whithersoever he went; he sank deeper and deeper into poverty, and died in the Fleet Prison.

Before he left he had the mortification to see Hannah and Luke married, while yet the trees were red and russet; and to hear the good wishes which followed them from rich to poor. Mr. Hartley was there, and gave the bride away.

Ere the week was out, the young couple visited Dugald in the prison, by special permission, and many times afterwards.

He knew them, and appeared gratified, but seemed to be no longer troubled by his position. He still clung to his pipes, and so solaced himself and other hearts more keenly alive to the sense of imprisonment. And who can tell how much good he unconsciously effected? Discipline was relaxed in his favour, and when the following autumn young Mrs. Raby's first born was baptised by his name he was permitted to visit the farm and pipe for the company.

Whether his scattered wits were recalled by the scene or the company, they could not tell; but his senses were restored in the short visit.

The return to prison after that brief taste of freedom and fresh air was too much for him; he sank into sadness, ceased to play his pipes, and lost his strength rapidly.

A gaoler had been well bribed to let the family at Hope House know if any change for the worse came over him. On Christmas Eve they thus learned that he was dying, and hastened to the poor piper's bedside in that stone cell, which even the money they gave freely for the purpose could not make comfortable.

He was sinking fast when they saw him; but rallied, asked for his pipes once more, began to play "The King shall hae his ain again,"[36] and dropped back dead as the Cathedral bells rang out the Christmas peal in honour of the birth of that great King who breaks the prison walls and sets the captive free.

But the piper never left the precincts of Elvet Bridge whilst a stone of the prison was left standing.

From the river side, up Elvet steps, along the bridge, and Magdalen steps, under the North Gate, and into the gaol his spirit was seen to pass every Christmas Day morning; and every midnight his pipes might be heard in the prison cells, playing his Jacobite airs, even when Jacobinism had died out.

The gaol came down, and now not a vestige of the old prison remains to mark the spot which had for so many decades been haunted by THE PIPER'S GHOST.

---

36 'The King shall have his own again.'

ST. CUTHBERT'S CUP

A LEGEND OF HELL-KETTLES, DARLINGTON

CHAPTER I

HUGH Pudsey was Bishop of Durham. Whether he was son or nephew of King Stephen is not decided; but it is certain that he lived in stormy times, and that stormy work attended and succeeded his translation from the Treasury of York to the Bishopric of Durham. The Conquest was a wrong of too recent date, and the rule of the intruders too oppressive for the Saxon monks of St. Cuthbert's shrine to welcome readily the Norman prelate nominated by their Norman king. His youth (he was but twenty-five), his secular life and conversation, the freedom of his morals (he had then three natural sons), his extravagance in dress, were all raised in objection; and as the monks at that time held the right of election, they might have set him aside in favour of one of their own body, if either Prior or Archdeacon, the rival candidates, would have waived his own claim to the episcopal chair.

Nor did he find that chair exactly cushioned with roses; at all events thorns were plentiful, and sharp enough to make him restless and uncomfortable. Shortly after his own installation, the election of a new Prior, in 1154, gave him hopes of quiet rule, for Prior Absolon was a man of inferior capacity and attainments, and too weak to resist strong hand or strong mind. But his hope was short-lived. Within the year Henry II had succeeded Stephen on the English throne, and with all his mother's wrongs burnt in his brain, he was not likely to look favourably on Stephen's protégé enthroned in the North, with a large body of feudal retainers to maintain his princely state.

Whether as a measure of annoyance, or of precaution against a possible foe, Henry commanded the prelate to render a return of the lands within his diocese held on military tenure, their occupation and values. To this Royal edict Durham owes the remarkable *Boldon Book*[37] still extant amongst its archives—the doomsday-book of the palatinate. This was on the marriage of the Princess Maud, and the pretext that of levying an aid.

Whatever was the King's true motive for desiring such return the effects were anything but prejudicial to the Bishop, who thus became more intimately acquainted with the condition and resources of his province. It drew him into closer relations with the knights and barons, and found clerkly work for those monks in whom inaction begot disaffection.

How he dealt with his contumacious monastics may be told in a few words. On one occasion he surrounded the Durham convent with a military cordon, and starved them into submission; on another destroyed their fish reservoirs, and later killed all their cattle in Bearpark.

Nevertheless, Durham owes much to his energy and public enterprise. He restored the borough of Elvet (destroyed by Comyn, the usurper), built Elvet Bridge, and completed the City Wall, and gave the inhabitants their first charter.

But he listened to tattlers and mischief-makers, and these made him irritable, distrustful, and finally impelled him to build himself a palace on the very verge of his palatinate—at Derlyngton—on the banks of the Dare (or Skerne).

Whilst these erections were in progress he was in progress too,

---

37 * *Boldon Book*: So called from the place where the survey was commenced —Boldon.

that is, he, a man embroiled with his sovereign, embroiled with his ecclesiastics, travelled in state with a large retinue to and fro to superintend and urge forward the works he had in hand; caring little how much he oppressed the Saxon franklins and serfs the feudal laws compelled to do him service. Posterity profited, but his subjects groaned under their bondage.

Amongst the secular vassals of the church none bowed more reverently to St. Cuthbert's prelate than Lord Eustace De Eden, of Castle Eden; none held him in less regard than did Sir William de Turp, who held adjoining lands in Eden Dene, and did knight's service to Eustace as his superior lord.

He was a stern, dark-browed, discontented man, was William de Turp, a man soured by disappointments, to whose lot had fallen land, but not the wealth to turn his barren acres to account, or maintain a Norman retinue sufficient to awe his Saxon feors and slaves into abject submission.

The death of Stephen had driven him from court, to the less congenial atmosphere of his own Thorpe,[38] where, but for occasional quarrels with warlike neighbours, his knightly armour seemed likely to rust.

Dame Elinor, his wife, was a mild, gentle woman, and it might seem at first glance they were unfitly mated. But in her presence his stern brows relaxed, and his moods softened. She offered no opposition to the will of her lord, and so they came not into collision. She was, as ladies of her rank were, the directress of the household; her daughters, Matilda and Emma, plied their rapid bobbins in the production of tapestry, or twirled the distaff amongst

---

38 * Thorpe: A farm or grange, together with the village surrounding or attached thereto.

their bowerwomen to spin yarn for the websters of Durham to weave into cloth for the family.

Dame Elinor was accomplished as the times went, having in a Norman convent learned not only to read and write, to embroider and spin, but to play the cithern and illuminate the missal she had herself transcribed; and more, she had learned to feed the hungry, shelter the houseless, and heal the sick and the wounded. And what she had learned she transmitted to her daughters, alike by instruction and example. They, however, differed in many respects; Matilda, with the dark eyes and hair of her father, had inherited also his lofty port, his ambitious longings, and pined for restoration to the courtly scenes of which the minstrels sang, and from which she in the fulness of her maiden bloom was excluded.

The brown-eyed Emma had few desires beyond the limits of their home and the beautiful dene. She was quiet and unobtrusive, and pious to superstition. This was not wholly due to the influence of the monks of St. Cuthbert, for though they were busied in building the chapel of St. James on the land in the dene, granted by Robert de Brus, and confirmed to them by charter from Eustace de Eden, and consequently drew largely on the hospitality of the surrounding proprietary, the few who cared to brook Sir William's surly welcome were of the class more inclined to join him is feasting and drinking than in fasting and prayer.

But in a natural recess, at the farthest extremity of the dene, lived Godric the Hermit, near enough to hear the roar and wash of the sea, yet sheltered from the fierce blasts which sometimes swept up the valley, behind the projecting rock, in a cleft of which his rude hermitage of wattled boughs had been constructed. Near and far had spread the fame of the holy man; pilgrims and devotees came by land and sea to ask his prayers, his blessing, and his counsel; and it was his influence which had moulded the plastic mind of Emma to higher and holier aims than those of mere earth.

Rarely, in those lawless times, did women above the peasant class venture far abroad unattended; but the tide of battle had hitherto swept other lands than those of the secluded dene, while for common marauders the Castle was too strong and well-guarded, and the Thorpe possessed little to repay a raid. So, in negative security, Emma was wont to pass to and fro unaccompanied by other than Getha her maid, save on those rare occasions when Matilda or Dame Elinor herself sought the cell of the good hermit for confession or consolation. There was little to distinguish the two damsels as they threaded the mazes of the wooded dene, or followed the common pathway by the stream, enveloped in long-hooded cloaks, save the texture of the homespun cloth, and the rich brooch which secured that of the mistress at the throat. But when the cloak was laid aside, and revealed the closely-fitting, open-sleeved tunic of embroidered linen, above the green woollen kirtle which drooped to the very shoes, the richly-ornamented pouch suspended from her gold-buckle girdle, the abundant hair which hung behind in two thick plaits far below her waist, contrasted strongly with the homely robe of Getha, long and loose, confined round the waist by a plain band of leather, and marked at once the difference of their rank and birth.

From the first dawn of womanhood Emma's wont had been to bring the pious anchorite such offerings in the way of eggs, honey, barley cakes, or fruit as would be most likely acceptable to one whose diet was spare to abstinence, and whose daily wants were supplied much as were those of Elijah by the brook Cherith. Little knew she that the stern ascetic never ate the eggs until addled, nor the cakes until mouldy. And for two or three years the budding maiden tripped lightly on her errands of charity and devotion with single-minded purpose; then when the bud blossomed into sweet seventeen, another element was introduced, another motive was superadded.

Her dress required more adjusting for the walk, and as she neared the hermitage her step was less firm, her colour came and went, her grace strayed timidly but expectantly, and within her breast was a faint fluttering as of the wings of an imprisoned dove.

We have said that many penitents and pilgrims sought the saintly Godric's cell; and one spring day, when the sun was high and the dene was vocal with the songs and twitterings of pairing birds, and the infant leaves were feeling their way into the sunshine, Emma and Getha were startled by seeing a light skiff moored within a short distance of the hermitage.[39]

Fain would she have retreated within the shadow of the woods until the boatman should have gone his way; but ere she could make her will known to her companion, the door of the hermitage opened, and she stood within a few paces of a well-formed, clear-eyed youth, whose length of cloak and length of yellow hair betokened him a Saxon, whilst the texture of the one and the golden fillet which bound the other bespoke his rank at least equal to her own. He had stooped in order to pass through the low doorway; but raising his head, an exclamation at once of surprise and admiration burst from his lips—he had not dreamed to see so fair a sight in that lonely place.

Their eyes met, and those of Emma fell abashed before his earnest enquiring gaze, whilst the quick blood flushed her face with

---

39 * The entrance to Castle Eden Dene in these days is much too confined to admit a boat—what it may have been so many centuries back is another matter.

the crimson veil of modesty, and her prompt hand drew closer the sheltering folds of her hood.

Rebuked by the action, the young man withdrew his ardent gaze, but not before his sudden exclamation had brought the hermit to the door also. Perceiving the maiden, and guessing the cause of her confusion, Godric advanced a step or two to meet her, saying, "Benedicite, my daughter; pass within with thy handmaiden. I will hear thy errand anon."

With one deep reverence to him and a second to the rude symbol of Christianity carved above the entrance, Emma obeyed, followed by Getha, who, turning to have another glance at the handsome stranger, overheard Godric say, as if in continuation, "And do thou, Alan, turn thy bark swiftly homewards, the winds will rise ere long. The sea-birds seek the land, and thou wilt need all thy strength to reach thy haven ere the storm comes on. Go, with my blessing to speed thy oars!"

"Nay, good father, thou are surely mistaken; the breeze has scarcely strength to ring the bells of yonder hyacinths; though I mind me it blew aside the folds of thy fair penitent's hood, revealing a vision of beauty to my unprepared sight. Holy father, cometh the sweet lady often to her shrift? And wilt thou not tell me what name to remember her by?"

"My son, my son, said I not ere now this would be a day of peril to thee? Go thy ways, whilst thou may. Ukillus de Hoton would scarcely care to hear that his beloved son had looked with fascinated eyes on the child of William de Turp. Go, and the blessed St. Cuthbert be thy shield."

Alan had been slowly (very slowly) loosing his tiny craft from her moorings, his thoughts running in rapid unspoken commentary on the hermit's words—"Peril! I fear me no peril greater than from those soft brown eyes!" But at the name of the damsel's sire he started. There was not much cordiality between the Saxon thane and the Norman knight.

"William de Turp!" he exclaimed in surprise; "William de Turp! I ever heard his heiress was dark and tall, and commanding as her imperious father. This maid seems timid and gentle as a cushat-dove. Her name, good father, her name?"

"She is the younger born, my son; I myself baptized her Emma, and, as thou rightly sayest, she does resemble the dove. But we waste words, and time; and thou hast none to waste. Pray to the saints to guard thee on the sea: thou wilt have need of prayers. *Pax vobiscum.*"[40]

The swift current of the Eden bore the frail skiff rapidly onward to the open sea, though the tide was on the turn, and breakers were advancing. The wind, too, had changed; the distant sky looked threatening; but Alan, the son of Ukillus, had been blinded to the aspect of the weather by that one brief glance from Emma's dove-like eyes.

Emma had withdrawn the inquisitive Getha from the open doorway before her ears had caught much more than the stranger's name; and assuming her young mistress to be as curious as herself, she decided in her pique to keep the information a secret.

During the absence of the holy man, Emma had laid her simple tribute of wild flowers gathered in the wood, blue hyacinths, sweet lilies of the valley, the purple orchis, the red-crane's bill, before the shrine of St. Cuthbert; and her short shrift over, Getha's prolix confession was austerely abbreviated by the hermit, who bade them hasten homewards, nor loiter by the way.

---

40 Peace be with you.

"Repeat thy Aves, Paternoster, and Credo to-night earnestly, if ever thou didst in thy life. Pray, too, for the souls of all who are dear to thee, my daughter," said the holy man, with more than his wonted solemnity. "I hear the first pantings of the storm wind, and I must to my knees, for I know that I shall hear more than the shriek of the whirlwind. Evil spirits are let loose, and the foul fiend himself heads his demon host. The Holy Virgin will protect innocents like thee, my pious child, but woe betide those whose path he crosses, whilst evil passions rage within their breasts!"

CHAPTER II

Struck by Godric's solemn warning, the two girls sped onwards; but ere they had compassed half the distance, the hermit's prescience was justified. At first a low moaning filled the shrinking woods, then with a sob and a shriek the blast came on and tore the budding branches and tender leaflets from the trees, which swayed, and writhed, and groaned, and tossed their arms abroad like human beings in extremity. The sky darkened, the rain came down, the torrent chafed and roared, their path was impeded by fallen boughs, and ere they reached the uplands and the Thorpe, their thick woollen cloaks were drenched, their long robes torn by the beating brambles.

At the first hut in the hamlet they rested a few moments to wring the wet from their garments and recover breath, and fain would Getha have remained by the serf's peat fire, but Emma, fearing her good mother would be anxious, rejected the suggestion that Mildred, the thrall's wife, or Osric, his son, might be sent on with an assurance of safety.

"They are dry and sheltered—let them remain so. We cannot be in worse plight than we are," answered she, with a consideration as rare in those times as in ours.

They found the Thorpe in commotion.

Two sea-fowlers, Edred and Oswy, driven from their occupation, had remained near the cliffs to watch the progress of the hurricane. They had seen a boat with a single occupant, tossed and driven by the winds and waves like a leaf upon the waters; nearer and nearer it came with every roller; though the oarsman strained and fought against the raging sea-horses with their manes of foam. But they raced with him to the rocks, and beat his bark to splinters, casting forth that they might devour him too. He was young and strong and nervous, and still fought for life with the billows. He grasped a rock, its shiny surface slipped from beneath his hand; again and again he strove, and at last maintained his grip. As he raised himself, clinging to the weedy boulder whence the next billow might wash him away, he heard the sound of a human voice from the cliff above.

At the risk of his life, Edred the fowler descended in wonted manner, secured a second rope round the half-drowned man, and, aided by his fellow above, contrived, with such assistance as the poor fellow could himself render, to land him safely on the cliff. There he sank exhausted. Between them they bore him away, until meeting a serf with a load of peat in his ox-cart, they removed part of the load, and carried him in the rude conveyance to the Thorpe, certain of Dame Elinor's approval.

Torn and drenched as were his clinging garments, they told he was of no mean order, and Dame Elinor—her pity for his helpless condition no doubt enhanced by his youth and comeliness—ordered fresh garments and a bed to be prepared, and busied herself about his restoration, the preparation of hot possets, and the dressing of cuts and bruises inflicted by the pitiless limestone crags; not forgetting to reward the brave men to whom the stranger owed his life.

In these active duties of matronly humanity, Dame Elinor almost forgot her own anxieties; but, as the senseless youth revived under her care, came back with redoubled force the consciousness that daughter and husband were both abroad exposed to the raging storm; whilst darkness was fast gathering over the earth.

So, when Emma and Getha reached the Thorpe, the hall door stood open, and, hurrying down the path, came several men with torches and horn-lanterns in quest of them.

Now was Dame Elinor perplexed. Fain would she have sent the serfs on to scour the country, and light the homeward footsteps of her lord; but his moods were capricious, and he might resent as prying interference any tracking of his movements, even though his own security demanded it.

Expressing her doubts to Matilda and Emma, each of whom gave a different opinion, she was overheard by Oswy the fowler, who, being a freeman, held the dread knight in less awe than did his own slaves. The man roughly but kindly volunteered to scour the neighbourhood with Edred, as if on an errand of their own, and should they encounter Sir William, render him what service he required, for the sake of his good lady.

The night wore on. Matilda and Emma had retired, the latter thoroughly worn out, and wondering if the rescued man were the same she had met on Godric's threshold.

The curfew sounded; torches and candles were put out, the servants crept to their straw beds in the dark, yet Dame Elinor was still a watcher for her lord. She still kept a taper burning on its spiked candlestick, but its rays were jealously guarded and scarcely afforded a glimmer whereby to con the missal she vainly attempted to read. The crickets chirped monotonously on the hearth, mice left their corners to feast on crumbs and fragments amongst the rushes on the floor, the grey owl hooted from the barn, bats flew against the horn windows, which trembled in the blast, that, piercing every crevice, shook the tapestry on the dais, and the mastiff in the garth howled ominously between the lightning flashes and peals of thunder which disturbed his canine dreams.[41] And still Dame Elinor was an anxious, fearful, solitary watcher.

In the fresh beauty of the springtide morn, Sir William, hawk on hand, and hound at heel, had gone forth with such attendants as he could boast, to join a hawking party assembled at Castle Eden by Lord Eustace. But all things went ill with the knight. Bishop Pudsey was there, and Robert Fitzmaldred, Lord of Raby, and his proud betrothed, Isabel Neville, of Brancepeth, were also among the guests, and my lord's jester did not scruple to twit De Turp on his scant retinue and their faded apparel. Then his mare cast a shoe, his hawk stooped not true to the quarry, and was not easy to reclaim, and Motley's coarse jests thereon were greeted with approving laughter.

In angry mood when far afield he dismounted, cast the reins to Bertrand his page, gave the falcon to her feeder, bade them "back to the Thorpe," then whistling his hound, strode moodily away in an opposite direction to chew the cud of his own bitter and wrathful reflections, heeding not, caring not, whither his footsteps led.

Wild, rugged and little cultivated was the east of Durham then; bleak moors, intersected with limestone rocks and picturesque ravines through which the mountain streamlets sought the sea, with some dark patches of primeval forest; oak and ash, elm and beech, and

---

41 * Garth: enclosed land near a dwelling; a courtyard.

here and there a sombre group of pine to tell of seed sown by Norseland invaders.

William de Turp was far from Eden Dene when he plunged into one of these thick woods as if to hide himself and his gloomy thoughts from mortal eye, regardless that not the spring leafage but gathering clouds made the shrouding darkness. Meanwhile he strode on, chafing, fuming, scowling, and uttering fearful maledictions on himself and the untoward fortunes which made him a fair mark for a fool's shafts. The storm broke in its fury, but to the raging storm within his breast it was but as the echo of a battle-song. He heeded not the crashing boughs, the drenching rain, the blinding lightning, the pealing thunder; the elements were at war with earth, but he was at war with God!

Lupus, his hound, crouched and whined, and slunk behind his master as in abject terror. He turned and with a curse kicked the poor brute. At once the forest seemed ablaze, the thunder rattled overhead, and a whirlwind rushed with terrific shrieks through the wood.

In the prolonged flash he beheld a tall figure leaning complacently with folded arms against the bare straight trunk of a lofty pine, where his eye had discerned no one the instant before. A lordly-looking man, with hawkish nose and lip sardonically curled, his hair and eyes black as midnight, the latter glowing beneath cavernous brows like coals of fire, his eyebrows (like two modern notes of interrogation) the slant lines meeting in the middle, then rising in a sudden arch from the curve of the brow towards the temples. It was a face to remember and dread. His dress was fearful as his features. From head to heel he was clad in what seemed black, but it was shot with a lustrous sheen of crimson, and its hue alternated with every movement. A drooping crimson plume was bound to his black cap by a huge carbuncle, whilst a second flamed on his sword-hilt, and a third clasped his cloak at the throat.

William de Turp, startled involuntarily, sought his sword, a movement answered by the strange knight with a mocking laugh, which seemed echoed in every avenue of the wood.

"So," said he of the crimson plume, "thou art at war with fate, and knowest not how to better thy fortunes!"

"Who are thou? and what dost thou know of me, or of my fortunes?" demanded Sir William, imperiously.

"Men call me variously. To thee I am thy friend of the Fiery-plume; and I am here to serve thee. Strike hands upon the offer!" and the dark speaker put forth his hand.

"I accept nor friendship nor service from strangers," rejoined De Turp haughtily, rejecting the proffered hand.

Again the mocking laugh rang through the forest, and a strange thrill ran through the knight's veins.

"Wait until Leo the Jew forecloses his mortgage, and thy lands and tenements pass from thee and thine for ever. But perhaps as Bishop Pudsey and his shavelings find seventeen marks to release Eustace De Eden from the grip of the Jew, thou lookest for like priestly aid in *thy* extremity?" suggested the fiery-plumed stranger with a leer.

"Now, the foul fiend seize Lord Eustace and the drivelling monks likewise, if that be true!" exclaimed the baited man impetuously.

"All in good time, my friend; but it *is* true as that thy bond and his alike fall due on Friday, and that thou art unprepared. But I owe these men no love, and would serve *thee*. Thou and I are near of kin."

"Of kin? I know thee not!"

"But I know *thee*," and the black eyes twinkled like fiery stars. "I know thou wouldst feed daintily, carouse merrily, drink wines, not mead or cider, have a full purse and a full retinue, with mettled steeds and costly raiment, wouldst vie with the baron thou servest, and have thy revenge on Leo, the Jew of York."

"*I would give my very soul for all thou sayest!*" broke impetuously and vehemently from the white lips of the knight.

"Give me thy hand upon the bargain, and thou shalt have all—and more than thou dreamest," said the tempter.

"If thou canst redeem thy pledge, here is my hand. But what dost thou require in lieu?" and he held out his hand, which the other gripped, replying with strange emphasis:

"No more than thou hast *proffered.* I have set my seal upon the compact. We are friends henceforth."

A scorching pain seemed to scar the palm he held, and when released the impress of his hand was redly marked on that of William de Turp. A nameless horror thrilled through the man's brain, for the first time conscious with whom he had to deal, and the awful nature of his contract.

Again that hideous laugh rang out, blue lightnings played amid the trees, and heaven's artillery rattled overhead. Heavy drops—not of rain—stood on William's forehead; and he who had braved the storm erewhile trembled at the new significance it bore.

"Nay, man, take heart, and give the Devil his due; he ever keeps his word," said his gruesome interlocutor, fitful flashes of bright crimson lighting up his robe and the three carbuncles, which seemed to flame in the darkness as he moved. "Take a draught of my wine; it will give thee courage man, and, *keep the cup*; it is my gift to thee."

A love of wine was William de Turp's besetting sin, nor food nor drink had passed his lips since morn; his throat was parched, his limbs were faint; a fragrant aroma floated from the cup; he could not resist the temptation; but taking the proffered vessel drank long and heartily, and as he drank seemed to become another man.

The cup or vase was of greenish blue glass, curiously constructed and ornamented. It narrowed bottle-wise at the neck, but round it ranged two rows of trumpet-shaped tubes, their slender tips closed, their wider ends opening like gaping mouths within.

"Mark well that cup, and guard it well; each lobe upon its surface is a horn of plenty. Dost thou lack wine, the upper row will give thee choice of vintage. Dost thou lack gold, or gems, or help, or counsel, seek them from the lower tubes. It is a gift of price, and will not lose its potency *until it finds its counterpart*: for it *has* a counterpart, fashioned by the same hand, but endowed with other and opposing properties. *Thou* art scarce like to meet its fellow. It is in safe keeping, and whilst thou keepest thy home from monkish intruders thy prize is secure. Farewell, my *friend!*"

He of the glowing eyes and fiery plume was gone; and but for the charmed cup within his clasp, and the burning mark on his right hand, William de Turp had thought the whole a dream.

CHAPTER III

With the dawn the household was astir. The patient night-watcher sought the rude pallet of the wrecked youth, subordinating her private troubles to the sacred duties of hospitality. She found him stiff and sore with his bruises, feverish, restless, yet unable to rise. No question had been made of his name or condition; but when in reply to his enquiries he was told that he was under the roof of

William de Turp, a troubled look settled on his face, across which flashed a sudden gleam of joy, as bright as it was transitory.

"Thy mother, good youth, will be anxious for thy safety. The men who brought thee hither wait in the lower hall, and would convey to thy home assurance of welfare, if such be thy desire and the distance within compass of willing feet. They bade me say thus much to thee."

"I thank them and thee, good lady. I have no mother, but Ukillus de Hoton will be full of apprehensions, which only the presence of his son Alan can allay. I must depart at once."

Better than the gentle dame did Alan know that the roof of William de Turp was no safe shelter for his father's son; and though Elinor felt bound as a Christian woman to press his stay until recovery, she yielded to his judgment, and her compunctious visitings were tempered by a sense of relied when in a hastily-constructed litter Oswy and Edred bore him from the Thorpe.

Other hands besides Dame Elinor's had helped to place his bandaged head and bruised limbs in the least painful position.

It was Emma who brought the softest cushion, it was she whose kerchief, steeped in scented waters, was pressed to his nostrils, and wiped the dew from his brow when he fainted on removal; it was she who undertook to bear assurance of his safety to the hermit; it was she to whom his last and most intense look of gratitude was directed, and the responsive blush on her fair cheek gave him more strength than all Dame Elinor's simples.

Who can tell whether accident or design left the maiden's kerchief in the litter? Who save a lover could tell how oft that kerchief, through weeks and months to come, was pressed to the lips of Alan.

Men might be cast in sterner mould in those days than in these, but they were men nevertheless.

The sun was high in the heavens, and the mid-day meal was waiting (to the intense disgust of the cook), when William de Turp entered his own hall, darker, sterner, gloomier than his wont. He bore no question even from his favourite Matilda, and when affectionate Elinor would have examined his scarred hand, he cast her off impatiently, muttering something of "hurt by a falling bough," with a gruff curse for "curious women."

None cared to ask whence came the vase of wondrous workmanship which he placed on the board at his right hand; or whence the mysterious dumb black servitor who displaced Bertrand as cup-bearer and page to the knight. But there were secret murmurings in the household, and from gossiping Getha to the meanest swineherd all marvelled why from the night of the great storm Lupus avoided his master's presence, and when called came reluctantly, whining and cowering.

Friday—the day dreaded by Dame Elinor and her daughters, who knew just enough of the mortgage to Leo, the Jew of York, to make them wretched—came, and with it came the Jew, mounted on a sleek mule, accompanied by a sumpter-mule, and guarded by four or five stout fellows who seemed more ready to give blows than to take them.

Dame Elinor and Emma were weeping together in her chamber at the sad prospect before them, and Matilda pacing the floor with clenched hands and angry hectic cheeks, when Getha came with hasty step to say Sir William demanded their presence in the great hall. Serfs and domestics were there before them, and there stood Leo the Jew, his customary cringe mocked by an air of secret triumph. Sir William, with a scowl upon his brow and a strange light in his eye, strode impatiently to and fro.

Waving the ladies to their seats upon the dais, and assuming his own, he said, "Leo of York, I owe thee thirteen marks, it is not so?"

"Thou dost," answered the Jew, briefly.

"And thou hast a mortgage on my lands and tenements for the sum?"

"I have."

"Thou knowest that money is hard to come by, Leo, that I have had losses and mischances—what grace wilt thou give me? If I pay thee part, how long wilt thou forbear to press for the remainder?"

"Not a day—not an hour! so help me Moses! Haf I borne the costs of a journeys from York to wait? Nay, nay, I must haf de monish or I foreclose."

William de Turp made a signal to his black mute, who with a salaam left the hall.

"Will not Hugh Pudsey, or his monks of St. Cuthbert, pay the costs of thy journey when they release thy bond over Eustace de Eden with seventeen marks? Eh! Jew?"

The Jew stood aghast! "How knew you of mine transactions with your lord? Hath treachery or sorcery revealed it?"

The knight's answer was a scornful smile. The mute placed a brass-bound casket on the table, which none remembered to have seen before. From it he took a handful of gold, and counting down thirteen marks on the board, said loudly, "I call all present to witness I pay these thirteen marks to Leo the Jew of York, in release of a bond he holds, since he will not give me grace '*for a day—for an hour*;' and now, Jew." said he in a changed tone, "hand me the mortgage, and the release, and take thyself and all thy belongings from my land ere the sun be an hour older, or I will hew thee limb from limb, and cast thy accursed carcase to the hounds."

Astonishment and fear fell on all, for the knight's poverty was no secret. The usurious Jew gathered up the gold, gave the lawful quittance, and without a second bidding hurried off to keep his appointment with Sir Eustace de Eden and the monks of Durham, more in fear lest the Sabbath of his race should find him trafficking than he was of the grim Sir William's threat.

That a half-drowned man, rescued from the waves, had received a night's hospitality under his roof, was too slight a matter to attract attention in the knight's mood, and the stranger's name and lineage did not then transpire.

Besides his hereditary land around the Thorpe, William held the manor of Oxenhall, near Darlington, under the Bishop of Durham. Under his tenure he had a horse-mill, and was quit of multure and service to the Bishop's mills, but his tenure bound him to certain services, such as ploughing, sowing, and harrowing fixed portions of the prelate's land, finding labourers in harvest-time, maintaining a horse and dog for the chase, and carrying the Bishop's wine. And seeing that four oxen were required for that service, not only must the quantity of wine have been considerable, but the roads in a deplorable condition.

Other terms in the feudal tenure under which Oxenhall was held necessitated the frequent presence of Sir William at Oxenfields, now that the Bishop's palace was in course of erection; and the only surprise evinced when he, accompanied by the mute, departed the following morning for Derlyngton, was that they were mounted on mettlesome steeds, black as Hamed's face, which had entered the Thorpe stables in the night none knew how.

If this errand was other than peaceful, none guessed it. But it so fell out that neither Leo the Jew nor the marks he had been paid ever found their way back to York. As he neared Northallerton, he and his escort were attacked by a band of armed men on sable steeds, their leader having fiery eyes and a crimson plume, and his companion a cowed wolf for his crest.[42] The battle was to the strong, and but one of the Jew's men escaped with life enough in him to tell the tale.

William de Turp rapidly grew rich and powerful; a band of retainers well mounted and caparisoned gathered round him at Oxenhall; those who had jeered and sneered at him in his poverty were well content to hunt or hawk with him, to feast and drink with him in his prosperity. If wondering whispers were circulated concerning the source of his wealth, they were silenced by the remark that the knight had been a new man since he had discharged his debt to the Jew. How that had been discharged none were prepared to say.

A new man, certainly; but scarcely a better man. As his wealth and power increased, as neighbouring knights and barons sought his friendship and alliance, he grew more saturnine and gloomy. The cloud never lifted from his brow; the wine he drank so freely from his singular cup never warmed him to geniality, but inflamed to fierceness, and many were the lawless deeds he and his retainers did under its influence.

The Thorpe would have been well nigh deserted had not Dame Elinor and Emma preferred its quietude to the noisy grandeur of Oxenhall.

Not so Matilda; she was born for command and admiration; and whilst her mother and sister sat calmly spinning or stitching by the banks of the Eden, she queened it at her father's side amongst barons and noble dames on the banks of the Dare. Isabel of Brancepeth, whose gecks and scorn of William de Turp had borne such strange

---

[42] * A seal of William de Turp bears a wolf passant, the tail cowed between the legs.

fruit, was the first to take the beauteous Matilda under her wing—a precedent rapidly followed by others. Minstrels sand her praises, knights splintered lances in assertion of her loveliness; and more than one put forth his claims to her hand. Amongst these the gallant Adam de Setoun shone conspicuously, and it was not long before Matilda herself betrayed her preference for her brave and courtly suitor.

In Matilda's lofty presence Emma's modest charms were little appreciated; but she seldom cared to quit the retirement of the Thorpe, and the heiress shone without a rival.

But deep in the recesses of the intricate dene Emma herself had lost her heart. Lost her heart and taken another in exchange.

Faithfully had she borne the rescued Alan's message to the hermit, and heard with echoing pulses his devout thanksgiving for the youth's safety.

"I had warned the son of Ukillus that that was a day of peril to him, and much I fear me that the peril is not past." And as he looked upon her kindling cheek he added, "I foresaw also peril to thee and thine; and in the visions of that night of storm discerned that *more than mortal foes* menaced the peace of thy house."

"Surely that brave but hapless youth can be no foe, good father!" she cried uneasily.

"Not a willing foe, my daughter, but the Saxon and the Norman are foes by birth, and thy sire holds his at bitter enmity. But tell me of thy sire. Hath aught befallen *him?*" And as he put the question he crossed himself devoutly and began to mutter an *ave*.

"Naught of evil, good Godric. He came not home until the storm had passed, and the young Saxon (she sighed) was far on his way homewards. But he brought with him a rare drinking-vessel, and a black slave, and—money to pay his debt to Leo of York."

"How acquired, thinkest thou? Men give not such things readily."

"We know not, holy father. He was more reserved even than his wont, and bore no question."

The white-bearded hermit shook his head. After a few moments' silent prayer he took from his girdle a small amulet.

"Take this blessed relic, my child; it is one of St. Cuthbert's beads;[43] wear it ever about thy person, and here (from a recess in his cell he brought a flask) is holy water, sprinkle the threshold of thy chamber night and morn. Desire that Dame Elinor come hither."

It so happened that when next Emma and Getha came in sight of the hermitage, Alan, the son of Ukillus, was loitering near the doorway, showing few traces of his battle with the billows; a fine stalwart man of some three-and-twenty summers, whom either Saxon thane of Norman baron might have been proud to own as son.

The recognition was mutual; their greeting constrained. The first natural expressions of thanks and sympathetic enquiry over, silence ensued. But Getha, stumbling over a stone, shook the eggs out of her baskets, and the laughter of the young couple at her dismay did more to break down the barrier of reserve than half-a-dozen formal meetings.

From that time their devotions took another turn, and before long confessions were made—but not to the venerable Godric; and Getha simpered, kept a discreet distance, and as discreetly kept silence; wisely or unwisely time would show.

Difference of lineage was forgotten, or if remembered, the fears so engendered but made their stolen meetings in the dene more precious; though many were the tears Emma shed on her pillow over the secret she dared not reveal to her mother—for fear of her father's anger.

---

43 * *St. Cuthbert's Beads*. Fossils from the black-slate at Lindisfarne: entrochi.

CHAPTER IV

Time sped on with its freight of human joys and woes. Seldom did William de Turp return to the Thorpe. Never but once did he set foot in his wife's chamber, and then, catching sight of the crucifix suspended by Godric's advice over the bed-head, he ran from the room with his hands clutched in his grisling hair, uttering a sharp yell—half-groan, half-shriek.

So, too, when he had dismounted at the hall door, he withdrew himself with a shudder from Elinor's embrace, and, pointing to the cross worn upon her breast, sternly bade her remove that symbol of superstition.

Bearing in mind the anchorite's injunctions, she did not dare to lay the cross aside, but concealed it within the folds of her upper garment; and the knight henceforth held aloof from his wife, even as Lupus still crouched and held aloof from him.

After a time he appointed one of his Normal vassals, named Rupert, chatelain of the Thorpe estate in his absence, deposing Nigel, the old steward, and assigning the new governor honourable place for bed and board. This man became an incubus on the household, serfs and feors groaned under his exactions and outrages. Dame and daughter shrank from his coarse familiarity. Complaint to Sir William was useless. His sole remark was, "Tush, tush! women are fools," accompanied by a scowl and a curl of the lip that forbade further remonstrance.

After his advent Emma's walks in beautiful Eden dene were restricted, her pious visits to the anchorite few and far between, meetings with Alan all but impossible. Whithersoever she turned she was sure to encounter the dark-browed chatelain; he seemed to dog her footsteps, and his free looks terrified her. Only in the privacy of her chamber was she secure from his detested presence.

The anchorite had long seen the growing attachment of the two young people, seen it with apprehension as to its results, but asceticism had not strained all the human blood out of his heart, which beat warmly beneath his iron jerkin; and pity mingled with his fears. He had been spiritual guide to both from childhood, had mortified his own flesh to spare theirs, and now, at Alan's entreaty, he left his cell, and, walking barefoot many weary miles, sought the mansion of Ukillus to break the intelligence and obtain his sanction.

What arguments he used it boots not to know; suffice it that the Saxon thane, though at first irate that his son should seek to wed the child of his direst foe, the man who had usurped his father's house and lands, softened at length, on the assurance that the maiden was pure as she was lovely; and that Godric would undertake to bend William de Turp to assent also—if Alan marred not all by his impatience.

"It is not meet that a devotee of Heaven should busy himself with marrying and giving in marriage; but I have a mission to accomplish, a soul to rescue, and your young loves will strengthen me to battle with the powers of darkness," said Godric, raising Alan, who had prostrated himself at his feet in humble thanks.

Alan insisted on rowing the aged hermit back to his cell.

About a mile from the outlet of the Eden, they observed two men, one of whom was dangling from the cliff by a rope. "See," cried Alan, "I owe yon men a life; yet, strange enough, they seem to think the obligation theirs, not mine. More thankful to have done me service than willing to be thanked."

"Their grandsire, boy, was thrall unto thy grandsire when these lands were his, and in giving freedom to the thrall he gave gratitude to his descendants.[44] *He cast bread upon the waters and thou hast found it after many days.*"

A signal from the younger fowler caused Alan to quicken his strokes.

They found Emma and Getha resting on a stone by the hermitage, the former wrapped in thought, the latter idly flinging pebbles in the stream. Emma started to her feet, joy chased disappointment from her face, as Alan sprang to her side, and, undeterred by the presence of either Getha or the anchorite, clasped to his ardent breast the beloved maiden, now his own by a father's sacred sanction.

It was long since they had met. On all sides there was much to be asked and answered. Emma told that her gentle mother, anxious at her pallor and dejection, had won her secret from her only to greet it with a flood of apprehensive tears. She told, too, how Black Rupert watched and haunted her; of his repulsive demeanour towards herself; of his oppressive rule; of the terror he inspired. Here Getha, in a voice subdued by fear, put in, "There is something awful and uncanny about him. The hounds whine when he goes nigh them, and two unbaptized babes have disappeared from the Thorpe since he came."

The hermit looked troubled. "Leave me," said he; "painful vigils, penitential prayers, and mortification of the flesh can alone enable me to conquer." Then extending his hands in benediction, he said, "Blessings be on both of you, my children, and St. Cuthbert guard you from your foes;" then abruptly entering his cell, he bolted close the door as if to shut out the world with them, and before they left the spot they heard the scourge in self-inflicted penance on the bare shoulders of the saint.

---

[44] Grandsire: paternal grandfather. Thrall: servant.

If ever Emma had needed protection through the Dene, Alan felt that it was necessary now. With one arm round her in affectionate guardianship, his ready sword in his right hand, and Getha close in the rear, he bore her company.

More than half the distance was traversed; when a sudden exclamation from Getha caused Emma and Alan to look up. Gleaming through the thicket above, they saw the evil face and eyes of Rupert leering down upon them with inexpressible malevolence. Alan darted forward, a fallen bough intercepted him; when he reached the spot the man was gone, but the echoes of a low laugh floated through the dene. Not until they reached the Thorpe did Alan quit his charge, and then with all a lover's lingering lothfulness to part.

Hastily retracing his steps to the boat, discarding the beaten track, bounding over one impediment, clearing another with his sword, he was suddenly beset by three or four men, who sprang upon him unawares. But his sword was out, and he was skilled in its use. Setting his back against an oak, he battled desperately, inflicting wounds with every stroke. Odds, however, will triumph over skill; he had received more than one flesh wound, when, with wild shouts, two men, armed with quarter-staves, came to his assistance. One of the ruffians fled. The others soon lay bleeding and disabled on the trampled ground.

A second time was Alan indebted to Edred and Oswy for safety.

There had been some love passages between Oswy and Getha, and seeing these men (known to be creatures of Rupert) skulking about the path she had taken with her mistress, love took alarm. He called his brother, and they followed in time to save, not helpless women, but a brave man, sorely beset.

Before the week was out, a mounted escort arrived with a peremptory summons for Dame Elinor and Mistress Emma to join Sir William at Oxenhall. To their terror, Black Rupert joined their escort.

They found Oxenfields in a bustle of preparation. On Christmas Day Matilda was to wed with Adam de Setoun, and but three weeks were wanting of the term. Much did Dame Elinor marvel whence came the costly silks, and furs, and jewels, so lavishly provided, not only for the bride, but for herself and Emma, and she shrank with secret dread from the suggestions of her own heart, as the warnings of Godric pressed upon her mind, coupled with the fitful moods of her lord, alternating as they did between savage sullenness and intemperate frenzy.

Even Matilda was not so blinded by the unwonted magnificence of her new surroundings as to shut her eyes altogether on the strangeness of their acquirement. Nor could she shut her ears to the whisperings of her attendants. In shoeing her palfrey, Wybert the smith had gruffly wondered where Sir William and his new followers got their horses shod, for none of them came to *his* smithy; and hazarded a remark that "*horse-shoes* mightn't fit *their* hoofs." The dyers and websters of Derlyngton commented with equal freedom on the hues and texture of Hamed's oriental attire, and the changing tints of black and crimson in that of De Turp's chief companion, a tall knight with a crimson plume, more than hinting that no human hand made the loom they were woven in.

Then the fierce revelry and discordant laughter of her sire and his new associates appalled her. She shrank and left the banquet hall when potations from his charmed cup made him fitter for the orgies of demons than for the presence of a pure woman.

In the privacy of their chamber, Matilda confided these rumours and her own vague misgivings to Emma and her mother; also that Adam de Setoun, anxious to remove her from such scenes, had pressed forward their marriage; and at the instigation of some holy man had fixed Christmas Day for the ceremony;[45] overruling her father's opposition.

Almost in the first hour of their arrival at Oxenhall, William de Turp took poor Emma to task on the sacred secret of her heart. He was seated beneath the canopy at the upper end of the supper table, his family and most distinguished guests ranged near, when, after he had quaffed deeply from the strangely-fashioned cup the turbaned Hamed offered on his knee, he broke forth:

"Soh! daughter Emma, thou hast dared to exchange love-vows with a Saxon, and he the son of thy father's foe! By this cup I swear thou shalt not wed him. Nay, weep not, girl, nor hide thy face; thou shalt have a husband ere long—but he must be of my choice. How say ye, noble friends; is the damsel likely to lack wooers?" and he roughly pulled aside the veil she had modestly drawn down to hide her tears and blushes.

There was an uproar of gallant oaths and flattering protestations; but loudest of all, and backed by glances which made her flesh creep, were the cries of devotion to the beauteous Emma from a dark knight in a varying suit of crimson and black; and the equally saturnine Rupert, who to her surprise was honoured with a seat above the salt.[46]

At once abashed and indignant, she rose from her seat and fled from the hall, followed by her mother and sister, and pursued by her two dread admirers, who nearing her seemed arrested by some

45 * On Christmas Eve, evil spirits are said to lose their power, nor regain it till Christmas Day be past.

46 * The salt-cellar separated the distinguished guests from their inferiors and the domestics. It was placed midway down the board.

invisible power, as she glided beyond the reach of their outstretched hands, and left them to exchange sinister glances of baffled rage. In after time she ascribed her escape to the amulet and cross she wore together.

Her father's intention so openly declared, coupled with the rumours afloat that Sir William had sold himself to the Powers of Darkness, filled the souls of wife and daughters with dread. Fain would they have sought aid from the saintly hermit, but lacked a messenger.

At length Getha found one in Bertrand, the discarded page. A few words written in Latin, on a slip of parchment, by Dame Elinor, were confided to his care, and under pretence of an errand to the Thorpe for some feminine gear, he was permitted to pass the warders.

He had not spared the spur, but midnight had long passed when he reached his destination. To his surprise and awe, he found the holy man, though it wanted but a week of Christmas, doing penances standing up to the neck in the stream before his cell, and wrestling as it were for victory over an unseen adversary. Hours elapsed before his austere vigils were ended; and Bertrand chafed with impatience.

"Bid Edred the fowler hither, and do thou return to thy mistress, and say Godric bids her 'Trust in God, and fear no evil!' "

Within the hour Edred the fowler was speeding with sure foot over moss and moor, through mire and wood, to Alan the son of Ukillus; and swifter still, as winged by love and fear, came Alan to the hermit's cell.

"Stay thou without," said Godric to Edred, admitting Alan, and closing door and shutter after him.

The cell was bare; the same stone serving Godric for a pillow as a seat, the bare floor being his bed.

Touching a stone in the wall, it revolved, disclosing a recess filled with strange matters. Godric thence lifted, with pious reverence, a greenish-blue glass vase peculiarly ornamented, *the counterpart of that in William de Turp's possession.*

"My son," said he, "mark well this holy relic. It was *St. Cuthbert's Cup.* How it came to unworthy me is not for thee to know. Suffice that it possesses rare qualities. The foulest water placed therein is purified, more aromatic and refreshing than the richest wine. Each separate open lobe pours forth a subtle power to strengthen and *revive a failing virtue.* And greater power than this it hath. Now, mark me! The father of the maid thou lovest, on the night of the storm which wrecked thy skiff, when nursing wrathful thoughts, fell within the power of the Evil One." Here both crossed themselves devoutly. "Blinded by his own fierce passions, he was unwittingly lured by the Demon to barter his soul for worldly gain. Satan proffered him a Cup, to all outer seeming the counterpart of *this*, but opposite as was the source whence it came. From every open mouth some grievous lust, some mortal sin is fed; it too turns filthy liquids into fragrant wine, but the draught maddens and corrupts. With the first draught William de Turp lost the right to his own soul. Nay, more; in his madness he has devoted the pure virgin thou wouldst wed to the Demon he serves."

Alan started: "Now, heaven forfend this should be so! Is there no remedy, good father?"

"Ay—an thou be prudent! Take this Cup, obey the instructions on this scroll, and all will go well, but falter not, whatever should appal thee. I have been loth to surrender St. Cuthbert's Cup for so sinful a man, but to save a human soul is work for an angel. May it be weighed in the Divine balance against my sins!"

Besides the wedding festivities, those of the church and the season had commenced. The Bishop's new palace at Derlyngton was all astir with guests. Prior Absolon, and such of the monks of Durham and Finchale as could tolerate their secular prelate for the good cheer he provided, mingled with the barons and knights he drew around him. The houses in Oxenfields and Darlington were bright with holly and ivy; the poorest hut had its yule-log lit with a brand from the last Christmas fire.

From the palace of the Bishop and that of the Neville's, from the hall of William de Turp, provisions were distributed, so that the meanest hind or serf should feast on the day of the blessed nativity. Fires blazed in the streets and the frozen fields, and oxen were roasted whole, whilst barrels of ale were there for whomsoever would. And in the lordly halls the boards groaned with good things.

At Oxenfields spacious lists had been erected for morris-dancing and mumming,[47] for football, wrestling, and other rough pastimes, and at either end raised seats had been erected for William de Turp and the bridal party, and for the Bishop and his friends. The Abbot of Misrule and his rough followers swarmed everywhere.

It was the third day of the sports—Christmas Day, 1179, the bridal-day of Matilda de Turp and Adam de Setoun. In a joust the previous day, the bride's father had been thrown from his horse. The slight hurt he received served as a pretext for absenting himself from the wedding ceremony; but when the gay cavalcade returned from Derlyngton Church, where not only Ralph the Vicar, but Prior Absolon and the Bishop himself assisted in binding the pair together, he seemed blythe as the best, and, for once, the moody puckers were smoothed from his brow.

[47] Lists: palisades used to enclose an area for a tournament.

He of the crimson plume was within the lists, Black Rupert, and a score of William de Turp's fiercest followers; but men jestingly said they seemed to have no relish for peaceful Christmas games, and had, one and all, the look of beaten curs. Nor was Hamed so brisk as his wont.

As the bridal party approached, Emma, holding her sister's veil, caught sight of a Saxon gleeman close beside her father's seat, and a flush of joyful recognition flashed across her face.

"Wine, wine, to drink health to the bride and bridegroom," cried the knight.

Hamed was not at hand; but the Saxon gleeman held to the knight what seemed his charmed cup. "Why, how is this, knave?" said he, as if amazed that other than the mute should bear his drinking cup; but—he raised the cup to his lips and drank.

There was a stir amongst his troop. He drew his left hand across his brow as if to recall some scattered thought. At that instant Hamed thrust *his* vase before William. The two cups had come in contact! An unearthly groan seemed torn from him of the crimson plume.

"Heaven and earth!" exclaimed Sir William, starting to his feet, St. Cuthbert's Cup still in his clasp. "What new sorcery is this? Are my senses leaving me?"

"Nay, rather coming back Sir Knight. Drink again, I pray thee, drink!" said the Saxon gleeman.

De Turp hesitated, looked from one vase to the other, at the imploring eyes of the mute, wavered in his choice, when the gleeman (or rather Alan) began to chant solemnly—

> Place *this* cup to the living lip,
> The sins of the past from his soul shall slip;
> Place *this* cup to the dying lip,

The soul shall escape from the Devil's grip;
Keep it close to the lip of the dead,
While centuries three shall be fully sped,
That soul shall be freed from the taint of sin,
And Paradise open to let it in!

The knight listened, raised St. Cuthbert's Cup again to his parched lips; again drank freely.

As he did so, Ralph the Vicar from behind poured a chalice of holy-water into the demon's vase.

It split to shivers on the instant with a sound that rent the air. A yell burst simultaneously from the shrinking mute and from the Crimson Knight. All nature seemed convulsed. The sky darkened, thunder rattled overhead, blue lightnings played and quivered on the ground, the earth within the lists shook, rent, then emitting sulphurous fumes, rose high above the tops of houses, tower or steeple. Then, breaking in the centre like a crater, swallowed up the Foul Fiend and his demon troop.

Black Rupert and Hamed disappeared at the same time.

Men were affrighted, women and children shrieked and ran for their lives, Bishop and monks told their beads in fear and trembling. The bride clung to her husband, Emma to the strong arm of Alan, and Elinor, throwing herself at the feet of her husband, murmured, "Saved, saved!"

All that Christmas Day the earth remained high above the tree tops. At noon the following day it sank, but where had been green pastures were four large round pools, filled with brack and sulphurous water; water no animal would drink, no housewife could use to wash an infant's face, or cleanse the household linen, or mix with the bairn's porridge, since it curdled milk. Few cared to pass those pools after dusk; and the evil name of Hell Kettles clung to them.

St. Cuthbert's Cup made William de Turp indeed a better man. Thankful for his deliverance, he grew grateful to the agent, and ere a month had sped gave Emma to Alan with a blessing, in the presence of Godric the Hermit and Ukillus the Saxon. For her dower he gave (Matilda, his heiress, and Adam de Setoun confirmed the grant) "one toft in vill of Hadene, and twenty-four acres of land. Twelve acres free of all service except that due to the King from one ox-gang in Eden,"[48] as witnessed many noble names.

In his penitence he gave by seven several charters grants of land to the Chapel of St. James, in Eden Dene.

St. Cuthbert's Cup was guarded with religious care, and in William de Turp's dying hour it was held to his lips by his daughter Emma.

Nor did their pious care end with his death. Herself and Alan by turns "kept the cup to the lip of the dead" until the very earth closed over his mortal remains and the Cup likewise. And so they left it with him in his grave within the precincts of St. James's Chapel, in Eden Dene; and on his tomb was carved the text, "Joy shall be in Heaven over one sinner that repenteth, more than over ninety-and-one just persons which need no repentence."

Edred and Oswy had been well cared for; and by the time Alan's son Walter was born, Getha was the wife of Oswy. Nigel, the steward, and Bertrand, the page, had been reinstated, the knight's great care having been to make restitution for wrong.

The monks of St. Cuthbert are no more. The chapel of St. James is gone; whether destroyed by time or the more ruthless hands of

---

48 Toft: homestead. Vill: a township or village. Ox-gang: an area of land that a single ox might plough in one year.

man is not known; but the torrent still flows to the north of the ruins, and on the banks of the little dene, through which it falls, a workman, in 1775, digging here, came across a skeleton, with a vase of thick greenish-blue glass adorned with remarkable tubes, to which a fragrant aroma still clung, placed to the mouth of the skull. And Hell-Kettles may still be found in Oxenfields, three miles south of Darlington.

THE FAIRIES' CRADLE

CHAPTER I

IN the south transept of the large and venerable church of Houghton-le-Spring may be seen the mutilated effigy of an armed knight, who bears a shield upon his left arm, whilst his right hand touches the hilt of the sword suspended from his girdle. Before the stone was removed to its present location, the cushioned head rested in a recumbent position on an altar tomb within the same arm of the crucial edifice. The lower limbs are gone, but once they lay there in their mail, crossed as befitted a knight who had fought in the Holy Wars; and strange stories were afloat that ever on the eve of St. Barnabas the image was covered with a dewy sweat, as if the very stone sympathised with the agonised soul of the man who lay in dust beneath. The armour the knight had worn in life, which hung suspended over the monument, creaked and groaned in unison, while the rigid face grew livid and mobile as the moonlight rays shot through the narrow lancet windows upon it. Time has closed the lancet windows, banished the armour, destroyed the tomb, defaced the scull-capped figure, as if eager to blot that man and his deeds from memory; but the minstrel and the historian who have fought with time to rescue Sir John-le-Spring from oblivion, and have won the victory, point to this relic with warning fingers.

Some of these chroniclers suppose that the Le Springs gave their name as an affix to the parish of Houghton; but it is much more likely that the first of these Norman intruders took his surname (when surnames were rare) from the chalybeate springs within his limestone manor, and that Sir John's parental ancestor was known as Henry-of-the-Spring, simply to distinguish him from some other proprietary Henry in the locality. This same knight Henry-le-Spring (or L'Espring) had married about the year 1254, Mary, the daughter and heiress of Roger Barnhard, High-constable of Durham. He carried his wife to his fortified manor-house close by Houghton burn, and there in process of time she became the mother of two sons, Henry the elder (of whom genealogists make no mention), so named after father and grandfather, and John, born five years later, whose baptismal name was given in grateful remembrance of the monarch who (ever ready to bestow what was not his own) had granted the manor of Houghton to his courtier Henry.

It might have been that the very name had a taint in it, for John-le-Spring had scarcely passed the age of whipping-top, caylys (nine-pins), and ball before his envious disposition broke out in open resentment of his brother's priority of birth, and consequent advantages, real or imaginary. He hardened his soul against the gentle teaching of his lady-mother, and scorned the holy precepts of the good monk, Robert Kellaw, who came at times over moor and hills from Durham to see what progress the boys made alike in their Latin and religion. But the piety and learning of the young monk made less impression on John than did the pride and gorgeous state of Bishop Beck in his visitations. The latter appealed to the eye, the former to the understanding, and his senses were open if his heart was closed. He longed for wealth, for the power and luxury it gave, and inwardly chafed more and more that the patrimony would descend to his brother, in right of primogeniture, whilst he must be content with a portion of his lady-mother's inheritance.

It was in no spirit of emulation that he strove to cope with Henry in his manly sports and games before the down was well tinted on his chin. He would ride and wrestle, and combat and tilt with him, until long practice made him equal in skill, if not in strength. Those were rough times; a man's own arm was needed to protect his life, and blows came readier, and had more weight than words. So the good old knight, when not doing feudal service in the battle-field, was well pleased to watch and direct these contentions at home; but his brow would cloud, and his voice stop the contest when he saw that John grew fierce and savage in the fight, and took advantages not in accordance with Sir Henry's code of chivalry.

Much of the land which is now open moorland or cultivated ground was then thick forest, peopled with red-deer, wild kine, and foxes. Roads were few, and primitive as the vehicles which traversed them; but horses' hoofs and peasant feet trod pathways to shorten distance between castle and thorpe, grange and hamlet.

Like other gentlemen of his time, Sir Henry-le-Spring filled up his peaceful leisure with hunting and hawking, his lady joining with him in the latter sport, though she and her bower-women preferred shooting conies (rabbits) with bow and bolt to the rougher sport of the chase. The sons followed where the sire led, though John turned on a scornful heel when Henry sat down to read a book, borrowed from Father Robert, or the Rector of Houghton. He was never far to seek when there was a living creature to pursue or to destroy.

It fell out that in one of their hunting expeditions, when Henry was about six and twenty, the two brothers had the good fortune to rescue a fair maiden from the attack of a fierce red bull. She was a distant relative of the noble house of Neville, a visitor at Brancepath Castle, separated from her own party by a wilful palfrey, and driven farther into the forest by the bellowings of the wild bull, which tore up the turf and snapped the lower branches of the trees in his progress towards her. The infuriated beast, maddened, no doubt, by its scarlet housings, had already ripped open the palfrey's side, and lowered his horns for an attack on the lady, when a thrust from a stout hunting spear arrested him, and he turned his fury against his assailant, only to be staggered by a second thrust on the other flank. The blood flowed, but the wounds were not vital, and the rage of the savage bull was terrific.

The brothers were themselves in peril. At length, with well-directed aim, Henry drove his spear right to the heart of Taurus, and with a snort and a quiver he fell to the earth, dyeing the bracken crimson with his blood.

The Lady Isolda had a fair face, and fair revenues, and when her gratitude and that of her friends eventuated in a treaty of marriage with Henry, John had much ado to conceal his rancour, for he coveted both the damsel and her gold. But it had been Henry who had disentangled her from her dead palfrey—Henry who had sprinkled her unconscious face with the water John had brought in his casque; and when sense returned, and the light of reviving life came into her pure grey eyes, Henry's arm supported her, and in the deep brown eyes bent over her she saw love leap as it were out of the windows of his soul to light up hers once and for ever.

Another pair of brown eyes were also fixed on her, but with admiration of another type, from which she shrank abashed, and the eyes, like the uncovered locks, had a redder glow in them. The face was more delicately chiselled, but the lips were fuller, and there was a deep dimple in his chin which might attract others, but not her.

It is needless to tell the many crafty arts by which John strove to oust his brother from Isolda's heart and woo and win her for himself, or his bitter anathemas when his treachery was revealed upon their marriage morn by Ursula, Isolda's nurse, whose fidelity he had endeavoured to corrupt. His pride took fire at the disappointment and exposure. Without a word of farewell, and with but one attendant, he took horse, and, vowing "never to return until he could rule where he had been ruled," bent his steps southward. He was barely twenty, and had not yet won his spurs; but, having resolved to join the crusaders and set distance between himself and Durham, he crossed over to France, and took service in the train of a noble knight preparing to start for the Holy Land.

No doubt his mother mourned her absent son, and not the less so that he went away with discontent in his breast; but father and brother alike looked on war as the only true path to distinction, and priestly training had strengthened the current belief that through the Holy Land lay the soldier's road to glory and salvation.

If Isolda missed him, it was with thankfulness. She possessed an amulet, the gift of a Syrian emir to her grandsire, which enabled her to test the truth of those around her, and it gave her reason to mistrust *him*. He would have come between herself and Henry, and on her doating happiness she could not have brooked intrusion. Five years elapsed before their only child, a baby-girl, came to brighten up the dull Manor House. No marvel that her birth furnished excuses for unwonted festivities. Between Dame Ursula and Lady-le-Spring ensued a generous rivalry which should do most honour to the young stranger; but the good nurse, by virtue of her functions, was mistress of the ceremonies to such visitors as were admitted to the lady's chamber; one of the bower-women dispensing the *caudell* (spiced drink) and groaning cake to the gossips of the village who thronged the lower hall.

There was little privacy then, even for the sick; the lady's chamber being also a reception-room, the bed (only separated by curtains from the rest of the room) often serving as a seat by day. In this room, too, at the foot of the bed, was the huge carved coffer in which was kept money and valuables, and against the wall a bulky cabinet to match. Here she would assemble her maidens for spinning or embroidery after the noontide meal, and here receive her private friends, and thus did Lady-le-Spring in her bower.

The Lady Isolda was an orphan, and the few friends she had were denizens of Northumberland. No little surprise, therefore, was excited when the Lady Isolda summoned her husband to her bedside, and said to him, in a low, sweet voice, "Henry, I have a dear friend, the tried counsellor of my mother; if not adverse to my lord's will, I would fain invite her to the christening feast."

"Be it even as you list, sweet dame; the mother who reared so gracious a daughter cannot have had evil counsellors. But how is the lady known? and whence shall I summon her?"

"The Lady Bell lives in retirement, Dame Ursula alone has the clue to her retreat, she will convey our wishes."

Henry-le-Spring bent his bearded lip to his wife's brow. "It is a strange request, fair Isolda, but so submissive and discreet a mate should have all her lord's trust. Be it even as you list."

Within the chamber was a cage containing a pair of pet carrier doves, which had come with the Lady Isolda's gear on her marriage. Ursula was summoned by her lady's silver whistle. At a signal she took one of the doves from its cage, fastened Isolda's amulet (a jewel of pearl and emerald, shaped like a lily-bell) beneath its wing, and opening the narrow casement let the bird fly, Henry-le-Spring standing by the while.

The sun was setting when the bird went forth; the shadows of night had closed on the Manor; the drawbridge was up, Lady-le-Spring had herself, as was her nightly duty, seen all outer doors locked and barred, and taken charge of the keys; seen the fires covered, sent the servants to bed, and had the candles brought back to be extinguished safely in her presence.

A night-lamp was hung on its croch in the Lady Isolda's chamber,[49] and the last good-night was being said by Henry to mother and babe, when there came a flutter of wings at the narrow window, and a tap on the panes.

The dove had returned weary, with a lily-of-the-valley in its beak, and the amulet shifted to the other wing.

"The Lady Bell consents, I know the token; Henry, dear lord, good night." Isolda turned a well-satisfied head on her flock pillow (feathers came into use later), whilst her lord, lighted by a foot-page with a lantern, trod the long stone passage and left her to repose; not, however, without some stirrings of curiosity anent the lady-friend of whom he had heard nothing before in all the five years of their marriage.

CHAPTER II

The child had been born whilst the March winds were blowing, and the eighth day appointed by the church for the baptismal rite happening to fall on New Year's Day, the 25th of that month,[50] the triple festival called for more than common rejoicing. Lady-le-Spring had doubled the weekly dole of bread distributed each Friday to the poor, Sir John had promised to all comers ale and beef *ad libitum* at the christening, and huge fires were laid down on the open

---

49 Croch: hanger.

50 * *New Year's Day, Old Style*, fell on Lady-day.

ground beyond the drawbridge to roast sheep and oxen whole. Henry-the-Reeve (who held two ox-gangs of land of twenty-four-acres each), besides gathering manorial-dues of hens and eggs, acted as Sir John's locum tenens, sending messengers hither and thither, ordering and countermanding in all the importance of office and the occasion. The warrener and his men came in laden with venison, hares, and rabbits.[51] The falconer and his mate brought home the heron and moor-buzzards, struck by the falcons of Sir Henry and his son. Trout were flushed from the burn, and salmon from the Wear. Will Milby, who paid 10s. a year for his malting and brewery, was heard to say over his steaming vats he "hoped there would be a fresh baby at the Manor every year, and he should go rent free." More grain was sent to the miller than the water-mill would grind, and Ralph Hodgson was despatched to Durham to bring from Elmete (Elvet) bread and provisions beyond the range of home produce.[52] Not even the wedding had created such a commotion. Lady-le-Spring seemed to forget her years, so active was she amongst her bower-women and handmaidens. Her shrill silver whistle was heard, now here, now there, the floors were swept under her superintendence, the long-table and benches were cleansed, fresh rushes strewed on the floor of the great hall; perfumed napery was drawn from the coffer, the dressoir or sideboard adorned with plate and Venetian glass; and her own hands relieved the anxious cook in the preparation of confections and composite messes, the very names of which are expunged from our modern cuisine. Even the poor little turnspits

51 Warrener: a person who farms or hunts rabbits professionally.

52 * Doubtless as here the assize of bread was held, here would other merchandise be sold—and the present name be a corruption of Ell-mete—an ell-measure.

looked at the cooks with languid eyes from between the bars of their revolving prisons, and with outstretched tongues and plaintive yelps seemed to ask if the roasting would ever be done.

Indeed, but for Dame Ursula, the sick lady, nay, even the little stranger about whom all the fuss was made, had like to have been overlooked and neglected in the commotion.

A gay procession swept up the aisle of the large church. Lady Neville as chief sponsor, in a richly-embroidered robe, presented the babe to the rector, whose cope and chasuble were gorgeous to behold,[53] and there was no lack of gallant knights and fair dames; but the Lady Bell, about whom the young mother had seemed so anxious, delayed her coming.

The bells pealed merrily, as the sacristan and his mates vigorously plied the ropes, and little Mary, who had cried lustily (a sign of grace) during the ceremony, was being carried in state from the church to the Lady Isolda's litter, beneath a spreading sycamore, as a courtly cavalcade made its appearance on the bridle-path from Hetton.

There was a general pause and a murmur of surprise amongst the mounting party at the church gates.

Isolda pressed her husband's hand as he gallantly helped her into her litter, and whispered "Henry, the Lady Bell." At the hint he stepped forward with doffed beaver, to greet his unknown guests with courtesy befitting their evident rank and his wife's friends.

Foremost rode the Lady Bell and three attendant knights in complete armour. The lady, of graceful but diminutive stature, rode a milk-white palfrey; above her kirtle of snowy white she wore a closely-fitting tunic of pale green, with a gauzy veil and head-dress

---

[53] Cope and chasuble: liturgical vestments.

of like hue. The housings of her palfrey were also green, sprinkled with many coloured flowers. As variously hued were the garments of the damsels in her train, but all wore tunics and head-gear of bright green. The fashion of the robes was varied in their singularity, their texture was delicate, and not a lady in the manorial party could so much as name their fabrics. A single diamond, clear as a dew drop, or her own bright eye, glistened on the lady's forehead, her only jewel.

Of the three knights, one, mounted on a coal-black steed, had armour of a strange pattern equally black and shining; the second, on a bright chestnut, wore a suit of polished steel elaborately wrought; the third, mounted on a dappled-grey, was clad in a suit as bright as silver but of a darker hue; yet each wore a scarf of the lady's colour—green, and each esquire and foot-page had also a scarf of green crossed over his dusky brown doublet.

The Lady Bell bent gracefully in acknowledgement of Henry-le-Spring's salute, then in a voice low and sweet, yet clear and shrill as wind rushing through a crevice, she said, "We are somewhat tardy, good sir, yet we trust we are in time to pay our respectful devoir to Sir Henry-le-Spring and his lady, to yourself and Lady Isolda, no less than to bless babe Mary who has brought us hither."

Henry bowed, and she continued, in introduction, waving her lily hand towards the knights on the chestnut and grey chargers, "My brothers, Sir Ferris, from the Cleveland Hills, Sir Plumbius, from the depths of Weardale, and here," she touched the black knight's glove, "My brother, Sir Carbo, who has a home with me here and there beyond the narrow limits of a palatinate, and is as welcome everywhere."

A gleam of fiery eyes shot through the bars of his visor as she spoke, and so warm was his salute to Henry that his heart kindled responsively as he led them to his father, Sir Henry.

Genial and courteous was the host, right noble was the feast; and if the royal peacock with its plumes outspread did not grace the board, a snowy cygnet did.[54] There were soups, and fish, and game, and poultry, solid joints; and dainty messes, patés, and blanc mange, and manchets of the finest wheaten flour.[55]

Ere the guests were seated, bowls of scented waters were handed round wherein they washed their hands, drying them with graceful motions in the air; and when the practised carver, with no more than a finger and thumb on the meat, dismembered poultry or sliced ham and beef, the viands were handed round, each gentleman shared his platter with the lady next him, and fingers and daggers did duty for those luxuries of the future, forks and table-knives.

And how those fourteenth century gentry did feed! And how Sir Henry-le-Spring and Lady Mary did press their hospitality! And how the haughty Ladies Neville and Belasyse looked askance and whispered their scornful "who?" and "whence?" as they marked the dainty abstemiousness of Lady Bell, whose slight repast was washed down by no stronger liquor than pure water in a tiny crystal cup supplied by her own foot-page. Even Dame Laton exchanged glances and shrugs across the board with Dame Isabell-de-Wessington and her husband Robert, and in the curiosity excited the blind minstrel in the chimney corner twanged his harp and sang his lays of love and war, as little heeded as the iron dogs which kept the burning brands together on the hearth.

But we linger too long over the feast. Let us leave the old knight and his jovial companions to quaff their wine, and with the father

---

54 * *Snowy Cygnet.* It was customary to send these birds to table with a covering of their own plumage.

55 Manchet: bread of highest quality.

follow the Lady Bell and her stalwart brothers from the dais of the escutcheoned hall to the tapestried chamber of Lady Isolda. Fatigued with the exertion of the day, Lady Isolda received her guests reclining on her couch; but Dame Ursula was in high feather, and with little Mary in her arms moved with smiling face from group to group, as proud and mindful of her charge as of the largess which found its way to her ample pocket.

The two dames stood before the cage of the carrier-doves, Ladies Neville and Belasyse arranged the pieces on a chess-board, all seemingly engrossed in conversation, yet listening with ears and eyes open to all that was passing. Rowland Belasyse, a handsome, curly-headed seven-years old urchin had slipped from his lady-mother's side, and clinging to Dame Ursula's kirtle, kept close to the wonderful baby, round which Lady Bell and the three strange knights clustered. As Henry entered she was clasping round the infant's throat, by a chain of fine fillagree, a gold amulet, strikingly similar to that worn by his wife, chanting the while in a thin piping voice—

Guard, Mary, the gift of thy friend Lady Bell,
'Twas wrought in the East with a magical spell;
It has virtues thou wilt not for years comprehend;
Unerring, 'twill show thee the foe from the friend.
The pearl will turn black and the emerald white
If danger but threaten by day or by night.
It endows thee with powers to come and to go,
Unseen as the wind, and unheard as the snow;
But holiness, cleanliness, purity, thrift
Must be hers who would dare use so potent a gift;
And seven, and seven, and seven again
Are mystical numbers to strengthen the chain.

And the babe we endow in *our* cradle must lie
With the stars for its watchers, its canopy sky.

There was a deep hush in the room as the Lady Bell's white kirtle gave place to the bright mail of Sir Ferris and Sir Plumbius, and clear metallic voices followed her reedy pipe—

Time will come, and need will be,
Then remember me—and me.
From our hills we press to aid—
These, our tokens, smiling maid.

Each fat little hand closed over something—Henry could not see what. The Black Knight then touched the baby's brow, smoothing the curls of Rowland Belasyse with the other hand; and in tones hollow as if they came from the depths of a pit, he said,

Babe and boy, I bless ye both,
Looking to a plighted troth;
And my gift on both bestow—
Lapse of years its worth will show.
Rowland, *you* my token take;
Thine for this fair damsel's sake.

The Lady Bell pressed her tiny hand on that of Lady Isolda, "Farewell! health, peace, and happiness to thee and thy brave husband; remember thy duty as wife and mother, Lady Isolda, and doubt not the fulfilment of ours. Sir Henry, the sun is westering, we crave your leave to depart."

There was a rush to the window to watch the cavalcade cross

the drawbridge 'mid the loud hurrahs of the feasting crowd beyond; and then another rush to see the gifts bestowed with so much parade. And then, what a murmur of disappointment and contempt!

One little fist held a piece of ironstone—the other merely a scrap of lead ore.

Lady Neville turned up her nose, "So much for Lady Isolda's friends!"

"Come hither, Rowland; what marvellous boon has that black knight bestowed on thee besides his prophecy?" cried Lady Belasyse, derisively.

The boy displayed a torque of a black substance, in the polished sheen of which a lambent flame seemed to play—perhaps caught from the rays of the setting sun.

His mother would have taken it, but the boy held it fast.

"It is baby Mary's as well as mine. I must take care of it, and when I am a man I will wear it in my casque, and fight to defend it, as a true knight should."

"That's my brave boy! And so you shall! and let those who dare take it from you!" was the exclamation of Sir Hervey Belasyse, who had entered the chamber in time to hear the colloquy.

And the boy did keep his token, as carefully as Lady Isolda preserved the despised pieces of ore; he with a precocious sense of chivalry—she with a knowledge that they were fairy gifts.

CHAPTER III

Years sped, during which no message of affection or enquiry came from the Crusader. A stray palmer or two sought shelter under the hospitable roof, and repaid their entertainers with current reports of his knighthood, of the bravery of Sir John, and the fluctuating fortunes of the Christian arms. Then Europe rang with the news that the Soldan had wrested Acre from the soldiers of the Cross, and driven the Crusaders out of Syria like flocks of worried sheep. But still Sir John came not, and the old people mourned him as dead. In vain Isolda and Henry strove to comfort Lady-le-Spring. She felt that if not dead he was a prisoner, and under the terrible supposition (for Oriental dungeons were awful things) the mother drooped and died.

Meanwhile Isolda's child grew in strength and loveliness. It is true both the Henries were disappointed that no boy came to transmit their name and honours to posterity; but that did not prevent the black-eyed beauty becoming the pet of the household. She was winsome and engaging as her mother, fearless and truthful as her father; and, as her character developed with years, displayed a precocity of intelligence and information not to be accounted for either by the book-lore supplied by good Father Robert or the housewifery instruction of mother and grandmother, or Dame Ursula to boot. Then she escaped the ills of ordinary children, or felt them lightly. If she so much as cut her finger, the blood stopped instantly, and no cicatrice was left. If she fell, where another child would have dislocated a limb, she got no more of a bump than would teach her caution.

Those wise in such matters attributed it to fairy guardianship, and strangely enough, twice had she disappeared overnight, only to be found the next morning in a singular oblong hollow at the top of a green mound or cairn fully three miles from the Manor House, in a field near the angle of the Eppylynden (Eppleton) and Houghton Lanes, on the way to Hetton, called by tradition the Fairies' Cradle.

To this spot the superstition of the time attached the belief that whosoever slept therein at midnight would be under the protection of the fairies, whose subterranean palace lay beneath, and free to join their revels on the grassy mound. But tradition also added that only the pure in thought and deed could lie therein with safety, and woe betide the incautious wight who, with an evil or revengeful thought in his heart, ventured even so far as to step upon the haunted tumulus.

So the country people kept aloof from the spot after dark, and no ploughshare was ever drawn within a goodly circuit of the mound.

The first of these disappearances occurred when Mary was but seven months old. Henry-le-Spring, his wife, and child, with their attendants, were returning from a visit to Brancepeth Castle; and notwithstanding Isolda's remonstrance, some unaccountable vagary prompted him to travel through the October tinted woods and over the moors of their own demesne in preference to the more beaten and traversed highroad through the city of Durham.

At that period much of the country was uncleared forest; and Bishop Beck underwent a heavy penalty some years later, for daring to despoil the woods and use the timber for smelting purposes. It was also unsafe to travel unguarded. Therefore the attack of armed men on their escort shortly after they had passed Hetton and Eppylynden was no uncommon incident of a journey.

The contest was sharp and well disputed, plunder being the apparent object; but in the end the robbers were driven off, leaving two of their troop dead on the ground.

During the conflict the shrieks of women were unnoted, but it was then discovered that Lady Isolda lay in a deep swoon, and that the infant had been carried off from the litter. The confusion that ensued was indescribable. Horsemen dashed hither and thither, but in the dusk pursuit only ended in failure, and the return of the disconsolate couple to the Manor without their child.

Leaving the women in safety, Henry and his followers set forth to renew his quest, and were returning dispirited in the dappled dawn, when they overtook an old peasant woman, with a basket on one arm and the recovered child, wrapped in a rich green mantle, on the other.

She said she had been gathering mushrooms on the Fairies' mound, where they grew thick, and to her surprise found the babe fast asleep in the hollow. She knew it was Mary-le-Spring, because she had been wakened out of her sleep by the fight, and a wounded man was then lying in her hut, who said the bairn was gone.

Surely the good woman had mushrooms in her basket, and the man found in the hut was one of Sir Henry's own retainers. There could be no doubt of her veracity. Questioned farther, she said, "Only ill-folk need fear the little-folk, and mushrooms grew thicker there at sunrise than anywhere about. And that fine green robe was on the bairn, none of *her* spinning." The old mushroom gatherer had cause to bless the child-finding, a double dole being henceforth hers, with wood and wool to keep her warm for the winter. Isolda and she agreed in supposing that the "little folk" had rescued the babe from the ruffian who had carried it off, either from revenge or to claim a ransom.

The second event happened shortly after Lady-le-Spring's death, while Sir Henry and his son were at the court of King Edward. Her godmother, Lady Belasyse was at the Manor; Rowland, a fine boy of fourteen, was about to take service under Sir Henry, as was the custom, and was there also.

It was Mary's seventh birthday. Rowland had renewed his acquaintance with the playful damsel, and was proudly vaunting to

Ursula, by the great hall fire, the noble deeds he meant to do in her defence when he was strong enough to wield his father's sword and battle-axe. "Where has the doughty squire of dames left the fair damsel he intends to champion?" asked Lady Belasyse, who had overheard him.

The inquiry sent him off to peer and peep into all the nooks and corners of the irregular mansion, from the very battlements to the buttery, where she had been last seen helping to distribute the week's dole. But as the boy's cry, "Mistress Mary! Mistress Mary, where art thou?" rang through the corridors meeting no response, an alarm was given, and the search became wilder and wilder.

There was weeping and lamenting in hall and bower when night fell, and the daughter of the house was still to seek. But comfort came to Lady Isolda at midnight with a tap at her window and a piping chant, which Lady Belasyse and Ursula mistook for the wild March winds careering round the mansion, and beating at the casement:

> The Fairies' Cradle is soft and green,
> There little Mary lies at rest,
> Lulled to repose by our Fairy Queen,
> Safe as bird in its downy nest.
>
> What she is dreaming lip may not tell;
> What is learning her life will show:
> The foster-child of the Lady Bell
> Fearless lies where the daisies grow.

Thither, at Isolda's instigation, the domestics sped in all haste, their torches flaring in the wind—Master Rowland, at his own urgent entreaty, one of the foremost. It was he who, when the men hung back, pressed up the mound as if he had been storming a fortress; he who, finding the maiden there, wrapped as before in a thick green mantle, uncovered her face and wakened her with a kiss upon her warm, white forehead.

Mary's own account was, that as she gave the old mushroom gatherer her dole of bread, a pretty white rabbit, with pink eyes, frolicked before the buttery-hatch. She tried to catch it, but it ran round the buildings, she following; then it crossed the drawbridge, and led her on, and on, forgetful of distance, until her little feet were weary, and when it disappeared in the hollow on the mound, she just lay down to rest on the soft grass, and forgot everything.

If Lady Isolda pondered over this in silence, Lady Belasyse rated the bairn in good set terms, and Ursula followed suit; but Mary bore their chiding meekly, and when Rowland found her weeping in the garden by herself, he consoled her with promises to take her part when he was older.

The Le-Springs returned from court, but not to the continuous calm they had anticipated. The Scotch King Baliol, exasperated by King Edward's mortifying exactions, broke loose from fealty. His chieftains crossed the borders, and carried into England's northern counties terror and confusion, burning and destroying all before them. In vindictive frenzy, Edward summoned an army for retribution, and the warlike prelate, Anthony Beck, rousing the vassals of his palatinate, joined him on his march, with a contingent of 1,000 foot and 500 horse, amongst whom were Sir Henry-le-Spring and his son. Rowland Belasyse followed as the younger one's foot-page.

The old man fell in the first conflict. At the terrible massacre of Berwick, an arrow shot from a factory occupied by Flemings pierced his brain, and he dropped from his saddle dead. Exasperated,

Edward ordered the building and its brave defenders to be given to the flames, and the cruel mandate was carried into effect, but the savage holocaust could not restore the father to his son. Henry himself, throughout the campaign, seemed to bear a charmed life. Alike in Berwick and Dunbar, the silver owls upon his sable surcoat were so many targets for the shafts of the enemy; but the arrows seemed to glance from his armour, the battle-axe which splintered his casque, spared his skull; and he came back safe in life and limb to clasp his loving wife and child.

Rowland Belasyse was not quite so fortunate; he was brought back to the Manor with an ugly wound in his shoulder, received whilst assisting in the removal of Sir Henry's body, and aggravated by neglect. But Dame Ursula and Isolda were skilful chirurgeons, and it healed much sooner than the wound in his heart from Mary's pitiful eyes, child though she was.

"My husband, I do not find the woollen doublet thou wert wont to wear under thy buff-jerkin?"[56] said Isolda, with unwonted anxiety, after a careful search amongst the warrior's mails.

"There was something in the lining which chafed me under my armour; I bore it during all the heat of battle, but after our fight at Dunbar, in my irritation cast it from me. I think I gave it to a poor wretch who was half-naked."

Isolda looked blank.

"Nay, do not look so grave, dear wife," he continued. "What matters the loss of a garment when thou hast got thy goodman back unscathed. I would have given every robe in my mails could I have brought our good sire home as safely."

Isolda's white arms clasped his neck, "Henry, in that cast-off

56 Buff-jerkin: a close-fitting, buff-leather jacket worn by soldiers

garment lay thy safety. I had sewn my *amulet* within its lining in my fear for thee. It was perchance that which chafed thee. Alack! that I did not avise thee of my precaution."

Much did Isolda grieve in secret over the loss of the amulet, regarding it as an evil omen.

Two more years ran their course, and Mary, progressing towards her teens, grew in grace and beauty. The ordinary ailments of childhood had passed her lightly as dew from a rose-leaf. She was tall and stately, and at twelve, the black-eyed, black-haired maiden had the port and bearing of fifteen, with the purity and innocence of a babe. She had learning and knowledge never imparted by the good monk, who had been her father's tutor; the flowers on her tapestry seemed to vie with those of the garden; she spun a finer thread than any maiden in the district; music seemed to flow from her fingers as she touched the lute; and the villagers she visited on errands of mercy used to say there was comfort in her voice, and healing in her touch. She had not lain in the Fairies' Cradle for nothing.

There was another call "to arms" when William Wallace drew his sword for Scottish freedom; and neither Sir Henry nor Rowland were likely to lag behind.

And now did Isolda anew lament the loss of her precious amulet. Fain would she and her daughter have pressed him to take Mary's, but he would not hear it. "Only cowards need charms," he said proudly. "A soldier's best amulets are a good conscience, a good cause, a good sword and shield."

Rowland Belasyse, now his esquire, was as doughty at nineteen as his leader at thirty-eight, and kissed away Mary's tears when she urged him to wear her fairy gift, if her father would not. But he was willing to exchange rings with her before he went to war, and to take her promise to love him ever and be his wife one day. And in Isolda's bower, disordered with hasty preparations, father and mother ratified the contract (those were days of young betrothal), the latter smiling through her tears, as memory brought back the prophecy of Sir Carbo and Sir Plumbius, those knights of Faëry.

How are victories won by kings? Ask the widows and orphans whose dead lie unburied on the battle-field, for kites and corbies to batten on! Ask the widows and orphans whose cries and lamentations are heard when the loud pibroch and the clashing cymbals are mute; heard when the roll of the drum, the whiz of the arrow, the crash of the battle-axe have ceased to madden the pulses of men and make them savages! Ask Isolda and Mary-le-Spring how Edward the First won the battle of Falkirk, and achieved his victory over Wallace? Ask the young esquire who came back wounded nigh unto death, leaving his chivalrous master under the crimsoned turf of Scotland!

CHAPTER IV

Still no tidings of Sir John. An inheritance waited him, yet he came not to claim it. Fain would King Edward have laid his paw thereon; but Bishop Beck resented interference with a fief of his church, and the barons of Brancepeth and Belasyse openly resisted the spoliation of the widow and orphan. Little did Edward dream the thorn Sir John-le-Spring had long been in his side, or the ample reason he had for confiscation, or he would have clutched and kept Houghton in spite of bishop and baron.

So Lady Isolda and Mary remained the virtual owners of the manor, Sir John's death taken for granted; and Rowland Belasyse, when long convalescence left him no longer pretence to linger at a lady's apron strings, bent his footsteps homeward. But the turreted Manor House was to him a casket enshrining a priceless gem, and occasions were not wanting when either alone of with his lady-mother he came hither to assure himself of its safety.

Fain would he have had the gem in his own keeping, and he urged upon Lady Isolda royal precedent for early marriages, and Mary's premature development in mind and person. The mother would hear no word of marriage until Mary should be at least eighteen; and Mary knew no higher duty than obedience.

The lady had cause to repent her decision at a time when neither Rowland, not Sir Hervey Belasyse, nor yet the Lord of Brancepeth were at hand to take her part. Every scattered limb of the martyred Wallace had had a separate tongue to call Robert Bruce into the field; and Lady Isolda's friends were with Sir John Warrenne across the borders, stopping the tide of freedom with the bodies of slaughtered men.

Lady Isolda was busy with her maids, apportioning their tasks, and Mary (sad at heart, for her amulet foreboded evil), under the instructions of Father Robert, was assisting him to illuminate a rare manuscript, when the clatter of hoofs on the drawbridge, and a loud blast on the horn at the gate, caused them both to look from the oriel.

An armed man, arrayed in black and silver (the colours of the Le-Springs), attended by a bodyguard, loudly demanded admission in the name of *Sir John-le-Spring!*

The monk rose. "Let me deal with this, dear lady. Unless Sir John be alive, which I misdoubt, this must be a robber's feint to gain entrance for plunder."

The hall-door stood open; he descended the steps, and,

approaching the gate, held parley through its small grated window, whilst Lady Isolda and Mary, amongst the white-faced maidens, held their breath in dire expectation.

"Who are thou, and what is thine errand?"

"I am Robert Lascelles, esquire of Sir John-le-Spring, and I come to take possession of his Manor of Houghton-le-Spring, with all revenues pertaining, to hold in his name until it be his good pleasure to appear in person.

"These are not days to take a stranger's word for proof, Robert Lascelles," answered the monk; "produce thine authority."

To the astonishment of all, the black-browed stranger drew a slip of parchment from the pouch of his girdle, and passed it through the grating. It was a legal authority, signed and sealed by Sir John-le-Spring, for the bearer, Robert Lascelles, to take possession in his name. Father Robert, who had himself instructed the brothers in penmanship, could well attest the crabbed signature, whilst mother and daughter, clasped in each other's arms, shuddered with dread.

"Sir John-le-Spring has long been dead to his family, if not in fact. In the name of the Church, which is bound to protect the widow and orphan, and in the name of the Lady Isolda, I ask some further token, before——"

He was interrupted by Robert Lascelles. "Bear that token to the dainty lady, and bid her remember the wild bull of Brancepeth;" at the same time a small glove, richly embroidered with seed pearls, was thrust rudely in the monk's face.

It was the missing glove of the Lady Isolda, stained with the blood of her palfrey! John-le-Spring had drawn it from her hand in her swoon, the better to chafe her fingers, and had kept it with a constancy worthy a better love.

There was no further question of authority. The gate was thrown open, and Sir John's claim admitted.

At once Lady Isolda gave orders for refreshments to be served in the great hall, and seeing the free looks Robert Lascelles cast upon Mary, dismissed the maiden to her chamber. Then turning to her brother-in-law's agent, she said, with an effort, yet still with dignified calmness, "This demand is somewhat sudden and untoward. What space of time is permitted for the collection of my personal property, and the arrangement of my private affairs, before I and my daughter retire. My home and lands in Northumberland have been laid waste by the incursive Scots; I shall seek refuge with my cousin, Lady Neville, for a brief space. I trust an escort of our old retainers will not be despised me."

"The Lady Isolda and Mistress Mary are expected to retain their positions in the Manor House." There was a covert sneer on the man's face which cast a doubt on his bland words.

"I thank Sir John, but I have ample means, and prefer to retire," was her quiet but resolute reply.

"Pardon me, Lady Isolda," rejoined the agent, his sinister smile spreading, "Sir John's commands are peremptory. You cannot be permitted to quit the mansion."

"Cannot be permitted!" exclaimed the monk and lady in a breath.

"No! By Henry-le-Spring's will, made and signed on the heights of Falkirk, on the eve of the battle, under presentiment of death, and entrusted to a friend, Sir John, if living, was appointed sole executor of his estate, and guardian of his daughter Mary."

Isolda's eyes flashed. "This is a conspiracy. My dear lord made no such will, or Rowland Belasyse would have known it."

"This must be looked into!" cried Father Robert.

"As you will," said Lascelles, with a contemptuous shrug.

"There is the document," throwing it across the table.

The will was brief, but decisive; and in all faith and brotherly love gave stringent powers to Sir John over all which he possessed, either in his own right, or in right of his wife, in trust for his beloved daughter.

It was duly signed, attested, and sealed with the arms of the Le-Springs. So far as Robert Kellaw saw, there was no disputing it. The two attesting witnesses had fallen at the siege of Stirling; and much as he and the distressed widow might doubt a deed so long held in abeyance, they were not in a position to disprove it.

Not since the tidings of Henry-le-Spring's death had reached his widow had so sad a scene been witnessed in Lady Isolda's chamber, when the good monk, whispering pious words of comfort, led her thither, lest she should swoon in the presence of the intruders. Yet the gleam of exultation which shot after them from Robert Lascelles' sinister eyes had been unseen. It was Isolda's memories of John-le-Spring which assured her heart of treachery and fraud.

Henceforth the Lady Isolda might regard herself a prisoner, seldom breathing the fresh air beyond the range of the Manor garden. Did she cross the drawbridge even, for Sunday or Saint-day service at the church, Robert Lascelles was at her elbow, and his presence marred her devotion; while so free was his manner towards the shrinking Mary, and such were the roystering habits of his followers, that at length she began to wish even for the advent of John-le-Spring as a safeguard from insult.

But what of fairy gifts? Had the amulet lost its power? Lady Isolda's own talisman was gone; but had it remained she might have scrupled to use it. Under the priestly influence of Father Kellaw, she had begun to doubt the lawfulness of accepting aid from ethereal beings beyond the pale of the Christian Church; nay, even to fear lest they should be but the specious delusions of Satan. Yet, had it been otherwise, maternal love would not have permitted her to purchase immunity for herself by leaving Mary unprotected in the den of the wolf.

"The King is dead! Long live the King!" John-le-Spring is back, the ruler of his ancestral home! What treason had he committed that had kept him from showing his face whilst the long-armed vengeance of Edward I could be dreaded?

At all events the monarch's breath was scarcely gone ere Robert Lascelles, with scant ceremony, announced the arrival of Sir John to Lady Isolda and her daughter. The new lord had the same foxy hair and beard as of yore, the same sensuous mouth; but the eye was more shifty, the voluptuary more marked in the smooth face; and ever and anon he would start and glance over his shoulder, as if he feared a spectre stood behind him.

He was marvellously gracious; but it was soon apparent a new persecution had commenced. He renewed his advances to Isolda, offering to obtain a dispensation from the Pope for their marriage. Prisoner though she was, Isolda turned a deaf ear to him, and in this Father Kellaw supported her. Sir John fumed and swore, and would fain have kept the monk out of the Manor; but somehow there was a drop of craven fear in his heart, and he, a vassal of the Church, dared not defy it openly, for reasons known only to himself and one other.

The death of Edward and the dispersion of the army brought Rowland Belasyse back, panting to embrace Mary as his wife after his more than Jacob's probation. Picture his dismay when Sir John refused to ratify the contract agreed to by his brother; and, moreover, asserted that Mary had consented to espouse his faithful follower, Robert Lascelles!

Old Ursula had hobbled into the hall during this colloquy, and contrived by a meaning shake of her palsied head to give a denial to Sir John's assertion. Damped, but not despairing, Rowland mounted his steed in a mist of passion and perplexity. He turned his head as he crossed the drawbridge to see Lady Isolda, pale and tearful, wave her kerchief to him from the oriel in her chamber.

Wrapped in thought, his horse was left to take its own course. It took the road towards Hetton. The last dwelling in Houghton was past; there was no human being in sight. Did his ears play him false, or was that his Mary's voice calling him by name? Was that her touch upon his arm?

"Rowland, my beloved, it is Mary speaks"—and lo! Mary rode beside him, paler, thinner, but lovely as ever.

In an instant he had dismounted, lifted her from her palfrey, and, straining her to his breast with impassioned ardour, covered her crimsoning face with kisses. Then followed a shower of questions, interrupted by fresh kisses and answers, in which Mary told all the wrongs and indignities she and her mother endured. "My amulet frees me to come and go," she said; "yet I cannot wander far lest I should be missed, and I cannot leave my mother to suffer alone; and she will not use it to escape."

"She would be less than a mother if she did, sweet Mary."

"But I am safe, perfectly safe, Rowland. I have slept thrice in the Fairies' Cradle since I was seven years old, once when I was seven months old, and again at fourteen, and lastly this year at twenty-one, and each time the Fairy promise of protection was insured for seven years.

"Protection! and yet in the grasp of your smooth-faced wretch of an uncle!"

"Yes! Rowland, safe! They may annoy, may threaten, but they cannot harm me. I only fear for my mother, who has not such security."

She opened a basket suspended from her saddle, and let forth a carrier dove. "See, Rowland, that bird will bear hither my messages to thee; and if thou be willing, my amulet also. It is not maidenly to meet thee here alone, but shielded by that talisman thou mayst enter the Manor boldly so long as thy purpose be pure; and with the Lady Isolda thou mayst concert some plan to free us. But thy horse must be left with a trusty attendant at a safe distance, since apart from the wearer of the talisman horse or garment will be visible. Yet, Rowland, know thou canst not come unseen into *my* presence. I have been free of the Fairies' Guild since my first dream in their Hetton Cradle, it would task a potent talisman to veil my eyes."

Those were not days when strong men made light of unseen spirits, or magic spells. He felt the truth of all she uttered, as he knew her incapable of falsehood; and longing for any mode of access to the home she brightened, assented to the transfer of the talismanic lily-bell.

"And now I must depart, ere the sun goes down," she whispered, breaking from his clasp. "The amulet confers invisibility, but not the power to lower a drawbridge, cross a moat, or pass through barred doors."

He lifted her gallantly to her saddle, and after a lingering farewell they parted, and as she vanished she murmured the spell—

Safely come and safely go,
Unseen as wind, unheard as snow.

CHAPTER V

In changing owners the Manor House changed its character. Sir Henry's invited guests had been of the nobility and chivalry of the North; the casual guests who sought his hospitality, of every grade, but mostly the indignant poor, and for these last there was ever a warm welcome in coming, a filled wallet and a whole garment at departure. Sir John entertained other guests, and a different feeling; he wore no robe of charity to cover his sins; perchance he held that the Paynim blood he had shed absolved him from all other Christian duties.[57]

He converted the peaceful mansion into a fortress, placed sentinels at every outlet, and on the turret; oppressed his tenants and vassals with his exactions; and lavished ill-got wealth in luxury and riot.

One by one the more noble of Lady Isolda's bower-women left her service, scared by the bold manners of the knight's companions. Sir John would fain have replaced them with creatures of his own, but the lady was firm, and preferred waiting on herself, with a maiden or two from the village as aids. Dame Ursula was getting old, and could barely hobble on her crutched stick from room to room. But she kept the maids in order, and guided the household thriftily, now Lady Isolda refused to preside, and to the maids' chamber Ursula was better than bolt or bar, for rude men not afraid of God were somehow in awe of her; yet she was no shrew, and had but a feeble voice. But she was motherly, and the coarsest of these men remembered, perchance with remorse, mothers and grandames, dead or far away, and slunk abashed from her rebuke.

---

[57] Paynim: a heathen or pagan.

The third Christmas spent at the Manor by its new master terrified the women. Feasting and wassail, yule-log and holly-bush, mimes and minstrels had been of old. But now the license of games and mummeries, indecent jests and buffoonery, beyond even the ordinary coarseness of the age, drove the ladies from the hall, amidst peals of laughter from Sir John and his worthy associate, Robert Lascelles. Something of this had been the previous Christmas. But now the mirth grew uproarious, until the noise penetrated to Isolda's chamber. Then, in their cups, the worthies quarrelled, and swords were drawn, the man taunting his master with an unfulfilled promise.

"I tell thee, nave, I broke no promise. I said thou shouldst have the wench an' thou couldst win her."

"Win her! sayst thou? I have no dainty words for dainty misses. I have hot blood, and am for hasty wooing. But not even a midsummer sun could thaw such an iceberg. Were she once my *wife* I could bend her to my will. But Sir John-le-Spring grudges his niece's dower to his old comrade!"

"Now, by the fiend, thou liest! An' thou wouldst have the girl, take her. I have heard a woman shriek ere now, and will not bar thee."

Once more the swords were sheathed, the red hands clasped in amity, cups were drained to the success of the foul compact, and the drunken men-at-arms hiccoughed their approbation, as Robert Lascelles, heated with wine and passion, rushed from the hall.

But there were old retainers of Sir Henry, whose blood had long boiled with indignation, who put their hands upon their swords with meaning looks.

In the Lady Isolda's bower there was calm—and a visitor, with such happiness as that visitor could make. Ursula had gathered the maids round their own chamber fire, and whilst sipping spiced ale, kept them alive with old-world tales. They took no note of the impetuous step which passed their door to stop at the Lady Isolda's.

"Who knocks?" was the answer from within, as a dagger hilt rapped loudly on the oak.

"A messenger from Sir John," was the reply. Robert Lascelles was sober enough to know that he was on the wrong side of a barrier almost as strong as a girl's will.

There was a whispered conference in the room.

"It is a late hour. I will hear the message on the morrow."

"It must be heard to-night, should the door be forced for its delivery!"

Lady Isolda hesitated. Her friends, Ralph Neville and Hervey Belasyse were away at Westminster, her husband's will, which left herself and a child penniless in the hands of his brother, bound her fast. She could but temporize until deliverance came.

"Let him come," was whispered in her ear, by the invisible friend at her side, who had crossed the ice-bound moat to spend his Christmas with his betrothed.

The wooden bolts were one by one withdrawn. Robert Lascelles stalked in; his eyes bloodshot, his face inflamed, his purpose black as his sable suit. Lady Isolda stood between him and Mary.

"Your message, Sir!"

"My message? This. I am to have Mistress Mary to wife an' I can take her! I have waited long enough, been flouted oft enough, but by St. Oswald I wait no longer. Stand aside, good dame. Mistress Mary goes with me to-night, will she, nil she!"

He had thrust Isolda aside as a reed, and put out his other arm to clutch the loathing Mary's waist—all at once his arm relaxed nerveless; his face blackened; his lips parted; his eyeballs glared; the grip of a muscular but unseen hand was on his wicked throat, another on his shoulder, he was thrust backwards through the doorway, and hurled out against the opposite wall of the corridor. There was a heavy fall, a groan, and silence.

The door was closed against intrusion, but it might as well have stood open. No one came to see how so good a comrade fared. No shrieks had been heard, and the jest went in the hall that he had won a mistress easily.

An hour later he crawled to his own chamber, a beaten cur; ashamed to face his mates and tell a story none would credit; his wicked purpose shaken for the time—but only for the time.

As he foresaw, he was jeered and bantered when he told of an unseen hand grasping his throat, even when he bared the blackened marks. "Thou'st had a drunken fit, man; or a tussle with the foul fiend himself. It's like enough," cried Sir John, with a mocking laugh.

"Ay, like enough," exclaimed another; "the Devil will have his due some day, and there's his sign manual across thy weasand as a token."[58]

"He'll have his due of thee, then, John-de-Weardale, and Sir John-le-Spring too, maybe, but he finds not me in your company; and mark me, Sir John, better face the foul fiend than me an' ye pay not what you owe, and send the girl to my hold in the Cleveland Hills before the year goes round."

"I tell thee to take her, man, take her! Sure thou'rt not afraid of a wench?"

The baited man's eyes glared. Sir John, reckless from his last night's riot, stretched his hand as appealing to those around him. "An' seem'st he not the very devil now? Good friend Robert, I never look to see a blacker fiend than thou."

---

[58] Weasand: the oesophagus or gullet.

"Then look to thyself, or forget not to pay thy bond!"

Robert Lascelles and his troop were gone. Their departure lightened the load of three heavy hearts. Rowland Belasyse, who, unseen, had remained to guard those so dear to him, reported the quarrel, and strengthened Lady Isolda's belied that Sir John detained them illegally, and that the man Lascelles held the secret.

Somehow, Sir John seemed to breathe more freely when his prime minister was no longer at his elbow, and the ladies were treated with less discourtesy. However, Isolda soon found this to imply a renewal of Sir John's importunities, and her temporary satisfaction ended. In her indignation she threatened to charge him before the bishop with forcible and fraudulent detention.

"Hard words, my lady, break no bones! Bishop Beck has but just 'scaped the regal lion's paw. He will hardly dare meddle with Sir John-le-Spring just yet, even should the birds of the air carry your charge. I have given you the chance to be mistress here once more. *Now*," and he ground his teeth, "I will bring a mistress over you."

Sir John took horse and rode away, leaving John-de-Weardale as his deputy. In less than a fortnight he returned, a lady riding by his side, whose robes of costly material were made in the very extreme of fashion; her amber silk under-skirt had a deep frill or flounce, the crimson upper robe swept the ground a yard behind her as she walked, her open hanging over-sleeves drooped almost to her knees; an embroidery of gold and pearls bordered each garment, and her shoes likewise embroidered, almost doubled the natural length of her feet, so long were the pointed toes. The compression of her waist in leathern stays made her movements stiff and rigid; then her eyebrows had been trimmed, her cheeks painted; her hair (as could be seen through its golden net) dyed; and from her hat, with brim curving upwards on either side, a flowing veil depended. On the simple-minded ladies, who were called into her presence as though she were a queen, this extravagant display made no impression; their minds were too full for envy, and the robes sat so ill upon the wearer admiration was impossible.

With this woman, Dame Maldred Fitzmaldred, came a bevy of bower-women, free of look, loud of voice, coarse of manner. To make room for them, Lady Isolda's maidens were dismissed, and the chamber she had called her own since she entered it a bride was usurped by the haughty leman of Sir John.[59]

When the household keys had been ungraciously demanded, Lady Isolda had charged Dame Ursula to surrender them to Lady-le-Spring, supposing this to be Sir John's wife; and in that supposition prepared unmurmuringly to resign her private apartment also.

The return of John-de-Weardale, after temporary absence, dispelled the illusion. There were foul charges and recriminations, oaths and maledictions, drawn swords and bloodshed in the hall, spurred horses dashing out over the bridge—and for what? A vile woman who had left one paramour for another—the poor esquire for the wealthy knight!

It was a dastardly and insolent deed to flaunt his shameless victory in the very face of the man he called friend, and under the cover of his own roof-tree. Had Sir John yet to learn that such wrongs ferment like yeast in the breasts of men, or that the most deadly foe is he who has been friend; or did he hold a charmed life, that thus he braved their vengeance? The imprisonment of Bishop Beck had made Sir John bold. Father Robert had been excluded from the Manor; and but for the freedom to come and go conferred by Mary's amulet on Rowland, the poor imprisoned

59 Leman: a lover or sweetheart.

ladies would have been solitary indeed. With him came glimpses of old happiness; and Maldred's petty malice fell innocuous. She had ousted the ladies from their chamber, and transferred them to an incommodious apartment with bare stone walls, rude beds, straw mattresses, rough chests for clothes and other women's gear; but coming intrusively to pry into their privacy, she stood aghast to see the transformation there. Tapestry, fresh of tint and texture, hid the grey stone; a bell-shaped canopy o'erhung a bed inlaid with ivory, and covered with a silken quilt of green and gold. A cabinet of strange device and rich in floral carving appeared to mock her wonder, and on the floor was the only carpet in the mansion.

Straightway she hurried to Sir John, and in a rage accused him of cozening her. Then summoning the household to the work, transferred the priceless furniture to her own use. Marvel of marvels, after a sleepless night on a hard couch, she woke to bare walls, a rush-strewn floor, and furniture of common wood. Back came the solid fittings of Isolda's time for her own use; back went the rude plenishing to the insulted ladies—and lo! all bright and glorious in hue and shape again, they filled that ugly room with beauty.

She impounded their wardrobes, dealing out linen and woollen raiment such as the peasants wore, and said that silken robes were not for dependents; but no sooner were the garments donned than they assumed fresh shape and texture, falling in graceful folds, and mocking art to imitate.

"Mother, the Lady Bell is still our friend, you see. Her lily wand has done this," said Mary, at this second transformation.

"Love, my child, may well convert a prison to a palace; and a modest wearer stamps her impress on her garb. Still, for thy sake,

I would that St. Cuthbert sent us deliverance. It is sad to see thy maiden bloom wasted in these walls."

And deliverance was coming, albeit not so swiftly as the lady craved. And Maldred, wearied of ineffectual attempts to lower their dignity or lessen their self-respect, perplexed and defeated, left them at rest while she plotted fresh mischief.

CHAPTER VI

Months went by. Sir John appeared besotted. His leman cast a glamour over him, and made the bad man worse. He left his helpless relatives in her unfeeling hands; lavished his means to gratify her whims; spent in dress and costly indulgence thrice his income; and, as though the Manor House was not spacious or sumptuous enough, built a summer bower within the garden bounds, and fitted it with luxuries from foreign lands, plunging himself in debt.

It so happened that Rowland Belasyse swam across the moat one bright May-day, when the drawbridge was raised, and passed invisibly on to the Lady Isolda's room, heedless of the fact that the water dripping from his garments left a wet track along the floor, scaring the men and maids who, in their wonder and alarm, raised a cry of witchcraft, a cry remembered well by evil Maldred. Rowland had brought good news. Bishop Beck was dead, and their friend Robert Kellaw had been elected Bishop in his room. From him they might hope for the succour denied elsewhere. And let it not be thought Rowland Belasyse had been inert or tame in his betrothed's cause. He and his steed had galloped from keep to castle, from castle to keep, to stir up friends in their behalf. But the will of husband and father, powerful in life, was powerful from the grave; and those barons who might have interfered were too intent on checking kindly exactions to embroil themselves with a neighbour.

But deliverance came when hope was gone.

One of Sir John's retainers, the bridgeward, fell sick, and was left to die, untended, like a dog. Old Ursula heard talk of him in the kitchen, and telling Mistress Mary, the pair sought the wretched loft where the sick man lay. Mary passed a cooling hand across his brow, and the magnetic touch appeared to check the fever. Ursula concocted healing messes, and between the twain the man in time recovered. Anxious to show his gratitude, he questioned Ursula if Mistress-le-Spring would not be too proud to accept a trinket from a poor man-at-arms. It had come to him, he said, in an odd doublet a good knight threw to him as he lay stripped and bleeding on the field of Dunbar. He had kept it in remembrance of the unknown knight.

Ursula's old eyes brightened. She saw in the trinket the jewel her mistress had lost, and rejoiced at its recovery, although she knew not all its properties. She recovered it not one whit too soon.

Sir John and his leman finding all efforts to humiliate Isolda and Mary fruitless—no menial task seeming to rob them of their native dignity—and feeling either their purity a rebuke, or a sense of insecurity crossing their conscious brains, began to long for their death. With the evil-minded to think is to do.

"Hast thou no skill in herbs, Maldred, to rid us of these meek-faced minions? I hate them!" and Sir John hissed out the words.

"Aye, marry have I, and the will to use them," was the quick response, as the woman's evil eyes glittered with satisfaction.

Isolda wore her regained treasure on her arm. That day, as her fingers touched the meat served on a solitary trencher for their mid-day meal, her hand stopped midway to her mouth. The pearls had turned intensely black, the emerald white. There was danger at hand! "Poison at last!" The exclamation and accompanying gesture checked Mary's hand also. The trencher was emptied from the window. A favourite staghound of Sir John's snapped at the meat, and died in agony within the hour. A Barbary ape brought home by Sir John shared the same fate the following day. One by one their household animals died; but the ladies lived and throve. The recovered amulet removed all difficulty in procuring wholesome food from the buttery unknown.

The consternation of Sir John and Maldred may be imagined but no remorse entered their breasts. They only chafed with every fresh defeat.

It was June the 11th, the eve of St. Barnabas. The air was hot and oppressive. The perfume of flowers and scented herbs wafted through the open casements of the summer bower where Sir John and Maldred were regaling themselves; spending the hours in wanton dalliance as they concerted a plan to accuse their captives of witchcraft, and so bring on them the awful judgment of the Church.

They might plan, but their long-tried victims were beyond their reach. The previous day Rowland had borne away the carrier dove. It had flown back with Mary's amulet beneath its wing. Ursula, feigning an errand to the village, persuaded Hugh, the grateful bridgeward, to lower it for her exit. Close behind her trod unseen her ladies with such valuables as they could carry. At the church they stopped, and entering the open doors, knelt in thankful prayer.

Rowland had horses nigh at hand, with a litter for the good dame whose feeble limbs had already been overtaxed.

To avoid observation, they took an unfrequented bridle-path well screened by trees. Barely were they in the covert, when a band of *Shevalds*, a new tribe of devastating robbers from the hills, dashed at full speed along the road they had just quitted.

Rowland had a precious charge with him, and dared not linger, but a man was sent back to watch the movements of the suspected desperadoes.

On they rode without pause in a straight line for the Manor House. The drawbridge was up, but at the cry, "For Cleveland and Weardale!" as at a signal, the man Hugh lowered it, and the horsemen crossed unstopped.

"With his leman in the garden bower," was Hugh's gruff answer to a question from the leader of the band.

Drowsy with wine and the heat of the June day, Sir John lay with his head on Maldred's shoulder, her wanton arms around him, dreaming of no intrusion, no mishap. Suddenly the curtains were rent from the doorway. The woman gave a shriek, Sir John awoke, two well-known men with gleaming swords and gleaming eyes were close upon him. His hand involuntarily sought his sword; but swords are not for sensual ease, and his was missing. Guilt had made a craven of the knight; he begged for mercy, begged it from the men he had taunted and mocked. But they were as hungry as wolves above a fallen leader. With every blow they struck they called a deed of blood or treachery to mind, and as they let out life through bloody doors added soul-tortures to his death-agonies.

Bloodshed and pillage in the lovers' bower, bloodshed and pillage in the mansion, the clash of swords, the shrieks of women, the groans of men, and flaming banners crimsoning the sky! Hark! "Belasyse to the rescue!" Le-Spring's retainers rally. Through fire and smoke they drive the Shevalds back, as Rowland and a motley force of men-at-arms and peasants dash in and turn the tide.

One man with a woman in his arms fights his way to his horse, calling his men to follow, and at their head dashes across the bridge, leaving the rest to their fate. Surely that was John-de-Weardale with the faithless Maldred!

The Shevalds had retreated, but now there was another foe to fight, a fierce untameable foe, that licked up blood like water, and made mammocks of masonry.[60]

Little of the Manor House was left when the fire was subdued. But Robert Lascelles, the assassin of Sir John-le-Spring, lingering after his comrades were gone, to dart from chamber to chamber for the fair prize he had reckoned on, had found himself a prisoner; Mistress Mary beyond his reach; himself denounced a murderer by the shrieking Maldred ere she had been carried off.

He was at once transferred to Durham Castle. There he was condemned to the rack. The very sight of the horrid machine opened his lips; and what a confession was his! It was he who had attacked the travellers and carried off the infant at Hetton, bribed by Sir John, who envied his brother's inheritance and happiness. Hotly pursued, he threw the babe into a hollow on a hillock, regardless of its fate. He had fought with Sir John when, under a feigned name, the traitorous knight had leagued with the Scots, headed incursions over the borders, and laid waste Isolda's lands. But it was Sir John himself who at Falkirk Bridge had struck his brother down with his own hand.

The will, said to be Henry-le-Spring's, was a vile forgery. A reprobate friar had been bribed to draw it up, and amongst them the false signatures were added. His brother's signet had been stripped from his dead finger by Sir John on the field of battle.

Here was a category of crimes to stain Sir John withal. Yet

---

60 Mammocks: fragments, broken pieces, scraps.

Lascelles was executed, being taken red-handed; whilst Sir John was buried in Houghton Church, and someone—it is said a woman who had once loved him—put a monument above his grave, and paid for masses for his soul.

Nor did John-de-Weardale escape. Bishop Kellaw, incensed at the ravages of the Shevalds in his diocese, vowed their extermination, and put his brother in command of a strong force to hunt them down. One of these soldiers killed John-de-Weardale in Holy Island, whither he had fled for refuge.

Whether the Fairies helped at the restoration of the Manor, history does not say, but it was ready for a grand wedding-feast long before Sir John's monument was carved.

It is said that Lady Bell and her train re-appeared on the occasion; that Mary's bridal robes, the envy of maids and matrons, were from fairy looms; that the wee guest's shrill piping voice recalled the christening feast, and reminded Rowland and Isolda that fairy gifts were not fallacies. As Sir Plumbius and Sir Ferris had predicted, "time and need" had come, and the hills of Cleveland and Weardale had sent men and steel to the rescue. And Rowland was told that Sir Carbo's flame-lit token was Mary's best dower to him. He would find the solution of the riddle if he dug deep enough below the clay of Hetton. Sir John had no children and no will, and Mary was heiress of the Manor, and the Fairies' Cradle too.

Rowland Belasyse did not take possession of Houghton-le-Spring undisputed. The monks of Durham would fain have recalled it as a lapsed fief; but the new law of Mortmain stood the young people in good stead. Then King Edward issued a precept to the bishop to "levy £20 of the goods of John-le-Spring, deceased, owing to Philip Morgan and others of the company of merchants trading to Florence." It was a goodly sum then, and Rowland paid it with reluctance; feeling that the merchandize had been for the woman who, but for the Fairies' amulet, had compassed his beloved Mary's death.

Centuries have passed since Fairies danced visibly round their Hetton Cradle, but long after they had disappeared the unshrived soul of Sir John showed its agony of remorseful guilt in beaded drops of sweat, which oozed from the carved image on his tomb on each anniversary of his red death—St. Barnabas' Eve, while a lurid haze filled the south transept, and the candles on the altar burned blue and dim. He had shed a brother's blood, and by man was his blood shed; he had robbed the widow and orphan, and he left neither widow nor child to lament him.

The very armour hung above his tomb Sir Ralph Neville tore down and carried off; and if Sir Ralph had to restore the armour and do penance for the sacrilege, it was but that it too might bear witness against the dead in the groans which came from the creaking coat of mail each St. Barnabas' Eve.

MY WILL

I was seriously ill; there could be no mistake about that. Dr. Godfrey had pronounced my symptoms alarming, and he was not the man to cry "wolf" before the wolf was in sight.

From a tour in the Highlands I had brought back to our home in Cheyne Walk (besides Anna my gentle wife, and Gilbert our high-spirited son) an intolerable, persistent cold, the result of too many baths of Scotch mist.

This I had neglected in the bustle of getting Gilbert off to school again, until it settled into acute bronchitis, attended with inflammation of the lungs.

The first note of alarm was sounded when Godfrey, our family surgeon (Dr. Godfrey we called him by courtesy), intimated to my poor distressed wife that he should like to consult with Sir James Ponder on the "case."

"Then you think Mr. Leslie is in danger, doctor?" put Anna, interrogatively, looking up at him with white and anxious face.

"Well—a—" and the doctor tapped his chin reflectively with three fingers. "The symptoms are not altogether so favourable as we could wish; and—a—it might be altogether more satisfactory for all parties if we had an additional opinion."

The "additional opinion" did not place matters on a much more promising footing.

"A sound constitution" was all on which Sir James relied to enable me to "pull through."

The second note of alarm was an intimation from Dr. Godfrey that it "might be as well to telegraph for Gilbert to return home without delay."

The final blast came from my old friend Matthew Sharp, when he asked me if I did not think I ought to make my will, and otherwise put my affairs in order.

I had known Matthew Sharp at least twenty years. When I married Anna he was groomsman, and he had stood godfather to Gilbert, who was now a sturdy lad of sixteen. He was a solicitor in Chancery practice, and had offices in Furnival's Inn, though his house was in Sloane Street, pretty near to our own. His son Albert had been sent to school along with Gilbert; visits between the two houses were frequent and *sans cérémonie*, and altogether we were very intimate friends indeed.

"Do not regard me as a bird of ill-omen, my dear friend, for this suggestion," said he, sitting by my bedside, stroking the Marseilles coverlet with one hand and looking across the room, not at me; "but it is always best to be on the right side—to be prepared for anything, in fact."

"Then you think me in a bad way, Sharp?" I murmured, feebly, in response, feeling as if he had given the sands of my life a shake in the hour-glass of time.

"We—ll—well. You know bronchial attacks are treacherous things; and as I said before, it is always best to be on the right side of the hedge."

"Certainly," was my sighing assent.

"You have signed too many leases to be frightened by a sheet of parchment; and are not silly enough to fancy you are signing your death-warrant in signing a will," continued he, still smoothing away at the quilt.

It was late in autumn. There was a good fire burning in my chamber, the temperature of which was regulated by thermometer. A shaded reading-lamp on a small side-table served to light Matthew, who sat with one knee crossed high over the other, as a support to the book which he used as a desk. As he sat by my bed-side, the blue damask curtain partially screened him from me, but I heard the scratching of his pen, and life seemed to ebb with every dip of the ink.

I devised all my real and much of my funded property to Bertie, on the attainment of his majority, with a suitable provision for his minority; my dear wife to have £800 per annum, for her sole use and maintenance for the term of her natural life, and the use of my real property until Bertie came of age. I also left her sole executrix.

Sharp, or his clerks, must have sat up all night; for before eleven o'clock next morning Matthew was there with the will all ready for signature.

Sir James Ponder and Dr. Godfrey were with me at the time; so Matthew sat in our morning-room with Bertie, who had arrived an hour before, fortifying him with all the platitudes of conventional friendship against the severe affliction which seemed inevitable, and comforting himself with wine and biscuit.

The doctors had barely left my room, accompanied by my anxious wife, when the lawyer entered—not, however, before he had caught Dr. Godfrey by the button-hole, on the staircase, and asked him to remain in the house to witness the will he was about to read over to me.

"In any case I should remain, Sir; our patient approaches a crisis. I hope you will not excite or weary him," answered the surgeon, as he went on.

I was too ill to pay much attention to the will, with its multitudinous "aforesaids" and "hereinafters," but the general tenor seemed all I had desired.

In the presence of Dr. Godfrey, Barton, our housekeeper, Annie and Bertie, I signed it; the two former being the attesting witnesses. And, notwithstanding my friend Sharp's assumption to the contrary, I did feel as though I were indeed signing my death-warrant.

I think Anna felt so too, for she hurried from the room, and I heard a sound of suppressed sobbing outside the door.

The effort tried and exhausted me. Nurse cleared the apartment. Dr. Godfrey remained downstairs. Mr. Sharp went away, carrying the will with him.

I might have died in signing that document; at least the bitterness of death seemed to have passed in the signature of the last sheet, with its formal renunciation of all my earthly possessions. Nothing troubled me—a sort of mental syncope followed; I lay listless and spent, my mind a blank. It may be I fell asleep.

If so, I slept ten or twelve hours. Anna was moistening my lips with brandy on a feather when I opened my eyes on drawn curtains and subdued lamp-light.

At all events I cheated the two undertakers who had quarrelled on the steps of Don Saltero's coffee-shop for the prospective right of burying me; and I got better.

I had, however, a long fight for it; and I think I had a fair chance of being spoiled by Bertie and his mother during the tedious months of convalescence.

Matthew Sharp was profuse in his congratulations; and I wonder now I did not detect the ring of base metal in them.

I certainly did think he changed colour and appeared fidgetty when I remarked casually one evening, while shuffling the cards for bezique, Anna playing and singing Longfellow's "Bridge" meanwhile—

"I say, Sharp, you were right, you see. Signing a will is *not* signing a death-warrant. I think I was an ass to leave a matter of so much import to the last moment; however, I am glad that you have my will all right and safe."

"Oh, yes, I have it safe enough, and it's a duty off your mind," said he, taking up his cards and considering them more irresolutely than usual.

Bertie had gone back to school, the domestic wheels ran in the old ruts, and the will I had made passed from my mind altogether.

Months went by placidly. Summer came in full force, and Londoners, to avoid the fate of traditional blackbirds "baked in a pie," were scattering hither an thither to cool themselves with sea or mountain breezes. Having had a significant dose of mountain mist to serve us for one while, we pitched upon Scarborough for our summer retreat, and packing began in earnest.

Then it was my will was recalled to my memory in an odd way.

I had not an overburdened mind, never overburdened my stomach, and as a rule slept well and dreamlessly.

The night was intolerably hot, and possibly that might make me restless. Be this as it may, I awoke in the middle of the night from a confused dream, a voice—that of Anna's dead father—ringing in my ear, "Look to your will!"

I jumped up in bed. There was no one in the room. Anna's breathing told me she was sleeping calmly.

With an amused smirk and a shrug of my unsuperstitious shoulders I lay down again, and soon dosed off; only to dream again, and this time more vividly.

I seemed to stand in front of our red-brick house in Cheyne Walk, yet not I myself, in the flesh, but in the spirit; and, gazing on it, beheld Anna and Bertie, both in deep mourning, at an upper window. As I looked I saw the dark building shudder, totter, and fall with a terrible crash, burying wife and son both in the ruins, despite my own frantic efforts to save them.

As I wakened, startled with the noise and the fright, I heard the same voice crying peremptorily, "Look to your will!"

August though it was, I shook as with an ague. My dear Anna was still composedly sleeping. I hesitated to disturb her in the face of a fatiguing journey, but I got out of bed, washed my face, walked about the room, and endeavoured to shake off, as so many superstitious cobwebs, the eerie sensations creeping over my otherwise practical self.

At length I succeeded, or thought I did, and once more stretched my long limbs between the sheets. Sleep again closed my eyelids, only to be rudely re-opened. Again my disembodied self seemed to stand gazing on our old habitation; wife, or rather widow, and son stood mournfully at the window; she clasped her hands imploringly towards me, and screamed as the house rocked and swayed, then fell as before with a hideous crash and a cloud of dust; and as I rushed forward appalled, a ghostly shadow of her father stood by my side, sternly and rebukingly pointing to the ruins as he peremptorily repeated, "Look to your will!"

This time I awakened Anna. A sort of shuddering horror was upon me. I could scarcely describe to her my triplicate dream for the nervous tremor which shook me. I seemed to hear the echoes of that exhortation floating away in the distance.

I need hardly say my fear was contagious, even before its cause was made known, her own hasty surmise hovering between illness and burglars.

Woman-like, Anna's faith in dreams was more developed than mine.

"Three times repeated," she murmured, "and with such a variation! I tell you what, Gilbert, that dream is not to be slighted."

Then, mother-like, her thoughts ran off at a tangent to her son—"I wonder if Bertie is well. I will write first thing in the morning."

"Oh! Bertie's all right. If anything is wrong, it is the will I made when I was ill. There may be some flaw in it. I will run across to Sharp's in the morning and ask him to look over it carefully; and perhaps get counsel's opinion upon it. I shall have plenty of time."

So that was disposed of, and we tried to sleep again, but we had been thoroughly aroused, and an hour or more elapsed before oblivion steeped our senses. Then we somewhat overslept ourselves, and breakfast was delayed.

As a rule, I linger at the morning meal, sipping coffee and *Times* paragraphs alternately.

I hurried over both. Nevertheless, when I reached Sloane Street I was too late for Sharp. He had been gone to the office ten minutes. I hesitated. Should I defer my visit to the lawyer's until our return? "Look to your will!" seemed to drift like a breeze through the doorway of the hall.

I looked at my watch. A hansom was passing; I hailed it; promised the driver a fee for speed, and was soon tearing away towards Furnival's Inn in hopes to catch the lawyer and our train both.

The clerks made such desperate efforts to appear busy on my entrance that I felt sure the mice were playing in the absence of the cat, without the announcement, "Mr. Sharp has not yet arrived, sir."

Twenty minutes at least elapsed before Matthew, smug and speckless, put in an appearance.

"Your cab will have outstripped my omnibus; besides which I was stopped by a wearisome client in the gateway," explained he, as he ushered me into his comfortable private office, important with a law library and japanned boxes, supposed to hold title-deeds, &c.

"And now what can I do for you?" he asked—

"Washing his hands with invisible soap,
In imperceptible water."

I rarely went to his *office*, save for business.

Notwithstanding the haste I was in, I could not plunge into my errand at once. I felt there was something ridiculous in confessing that I had been brought thither by so intangible a matter as a dream. After some preamble I blundered out—

"Well, the fact is, Sharp, I dreamed last night that there was something wrong with that will of mine; I wish you would just go over it; perhaps get counsel's opinion to see there is no flaw in it."

A curious expression stole over Matthew's face as I spoke, then he broke into as curious a laugh.

"You don't mean to say that you, Gilbert Leslie, rode here post-haste spurred by—a dream—a mere dream?" and he chuckled outright; "and that you would throw away cab-fare and counsel's fees for anything so absurd? I really gave you credit, Leslie, for more common-sense."

I felt somewhat nettled by his reception, even though convinced I should have laughed at anyone else who had been similarly swayed by a nightmare, and I think I answered rather snappishly.

"It is no imputation on common-sense to have a hastily-concocted will examined for security. I want no litigation over my grave; and should scarcely rest there if my neglect brought trouble to my dear ones."

"Oh! well, if you take that view of the case, you may be right. I will do as you wish. But—" and he glanced at a solid marble timepiece on his chimney-piece—"I thought you were off to Scarborough this morning?"

"So we are, and I have no time to lose."

I snatched up my hat and was off. But, though the attendant hansom dashed along dangerously, and Annie had a four-wheeler loaded with luggage waiting at our door, and stood herself on the step ready to get in, we reached Euston Square fully ten minutes after the train had started.

I felt myself looking foolish a second time that morning; and what with my restless night, the heat, and the hurry, was not in the most amiable of tempers. I am afraid I swore at my folly, in allowing myself to be sent such a wild-goose chase by a dream.

Annie was more philosophic than I.

"Never mind, Gilbert," said she, pleasantly. "On a mere journey for pleasure, one day sooner or later will make very little difference. Let us leave our luggage in the booking office until to-morrow. Travelling by this precise train is not a matter of life and death."

Not a matter of life and death? How little we mortals know the slight threads on which the issues of life and death depend!

Before night the whole town rang with the terrible news of an awful collision between *that precise train* and a luggage-train, in which carriages were smashed to splinters, and human beings sent out of life, crushed and gashed, and others back to life maimed, disfigured, shaken.

And we might have been among those, but for the dream which Sharp held in such derision.

A telegram in a late evening paper brought Matthew himself to Cheyne Walk, in a state of excitement and agitation, and with a face white as his own spotless shirt-front. The telegram had given no list of the injured, and believing us to have been passengers, he was too anxious to sleep until he had ascertained the worst.

So he said: and certainly his mental disturbance was peculiar—even "ascertaining the *best*," as Annie remarked, "did not compose him."

He had evidently received a great shock, from which he could not recover. Was too restless to remain to supper, but tossed off a glass of brandy-and-water hastily, and rushed away to "relieve Mrs. Sharp's mind." I have since put another construction upon his agitation that night.

Be sure our thankfulness at escape did not allow us to forget the dream which had mainly procrastinated our journey. But we were inclined to put a new interpretation upon it, and regard it as a means to save our lives, rather than as indicating an irregularity in my will; especially when Matthew Sharp assured me he had gone carefully over the document and found it perfect in all respects—the best and clearest will he had ever drawn.

We went to the sea-side; but not to Scarborough, and not until we recovered from the shock and horror which every fresh and pictorial representation of the terrible catastrophe had served to renew.

In about a week we found ourselves at romantic Ilfracombe, with nothing to do but enjoy ourselves thoroughly. In order to do this completely, I hired a small yacht, in which we, and a friend or two we met there, spent many delightful hours.

We had been in Ilfracombe about a fortnight when I experienced a recurrence of my memorable dream, in its complete form.

I was not likely to treat the warning lightly now. Both Anna and myself felt it boded evil.

A sailing party had been arranged for the day, but at the risk of offending our friends, I countermanded my orders for the yacht; would neither sail in her myself, nor permit my friends to venture that day. I was unmercifully chaffed, but I stood it well; and all the more stolidly when the freshening breezes got up into a gale, and the waves ran in with white crests.

Moreover, I relinquished the yacht, feeling a sense of danger in its possession.

A few nights later my dream troubled me again. I am a good swimmer, and it had been my wont to bathe every fine morning. I resigned my sea-bath with a sort of feeling that superstition was setting a seal on all my pleasures; but I never thought of obeying the dream-voice's injunction, "Look to your will," until it was repeated, when I had no pleasures to surrender from which danger could possibly threaten.

Then it was we gave up our lodgings, and returned to town, much to the astonishment and perturbation of Barton and the maids, who were deep in the mysteries of "autumn cleaning."

Leaving Anna to find her way through a labyrinth of inverted chairs and bundled-up carpets, I went at once to Sloane Street. I found Sharp's house in like condition. "Master and mistress at the sea-side. Gone to Tenby for a month."

The next day saw me pass under the archway of Furnival's Inn to my friend's office, where I had a conference with his managing clerk. He knew nothing of the will. Mr. Sharp had his keys with him, and must have it in his own keeping. He would communicate with his governor; and gave me his address that I might do the same.

Letters brought only the unsatisfactory answer that he would see me on his return; but quite six weeks elapsed before he did return, and I grew restless and worried by delay.

Then he was necessarily overcrowded with business. If I called at his office he was either engaged, or out, or busy, or had an appointment; or had some shuffling excuse. At one time he had left his keys at home, at another was taken ill as he unlocked his private safe; and finally, he told me he had mislaid the will when he had it out for examination, and could not find it; but as soon as he had got over his crush of work he would have a thorough search for it.

"You need be under no apprehension," he said. "You are in good health, and even if you were not, you could make a fresh will, if that did not turn up in the meanwhile."

"So I can," returned I, with the office-door in my hand, "and I think I shall take your advice."

And I did. I went straightway to Messrs. Shrewd and Cleare, solicitors, in Bloomsbury, and gave instructions for a fresh will. My dream had been latterly very troublesome, and I could not rest with "Look to your will!" perpetually ringing in my ears.

Moreover, I was so haunted with the reiterated idea of something wrong with the will, that I assented to Mr. Shrewd's proposition to commence legal proceedings for the recovery of the former will from Sharp.

There had been a coolness growing between the families, dating from our return from Ilfracombe, and extending even to Bertie and his schoolmate Albert Sharp, and now the rupture was complete.

I need not follow the sinuosities of the law in the struggle to recover the missing will, during which Sharp took an affidavit that it was lost; had been abstracted from his desk.

Suffice that it was recovered.

Something wrong with it?

I should think there was!

Sharp had substituted his *own son's name for that of our Bertie, had reduced the sum left to my dear Anna to a mere pittance, and put in his own name as executor and residuary legatee* in place of my wife's. That will would, indeed, have brought down my house—have made them beggars.

We had obtained possession of the precious sample of roguery through a sneak of a clerk who, smarting under some real or fancied wrong, turned upon Sharp, and sold his services to Messrs. Shrewd and Cleare.

Had it not been for Anna, Sharp would not only have been struck off the rolls but placed in a criminal dock. I was so exasperated at the treachery of the man I had known and trusted from boyhood.

His submission had been abject. His wife went pleading to mine—and she, kind creature that she is, forgave him for the sake of their daughters and son, whose whole lives would be blighted by their father's disgrace.

She thought he had had a lesson to last his lifetime.

I was not so sure of it; but I let Anna have her way, and left him to the whip of his own conscience.

But we held no contact with the Sharps in future.

Bertie was recalled from school, and sent to Cambridge.

I read my new will over myself carefully, and then submitted it to counsel to make assurance sure. I was never more troubled with dreams of anything "wrong" in that testament; and I never afterwards signed any document, no matter what, without first reading it myself.

JUDGMENT DEFERRED

CHAPTER I

ON BOARD THE BEGUM

A trading vessel—the Alcestis, from Bahia to Liverpool—found the Begum drifting helplessly as a log on the billows. Yet she was a stout ship, well rigged, and seemingly in good condition. When the look-out sighted her, Captain Somers changed the course of the Alcestis to come within hail of the apparently disabled craft. But only the scream of the curlew answered the loud "Ship, ahoy!" though the cry was thrice repeated.

Under the conviction that something was wrong with the silent vessel, he still bore down upon her. As they neared, his glass told him that the boats were gone from her davits, and that the man at the helm was the only visible creature on deck.

"Ship, ahoy!" again pierced the stillness. A handkerchief fluttered for an instant above the helmsman's head, and a faint echo seemed to come across the water.

A boat was lowered from the Alcestis. As the men pulled steadily towards the mysterious stranger, Captain Somers, who was himself in charge, saw that the figure-head was a woman, and next read her name, "The Begum."

Cries of horror burst from the lips of the boarders at the sight before them. Captain, mates, and a couple of seamen lay gashed and dead upon the deck, where pools and rivulets of blood lay black and festering; and, sad as anything to see, a fine hound stretched in their midst, killed, no doubt, in the defence of his master.

The man at the wheel—by his garb a passenger and a gentleman —was the only living thing aboard, and he had fainted as Captain

Somers stepped upon the deck, apparently from exhaustion caused by wounds.

The sun was broiling hot, and the stench from the exposed bodies was pestilential.

The first care of Captain Somers, after the restoration of the survivor, was to commit the slain reverently to the deep, and next to make such disposition of his own crew as would best enable him to take the Begum in tow, and so preserve the sound teak-built ship and cargo for her owners.

Some hours elapsed before the rescued man was able to throw any light on what was a manifest tragedy. When he did relate the story it was with shuddering horror and many pauses, yet with strange and almost studied precision.

"My name is Stanhope—Alfred Stanhope. I went to India with my parents when a mere child. They have been dead several years. I was summoned from India to take possession of a fortune, inherited and bequeathed to me by a relative; and after winding up my affairs in the Presidency, I embarked on the Begum with my private secretary, Oliver Craven. The Begum, Captain Manners, was bound from Madras to London, with a cargo of rice, silk, sugar, and spices. There was also specie on board, for consignment to English bankers. Myself and secretary were the only passengers. There was a sufficient crew to work the ship with ease, had Captain Manners been so minded.

"We had baffling winds at the Cape, and our voyage was protracted—not, however, to any alarming extent; yet Captain Manners harassed his seamen with fatiguing duties, which I, a landsman, regarded as excessive. I may be in error, having no knowledge of seamanship. On the plea that provisions ran low, the men were put on short rations, and the allowance of grog was diminished. I am not prepared to say it was not a necessary precaution, but the consequences were terrible!

"A spirit of discontent prevailed. We had called at Madeira for fresh fruits and water. One or two of the men sought leave to go ashore. It was denied, and denied harshly. I ventured to remonstrate with the captain; was told to mind my own business; he was master of his ship, and would do as he chose.

"One glorious morning, about a week ago—I have lost my count of days, but it was the 4th of August—I sat writing in my cabin, Selim, my dog, coiled on the rug at the open doorway. There was a trampling of feet overhead. He gave a low growl, sprang to his feet and rushed on deck, the first to hear the mutterings of the storm and the plashing of the red rain.

"The slumbering mutiny had broken out. I reached the deck unarmed, to find sailors and officers in fierce conflict, and my secretary, in the very midst, endeavouring in vain to quell the strife. Poor Oliver paid the penalty of his rashness. My faithful hound, rushing forward to defend him, fell a sacrifice at the outset. Before I could seize a cutlass, or strike a blow in self-defence, I felt a sharp sting of a bullet through my arm, and almost simultaneously a blow from a marlinspike stunned me.[61]

"I must have lain senseless an hour or more. I recovered to find myself stiff and sore, in a pool of blood, amidst silence profound and terrible.

"It was some time before I attained full consciousness of my awful situation. The Begum had been abandoned by her mutinous crew, and I had been left for dead—among the dead.

---

[61] Marlinspike: a pointed metal tool used by sailors to separate strands of rope or wire.

"I managed to creep to my cabin and obtain a draught of brandy. Fortunately, the bullet was embedded in the muscles of my left arm, and I contrived to extract it with my penknife. Doubtless, I did it clumsily; but I did it, and, moreover, plaistered and bound the wound."

"Had I not better examine it?" asked the surgeon of the Alcestis, rising, and coming forward.

"It is not necessary, sir," answered Mr. Stanhope, waving him back somewhat stiffly; "the wound is healing."

The surgeon coughed slightly, as he retired disconcerted, and Mr. Stanhope resumed:

"I discovered that the ship had been plundered, my cabin ransacked, money and valuables carried off. They had victualled their boats well. I could find no provisions beyond a few biscuits and a little water."

"I thought rice and sugar were part of the cargo?" suggested Captain Somers.

"Yes; but I was too weak and unskilled to procure them."

"Humph! they would be in the hold, and neither East India sugar bags nor rice bags are made of cast iron!"

There was a world of contempt for a land-libber's imbecility in the captain's tone.

"The ship tossed and drifted at the will of the wind. My situation was horrible. If I went on deck the open eyes of the dead men seemed to follow me. If I went below I could signal no passing vessel. On the second day I resolved to throw the bodies overboard. I shudder as I think of the result." (He did shudder, indeed.) "Round the corpse of Oliver Craven, my secretary, who deserved a far better fate, I wrapped a piece of canvas, and as well as I was able, having one arm disabled, dragged it to the side and pitched it over. There was a downward plunge, and then——"

"Some brandy for Mr. Stanhope, he is fainting."

Mr. Stanhope rallied, again waved back the officious surgeon, and continued:

"The canvas had slipped, and Craven's head and shoulders rose and fell with every wave that lapped the vessel's side, and life seemed to look out of the wave-washed eyes, from which salt tears ran down the white cheeks. It was an awful sight, yet it fascinated me. If I turned away, I was certain to look back, and as certain to see Craven's pale face and glassy eyes before me."

Mr. Stanhope drew his hands across his own as if to shut out the sight.

"Two days more, and a couple of friendly sharks rid me of the horrid spectacle. But not of that on deck, and I had neither strength of body nor will left to cast another corpse into the sea. Even poor Selim had to lie where he fell.

"In all that time no vessel hailed us to hove to. I saw sails in the distance, but what signal I could make was unheeded. I felt abandoned even of Heaven, and gave myself up as lost. Whither the sepulchral ship was drifting—into what solitary sea, I knew not.

"The sleepless nights spent below were haunted by visions of the scene on deck. Prayer seemed frozen on my lips, and morning found me at my post at the helm, with reality before me and my own certain fate in contemplation. The very sharks appeared to multiply and grow more ravenous as they followed steadily in our wake!

"When you found me, Captain Somers, I was on the verge of madness. My debt of gratitude to you will never be cancelled."

The statement made on their arrival in port to magistrates and shipowners by Mr. Stanhope, though precisely the same in all points of fact, was still more concise. He had recovered somewhat his composure, and told his tale with quiet gravity, and with none of the nervous tremor which had marked and broken the first narrative.

Yet, he must have suffered greatly, his hair and unshorn beard being white as foam when he was picked up, though he gave his age as twenty-eight, and in answer to surprised inquiry said that on the morning of that fourth of August his hair had been dark brown—a statement borne out by the reddish light in his cavernous eyes. He looked much older; but no doubt an Indian sun, as well as his terrible experience, were accountable for that.

He was apparently a man who had his feelings well under control, yet no effort could hide his perturbation and reluctance to revisit the Begum for the purpose of collecting his own papers and property; as also the luggage of his unfortunate secretary, of which he offered to take charge for transmission to the friends of the murdered man.

Of everything in the shape of money or jewellery, cabins and bodies had alike been despoiled; how Mr. Stanhope's watch had escaped them was a marvel. The owners of the Begum were prompt in their offers of cash for immediate use, but Mr. Stanhope had with him letters of credit, which had escaped confiscation, and which were duly honoured.

The story found its way into the newspapers of the time, 182—; and had he been so minded, Alfred Stanhope would have been pushed into notoriety. But this seemed repugnant to his feelings. He said, curtly—

"I decline to be made the hero of a tragedy." And again: "My own business requires my presence elsewhere."

Those who would have fêted and lionized him were disappointed, and whilst one half pronounced him sensitive, the remainder voted him haughty and imperious.

His stay in Liverpool ended with the official inquiry. That terminated, Mr. Stanhope sent on his luggage by carrier, and ensconced himself in a corner of the Royal Mail coach for transmission to London. It was a glorious day in September, but he shivered, though he was wrapped in a long, straight, fur-lined cloak which reached to his heels, and in which he shut himself up as in a sentry-box. The very sealskin cap on his head had flaps to cover his ears, and had there been another to cover his mouth, he could not have been more silent and self-contained.

A chirrupy little man on the opposite seat made sundry attempts to draw him into conversation, but failing, turned his attention to more sociable fellow-passengers. Not even when they stopped to change horses or alighted for refreshment was he more accessible. He ate and drank of the best, and paid freely, but his taciturnity increased, if possible, as they neared London. For a man about to take possession of an estate, his cogitations seemed to be of the gloomiest. It might be his past experience led him to fear legal thorns before the full-blown rose could be plucked, or, it might be, a feminine rose as thorny.

If so, he troubled himself in the one case unnecessarily. His credentials were indisputable. Recent investigation had already established his identity, and Messrs. Falconer and Robb, of Verulam Buildings, solicitors under the will, both remarked, "Mr. Stanhope's resemblance to his late uncle," so no impediments were thrown in his way; and he took possession with as little delay as the law permitted, confirming Messrs. F. and R. in their position as solicitors to the Stanhope estate.

Alfred Stanhope was by no means a poor man when he left Madras. His uncle's will had superadded money in the bank, money in the funds, and house property in town, to the old entailed mansion in Warwickshire, with its well-wooded and extensive grounds.

"I understand you have not visited Stanhope Court since you were quite a child," said Mr. Falconer to the new owner, as their travelling carriage passed through the lodge gates, and swept under a long avenue of limes, from which the leaves were beginning to fall.

"Not since I was five years old. My father and uncle quarrelled at the time, and afterwards held aloof. They were only reconciled when my father was about to sail for India some four years later."

"Your memories of the place will consequently be very dim," observed the lawyer.

"Very. I remember only an irregular building, large rooms, and gloomy passages, with a gallery of grim pictures, of which I was half afraid. But I have not to be told that its foundation was laid in Tudor times, and its latest addendum was when George the Third was King. I have memories, too, of a kennel of yelping hounds and a stud of hunters," continued Mr. Stanhope, half questioningly.

"Your memory does not deceive you," said Mr. Falconer. "The late Mr. Stanhope was an inveterate fox-hunter, and you will find stables and kennels much as he left them."

"Shall I? Then I shall make a clean sweep of the whole lot. Send them to auction before the week is out!" was the abrupt and somewhat acrimonious retort.

"Indeed! Then you are not a sportsman?" interrogated rather than asserted Mr. Falconer, with uplifted eyebrows.

"Not an English sportsman, certainly. He who has hunted the antelope, with the cheetah for his hound, and the tiger, with an elephant for a steed, will not care to ride pell-mell over hedges and ditches to witness the worrying of a fox!" And Mr.

Stanhope's lip curled unmistakably.

"You speak of the hunting-field with all the force of familiarity, until really, Mr. Stanhope, I can hardly realize that you left England so young," observed the solicitor, in some astonishment.

He was put down by the anglo-Indian's haughty sarcasm—

"Men who read, sir, need not travel the world for information on such topics."

"True, true!" assented his interlocutor, with the mental rider —"Hang his impertinence! He is as haughty as if he were the Great Mogul."

The haughtiness subsided into sufficient condescension, when stepping from the carriage he entered the wide hall, hung round with sportsmen's trophies, and, passing between a double file of servants, acknowledged their cheer of welcome, and the salutation of butler and housekeeper with almost the first smile Mr. Falconer had seen upon his face.

CHAPTER II
AT STANHOPE COURT

"Hush! The place strikes chilly as a vault!" muttered Mr. Stanhope, as the cheering subsided. Then aloud to the curtseying housekeeper (a buxom dame), he said, "I trust you have large fires, Mrs. Hudson. I have never been warm since I set foot in England;" and he visibly shivered under his fur-lined cloak, though there was an ample fire burning in the hall at the time.

"Yes, sir, in all the rooms. Mr. Falconer gave particular instructions, after our dear old master's funeral (how you do shiver, sir!) that the place should be kept well aired, and I trust you will find everything satisfactory."

"As satisfactory as English skies and heavy English masonry will permit, I daresay."

"Do you think the conjunction of an Indian bungalow and an English sky would be more satisfactory, Mr. Stanhope?" put in Mr. Falconer, with a sort of dry chuckle.

"It would be lighter, and brighter, and scarcely colder, sir," answered Mr. Stanhope, in a tone which "put down" the little, wiry, bright-eyed solicitor for the second time that day.

The housekeeper came to his relief. "Your chambers have been prepared, gentlemen, and dinner will be served in an hour—unless, Mr. Stanhope, you would prefer to go over the house at once.

Mr. Stanhope deferred the necessary tour of inspection to the morrow, and both gentlemen were shown to their rooms to refresh after their journey.

There were cheerful fires in bedrooms and dressing-rooms; and as the flames danced and flickered, they were reflected in well-polished furniture of dark mahogany, and swing-glasses in oval frames. But windows and tall four-post bedsteads were draped with dark velvet hangings, loaded with silk lace and deep bullion fringe; and doubtless to the man reared from boyhood amongst the lightsome fittings of bamboo and gauze, their heaviness was oppressive. He had declined the assistance of a servant, and now, instead of dressing, paced the room with his hand at his throat, panting for breath, and muttering in gasps, "What is the matter with me? The very air of the place might be tainted; it seems to stifle me. I can hardly breathe. But I must overcome it, if I would enjoy the good the gods have sent me."

The faint baying of a hound from the distant kennels smote his ear. He turned ghastly white, even to the lips.

"My God! what was that?" He sank into an arm-chair before the fire, in absolute faintness. "What a fool I am!" he murmured. "It is one of those infernal fox-hounds. I'll have none of their yelping about the old court."

He had thrown his cloak aside and sat there, a white-headed, white-browed man, with a dark skin, a massive forehead, a long, but not straight, nose; a straight upper lip, a close mouth, broad jaws, full rounded chin, and deep-sunk, red-brown eyes, that seemed to pierce the very fire to question it, so keen and searching were they. Yet, at times, they were furtive and stealthy as those of a panther; at others restless and timorous as a fawn's. Indeed, the entire face was one of many meanings, many expressions, and though Indian life, and the fearful tragedy aboard the Begun, had blanched his locks and lined his young face prematurely, there was no question he was a handsome man of fair proportions, on whom reserve and hauteur sat not ill.

He was still asking its secrets of the fire, when the second dinner bell rang. He started up, drew his hand across his brow, and flung his open palm outward, as if he threw something from him.

"I will brighten the dull place before I bring *her* here," was the burden of his thoughts, as he hurried his toilette.

A respectful servant was in waiting to conduct his new master to the dining-room. This was a long, lofty, dark-panelled apartment, with well-worn carpet, and three windows, across which ruby curtains hung in folds as massive as the antique chairs and tables. Between each window was a mirror reflecting the lights from its own candelabra, and the flames from the sputtering wood fire on the open hearth opposite, and—that which was the most conspicuous thing in the room—a full-length picture of a stalwart man, in a scarlet hunting coat, buckskin breeches, and top-boots. His one hand rested on the neck of a bay mare, a hunting cap and whip were in the other, and by his side stood a long-nosed tawny fox-hound.

As the picture caught Mr. Stanhope's eye he gave a perceptible start, and for an instant held his breath; but only for an instant. Coming forward, he apologized to Mr. Falconer for being a few minutes beyond time, and then turned to survey the painting more fully.

"My late uncle's portrait, I presume," said he.

"Yes," responded Mr. Falconer, "and, but for his sixty years and florid complexion, a marvellous likeness to yourself. Your grey hair assists the resemblance. It is astonishing how family features are transmitted from generation to generation."

Judkins, the old butler, with the freedom of long service, here struck in" "If I may be so bold, I would say as Mr. Stanhope here is more like to our old squire than to his own father; at least as I remember him before he went to Indy, three an'twenty years ago."

"Ah, that would be when my father and uncle parted in anger, never to meet again. Judkins, what wine have you there?"

The subject thus waived was not resumed. The picture had, however, a strange fascination for the new owner of Stanhope Court. Whenever he lifted his head his eyes sought it furtively, but with a look in which pain and pleasure mingled.

When the meal was over and the servants dismissed, the twain drew nearer to the fire, wine-glasses were filled, cigars lighted, and in the midst of the fumes they talked of many matters, mostly connected with the estate and the late fox-hunter's will.

"And you have no idea what was my uncle's motive for leaving Oliver Craven so substantial a legacy as two hundred pounds a year?"

"Not the slightest. Mr. Robb drew up the will, but received no instructions which gave a clue either to his reasons, or to the young man's connections or antecedents. He was simply described as 'Oliver Craven, sometime secretary to my late brother Alfred, in Madras, and now secretary to my nephew Alfred.' Our late client, though a jovial, social being amongst his fellow-sportsmen, was close and reserved in all personal and private matters. Have you no suspicion?"

"None. Craven came to India, bringing with him a whelp from the same litter as that in the picture"—pointing upwards with his cigar—"and a letter to my father, urging, as a special favour to himself, that he would push the fortunes of his protegé—a namesake, whose parents had been friends of his own. This was seven years ago. The young man said he had no recollection of his father, and that he was then in mourning for his mother. He served us with faithfulness and intelligence, and I lament, deeply lament, that he should have been so tragically cut off from the enjoyment of my late uncle's well-meant bequest."

"Of course, the money reverts to you in consequence of his death?" said the lawyer.

"I do not intend to touch it. I gather from letters and a miniature I found amongst Craven's luggage that he had been long engaged to a young girl in his own rank. I shall seek her out, and make the annuity over to her."

"My dear Mr. Stanhope, this is, indeed, noble. I——"

"It is justice, sir, not nobility," interrupted Mr. Stanhope, rising. "I will leave you to your wine, Mr. Falconer. I am unused to your mode of travelling, and must plead fatigue as my excuse for retiring early."

Mr. Falconer heard him address a servant in the hall.

"What dogs sleep on the premises—within the house, I mean?"

"Well, sir, there's Snap, the bull-terrier, an' Grip, the mastiff, an'——"

"Turn them all out before you go to bed, and see that no dog crossed the threshold again, as you value your place."

"Strange!" murmured the lawyer. "Fancy a nephew of old Noll Stanhope with an antipathy to *canis*. The old sportsman would have disinherited him could he have foreknown it."

"Strange!" echoed the chorus in the servants' hall. "Turn them animals out! Why, its enoof to make t'old master turn in his coffin!"

They might not have thought it so strange could they have seen through their closed eyelids and chamber-doors the stranger sight of their new master, in slippered feet and dressing-gown, in the dead of night, wandering about the deserted rooms below, and holding his light to the portraits in the picture gallery, as if to print them on his memory!

The formal tour of inspection took place the next morning, the housekeeper and butler acting as guides. They, no less than Mr. Falconer, were surprised at the tenacity of Alfred Stanhope's memory.

"He was such a little thing when he ran about the place last, and his nurse frightened him with that grim picture in the black frame."

They were in the picture gallery at the time.

"It *is* a grim picture. I can scarcely look upon it without a shudder even now," said he, in answer to the housekeeper's remark.

"No doubt recent events have given it force," observed Mr. Falconer. "The fierce, murderous eyes of Cain and the imploring ghastliness of the stricken Abel must be like realities to you."

"Like realities, indeed!" echoed Mr. Stanhope, in an undertone, as he turned away with a face scarcely less ghastly than that of the painted Abel.

There was a second portrait of his uncle, with the inevitable canine pet, close to the doorway; and by its side one of Alfred Stanhope's father, both taken in their prime. But he merely paused to note the resemblance between the brothers ere he stepped across the corridor (lighted at one end by a wide mullioned window, emblazoned with the Stanhope arms), and into the library.

Here he drew a deep breath, and sat down, as if to look around.

The door by which he and his attendants had entered lay behind him, in the extreme corner of the wall at his right hand. On the same side was the fire-place, originally open, but which had been closed in beneath the massive carved shelfless chimney-piece with glistening Dutch tiles, and fitted with a modern grate—that is, modern a century ago. The heat of the bright fire in the sweeping semi-circular grate shone on the polished tiles, and radiating, glowed afresh on the brass fender and equipments, and on the margin of polished oak-floor left bare by the square Turkey carpet. An immense mullioned window confronted the fireplace, and through the ermine and gules of its stained escutcheon the morning sun fell in ruddy patches upon the solid centre table. A ponderous escritoire held possession of the wall at his back, and before him stood open the chief door of the apartment, covered with crimson baize, spangled with brass nails, and through its two-foot vista he saw its duplicate closed. An army of old books, in good but dingy uniforms, were ranged in rank and file on shelves, which left no inch of spare wall uncovered. New books there were apparently none, and the place had the aspect of hasty furbishing up; yet, as Alfred Stanhope surveyed it from his high-backed arm-chair, a smile of satisfaction swept over his weary-looking countenance. He rose.

"Mrs. Hudson, I will thank you to have another table brought in, and let tiffin—I mean luncheon—be served here. In future, unless I have more than one guest, I shall take my meals in this library."

"Very well, sir, your wishes shall be attended to," said the housekeeper, as her master left the library, with Mr. Falconer in his wake; but turning to see her own amazement reflected in the butler's rubicund face, she clasped her uplifted hands with the exclamation, "Laws, Mr. Judkins, how tastes differ to be sure! When did old master ever put foot in the library, I wonder?"

"Well, Mrs. Hudson," replied the butler, sententiously, "what's one man's meat's another man's pison. Old master liked dawgs and hated books; the new master hates dawgs, and maybe likes books. It's all one to me, if he don't put a padlock on the cellar door, and turn all the old servants adrift."

Alfred Stanhope did not turn his uncle's household adrift. But he made a clean sweep of kennels and stables. Hounds and hunting-stud went under the hammer, and all superfluous trainers, grooms, and stable-boys were dismissed with pensions or gratitudes.

An open hand will atone for a close mouth and many eccentricities; and so, on the whole, Alfred Stanhope grew in favour with his dependents, though he preferred the companionship of books to that of fox-hunting squires, and sat shivering over the library fire, instead of warming his blood with a brisk canter in the crisp autumnal air, and started like a woman at the report of a gun or the bark of a dog.

CHAPTER III
OLD PAPERS

There were no railways to whisk people hither and thither, without notice or preparation, at the date of this narrative. Letters and messages did not fly on wings of steam and lightning. People and business went on in an easy jog-trot fashion, and no one then thought the world too slow or felt themselves the worse. Then newspapers were too dear, and too few, to find their way daily to every breakfast table; and their news was not always of the newest.

Thus it happened that when Mary Lloyd, schoolmistress, of Lupus Street, Pimlico, picked up a fragment of newspaper which had done duty as wrappage to a pupil's luncheon, and read thereon a report of the "inquiry into the mutiny and abandonment of the Begum," the inquest was over, and the survivor of the massacre quietly established at Stanhope Court.

Poor girl! It was well for her that it was Saturday, and that her scholars had separated for the week; well that she was alone when the direful paragraph met her eye, and felled her as with a blow from an unseen hand!

Her little maid-of-all-work, dish-washing in the regions below, heard the scream and fall, and rushed to her assistance, wiping her hands on her coarse apron as she ran.

Their lodgers were out, and the small domestic was at her wits' end, but she had sense left to raise the head of her young mistress from the uncarpeted floor, using work bags for pillows, while she ran for water to sprinkle her with.

As Mary revived, the tender-hearted maid replaced the side-combs which had fallen from the dark-brown ringlets, and looked ruefully at the tall Spanish back-comb which lay shivered on the floor. But she never doubted the truth of the explanation that the fall arose from a sudden dizziness caused by over-fatigue.

Two music pupils, coming an hour later, found her stretched on a sofa with her hair disarranged, "looking white and awful," and went home with their lessons deferred through their teacher's illness.

"Oliver Craven killed! Oliver dead! Her Oliver—her good, true Oliver, for whose sake she had kept single all these years; to whom she should have been married this very month! Could she ever bear to look again on the wedding-dress he had sent her, which was even then being made up? Oh, that she had listened to his pleading seven years back, and kept him in England—her husband, her own, her Oliver! Yet how *could* she marry whilst her poor paralyzed mother claimed her care? How burden him with such a charge? How stand in the way of his advancement."

So ran Mary Lloyd's conflicting thoughts as she lay on that chintz-covered sofa in her semi-scholastic back parlour in Lupus Street, with one hand over her tearless eyes and burning brow, holding together the head that seemed ready to split, and the other over the heart that seemed just as ready to break, in its desolation.

And she *was* desolate.

At the death of her father she inherited little besides a good education, a loving heart, strict integrity, a resolute will, and the charge of a paralyzed mother. He had insured his life for three hundred pounds, and with that and their tolerable stock of furniture, Mary Lloyd, with no relatives to assist or oppose, before she was eighteen took the house in Pimlico, let a portion to lodgers, and converted the remainder into a "School for Young Ladies." Had she waited twenty years she might have dubbed it an "Establishment."

It was during the settlement of her father's affairs that she met with Oliver Craven, clerk to a solicitor in Lincoln's Inn Fields. He was struck at once by the fearless energy of the young girl, and her untiring affection for her helpless mother. Of her beauty I think he only discerned that hers was the beauty of goodness; yet she stood above the common height, her limbs well-proportioned, her head erect on a somewhat full throat, her brow was broad and reflective, and if her nose was not classical, and her upper lip was somewhat stiff, the lines of mouth and chin were tender in their curves, and she had the very mildest of clear grey eyes.

The concern he had evinced for her friendless position, the desire he had shown to serve her, created an interest in Mary Lloyd's breast for Oliver Craven, and love was not far behind. He was her sole confidant, her sole counsellor in the many trials which beset her progress, and when he announced Oliver Stanhope's offer to send him to India under good auspices, a very earthquake seemed to rend them asunder and shatter the temple of her hopes.

But when her lover proposed to remain in England at the risk of his patron's displeasure her negation was final.

"I will wait for you, dear Oliver," she said, "any number of years, but I will not destroy your prospects, not can I burden you with the care of my mother, and so a double duty compels me to say 'Go.' "

And now that he was no more, for the first time she questioned the basis of her decision. It was she who had sent him to India; she who had been the cause of his death!

All that day and the next her mind was racked with torturing agony. With the Monday came her pupils and her duties, and in their obligatory performance the strain relaxed little by little, the violence of grief and self-accusation subsided; but the wound in her heart was unskinned, the void unfilled, and "Oliver! Oliver!" seemed written in red on every lesson-book, or slate, or copy she touched.

She substituted black crape and bombazine for the delicate Indian silk in the dressmaker's hands, and "the loss of a friend" was the answer to all inquiries.

A week later, a letter with a black seal, from Messrs. Falconer and Robb, made her formally acquainted with that which she already knew, and with the further fact that Alfred Stanhope, Esq., made over to her his right of succession to a legacy of two hundred pounds per annum, bequeathed by the late Oliver Stanhope to his young protegé, Oliver Craven, knowing her to have been his secretary's affianced wife.

Her wound bled afresh, and now she wept. Had Oliver but lived, how happy might they have been with such an assured income! Then she doubted her right to accept it, and after some correspondence, the solicitors, at the instigation of their client, assured her that she had no alternative—the deeds were already executed. If that was a fiction she was not lawyer enough to know it.

Her grateful letter of thanks was duly forwarded to Mr. Stanhope; but much as she wished to thank him in person, no interview had as yet taken place.

Yet such a meeting could not be far off, since, in a fit of very unusual confidence, he had told Mr. Falconer that he had been so much attracted by the miniature amongst Oliver Craven's papers, and the good sense of Miss Lloyd's letters, that he purposed making her acquaintance as soon as the first tumult of her grief had subsided. And Mr. Falconer having but a low opinion of woman's constancy, duly confided to Mr. Robb that he thought Stanhope Court would not be long without a mistress.

The last swallow had departed on his African tour, with the nightingale close in his wake; the green woodpecker laughed his loudest as old October gripped the trees with firm hands, and shook to the ground their crimson foliage; and along with the rustling leaves down went the hard dinner of the nuthatch from his claw, to be pounced upon by the merry squirrel gambolling at the roots of the oak, and stowed away for leisurely digestion.

The month was dying in a flood of gold and purple splendour when its last sunset glories fell on the escutcheoned window of

Stanhope Court library, and flecked with black spots and great crimson patches the papers spread on the oak table, and the warmly-clad figure bending over them.

Alfred Stanhope raised his head, and, as his eye rested on the exaggerated escutcheon tinging his papers, he cast himself back in his chair with a sigh of utter weariness; and, looking upwards at the window, murmured sadly; "Always the same; always those great red quarterings falling athwart my hands, staining my books and papers as if with great blotches of blood. It affects my sight; and but that all the crazy antiquaries in the county would cry out upon me, I would remove it. And then the motto mocks me with its 'A Deo et Rege!'[62] Well, well, 'familiarity breeds contempt.' I shall grow different in time."

The old escritoire was open, and he was apparently going over its contents to destroy or conserve at his pleasure. The paper before him went with a toss into the waste basket, as he laid his left hand on a packet of letters, yellow with age, and tied round with a faded ribbon. They were addressed to 'Oliver Stanhope, Esq.," in a cramped female hand, but no dated post-mark gave a clue to their antiquity or order, so he took up one haphazard.

He had taken it up listlessly enough, and paused with it half unfolded in his hand to ring his bell to have the fire replenished; but whatever he found therein—when the footman came to learn his pleasure—he sat with the square discoloured sheet held tightly in both tremulous hands, poring over it with eager eyes, too absorbed to note the entrance of the man or heed his twice-repeated query. But glancing prematurely at the signature, he started to his feet with an exclamation so sudden and vehement, that the servant went

---

62 *Meaning*: 'From God and the King.'

back to his fellows and said, with much commiseration, that "Master must have had a sunstroke or something in India, for he sure never could be right in his head. What with his fancies that dogs were growling when there was never even the ghost of a dog within the park palings, an' his shivering over the fire, an' starting and bouncing only to frighten honest folks, he never could be right in his upper story."

The man had jumped to a false conclusion; his master had as clear a head as any in the shire; but he had made a discovery such as would make any man leap to his feet and cry out, if he had a spark of feeling in him.

It was the old story of woman's weakness and man's depravity he read in those letters—the story of a silly girl caught in the toils of a dashing blade, allured from home, her scruples silenced by a clandestine marriage, afterwards repudiated as informal when satiety or jealousy needed a pretext to cast her off, and brand her child with illegitimacy.

The dashing blade had been Alfred Stanhope's sporting bachelor uncle; the disowned woman had signed herself—*Margaret Craven.*

CHAPTER IV
MARY LLOYD

November was but three days old when a knock, which made Mary Lloyd's heart beat, came to the door of the "Ladies' Seminary" in Lupus Street. It was Thursday, and her holiday afternoon, on which she only gave music-lessons. The last of her music pupils had gone home, the square piano was closed, and she sat down in her dead mother's rocking-chair by the fire to muse on her utter desolation—

desolation of heart and home; a void not to be filled by her pupils' love or the respect of their friends.

The face, paler and thinner than of old, was not improved in tone by her black dress; but what she lost in colour she gained in gravity and repose.

The little maid handed in a black-edged card, and before Mary could well decipher the inscription in the waning light, the visitor had followed his pasteboard into the dim room.

The man was so muffled in a long fur-collared cloak and a cashmere shawl worn over throat and mouth, as if to guard both from damp, that all she could discern besides was a mass of white hair, a dark skin, and a pair of searching eyes that seemed to look her through.

"Candles," she whispered to the maid, as she rose to receive the stranger.

The girl retired, closing the door behind her.

There was a momentary hesitation, caused apparently by the gentleman's reluctance to speak before the servant, during which Mary Lloyd contrived to spell out the card in the firelight. A smile of pleased surprise crossed her face.

"Mr. Stanhope," she said, advancing, "this is, indeed, an honour I did not expect. How pleased I am at this opportunity to express my——"

He stopped her with a deprecatory wave of his hand.

"The honour, Miss Lloyd, is mine."

What was there in the motion, or the tones, which came thick through the muffler to make her start?

The maid brought two mould candles in tall brass candlesticks, and placed them on the table.

"Will you not remove your wraps, sir; the room is warm?"

"After the heats of India, I find all rooms cold."

The door again closed. The girl's heavy step was heard to go downstairs. He loosened but did not remove his shawl.

"You wrote to me, Miss Lloyd, for a miniature and some letters of yours found amongst the effects of my late secretary?" There was a huskiness as of deep emotion in his voice as he added: "I have brought them with me."

Mary could scarcely trust herself to speak.

"Thank you, sir; you are very kind," was all that issued from her quivering lips.

"But"—he laid a packet on the table—"pardon me, I am most reluctant to surrender them. I have looked at your semblance until the image is painted on my brain and heart. I would not wrong the memory of your lover; yet time——"

She rose with an indignant protest on her lips.

"Mr. Stan——"

The next syllable was inaudible. The lips parted; but she stood motionless and rigid, unable to utter a word.

He has unclasped his cloak to get at the packet, and the shawl had fallen aside.

As she confronted him with eager, open eyes, and gasped, "*Oliver!*" he, too, started to his feet, and caught her fainting figure ere she fell.

She had made her discovery prematurely.

If kisses, showered on lip and brow and cheek, could vivify a swooning woman, surely his might have brought her back to consciousness; but she lay white and helpless in his arms so long he was fain to place her on the chintz-covered sofa, and look around for a restorative. A common bottle of smelling-salts stood on the mantelshelf, telling its tale of frequent need. Its application ere long brought back the colour to her cheeks, a faint sigh stirred the curl that had fallen across her face; her eyes opened, to rest on the grey-haired man kneeling by her side with anxiety, love, and dread striving for mastery in his countenance.

As the soft light came back to her eyes, he drew her head once more to his shoulder, and placing his hand on her mouth lest she should scream, whispered:

"For God's sake, Mary, darling, command yourself; it is Oliver, your own Oliver, who bids you be calm and cautious, as you love him."

She had thrown one arm around his neck, and was sobbing as if her heart would break, saying, in broken gasps between her sobs:

"They told me—you were—killed—I—I—Mr. Stanhope—he—I—do not—understand—they—the lawyers—he—oh, Oliver! Is it indeed you?"

"Yes, darling, yes—your own love come back for his sweet wife. You will be my wife, Mary, will you not? You will let nothing part us, will you?"

Kisses did duty for punctuation as he spoke, and Mary, in bewilderment and bliss, could only kiss him back in answer. The sea had given up its dead to her, and she in fullness of joy and gratitude was dumb.

In his face love and joy seemed dashed with a shadow of distrust—some haunting presentiment of evil appeared to contract his thoughtful brow as if with pain.

The maid in the kitchen waited impatiently a summons for the tea-tray. They sat, oblivious of common things, side by side on the sofa; she with her head on his throbbing breast lulled in a delicious calm; he, with his arm gripped round her waist, as if some powerful foe were about to wrest her from him.

The treacherous calm was soon broken.

"Mary," he whispered, as if nodding mandarins on the mantel-shelf were listening, "Mary, I have a strange tale to tell you, but first I want your solemn promise—your oath—to be my wife in the face of everything and anything."

"You have my promise, dear. You know my *love*; if that cannot suffice, what oath could bind me, Oliver?" She looked up proudly as she spoke.

"Hush, darling, not so loud! You must not call me Oliver, I am Alfred—Alfred Stanhope now."

"Alf—what? I do not understand.

"Do not look so strangely, Mary! I have a confession to make. Nay, darling, do not shrink from me. What I have done, I have done for your sake. Nay, listen! It is not so bad, after all.

"Mary, my love, I need not tell the dreadful story of the mutiny; you know it. But dearest, Mr. Stanhope was the one killed. I, your Oliver, was wounded and left for dead. As I dressed my own wounds with lint from his medicine chest, it flashed across my mind that he had not a relative to take his estate; that no one in England had seen him from a boy, and that if they had I bore a strong likeness to him. By his death I was deprived of an appointment, and if ever I got home could only wed you to poverty. Mary—Mary, darling, the temptation was strong! I resolved to personate him—to be Alfred Stanhope to all the world but you. I knew all the family traditions; I could not fail. I threw his corpse overboard, and then——"

"Then, Oliver Craven, after sufferings that should have taught the falsity of your policy, you took false oaths, before God and man, to magistrates and lawyers; and thought that *I*, the child of a Christian clergyman, would be an accomplice in your fraud. Better the deepest poverty than such dishonour."

She had gradually loosened herself from his clasp, and now stood before him erect, with indignation and shame burning in her else calm eyes. She seemed transformed, and he sank cowed before her.

"Mary, Mary, forgive and pity me! If I erred, it was for you. I would make you mistress of Stanhope Court, close the sad volume of your drudgery here, and fill your life with all that luxury or love could give."

"Had you come back to me an honest man, without a shilling in the world, I would have been proud of you, and love would have dignified drudgery. But now——" She crushed her face up in her hands in anguish unsupportable.

In vain he tried to move her. At length: "Mary," said he, in lower tones, "I am not the impostor you think. I made a discovery three days back which staggered me and nearly drove me mad. Had I not proclaimed myself Alfred Stanhope, I might yet have claimed the estate in my own right. *Oliver Stanhope was my father*."

"Your father?"

"My father, dear one. Whether his marriage with my mother was legal or a vile cheat I have yet to ferret out and prove to clear her fame. But I *shall* do it some day, I *know!*"

He would have taken her in his arms again, but she held him aloof and begged him to depart. He was abject in his entreaties. Then fear lest she should denounce his fraud took hold of him—the quiet woman so like a pythoness with scorn.

But he mistook her.

"Go, sir. No eloquence of yours can move my from my sense of duty. You have done me a wrong in opening my eyes this day. Dead, and buried in the everlasting sea, I mourned and worshipped you; living, the master of Stanhope Court, I can only strive to forget you. You have dropped your identity; I shall not recall it. Your secret is safe with me."

Hearing the outer door bang, the maid came upstairs to find Mary Lloyd on the hearthrug senseless, and the fire out.

She called loudly to the lodgers, and with their help the prostrate schoolmistress was carried to her bed.

Haggard, careworn, wretched, Oliver Craven—Mr. Stanhope —went back to his ancient mansion to envy the very lodge-keeper who opened the gates, his smiling wife and chubby children; went back to cower and shiver over his library fire, to hear the yelping of imaginary hounds, and fancy uncle, father, and cousin lurked behind him in the shadowy corners of the large room; to feel all the agonies of remorse deepened by failure; to feel his life bleak and barren henceforth. Himself a dry twig, having neither root, nor sap, nor leaves, fit only for the burning; scorned, contemned, despised by her for whom he had perilled his own soul.

During all that week he ate little; drink much he dared not, lest he should babble and betray himself. Then, to fly from his very self, he mounted a blood mare he had retrained, and dashed helter-skelter over the park, leaving his groom far in the distance, and coming home hours afterwards with his horse in a lather, to dine in solitary state.

He wrote a guarded letter to Mary Lloyd, signing only "Stanhope;" and again a second, but no answer came. Her silence struck him with a greater chill than her indignation. He posted up to town. In spite of the weather, which tried him severely, he began to take long walks, into the circuit of which Lupus Street was sure to come every half-hour.

There was something unnatural in the silence of Miss Lloyd's house for a school. No string of little misses issued forth at noon with bags and slates; no little faces peeped surreptitiously over the wire-blind; there was no echo of music-practice heard in the quiet street.

A light in an upper window at night—a doctor's gig calling morning and evening—filled his soul with agony and apprehension. The doctor's groom, thinking no wrong to take a fee like his master, let out that a young lady was "lyin' ill of brain fever, an' not like to get better."

Truly Mr. Stanhope's punishment had begun. What would he not have given for the right to penetrate to the sick room, and minister to the poor creature he had himself stricken down?

He introduced himself to the doctor, and then introduced a noted physician; laid Covent Garden Market under contribution, and sent in anonymously jellies and chickens sufficient to supply a household of invalids.

Youth and a sound constitution triumphed. In January, Mary Lloyd re-collected her scattered flock, and having aged years in those two past months, set herself resolutely to work as an antidote to care.

And now she wrote to Mr. Stanhope to reject emphatically the use of Oliver Craven's annuity.

It was in vain he urged that he owed her reparation, even if she persisted in rejecting him, and that Oliver Craven's money belonged of right to her. She returned for answer, "I can be silent without a bribe;" accompanied by the deed-of-gift torn in pieces.

"Firm as granite—and as silent, I know—is the rock on which I have wrecked my hopes," said he who to the world and to us is Alfred Stanhope. "But I will prove to her that I have legal right to bear my father's name, and to sit in his ancestral home; and I will make my name known and respected beyond a *posse* of fox-hunting squires."

CHAPTER V
AT THE BAR

All that year a demon of unrest seemed to possess Stanhope; he returned at last the calls of such county people as were not inveterate sportsmen. The Court was surrendered to upholsterers, and Mrs. Hudson rejoiced in preparations for the reception of guests to enliven the gloomy mansion. Women angled for the interesting man with the prematurely grey hair, burning eyes, aristocratic bearing, and fine estate; yet there was not a member of the Warwickshire Hunt but grieved over the degenerate scion of a race whose stud and pack had been the boast of the shire for centuries.

He visited, and was visited. He overlooked his estate himself, went and came, searching the registers of all the out-of-the-way churches in and about Doncaster, where Margaret Craven had met Sir Oliver Stanhope at the races; and he found time also to resume his law studies, and the examination and docketing of old papers.

Yet the shadow never lifted from his brow, and warmth never seemed to penetrate his chilly frame. To Mr. Falconer he had explained that he had been premature in addressing Miss Lloyd, who was not cast in the common mould; and that she had rejected alike his suit and settlement as insults. So true—and yet so false in everything!

So it got bruited abroad that Alfred Stanhope's gloom and eccentricities grew out of a love disappointed; and even his own servants accepted the story, his valet having somewhat to say of a miniature worn round his master's neck, and kissed and gazed at in supposed privacy.

And so the months went on to the anniversary of the day when

Oliver Craven and Alfred Stanhope changed places. The glorious sun poured in through the library window, and, as usual, the red quarterings stained floor and table as if with pools of blood; at least, so the nervously-sensitive man deemed. But he had just made the discovery of a *fact* which closed his eyes to fancies.

An old, worn register of the marriage of Oliver Stanhope and Margaret Craven, spinster, performed in the parlour of the Clifford Arms, Skipton, by John Knowles, Clerk in Holy Orders, and witnessed by Martha and James Cragg (the innkeeper and his wife). The letters were imperative demands for money by the said John Knowles, in consideration of his having falsely denied his priesthood to the young wife some two years earlier, at the bidding of the said Oliver, which demands were attended with threats of recantation unless further bribed to hold his peace.

At the precise moment when Alfred Stanhope was thanking God for one load taken from his heart, Mrs. Hudson ran to the butler in his pantry, white and trembling.

"Oh! Mr. Judkins, I declare I've just seen Oliver Stanhope and his dog walk from the picture gallery, and cross the corridor to the library door!"

"Nonsense, Mrs. Hudson! You're dreaming."

"I tell you I saw him; people don't dream in broad daylight. I mean him when he was young. He looked as if he had walked out of a picture frame. I declare I trem——Hark! what's that!"

The ferocious barking of a dog was heard from the library; servants, mindful of their master's interdict, rushed thither to remove the intruder. Opening the first door, sounds of scuffling were heard to mingle with the bark; a groan, a fall, and—stillness.

They found their master extended in a fit on the floor, the red lights from the window staining his face and hands, which still grasped the precious certificate.

His neckcloth was loosened; water was dashed over him; still he did not revive. A groom, with some knowledge of veterinary matters, drew a lancet from his pocket, and bared his arm for blood-letting, exposing a terrible scar. There was another on the throat.

As he plunged in his lancet he said, "Them's oncommon like dog-bites, them be. No wonder th' squire hates 'em mortally."

The bleeding doubtless saved his life, and the groom pocketed his reward; but Alfred Stanhope left the Court shortly afterwards and seldom returned to it—never in the autumn.

He took a house in Cavendish-square, and chambers in the Temple, and after the necessary study and formulas emerged a full-blown barrister, to the surprise of all his circle. He had turned to active work to shut out troublesome thought.

To Mary Lloyd he sent duplicate copies of all documents which attested his birth, and implored her, seeing indeed he was a Stanhope, to receive him once again. What tears, what anguish it cost her to deny him, how she wavered, he never knew; he only read her brief "I cannot," and crushed the letter up in a paroxysm of mute agony.

Had he needed briefs they would have been as rare as the dodo; he was rich and fashionable, and they came to him in shoals. Perchance after the first start his sound early-acquired legal knowledge, his acumen, and terse, trenchant eloquence might, in a measure, account for this. He rose rapidly, passing older and less influential men on the road, until his fiftieth year saw him appointed to a vacant judgeship. Envy and congratulations followed him to the bench.

Ah, little knew his foes or his flatterers of his haunted life, of the fits which grasped, and shook, and worried him, when August suns were bright and fierce! Little knew they of the miniature and marriage certificate worn together close to that man's heart. In the twenty years which had elapsed since he took possession of Stanhope Court, society had discussed and forgotten many romances more recent than his, and match-making matrons had given him up as impracticable for very many years.

His appointment was yet new, when in the Autumn Assizes he sat on the bench, for he first time, in a large seaport town within his circuit.

Amongst the names on the charge-sheet Judge Stanhope noted those of James Smith and Owen Nicholson, accused of piracy, mutiny, and murder on the high seas. There were a number of counts in the indictment, some of which dated back more than twenty years. A mate, who had turned informer, was the chief evidence against them.

The judge was observed to flush frequently during this trial, and to make several efforts to taste the water in a glass before him, yet to pit it down ere it reached his lips.

The piracy was the more recent offence. The prisoners, with others not in custody, had taken forcible possession of a barque, to which they were attached as able-bodied seamen, had put the captain and officers ashore in the Antilles, and, hoisting the black flag, had committed outrages enough to hang them three times over.

It is with James Smith our story lies. Under the *alias* of John Jackson, he had formed an item in the crew of the Begum. He was now indicted for that, with others not in custody, he had, on the 4th August, 182—, in the spirit and act of mutiny, murdered, or connived at the murder, of Captain Manners and certain other officers of the said Begum, together with one Oliver Craven, a passenger.

The prisoner pleaded "No guilty;" but the evidence of the informer was too strong to be shaken. The jury, without leaving their box, declared the man guilty on all the counts. At this stage the judge, who was evidently ill, appeared scarcely able to proceed with the case.

As he put to each prisoner in turn the question whether he had anything to say in arrest of judgment, the court was electrified by the change which came alike over the prisoner at the bar and the judge on the bench.

"Ay, my lord, I have this to say, that I am *not guilty* of the murder of Oliver Craven, and that *you, Oliver Craven*, sitting there alive, to judge other men, know it! And I accuse *you*, my lord, in spite of wig and gown, or the murder of your master, Alfred Stanhope, as was our passenger on the Begum!"

His words rushed like a torrent of lava through the breathless stillness of the court; and the very officials, who pressed forward to check him, themselves fell back at the wave of his brown hands, and his impetuous speech.

"Ay, ay, my lord," he cried, "for all so grand as you sit there, I know *you* and you know *me*. Didn't I see you steal up the companion-ladder and shoot Mr. Stanhope down with his own pistol? And when your master's dog sprang upon you, and would have worried you, didn't I shoot the brave beast through the head to save the life of the sneaking cur as wasn't worth it? And if we left you aboard to take your chance, what better did you deserve? Who made the men discontented first? You, Oliver Craven! I call God to witness I tell no lie!"

The officials rushed forward to stop him, but at this juncture a low growl was heard in the court. All eyes were turned to the bench, towards which the prisoner pointed with an excited gesture, and a quick—"See! See!"

The impalpable form of a man, who might have been Judge Stanhope's younger brother, stood by his side, fitting a halter round his neck; and there, too, a tawny foxhound crouched in act to spring.

Horror fell upon the court.

The face of the judge purpled, foam issued from his mouth and flecked his scarlet robes, and from his black and gaping lips came a sound more like a bark than aught human.

He fell forward, snapping at those who would have supported him.

The court was adjourned; the sentence of the prisoners deferred.

But the judge was carried from the court to die in his robing-room—according to doctors—of hydrophobia, the virus of which must have been for all those twenty years lurking in his veins.

Can we say that judgment had been deferred in this case? If so, it had been pronounced at last—and executed!

In a will made many years before, he had left Stanhope Court and all which is contained to Mary Lloyd. But the quiet maiden lady refused to administer, and the place—with its evil reputation of being haunted—passed to strangers.

A DOUR WEIRD

CHAPTER I

FORETOLD

"LASSIE, beware how ye wed! Ye will hea walth o' wooers, for weel the bees ken whar to find the honey; an' amang them I see a braw Cummerland lad haudin' a pleugh, but ye aye turn awa'. Ah, weel! A dour weird lies before ye, an' ye choose wrang. Again I hear the sound o' the pipes; see the fluttering o' the tartan, an' anither braw chiel wi' dirk an' claymore, an' the front of a Wallace—an' from *him* ye turn not awa'! I hear, too, the clash o' swords, the roar o' battle. Ah, lassie, I daur na tell ye a' I see. But there's a leal an true guidman for ye, there are brave bairns, an' ye sall die on your ain bed under your ain roof, an' yer ain flesh an' bluid sall close your auld e'en. But, mark ye, lassie, gin ye quit Cummerland ye sall never see your bonnie face in the Eden again, never sit on your father's hearth-stane mair, an' whar ye were born ye will na' be buried. I wad tell ye mair, but it is na' weel to ken a' the weird ye maun dree."[63]

---

63 *Meaning*: 'Girl, beware how you wed! You will have plenty of wooers, for well the bees know where to find the honey; and among them I see a fine Cumberland lad holding a plough, but you always turn away. Ah, well! A hard fate lies before you, if you choose wrong. Again I hear the sound of the pipes; see the fluttering of the tartan, and another fine fellow with dirk and claymore, and the front of a Wallace—and from him you do not turn away! I hear, too, the clash of swords, the roar of battle. Ah, girl, I dare not tell you all I see. But there's a loyal and true husband for you, there are brave children, and you shall die on your own bed under your own roof, and your own flesh and blood shall close your old eyes. But, mark you, girl, if you quit Cumberland you shall never see your pretty face in the Eden again, never more sit on your father's hearth-stone, and where you were born you will not be buried. I would tell you more, but it is not good to know all the fate you must endure.'

Thus spoke, with impressible tone and varying expression, Margery Grant, the noted Scottish spae-wife,[64] to Susan Gray, of Wetherall, whom she had met casually on the bridge over the Eden, and, as if impelled by some resistless power, had clasped by the wrist and drawn out of observation to the water-side, where Corby Castle towered high above them.

It was the shadowy hour when day weds night, and the young heart is most susceptible of outer influences. Shadows of rocks and trees deepened in the watery mirror beneath, in which a single star was looking for the new moon, and a faint breeze went like a whisper through the woods, as the mysterious creature, muffled in a shepherd's plaid, threw into the stream of the girl's life a fateful stone to ruffle its surface for evermore. The whole country-side stood in awe of Margery, who, by sprinkling water from a holy well on the sick, cured disease, who held the key of the future in her grip, and yet never blighted man or beast with the glance of an evil eye. No wonder, therefore, that Susan's natural awe was intensified by the accessories of time and scene; which gave dramatic effect to the witch-like crone's tones and gestures, and impressed her voluntary communication on her young hearer with all the force of revelation.

She was but sixteen at the time, as bonnie a lass as any in Cumberland; frank, fearless, and independent; a girl after Farmer Gray's own heart; but a change fell upon her that night, and that old sybil made or marred her fortune. For Susan Gray was born in the last century, when Superstition walked boldly through the land, sat in high places, and had his strongholds among the mountains of the North. The picture drawn of the "braw chiel wi' the front

64 Fortune teller.

o' Wallace" haunted her imagination. She had longings to see the world whence came the fine visitors to Corby Castle; and had in her mind an ideal not to be approached by any Cumbrian lad she met at Carlisle fair or market.

People—there are people everywhere—said she was too proud and independent; but when the croakers prognosticated that "Pride would hev a faw,"[65] the farmer answered briskly, "Then independence wull pu her up agean. I'se held my awn, an I mean te deu, and Susan wull ho'd her aw too, or I's mista'en."[66] At one-and-twenty she was a study for a painter, in her full dark skirt and short linen overgown. Her bust was full and round, her form erect, her head well poised, her step springy; health tinged her somewhat high cheeks and shapely arms, the hair braided smoothly beneath her linen cap was brown, only one shade lighter than the bright, dark, steadfast eyes which so plainly had a will in them.

By this time, however, her father had begun to think a little less independence might be quite as satisfactory, as one after another wooer was sent adrift with a hole in his heart, to sink or swim, until only one remained. Reckless Rob had enlisted, Stephen Heskett consoled himself with Dinah Bleckett, Watty Carel made her cousin Tib his guidwife. Only Dick Dalton, of Stainbrig, still hung on her footsteps, and loitered in the kirkgarth on Sundays,[67] sighing if she spoke to another, reddening if she smiled on him—six feet of shyness! Dame Gray, amongst her many duties on the farm, yet found leisure to lament Susan's lost

65 'Pride would have a fall.'

66 'Then independence will pull her up again. I've held my own, and I mean to do, and Susan will hold her own too, or I'm mistaken.'

67 Kirkgarth: churchyard.

chances. Bell, her youngest sister (who had more than an eye on Dick Dalton), twitted her openly, until her father asked her if she meant to remain single all her life, or to take up the crooked stick at last.[68]

At this she only tossed her handsome head, and with a light laugh replied, "Mappen I may."[69]

It was the very fear of taking the crooked stick that had kept her single; she was by no means so unconcerned about the future as she assumed to be. As she sat by the light of the peat fire in winter, or by the open door in the long summer evenings, spinning the wool from her father's sheep, or knitting his long grey hose, her soul filled with anxious longings to see the "braw chiel wi' the front o' Wallace." How could she make choice between swordsman and ploughman unless she saw a chance of both? Now and then an officer on his way to Corby Castle addressed her with familiar admiration, but only the uniform was braw; and the expected soldier-laddie had not made his appearance.

As the time went by she began to think she might as well make up her mind to sit up at night after the old folk and Bell had gone to bed, and when next she saw Dick Dalton's wistful eye looking in at the curtainless window, to open the door to him, and to acknowledge him her sweetheart in old Cumberland fashion. He would have a better farm than theirs when his father died, and that he loved her well she knew.

Still the forecast of the "dour weird" made her hesitate. What if she waited until St. John's Eve, and tried her fortune, as other lasses did, before she decided? Midsummer was close at hand.

---

68 A crooked stick: a worthless, idle or dishonest man.

69 * May happen, probably.

With Susan thought resolved itself into action; but when St. John's Eve came, and she prepared to question fate, tales of terror and mischance to venturous maids whose timidity overcame their courage flashed across her brain, and her heart beat fast with superstitious dread. Still her purpose held. Unknown to human being (for that was imperative) she provided in secret for the silent midnight supper, which her pre-ordained husband was expected to partake with her, either in the flesh or the spirit.

At noon she prepared this with an impromptu attempt at divination, profoundly credited in the North. Whilst shelling peas, she found a pod containing the mystic nine. This she suspended over the doorway, watching eagerly for the first male foot that should cross the threshold. She helped her mother with the cookery as if in a dream. Presently a child's cry was heard, and little Alick Carel came into the kitchen with blood on his face and frock, sobbing aloud. He had fallen and cut himself.

It was nothing disastrous, but Susan, blanching and trembling, stood motionless, until restored by the asperity of Mrs. Gray's renewed command, "Git a piggin o' watter an' wash the lal bairn's feace, an' dunnet stond theear like a fuile."[70]

The water was brought, the little fellow bathed and soothed, but Susan did not regain her composure. What might the blood portend? It was an ill omen in any case, though she knew no one whose name began with A. C.

Strong and hearty as she was, her forebodings so unnerved her that she was allowed to retire early to rest on the plea of sickness (her fast unbroken as a condition of the midnight incantation),

---

[70] *Meaning*: 'Get a pitcher of water and wash the little child's face, and don't stand there like a fool.'

with no further remark than the bantering chance hit of her father, "Thou snafflin', thou'st niver due for a sowdger's wife, gif thou tworn seec at the seight of a drap o' two o' bluid."[71]

She preserved silence by counterfeiting sleep when Bell came to bed. But there was little thought of sleep. For the first time within her memory, she lay awake counting the time by heart-beats more than by the drowsy clock below.

Long after the last stroke of eleven had died away, she slipped warily from her sleeping sister's side, dressed quietly in the moonlight, and stole downstairs, her face whiter than the muslin kerchief which covered her heaving bosom. Her first care was to rouse the fire, kept alight on the hearth by the "gathering peat." Then she spread a home-spun, grass-bleached cloth on the three-legged table, laid on it bread and cheese, and the "dumb-cake," mysteriously baked by herself for the awful ceremony, a jug of ale, two drinking horns, two wooden platters, and two knives. After placing two stools at the table with fingers trembling at their own daring, she drew back the thick wooden bolt, pulled the door open wide, and took her seat at the board five minutes before midnight, with her pale face turned towards the door.

Her breath seemed to thicken, and her heart to beat louder with every pulsation of the pendulum behind her, whilst the effort to maintain rigid silence became insupportable.

Afraid to look at door or window, her eyes wandered from the glowing fire to the rafters. She counted involuntarily the pendant hams and flitches, the oat cakes in the cratch, the platters and mugs on the shelf; but at the first stroke of *twelve*, her eye was arrested

71 'You snuffling, you'd never do for a soldier's wife, if you turn sick at the sight of a drop or two of blood.'

by a man's face at the window—*not* Dick Dalton's.

Before the last stroke ceased to vibrate, a Highland soldier in full costume presented himself in the doorway, and receiving no answer to his first free salutation, "How's a wi' ye the nicht?"[72] doffed his plumed bonnet and bent his tall shoulders to enter.

Fain would Susan have fled, but fear glued her to the seat. Had she indeed evoked from the spirit world this "braw chiel" to share her charmed repast? "Are ye expectin' the guidman, lassie, that ye sit by your lane sea late?"[73] questioned he advancing.

Susan's lips were compressed as much by resolution as terror.

"Are ye frightened, my bonnie doo, that ye sit there a' in a swither? Ye need na, lassie; Archie Cameron is no the chiel to harm man or woman, save at the word o' command, an' on the field o' battle."[74]

He drew his lofty figure up proudly as he uttered his own name. Like a flash, the initials struck her as those of Alick Carel; so, too, came the swift thought that here was "the front o' Wallace," and the warm blood rushed to cheek and brow only to retire, leaving her pale as before. That this was mortal man had no place in her thought.

"The guidman's unco late," he resumed, "but maybe, lassie, it's a sweetheart ye're waitin' for, an' ye did na' luik for a stranger. But neither guidman nor sweetheart wad grudge bit an' sup to a

[72] *Meaning*: 'How's it with you tonight?'

[73] *Meaning*: 'Are you expecting the master of the house, girl, that you sit by yourself so late?'

[74] *Meaning*: 'Are you frightened, my pretty dove, that you sit there all in a quandary? You need not, girl; Archie Cameron is not the fellow to harm man or woman, save at the word of command, and on the field of battle.'

tired sodger-body wha's lost his way in the mirk."[75]

He had seated himself opposite to her, and did not see, as she did, pressed against the small panes of the window the face of Dick Dalton almost as ashen as her own.

"Gin ye canne speak, or daur na speak, gie me a sign that ye hearken till me, an' that I am welcome to sup wi' ye."[76]

Terrified as much by the sight of Dick Dalton at that unwonted hour as by the apparition before her, she bowed her head from sheer inability to hold up. Taking it as a sign of assent, her visitor helped himself plentifully to the cake and cheese, poured out a horn of ale, and before drinking, nodded to her, saying heartily, "Here's till ye, bonnie lassie; wussing ye a kind guidman, an' suin!"[77]

Quite three parts of an hour had fled, when, pushing aside his platter, he rose, and drawing nearer, said, "Mony thanks, my bonnie lassie, for your hospitality, for ye *are* bonnie, gin ye hae no that muckle to say. Gin the guidman had bin at hame, I wad hae asked for a night's lodgin', an' a hantle o' bracken for a bed; but ye are a' alane, an' a maiden's guid name is suin tint, so Archie Cameron wull aye march awa', lest he sould rob a guid an' fair lassie o' her best tocher. A dirk wadna wound mair than those bright e'en, an' I'll ne'er forget this night, nor thee, puir dumb lammie. An' noo,

---

[75] *Meaning*: 'The master of the house is very late… but maybe, girl, it's a sweetheart you're waiting for, and you didn't look for a stranger. But neither husband nor sweetheart would grudge food and drink to a tired soldier who's lost his way in the dark.'

[76] Meaning: 'If you can't speak, or dare not speak, give me a sign that you harken to me, and that I am welcome to drink with you.'

[77] *Meaning*: 'Here's to you, pretty girl, wishing you a kind husband, and soon!'

tak' this ae kiss fra' Archie Cameron to keep him in mind."[78]

As he stooped to touch her reddening forehead with his lips, a groan and a rush outside were audible. Susan's overstrained nerves gave way. She dropped from her seat in a swoon as the handsome Highlander started after the retreating figure of despairing Dick Dalton.

The cloth and its contents, dragged from the table when she fell, and the clatter of falling wood and delf, roused the household. Alegar[79] and burnt feathers restored her to her senses, but no explanation would Susan vouchsafe: maidenly shame and superstitious dread alike kept her silent.

The farmer and his dame from their box-bed in the adjoining room had overheard a man's voice and step, and congratulated themselves that Susan had opened the door to Dick at last. When Dick held aloof, and kept silent, not caring to witness or proclaim the supposed triumph of a rival, they just as sapiently concluded that the brief courtship had resulted in a lovers' quarrel, which they looked for time to heal.

The girl's secret preyed upon her. No neighbours spoke of a Highland soldier seen in the village. No Scotch regiment had been quartered in Carlisle. The mystery strengthened her belief in the supernatural.

---

78 'Many thanks, my pretty girl, for your hospitality, for you *are* pretty, if you have not that much to say. If the master of the house had been at home, I would have asked for a night's lodging, and a quantity of bracken for a bed; but you are all alone, and a maiden's good name is soon lost, so Archie Cameron will always march away, lest he should rob a good and fair girl of her best dowry. A dirk would not wound more than those bright eyes, and I'll never forget this night, nor you, poor dumb lamb. And now, take this one kiss from Archie Cameron to keep him in mind.'

79 * Alegar: what we call vinegar was formerly made from sour ale and called alegar; it was only vinegar when made from wine.

Every wave of the golden hair, or glance of the clear blue eyes, every feature of the manly face, or motion of the stalwart form impressed upon the retina, had left only the conviction of a phantom drawn thither by a potent spell. Would the living man ever appear?

She grew fitful, restless. Weeks, months rolled on. The sight of little Alick made her shudder. Dick Dalton, his jealous fever over, again hung at her heels, but no Archie Cameron came wooing to Wetherall.

She took to wandering by the Eden after the kye were milked and her work done;[80] and gossips meeting her on the bridge smirked to think that it lay midway between her home and Stainbrig. It was there, however, that Margery Grant had planted a thorn in her breast, and inchoate yearnings to meet and further question the wise woman prompted these twilight rambles.

It fell out that one evening as she stood by the water side, within the shadow of the bridge, knitting mechanically, and looking dreamily into the stream, asking herself if it were right that leal Dick Dalton should be set aside for a cantrip ghost, the fateful old crone touched her on the shoulder.

"Weel, Susie Gray, an hae ye no made your choice yet?"

Susan started, the witch-like woman had come upon her so stealthily, the grey plaid in which she was wrapped leaving her outline dim and indistinct in the twilight.

"Ah, no, dame, but," Susan's voice sank to a whisper, "I've seen the wraith o' the Hielan' sowdger."[81] Then she poured into the wise woman's ear the secret she had kept from her own friends, nay, almost from her own heart, that she was in love with the ghost she had

80 Kye: cows.

81 *Meaning*: 'I've seen the wraith of the Highland soldier.'

invoked. Not that she *said* so, but it needed no witch to infer so much from her eagerness to overleap the present and pry into futurity.

Margery's reluctance only made Susan more eager; but when, with a motion as if she washed her conscience of the consequences, and a "Weel, lassie, wilfu' is aye waefu', ye maun gang your ain gate,"[82] she proceeded to unfold certain spells and incantations to bring the future husband near, Susan shuddered, the remembrance of St. John's Eve having lost little of its terror.

The witch warned even while she instructed, but her own faith in the diablerie she taught was more powerful than argument.

Susan had, however, been brought up reverently, and the dread of doing that which was unholy, coupled with fears for the result, stayed her hand for many days.

Yet, impelled to tempt fate by something stronger than her reason, one Friday, about the middle of September, she rose at midnight, took an apple from her coffer, knelt down in the darkest corner of the room, and *stuck in the apple nine pins*, muttering in a voice too low to awaken Bell—

I stick thur pins i'ma luive's heart,
I wish ilk pin may pruive a deart,
T' gev him nowther rest nor peace
Till he cum to me an' bring release:[83]

commencing the incantation with the first pin and ending with the last. Then she wrapped it up and hid it amongst the clothes in her kist.

---

[82] *Meaning*: 'Well, wilful is always woeful, you must walk your own way.'

[83] *Meaning*: 'I stick these pins in my love's heart/I wish each pin may prove a dart/To give him neither rest nor peace/Till he comes to me and brings release.

Cold dew stood on her forehead, and she trembled so violently as she crept into bed that Bell awakened and asked in some concern if she was ill.

Day after day went by, but no lover, save the inevitable Dalton, came near the farm, yet Susan seemed wilfully determined to read her riddle her own way.

It was the season for laying in the winter stock of fuel. The peat had been cut, dried, brought home, and stacked with all the importance of a harvest; and all being done, there was a festive gathering for fun and frolic in the farm kitchen, as was wont on Halloween.

It was the night for spells and cantrips, open or concealed. Nuts were burned in pairs on the hearth, apples pared, and the unbroken rind thrown over the shoulder to indicate the true love's initials; boiling lead poured into water to reveal his occupation. As Susan poured her lead, it shaped itself into what the general voice called a scythe-blade, but what she herself held to be a sword.

Afraid to do her spiriting alone a second time, she prevailed on Bell to leave the party by stealth, and "sow hemp-seed" round the byre while she made the circuit of the barn on a like errand; an act supposed to need swift limbs and steady nerves; and never had she felt her courage at so low an ebb.

The night was gusty, the oaks and elms creaked and groaned, the trailing pendants of the ash swept like dishevelled tresses on the wind, dark clouds scudded across the sky, and through the changing rifts the moonbeams fell in fitful rays. It was an eerie night for such spells, to those who held that evil spirits were abroad to do the hests of man.

The fortune-seekers had not quitted the noisy kitchen wholly unperceived. At a sly hint from the farmer, Dick followed; and, after hesitating which way to take, turned to the left, lured by the flutter of a petticoat.

He ran, overtook the flying damsel, caught her in his strong arms, bent his head to inflict the penalty—and lo! he touched the lips of Bell. If he muttered an oath at the disappointment, Bell never betrayed him. It is certain she returned to the house radiant, accepting the omen in its fullest significance.

It was long before Susan re-appeared, and then in a state of extreme agitation, Twice had she made, in expectant trepidation, the circuit of the barn, one side of which was abutted on the lane, fenced off by a low wall of uneven stones. As she ran past for the third time, scattering imaginary seed, and with her head turned over the left shoulder, repeated the formula—

> Hemp-seed I sow, hemp-seed I hoe,
> Let ma future guidman cum ahint and mow,"[84]

an unsuspected listener leaped the wall, saying—

"Gin ye hae fand a tongue for siccan a Halloween cantrip, lassie, Archie Cameron was be a fuile to miss siccan chance!"[85]

A sudden gleam of moonlight fell on his face and plume, the flying maid felt that she had again raised the spirit that was a fate to her, and with an apprehensive scream fell prostrate in his path.

When she came to her senses the Highlander was sprinkling water on her face from a tiny beck close by, whither he must have borne her. He knelt upon the turf, his arm supported her, and the well-remembered voice strove to allay her apprehensions with the

---

[84] *Meaning*: 'Let my future husband come behind and mow.'

[85] *Meaning*: 'If you have found a tongue for such a Halloween spell, girl, Archie Cameron would be a fool to miss such a chance!'

assurance that he was no wraith but solid flesh—a living and breathing man.

Whether she was spell-bound or only faint she knew not: she could neither rise nor call out; the effort she made to free herself only inducing a tighter clasp.

"Nay, lassie, ye dinna gang till ye tell me your name, an' your faither's name, that I may ken what to speer for. I hae thocht mair an' suffered mair ower the white-faced dumb lammie I supped wi' o' St. John's Eve than I wad care to thole again. I hae been like a hen on a het girdle for mair nor three weeks, an' hadna orders come for the Seventy-first to garrison Carlisle, I maun e'en hae deserted, sin' I could get na leave o' absence, an' I couldna bide langer awa' frae ye ony gate."[86]

Susan thought of the apple in her coffer, and assigned to witchcraft that which was due to the more subtle power of first-sight love.

He held her fast. "Your name, my canny lassie? What do they ca' ye at hame? Wunna ye speak? Hae ye lost your tongue agen? Ye had fand it a wee syne. Tell me your name, or I maun kiss it frae your lips."[87]

Afraid lest he should put his threat into execution, she stammered out, "Susan Gray;" at the same time struggling for freedom.

---

[86] *Meaning*: 'No, girl, you don't walk till you tell me your name, and your father's name, that I may know what to ask for. I have thought more and suffered more over the white-faced dumb lamb I drank with on St. John's Eve than I would care to suffer again. I have been like a hen on a hot griddle for more than three weeks, and had not orders come for the Seventy-first to garrison Carlisle, I might even have deserted, since I could get no leave of absence, and I couldn't remain longer away from you anyway.'

[87] *Meaning*: 'Your name, my gentle girl? What do they call you at home? Won't you speak? Have you lost your tongue again? You had found it a short time ago. Tell me your name, or I must kiss it from your lips.'

"Susan, my fluttering doo, I'll gie ye liberty noo, but ye ken I cam to mow the hemp-seed ye were sowin', and so hae guid right to mak' your lips my ain."[88]

A kiss fell upon her lips. The strong arms released her; and in a swirl of undefined emotions she fled into the house without even a response to his "Guid nicht!"

Dalton, coming to seek her, saw her break from a soldier's arms, and remembering the supper scene he had witnessed, turned back sharply, to devote himself to Bell for the rest of the evening, in the very revenge of jealousy.

Her lover's paraded defection was lost upon Susan, whose usually firm mind was almost shaken from its balance by the daring act of the night, and its mysterious climax. Man or ghost, the soldier had been drawn thither by spells too powerful to resist, and how far they had been lawful she dared not think. Surely she had not been tempting the devil to her own destruction? Surely the uncanny witch-wife had not beguiled her into the clutches of the foul fiend, and so brought the "dour weird" upon her! In shuddering dread she retreated to her room, and kneeling on the white boards by the bedside put up an involuntary prayer for mercy and forgiveness.

Moreover, she resolved to take Dick Dalton into favour at once, little as she cared for him, and so blot the Scotch soldier from her memory for ever.

Alas! for her resolution. Dick Dalton perversely kept away from the farm, and Corporal Cameron contrived to accost her in Carlisle market on the Saturday; to be the frequent bearer of messages from his captain to the hospitable owner of Corby Castle,

---

[88] *Meaning*: 'Susan, my fluttering dove, I'll give you liberty now, but you know I came to mow the hemp-seed you were sowing, and so have good right to make your lips my own.'

and, his road lying past the farm, to scrape acquaintance with William Gray himself.

In less than a fortnight he was not only at liberty to open the gate and walk into the house, but was welcomed to the ingle nook, as news-bringers from the outer world were welcomed in places and times remote from post and press.

Nevertheless, the November sky did not lour more darkly, nor the Eden swell and foam with chafing rains more threateningly than did Farmer Gray with wrath, when some six weeks later Archibald Cameron asked leave to marry his eldest daughter, having her full concurrence.

He spluttered and fumed with impotent rage, ransacked his Cumbrian vocabulary for invectives wherewith to batter the inauspicious wooer, and made it quite sufficiently apparent that his "veto" was decisive.

The corporal had, however, taken too many hard knocks in his time to mind hard words; and if the imperative farmer had a dominant will, the canny Scot was blessed with a cool temper and tenacity of purpose.

Susan, standing by the open door with the hood of her grey duffel cloak drawn over her head, as a protection from the weather, heard every word of the colloquy, her heart beating time to her father's temper. Her breath came with a quick gasp as Archie's last speech fell on her ear.

"Ye may as weel keep your breath to cool your parritch, farmer; what maun be, maun be, an' ye canna wipe oot Archie Cameron from your bairn's weird as ye wad rub the ruddle fra a sheep's back. An' lang ere I pit a foot ower your doorstane, I hae seen our bonnie Susan an' myself kneelin' thegether th' kirk, before the meenister, as man an' wife. Nay, man, ye need na' laugh sae scornfully! Ye wunna be gifted wi' the second-sight, but before Heaven, I hae seen this mair than ance or twice, an' a fated weird is stronger than will of man or maid. Fair ye weel, farmer, ilka ane maun gang his ain gate."[89]

"Dinna greet, Susan lassie," whispered Cameron, interrupting his soothing words with kisses quite as consoling, ere they parted in the lane. "We maun bide a wee; your father may change his mind ere lang. He canna fight against predestined love like ours. So gang ben oot o' the rain, my ain love, an' aye put your trust in an ;'er-ruling Providence."[90]

The passionate tears had burst like a thunderstorm and were gone. And now broke forth speech as passionate, born of love and self-will, in which she avowed her determination to be his in spite of father or mother, or even fate itself. She stood erect before him, a hand in each of his, her upturned eyes flashing, responsive to the calm resolution in the eyes looking so far into the depths of her own.

Her father met her on the threshold, and enforcing his will with a leathern bridle, which he laid across he shoulders, using words that fell harder than blows, so crushed out the last spark of obedience.

---

[89] *Meaning*: 'You may as well keep your breath to cool your porridge, farmer; what must be, must be, and you can't wipe out Archie Cameron from your child's destiny as you would rub the ocher from a sheep's back. And long before I put foot over your threshold, I have seen our pretty Susan and myself kneeling together in church, before the minister, as man and wife. No, man, you need not laugh so scornfully! You won't be gifted with the second-sight, but before Heaven, I have seen this more than once or twice, and a fated destiny is stronger than will of man or maid. Farewell, farmer, every one must walk his own way.'

[90] *Meaning*: 'Don't cry, Susan girl… We must wait a while; your father may change his mind before long. He can't fight against predestined love like ours. So go in out of the rain my own love, and put your trust in an over-ruling Providence.'

When the "Kersmus cairdins" came round,[91] and the huge "yule log" blazed and crackled on the wide hearth, mocking the feeble rushlights in the tin sconces amongst the evergreens on the wall, Dick Dalton sat once more among the players, but only Bell supplied the hot ale, and Dick's jubilant mirth, like his love-making to her, was somewhat overdone.

Susan was gone! She had married the soldier against her father's will, and he had discarded her: driven his favourite daughter forth with furious threats of violence if ever she should darken his doors again.

As she fled from his frenzied wrath through the blinding snow to seek shelter and protection in her husband's quarters in Carlisle, she was haunted more by her mother's piteous tears than by her father's denunciations. Surely, the "Dour weird" had already begun to fall.

CHAPTER II
FULFILLED

In Archibald Cameron's large frame was a large heart, and he cherished, well as he could, the woman who had left home and friends for hm. But a soldier's wife finds more thorns than roses in her path, even in times of peace; and Susan, on a baggage wagon, or tramping for miles on foot with a babe in her arms, cast many a regretful glance back towards her comfortable Cumbrian home; and her wonderings if Dick Dalton had taken a wife to Staneley farm were much more frequent than her steadfast husband might have approved.

[91] In the humblest Cumbrian cottage, even where a board laid across the players' knees has to do duty for a table, cards are played at Christmas time.

Years passed; wandering, restless, adventurous years; years full of hardship, sufferings and trials, of all but repentance; for Susan had a good husband and did not repent. Archibald was promoted. Sergeant Cameron's wife wrote home to her mother a long, proud letter abounding with love for her husband, but asking no forgiveness, expressing no contrition. Yet the letter told that she had named her fourth son William, after her father, and that she never forgot her home friends in her prayers, as she still loved them all dearly.

That letter was never answered and no second was ever written. The affection thus tacitly rejected by those she had left now concentrated on the dear ones around her. The love kindled so mysteriously never flickered or died out; she was devoted as a wife and mother, as frugal, industrious, and heroic as the partner of a soldier's fortunes should be.

Cameron himself, a compound of religion and superstition, a man of iron will, held tight rein over his family; even Susan's will yielding to his, although she did resist the curb at times.

But for a soldier's wife, she was singularly fortunate in her domestic relations, and old Margery's prophecy slipped from her memory.

Each son joined the regiment as he stepped out of boyhood, Willie, her golden-haired Willie, entering the ranks at the very commencement of the Peninsular war. His brothers were tall and stalwart like the sergeant; Willie, her latest born, was of slighter build, and in his face she saw a reflex of her mother's. Thus it was that apprehensions of the "dour weird" stirred in the secret depths of her soul, quickened no doubt by the subtle instinct of maternal love. These apprehensions were strengthened by a change which came over her husband. He became gloomy and silent, his "religious exercises" took a more sombre tinge; yet, underlying all was a pitiful tenderness towards his family, which showed some deep feeling at work.

Five finer or braver men were not to be found in the ranks of the Seventy-first Highlanders when they landed in Portugal, in the August of 1808, but only Archibald and Willie came unscathed from Vimeira. As the season advanced, their retreat, hungry, ragged, and shoeless, over mountain snow or through drenching rain, told upon all—most on the boy. Susan herself seemed endowed with supernatural strength; she had water for the thirsty, bandages for the wounded, consolation for the dying.

Christmas came, pitiless, fearful; and Susan, contrasting the misery of their condition with the Christmas hearth by the silvery Eden, began to realize the truth of the witch-wife's forecast.

During a brief bivouac, Susan made her way from the baggage towards a small, ill-conditioned fire, round which Archie and their sons were grouped, sharing its little warmth with many comrades.

She found her husband sitting gloomily apart, his eyes fixed, intently fixed, not on the fire, but on the space beyond, with the strange, unearthly aspect of one who walks in his sleep.

"Archie, my man!" said she, wonderingly, "Archie!" laying her hand upon his shoulder.

To voice and touch he was alike insensible.

Presently he rose, muttering as if to himself, "Four! four! ken ye wha's the fourth?"[92] He turned his bonnet, reversed the position of his plaid, still keeping his eyes fixed on vacancy, "E'en as I thocht, e'en as I thocht!"[93]

The words dropped slowly from his rigid lips, accompanied

---

[92] *Meaning*: 'Four! four! do you know who's the fourth?"

[93] *Meaning*: 'Even as I thought, even as I thought!'

by that short upwards and downwards shake of the head which confirms ill fears.

Experience had told Mrs. Cameron that a visitation of second sight was upon her husband, and although an undefinable sense of horror and dread crept over her, as she stood with clasped hands and drawn breath watching him, she dared not attempt to rouse or disturb him until the vision had passed.

His sons and one or two comrades rose form their places on the ground, and drew closer as spasm after spasm convulsed his face and herculean frame. At length his limbs became rigid, then relaxed, and with a sigh of infinite relief he sank upon the ground exhausted, murmuring, "Not a', not a'—thank God! for puir Susie's sake."[94]

Susan, kneeling by his side, chafed his rugged hands in hers and peered anxiously into his face with the question, "What have you seen, Archie?"

"Dinna ye ask, guidwife, dinna ye ask. Sorrow comes aye suin enough. I hae had a wasfu vision. But I wunna gar ye greet ower suin."[95] And with a short wave of his hand he dismissed the subject.

It was on the fifteenth of January, the eve of the memorable battle of Corunna, when he referred to it again. Sir David Baird's troops formed the right horn of the human crescent extending between Betezos and the heights of Corunna, waiting for the morrow. Susan, as usual, moved about actively amongst the emaciated men, ministering to their wants with the feeling that common misfortune was kinship.

---

94 *Meaning*: 'Not all, not all—thank God! for poor Susie's sake.'

95 *Meaning*: 'Don't you ask, wife, don't you ask. Sorrow always comes soon enough. I have had a woeful vision. But I wouldn't make you cry too soon.'

The night was closing in when Archibald caught her by the hand, saying, in low tones, "Susan ye hae aye been a guid wife, an' a guid mither to the bairns, an' I wad ill like to part frae ye without my blessing to comfort ye when ye are left yer lane."[96]

"Alane! Archie, what dae ye mean?" she gasped, clinging to him with strange premonitory dread, infected by the solemnity of his tone and manner.

"Ah, Susan dearie, ye maun e'en pray for strength. Ye hae muckle sorrow to thole. I hae seen the smoke o' the comin' battle, an' sword an' bullet do their foul work on a' ye love—an' hae seen it for the third time this vara night."[97]

"It cannot be! I'll not believe it!" burst from the poor woman's white lips in all the agony of full belief in his previsions. "*All!* did he say, *all*?"

"Ay, danger threatens a', an' ye maun take tent o' your ainsel. But in a' His dispensations, the Lord remembers mercy, an' a remnant may escape. I saw four stark in death, but the face of one was aye turned awa'."[98]

"But yoursel, Archie, yoursel?"

"I turned my plaid as auld seers advise, an' the plaid in the vision was turned also!" was his impressive answer.

---

96 *Meaning*: 'Susan, you have always been a good wife, and a good mother to the children, and I would ill like to part from you without my blessing to comfort you when you are left by yourself.'

97 *Meaning*: 'Ah, Susan dearie, you must even pray for strength. You have much sorrow to endure. I have seen the smoke of the coming battle, and sword and bullet do their foul work on all you love—and have seen it for the third time this very night.'

98 *Meaning*: 'Yes, danger threatens all, and you must take care of yourself. But in all His dispensations, the Lord remembers mercy, and a remnant may escape. I saw four stark in death, but the face of one was always turned away.'

Susan wrung her hands, doubting not the premonition; but over their farewells, and the subsequent parting with her sons, we must draw a veil, such a veil as Susan was bidden by Cameron to hide her emotion with, lest she should damp the courage of his brave lads.

Night—morning—passed. Noon came. The French brought their guns to the front and opened fire. An attack on General Baird's division followed rapidly, and the bloody work began in earnest; the gallant Seventy-first, in spite of wounds, privations, and fatigue, showing they could yet fight and die like heroes.

At no great distance Susan was posted on a rising ground whence she could watch the conflict; ready to tend a dear one if disabled, but with a feverish, anxious, despairing look in her eyes none ever witnessed before. During the heat of the engagement, Sir James Baird was borne past her, his arm shattered by a grape shot.

Eagerly she questioned the bearers. Prompt but terrible was the response, "Sergeant an' three o' the lads down." They had fallen before a charge of cavalry.

Hardly waiting till the tide of battle receded, Susan rushed like a mad woman to the field, searching, with panting heart, amongst the dead and dying, hoping without hope, to find son or husband surviving. The first sight which met her eager eyes was the prostrate form of her darling Willie. He had just dropped, wounded by a stray shot; but he seemed on the point of expiring.

Tenderly she raised his head, and put a can of water to his blue lips; but ere a wound could be examined, a party of the enemy's cavalry in full retreat swept like a whirlwind over the field, leaving Susan barely time for the cry of despair with which she threw herself as a shield across the body of her boy. She felt the cruel beat of iron hoofs, then lost the power to feel.

A remnant of their shattered company, searching the field at the close of the battle, found the poor creature as she lay gasping, an arm and leg broken, a gash on her forehead, bruised in every limb. They raised her gently, and bore her carefully as haste would permit to one of the transport ships in the harbour, for not one man in the corps but respected the motherly wife of Sergeant Cameron.

Rough as was army surgery in those days, she bore the setting of limbs and the dressing of her wounded forehead with unflinching fortitude: anxiety for her beloved ones over-riding bodily pain.

Her tremulous inquiries were at length set at rest—But how? God help her! Hers was indeed "a dour weird." Husband and three sons had been found in one heap, *dead*. Of Willie, her youngest born, there was no trace, but there was little hope that he survived. There were men too disfigured by trampling steeds for recognition—he might be one.

How she endured her mental and physical agony was a marvel to the rough men around her. She gave no demonstrative utterance to her sorrows, but it is no doubt they retarded her recovery.

Months elapsed before she was able to quit the hospital to which she had been consigned on landing at Deal; and then she found herself cast upon the world, homeless, friendless, and almost penniless.

An old piper of the regiment named Rae, a Paisley man, got a memorial drawn up, which Colonel Cadogan endorsed and forwarded. But great is the inertia of circumlocution! No pension, no recognition of any kind came to the stricken heroine, the wife and mother of heroes. Susan Cameron was left to drift, one of England's many martyrs to martial glory.

She was herself too independent to persist in importunities. For the same reason she scorned in her distressed widowhood to crave help of the relatives who had disowned her when a cherished wife. Had Colonel Cadogan remained in England, Susan's case might not have been overlooked, but all things conspired against her. In May the Colonel and Piper Rae also were included in the draft from the Seventy-first sent back to the seat of war.

Ere they started, the friendly old piper bestirred himself to raise a subscription amongst his comrades for their sergeant's widow. The money was given freely, and pressed upon her as a farewell token of respect, else her native pride had certainly ignored her poverty, and prompted its rejection.

Susan, in humble but sombre widow's weeds, watched the two frigates sail from Deal harbour, bearing with them her only friends, and as the hulls sank below the horizon she felt her heart sink with them. A friendless, childless widow, with enfeebled frame, and shattered constitution, she was realizing in all its force the "dour weird" which had followed her choice of a husband. Yet, keenly as she felt her situation, there was no looking back with regret to Dick Dalton.

She was more engrossed in contemplation of Margery Grant's prophecy, and her own slaughtered husband's second-sight previsions. Like Pandora's box, there was Hope at the bottom. What had been true in part, might be true in all. Cameron's eerie vision had shown but *four* slain. Where was the fifth, the lad whose corpse had not been found? Might not *he* be the one of her ain on whose breast her dying head was to pillow?

Nerved by this hope she bent her steps northward, a woman aged by afflictions, not years. Her small store of money she sewed in the lining of her stiff bodice, keeping a small reserve for use, and too poor to pay coach-fare, took her way on foot to Edinburgh, hoping to find a welcome amongst her dear Archibald's friends.

Pass we over the long and weary journey, the perils of the road, her expedients to pay honestly, yet without money, for temporary accommodation at wayside farm or inn. Her knitting pins were bright with use, and her rapid fingers far outstripped her poor lame limbs on the homeward journey.

A June sun was blazing in the sky when the footsore wayfarer turned into the bye-lane which led from the Carlisle road to Weatherall and Stainbrig, impelled by strong yearnings towards the place of her birth and the home friends from whom she had been so long estranged.

Alas! for the re-visitor! What found she? A grave in the kirkgarth, where slept her mother. A new wife on her father's hearth; Bell reigning in the Dalton farm. Change everywhere, the saddest in herself, to whom no old friend stretched out a hand in recognition or greeting.

Sad and sick at heart she laved her heated brow and feet in the little beck whence Corporal Cameron had baptized her to himself on that fateful Michaelmas eve; then, without a sign, she turned her back for ever on Cumberland and all that it contained.

Her funds were low when she reached Edinburgh. But Susan's unconquerable spirit was not the one to flag at her journey's end. Of Cameron's relations she found but one, a far-awa' cousin, a shopkeeper in the Luckenbooths. Here kinship was a passport; she was welcomed hospitality for her dead guidman's sake, poor though she was.

It was not in Susan's nature to outstay her welcome. Her first conversation with Dugald Cameron convinced him she had not come to be a burden. If her misfortunes and sufferings excited benevolent sympathy, much more did her independence win his esteem. From a friend of his she obtained, at a nominal rent, a small cottage at the foot of Salisbury Crags, which her well-hoarded money just sufficed to furnish with absolute necessities. These comprised a camp-bed, a three-legged table, a couple of chairs, a low stool or two, a kist for meal, and another for clothes, a girdle for bannocks, platters, pots and pans. To these she added a spinning-wheel and a small stock of poultry.

And now began another phase of Susan's eventful life. A kindly word dropped here and there by Dugald Cameron soon found the sedate soldier's widow purchasers in Edinburgh for her eggs and chickens. Then, while her hens clucked, her knitting-pins twinkled, and her spinning-wheel hummed, and for some years she held her head bravely, a woman who, but for the injuries she had sustained, would have been in the prime of life and activity.

But the "dour weird" had fallen heavily. In the twenty-three years of her wandering life, the horrors she had witnessed, the shocks she had received, the heats of India, the snows of Corunna, had told on her constitution, and at forty-three she bore the stamp of another decade. She had exchanged a stirring, gregarious life for monotony and solitude. The drowsy hum of her wheel, and the tic-tic-tic of her knitting pins filled up no vacuum, but followed in low undertones the sorrowful or anxious train of her thoughts from the bloody battle-field, where husband and sons were lost, to that speculative region occupied by her boy Willie, and that one word, "missing;" her anxious unsatisfied yearnings only giving poignancy to her desolation.

She had lived about three or four years at St. Leonards, when an unexpected stone was thrown into this continuous current of thought, breaking it up into whirling eddies.

With a basket of eggs balanced on her head, one fine spring morning she bent her steps towards Edinburgh, busily knitting a blue worsted overall the way, as was her wont. Where the wall of the King's Park skirted the high road there was a stile for ingress and egress.

Seated on this was a poor feeble creature, whose age, computed by wrinkles and decrepitude, must have been nearly a hundred, gasping and struggling in the tearing grasp of an asthmatic cough. Her plaid and mutch were displaced,[99] her grey hair straggled over her face and neck, her skirts were torn and bedraggled. She had evidently passed the night on that inhospitable bed, too weak to pursue her journey.

Susan's compassion was stirred. "Mother," said she (her Cumbrian dialect had worn itself out in her long march over the world), "you seem weary and faint; drink this." She had unslung the canteen she still carried camp-fashion when she went abroad, and presented a draught of milk to the parched and palsied lips. "Are you far from hame? Can I help you?" proffering oat-cake from her wallet as she spoke.

The poor creature munched it eagerly, murmuring between each mouthful, "Eh! woman, but ye're gude an' kin'! but ye dinna ken wha ye hae gien your awmous to, or may be ye wad hae left the feckless auld witch-wife to die her 'lane. Sair worn am I wi' my lang journey ower mair than ninety miles o' life, an' hame canna' be far awa'. But wha cares a bodle gin Margery Grant dies by the roadside, wi' a stane for her pillow, or amang the green rashes o' a festerin' pool?"[100]

Susan recoiled with a start. "Margery Grant!" Could this be the same who had spaed her fortune full five and twenty years before?

---

[99] Mutch: linen cap.

[100] *Meaning*: 'Eh! woman, but you're good and kind! but you don't know who you have given your alms to, or maybe you would have left the feckless old witch-wife to die alone. Sorely worn am I with my long journey over more than ninety miles of life, and home can't be far away. But who cares a bodle (a copper coin) if Margery Grant dies by the roadside, with a stone for her pillow, or among the green rushes of a festering pool?'

If so, she who had then foretold the "dour weird" was surely the one to lift the veil now and set anxiety at rest.

"Ay, woman! Margery Grant! Does the name sting thee? It's like, noo ye ken me, ye grudge the bit and drap that hae keepit the life in the auld doited body. Weel, weel, it's muckle time I won hame."[101]

"Nay, Margery, if the fortune ye telled me lang syne did set my silly head running on soldier laddies, ye aye warned me to beware how I wed. There is no fleeing from fate, and I had more than one token. But truly the 'dour weird' ye foretold to the thoughtless lass on the banks o' the bonnie Eden had been a dour weird indeed!" and Susan shook her head mournfully.

The old woman strove to rise. Mrs. Cameron helped her to her feet. Margery put her hand to her forehead with a gesture indicative of recurring memory. "Eh, woman, but I mind it a noo. Ye ken, I spake o' a sweet drap o' comfort i' th' grunds o' th' bitter cup. But I trow it's weary waitin' at mirk midnight for the sun to rise."[102]

A deep sigh testified Susan's assent.

Loth to leave the decrepit old crone to perish from neglect, she took her basket on one arm and Margery on the other, and retrod the path to her cottage, with a hasty resolve to shelter the forlorn castaway, whose word had so deeply influenced her life.

Margery's tottering steps made progress slow. The neat cottage once reached, Susan seated her charge on a low chair by the ingle, with a corner of her plaid fanned the gathering peat on the hearth

---

[101] *Meaning*: 'Yes, woman! Margery Grant! Does the name sting you? It's likely, now you know me, you grudge the food and drink that has kept the life in the old stupid body. Well, well, it's about time I was home.'

[102] *Meaning*: 'Eh, woman, but I remember it now. You know, I spoke of a sweet drop of comfort in the grounds of the bitter cup. But I know it's weary waiting at the pitch black of midnight for the sun to rise.'

to a glow, and, putting some sowens into a saucepan,[103] soon set a smoking bowl of porridge before her charge.

Susan never did things by halves. The morning was advancing, and her errand could not bide. As a safeguard against fire, she put the old spae-wife in her own bed, left food and drink within reach, mounted her basket and again set off towards the city, the grateful thanks of a rescued fellow-being lightening her load.

Housed, warmed, and fed, Margery Grant recovered, and Susan was no longer lonely. Then she had to work for two, so had less time to brood over the past, and faith in Margery's hopeful previsions kept her up wonderfully. Indeed, she had need of some mental support, the persecution which followed the old fortune-teller appearing to cast its shadow over her protectress.

That which should have been her highest honour only aroused credulous suspicion; the slight halt in her own gait, the knowledge (gathered in many lands) of strange herbs and simples, her style of dress (the wallet and canteen to wit), all marked her out for the shafts of ignorance and superstition, which, in time, made themselves felt; and the "twa witches thegither,"[104] as the country folk dubbed them, sank to extreme poverty. Through this Mrs. Cameron struggled nobly, asking no alms, accepting no eleemosynary aid, though penury sat down by her side with sharp threatenings to put out the fire, and sweep out the meal kist.

Five or six years passed, when Margery, quick to note her friend's despondence, roused like the flickering of a spent candle, and stood before her, the embodiment of an ancient sibyl, the fire of prophecy in her eye and on her cheek. Pressing one withered

103 * Oatmeal steeped in water.

104 Two witches together.

hand on the other's shoulder, she spoke in earnest tones—

"Susan Cameron, look up! Dinna fash yoursel' wi' care for the future. Ye hae been to me as the widow of Zarepath to Elijah, and fear not that *your* cruse o' oil shall fail or your meal be spent in the barrel, till the Lord sendeth his blessed rain on the earth. An' it's comin' Susan, comin'; I see the sma' wee cloud that comes to shed on the dry wilderness o' your existence the tender rain o' new life. Susan woman, ye shall be fed an' clothed, and see yer ain when these auld limbs lie under the mools. I see your gowden-haired Willie comin', comin', but he's far awa' yet, an' there's sma' glint o' gold in his pouch, or in his locks."[105]

Susan started to her feet in awe and expectation. Margery uplifted a finger to bespeak attention.

"Hark, did ye no' hear the rustlin' wings, and the weird voice o' the angel o' Death callin' the auld witch-wife to rest? Hark!"

The upraised hand dropped, the fiery eye dimmed; the glow of inspiration on her cheek faded to a dull grey; the frame collapsed, and that which Susan caught ere it fell was but a relic of Margery Grant.

In the old woman's leathern stays was found gold enough to bury her and leave a surplus, doubly acceptable to Susan, whom starvation and rheumatism alike held in their grip. It enabled her to make her house once more weathertight, and to renew her stock

---

105 *Meaning*: 'Susan Cameron, look up! Don't trouble yourself with care for the future. You have been to me as the widow of Zarepath to Elijah, and fear not that your jar of oil shall fail or your meal be spent in the barrel, till the Lord sendeth his blessed rain on the earth. And it's coming, Susan, coming; I see the small cloud that comes to shed on the dry wilderness of your existence the tender rain of new life. Susan woman, you shall be fed and clothed, and see your own when these old limbs lie under the earth. I see your golden-haired Willie coming, coming, but he's far away yet, and there's small glint of gold in his pouch, or in his locks.'

of meal and fuel. Yet she missed her old companion sadly, and would gladly have gone on working and pinching for both to have kept the helpless old woman in the ingle nook.

As moons and seasons waxed and waned, and even years rounded bringing no tidings of her missing son, her heart at last began to fail, and with it her energy. Twelve long and weary years had worn out hope, and the "dour weird" pressed heavily.

Sea and land were bathed in the glowing light of a July midday sun. Sheep and cattle sought the shade of rock or wall or tree. Grass and leaves alike seemed fainting with the heat. Susan Cameron sat with doors and window open, inhaling the breath of the honeysuckle she had trailed round the porch in memory of her old home; knitting but slowly, heat and old memories overpowering need.

Her fingers moved mechanically, her eyes looked out on parched pasture land, distant heather and grey rock. Then came into the scene a poor crippled emaciated wayfarer, toiling painfully along, his forehead bandaged, his arm in a sling; his form bent with fatigue or disease, not age. There was just so much shape and colour left in his rags as told he had been a soldier.

The soiled red jacket caught her eye like magic, set her pulses in a strange flutter, and roused all the woman within her. No matter his regiment; he was a soldier, and in distress, and that was sufficient claim on her sympathy. Might not her own boy be a wanderer somewhere!

She had put down her work and risen to meet him ere he approached, and faintly, as one at the last gasp, implored "Drink and food, for the love of God."

Susan's heart was too full for speech; she pointed to the wooden bench outside the cottage, and soon held to his parched lips a bowl of meal and water.

"Here, my poor fellow, drink this. It may serve to keep life in you, and it is all that war and an ungrateful country have left the soldier's widow either for herself or others."

He had taken the bowl eagerly in both hands. As he raised his head and the vessel in the act of drinking, his eyes encountered hers, the tones of her voice fell familiarly on his ears.

The bowl dropped. With one wild cry, "Mother!" he put forth his arms; Willie was gathered to the loving heart which had longed for him, hoped for him, prayed for him through twelve unanswering years; the bandaged head rested on the motherly breast where his golden curls had nestled in infancy.

Here was new life for Susan. She laughed, wept and caressed him by turns. But the growing pallor on his face warned her that emotion was overpowering him. With one strong effort of will her demeanour changed, there was dread as well as affection in the quiet care with which she led him to old Margery's cushioned seat, and, having revived him with a fresh draught of her only beverage, ran, despite her lameness, to her nearest neighbour, to procure with her last coin food and whisky, and to dispatch a bare-legged callant to her friend in the Luckenbooths.

The stimulant might not have been loyally dutiful to King George, but it did good service to his loyal subject. His faintness passed away, and the soldier rallied sufficiently to partake the first substantial meal he had had for days.

After a sound sleep on Margery's comfortable pallet, evening found him another man. Wan and emaciated he was, certainly, but the dust was gone from shoes and garments, a needle had drawn the rags into place, his face was washed, his wounds were dressed and re-bandaged; happiness lit his blue eyes, which followed his mother's every movement with a restful satisfaction not to be described.

See Susan stroking his wasted hand as she sits on a low stool by his knee, endeavouring to trace in the worn features of her recovered treasure the fine boy she remembered.

"Ah, Willie, dearie, want and wounds are sair disfigurers. I see little of the golden-haired laddie I left in his blood on the fatal field of Corunna!"

"I have brought back my heart, dear mother, and my hands to work for you, when I grow strong again. But consider what I have endured since then."

And what had that been? He had roused from a temporary stupor to find himself covered by what he deemed the mangled corpse of his mother; he had dragged himself away to a place of safety; a party of the enemy crossing the field had carried him off with them; and for two years he had endured the miseries of a French prison. Then he was exchanged. Could learn no tidings of his family save "death, death." Believing himself alone, he re-entered the army, was sent with his regiment to Canada, was tomahawked by an Indian at Fort Erie, and only escaped scalping through a timely musket-shot which brought down his savage adversary. His wounds cured, he was draughted from the intense cold of Canada to the intense heat of the West Indies. Had an attack of yellow fever. Wounded and diseased, was at length permitted to exchange into a regiment returning home. Shortly afterwards the regiment was disbanded, and without pension or remuneration he was cast adrift, a crippled beggar, one of England's incongruities—its glory and its shame.

This is but a condensed outline of the wanderer's story, told less connectedly, and with details which made his mother shrink and shudder. The moon was rising as it drew to a close, and silent thanksgivings were rising from Susan's heart as she caressed the straggling curls the scalping knife had spared, when a quick light step was heard on the threshold, and the callant she had sent to their kinsman rushed in crying out, "Braw news, Meestres Cameron! braw news!"[106]

Close at his heels came Dugald Cameron puffing and blowing, out of breath, but waving a paper in one hand, his bonnet in the other.

Speech was impossible, he thrust the paper into Susan's hand, tossed his bonnet across the kitchen, grasped Willie by both hands before he could utter a word of congratulation, altogether in a state of excitement very foreign to douce Dugald Cameron.

It was a document from the War Office. Unknown to Susan, her staunch friend Dugald had for years worried the powers that be (as he said "like a collie-dog at the heels o' a flock o' sheep") until he forced recognition of her claims. That paper confirmed the right of Sergeant Cameron's brave widow to a liberal pension.

Thus was her joy crowned!

Tears of gratitude fell from Susan's eyes that night as she opened her kist, and drawing thence with much solemnity Sergeant Cameron's well-kept Bible, laid it reverently on the table before their son.

"Willie, my boy, let us both return thanks for doubled mercies. For me, I thank God heartily that my long-lost boy is given back to be the comfort of my old age, a token that my 'dour weird' is past."

Their hands met and clasped over the holy book.

"My own Willie!"

"My dear mother!"

That clasp was for life. There was no more parting until the grey-haired woman laid her dying head on the breast of her son in after years.

---

[106] *Meaning*: 'Fine news, Mistress Cameron! Fine news!'

THE WHITE WOMAN OF SLAITH

CHAPTER I

SUPERSTITION dies hard, and who shall say that when Superstition dies, his twin sister, Veneration, will not droop and languish over his bier? But nowhere does superstition linger longer than among the fisher-folk of the far north. The men who "go down to the sea in ships, and occupy their business in great waters," not only "see the works of the Lord, and His wonders in the deep," but they leave behind them ashore women sensitive as barometers to every change of wind and weather, keenly susceptible of all that may affect the husbands, and fathers, and brothers who risk their lives that they and others may live. And they also leave behind them children to be influenced by all they hear and see, and to catch up and transmit every eerie whisper that may fall from their elders.

So from generation to generation the wind has had voices for the fisher-folk that the trading townsman could not hear, and the wreathing mist has held shapes the city matron could not see; voices and shapes of awe and mystery, powerful to bless or ban.

Such may have been the "White Woman of the Wreck," of whom the hardy fisher-wives of Slaith to this day speak in undertones, lest the very utterance of her name should bring the ill-omened spirit amongst them.

Yet only once has she been seen within living memory, and a grey-haired woman keeps the record in her heart.

Far back, when Hilda Sanderson's grandfather was a boy, when the fishermen's huts were not perched here and there upon the rocks to be out of reach of the tide, but looked out from beneath the cliffs on a fair expanse of sand and shingle and a land-locked bay, was the White Woman seen for the first time, and *in the flesh.*

Rude and uncultivated as are the fisher-folk of Slaith in these our times, civilization is yet making its mark on the young; but in those bygone days the dwellers on too many of our coasts looked upon all spoils of the ocean as their legitimate right. So at Slaith, when a fierce north-easter ravaged the coast and kept yawls and cobles at home, the storm would bring as sure a harvest as was won from the deep on those moonlight nights when the herring-boats were out. And notwithstanding the abundance of coal in the wild region around, frequent wrecks made wood the common fuel; it was plentiful, and cost nothing but the gathering and stowing away.

Never had come storm to Slaith at once so productive, or so disastrous, as that which spread its lurid banners over the sky one September evening more than a century ago, warning the busy fishermen to put back and haul their craft high and dry upon the beach for safety. Only one boat, which had set sail in advance of its fellows, disregarded the storm-signals of the sky and pursued its course, whether in recklessness or confidence is not known.

The purple clouds gathered over the crimson glare, the wind came howling up, driving blacker masses of cumuli before it, and night set prematurely in over land and sea.

The village, sheltered on the north and west by a steep, stern ironstone cliff, which spread its protecting arm far out to sea in a formidable reef or "neb," was all astir. Men and women gathered on the beach intent on hauling up the boats, securing nets and tackle, and speculating what luck the sea had in store for them, as it broke in foam and froth on the hard rocks and ran in almost to their feet.

Yet, mingling with the crowd and these speculations, came one short-skirted fishwife to the beach with wildly anxious eyes, and hands pressed on her throbbing breast, for Robert Blackburn's boat had not come back with the rest, and it held her husband and her boys. Only the youngest clung to her woollen skirt, and added, with his questions, to her fears and agony.

As the waves leapt up to meet the vivid lightning darting from the clouds and dancing on their crests, she could discern through the blinding rain a disabled ship struggling amid the billows, and she felt how little hope these was for her husband's coble in a gale before which so large a vessel was driving to destruction.

Yes, driving helplessly on towards the Neb, and never a boat or a hand put forth to the rescue, though the minute gun boomed in solemn appeal above the roar of the elements; though shrieks and cries for help were borne in by the wind as the doomed vessel was hurried nearer and nearer to its fate; and though the lightning flashes revealed the white figure of a woman lashed to the broken mainmast, and hapless sailors clinging to the bowsprit and rigging.

Nearer ran the ship to the outlying reef, and nearer to a crowd of stalwart men who knew the coast, were inured to danger, and lacked neither strength nor courage to risk life or limb in saving life—but only *the will.* True, the danger was imminent, the risk great, the men had families dependent on their lives, and—if none were left to tell the story of the wreck, better luck would be for the village. So cries and shrieks fell on deaf ears. Not even the piteous adjuration "For God's sake!" which came with strange distinctiveness across the waters as the vessel struck, had power to move a man. Maggy Blackburn ran from one to another beseeching pity for the lady and the helpless crew, as they might hope for aid in like straits, as *her* husband and sons might be needing aid even then!

Sullen silence, or gruff admonitions to mind her own business were the only response. Even the women turned away, the greed of gain, the hope of spoil, stronger than womanhood.

Morning dawned on a cold, gray sky, a receding tide, a placid sea, a fishing village nestling under rugged cliffs, with a long reach of smooth sand between the cottages and the narrow strip of boulders and shingle, and the outstretched arm of the Neb, looking innocent as any other benevolent protector.

It dawned also on smoke uprising from cottage fires kept alive during all the storm and tumult; on a sea and beach strewn with wreckage; on men and women wading into the surf to bring ashore boxed and bales within reach of arms or boat-hooks; on boats, well manned, steering amongst the rocks and shallows, or even into deeper currents around the Neb, to pick up jetsam and flotsam before the coastguard or the lord of the manor should come on the scene with a legal claim.

It dawned on the half-naked bodies of drowned sailors swaying hither and thither with the undulating waves, or lying disfigured among the rocks, among weeds, and tangle, and inquisitive lobsters black as undertakers. It dawned, too, on a tall, slim woman in a white clinging garment, her head and shoulders wrapped in a grey shawl, from beneath which her fair hair had fluttered and lay in wet, loosened tresses on the sand, where the tide had landed her and the broken mast together. Landed only to lie there unnoted and unregarded, although when the sun kissed the pale lips and eyes they opened to the light and warmth, and perchance a hope of deliverance thrilled through the half-insensate form.

It came not until too late. Maggy Blackburn and her boy retreating to their hut when the ship struck, had spent the intervening hours in weeping for the dear ones they never expected to behold again; and not until the sun was fairly up, and the boy had cried himself to sleep, did she venture forth to see the devastation night, and storm, and pitiless men had to answer for.

Far along the beach, away from the busy knots of wreckers, she found the White Woman lying, to all appearance, dead, A compassionate tear fell on the pale upturned face, and a word or two of pity dropped from the rough fishwife's lips—in her own grief sympathetic.

As she spoke, a pair of lovely blue eyes slowly unclosed and rested for an instant on her own in mute thanksgiving.

With a cry of surprise, Maggy strove to loosen the bonds which held the frail form to the mast. In vain! loving hands had tied them too securely, and the wetted cordage would not yield.

She had no knife. Rising to her feet she put her hands to her mouth and sent a loud halloo across the sands for help. Again and again she called. Her call was disregarded. A large cask was being rolled over the grating shingles.

At length an answer, prefaced by an oath, was shouted back. "Mind thy own business, Maggy Blackburn, an' let th' woman be."

But Maggy, tender in the hour of her own dreaded bereavement, stooped to whisper, in ears which might or might not be conscious, the nature of her errand; and ignoring the belief that ill-luck follows the restoration of the shipwrecked to life, she sped along the sweep of sand to her own home for a knife, lest a churlish refusal might meet her on the beach, where knives were in active use.

Blachburn's cottage was mounted on a ledge of rock above the rest of the village, and was less accessible, and though Maggy was strong and swift of foot, swifter-footed Death outran her. *He* had severed invisible cords, released the struggling spirit. It only remained for Maggy to release a stiffening corpse, bear it reverently beyond reach of the tide, and compose the dead limbs for burial, woefully wondering the while who would perform the like office for her Robert and his boys.

Intent on her melancholy occupation, absorbed in her own anguish, she heeded not the noisy group near the Neb quarrelling over their spoil, until a loud "Halloo" arrested her attention. Turning round, she saw a young fisherman's hand pointing seawards, and some instinct prompted her to fall on her knees with uplifted voice and hands. She felt rather than knew the distant sail for their own.

Robert Blackburn and his sons were safe, though their boat had sustained some damage. They had found a haven close at hand on the first outbreak of the tempest.

But what of the good ship that had gone to pieces on the Neb?

What the billows had spared the wreckers had industriously stowed away in secret caves and cellarage, till scarcely a spar remained afloat to tell the mournful story. And after the White Woman and the sailors washed ashore were buried in the sands there was rejoicing and carousal. "That was a lucky day for Slaith," they said, as they sat round fires supplied from the timber of the wreck; "drowned folk were not likely to dispute possession of their harvest, and no man living had put in a claim."

And as the "last lucky day," it was remembered and spoken of with regret as the winter nights drew on; and of all the good ships lost on our northern coasts, not one went ashore at Slaith that had not sailed from it. No more luck of the kind came in their way. Even the take of fish grew scanty and precarious; and a rumour got about that a supernaturally tall woman in a long white clinging robe, whose head was muffled in a grey shawl, was sure to stand like a beacon on the uttermost point of the Neb whenever a storm was brewing, and with the motion of her white arms in the air warn approaching vessels of their danger; and that she had been seen to finger the nets as they hung outside the huts to dry, when they would break like tow and let the fish escape.

Certainly the nets were always under repair, and the boats; and when the weird white figure was seen on the Neb, like a wreath of mist or spray, there would be apprehensive whispers in the village of the White Woman of the Wreck, and a sense of ill-luck spread its gloom and discontent over Slaith.

It made itself felt in envious antagonism to the Blackburns, who somehow seemed to prosper where others failed, and to be thriving better without a share of the great wreck's cargo than any of those whose cellars had been filled with her merchandize and stores. Silk had mildewed, casks had leaked, and fruits had been damaged by the sea-water.

"Nothing, however, seemed to go wrong with the Blackburns," was said with a grumble, not only at the firesides, but openly to Maggy and Robert both; and they were so often twitted with being "above their neighbours" in more than their dwelling, that as the ill-feeling spread, whilst the seasons went their round, the elder and younger Blackburns alike ceased to grumble at the extra distance and rugged path to their abode, since it kept them apart from ill neighbours.

A year had almost gone by since the day of the great wreck, when Robert Blackburn lamed his foot stumbling over a coil of cable on the beach, at the same time that his two up-grown sons lay tossing on their pillows in the burning arms of fever.

A sad and anxious week this for Maggy, watching her sick, with only Cuthbert, a lad of thirteen, to run to and from the distant apothecary, hew her wood, or draw her water.

His brothers had been three days in bed when he was sent in the early morning for water from the beck-spring. The village lay asleep at the foot of the rock; the boats, which had not been out over-night, were hauled up high on the beach—that beach which seemed to have narrowed so considerably; and a thick haze rested on the slightly heaving sea.

Something of this crossed the boy's mind as he came down the hill with his pail, and noted the high-water mark left by the receding tide.

Suddenly he beheld—as if she came out of the very mist—the tall White Woman of the Wreck glide over the sands and shingle, and touch the stern of every boat as she passed, with one omission—that of his father; and then with a sweep of her long arm towards the line of cottages, glide away silently as she came, leaving Cuthbert so dazed he could scarcely find words to tell his mother what he had seen.

"Not a word to them inside!" she said, as she met him on the threshold. She, too, had seen the White Woman from her own door, and her heart sank lest Betty Rae's ill-savoured words should be true and their own luck indeed be on the turn. What if the omen should be to them, and her sons be taken from her?

Private forebodings did not, however, stifle her goodwill to others. Cuthbert was despatched to the awakening village with the intelligence, and a word of advice for the men not to go to sea that day. Her messenger was greeted with incredulity and scorn. The Blackburns were not in favour, Maggy's motives were suspected, her story disbelieved.

"Are our wives to have empty creels because Maggy Blackburn's men-folk are laid by and canna work?" asked Peter Rae, the man who twelve months before had bade Maggy "Let the woman be!"

Cuthbert went back with a laugh ringing in his ears, and a hint that his mother had picked a convenient time for ghost-seeing.

Nevertheless, her message had not been wholly thrown away, however much her motive might be suspected. There was an absence of ordinary alacrity in preparing the boats for sea, and a disposition to talk rather than work. One old fisherman, with a weather-beaten face, whose name was Sanderson, declared that neither he nor his sons would put to sea that day. "Better lose a take of fish than a' our lives, and' there's no kenning what mischief's afloat if th' White Woman has been seen."

There was a sneer at the Sandersons. Nevertheless, one or two young fellows held back at the last, and a yawl or two sailed without the full complement of hands—the Raes for one.

It was a memorable day for Slaith.

When the sun reached its meridian, sea and sky were all aglow like molten gold, and the women on the shore, led by Betty Rae, laughed the stay-at-homes to scorn as they themselves went about their household ways panting with the unprecedented heat.

Maggy was thankful when a breeze came landward with the returning tide and through the open door to fan the flushed cheeks of fever; and not she only. But with the breeze came a little cloud out of the distant wave, and deepened and darkened and spread as the breeze swelled and mounted to a gale, and the long rollers of the advancing tide swept in on the shore, mounting higher and higher, and breaking on the Neb as though trying their strength on the rock and disputing its right to bar their progress.

The Sandersons said they saw the tall White Woman on the shore waving her long arms and beckoning to the waves. Calling all hands to help, they drew their own coble and the Blackburns' higher and higher up the beach, now alive with frightened fish-wives wading in the surf to secure cables and tackle, nets and creels, hitherto supposed to lie beyond the highest tide.

But on came the rushing water, on and on as the daylight went, one and on in the darkness of night, white-lipped and roaring. Then there was a sudden stir within the cottages, as the water crawled in at the open doors an put out fires on the hearth.

A sudden stir, with lanterns and flaring torches, to bear the infant and its cradle, the grandmother in her chair, and household goods anyhow up the rocky pathway to security; a stir all too late and too hurried in the darkness to save all of life or property. The whole shore was invaded by sea.

Morning broke on desolation. Weeping women and children up on the cliffs looked in vain for their homes down below. The village had been swept from the sands.

The two cobles had held to their moorings and were but little damaged; of the picturesquely grouped cottages only ruins mingled with weeds and tangle were visible. No four walls were standing that were not, like the Blackburns', perched on the cliff.

There ran at last a shuddering reminder through the shelterless crowd that it was the anniversary of the "great wreck," as Betty Rae was missed from their midst, and a bundle of blue and red that had once been a woman was found amidst the debris of the Raes' dwelling. And as hour after hour, and day after day went by, and never yawl or coble came back to tell the secrets of the night or of the devastating storm, the homeless women, whose orphaned children clung wailing to their skirts, in their own agony envied the lot of Maggy Blackburn, whose men-folk were spared to her. And not a few remembered that, of all the village, she alone had shown compassion towards the White Woman of the Wreck.

Slaith—the original Slaith—was gone; homes and people: and the White Woman was seen no more by *that* generation.

CHAPTER II

A new Slaith arose. Not immediately, and not on the sands. In spring and autumn the sea had possession of the old site at flood-tide. Of the bereaved families who had found refuge in holes and caves among the rocks, some wandered inland; others, who had means or a man left, began to build cabins here and there on the irregular hillside. Buxom or energetic widows attracted husbands from other stations on the coast. There were marriages and intermarriages, notably between the Blackburns and the Sandersons. Even Raes' only surviving son (the one who had stayed ashore), having wherewith to purchase a new boat—secret spoil of the great wreck—had not far to seek a wife, who scouted the suggestion of ill-luck.

The new village rose under other auspices. The patriarchs of Slaith would have no wreckers in their midst, the awful visitation of the White Woman of the Wreck serving as a deterrent, so long as an eye-witness remained to verify the story he handed down to future generations.

So long as Cuthbert Blackburn, the last survivor of the great storm, sat in the chimney nook, and related to his listening grandchildren how, with his own young eyes, he had seen the white woman with the grey shawl cut away from the broken mast to be buried; and how, a year after, to a day, he had beheld the shadowy form of the dead and buried woman, but tall as a ship's mast, glide over the sands, shake a threatening hand at the village, and touch the stern and sails of every foredoomed boat; the listening children would edge closer to each other, look fearfully around, and hold their breaths in awe.

And so long as the old man could totter about, with the wind playing amongst his grey locks, never a Blackburn or a Sanderson was known to bring other than a legitimate cargo ashore, although smuggling was openly connived at by people of note and respectability on the coast and inland.

But when the old grandfather was laid to rest, the White Woman might have been laid to rest also. She had lapsed into the airy region of tradition, and, in the daily duties and anxieties of fishermen's lives, the very awe her name had inspired was fast dying out. And no wonder. Seventy years had almost rounded their circuit since the sea made its obliterating inroad upon Slaith. Cuthbert's youngest grandchild, Hilda Sanderson, was a blooming maiden of eighteen—golden haired, fresh coloured, firm of foot, and round of limb—as ready to wade in the surf as a water nymph; and she carried on her shoulders the wicker fish creel, suspended by its strap across her forehead, with a grace peculiarly her own.

Eighteen. And nine years had gone since she, her grandfather's pet, had, for the last time, wandered with him on the shore, and drunk in his never-failing recital, as, with his stick, he pointed to the end of the Neb where the ship went down, marked out, as on a map, every detail of the scenes he had witnesses, and cautioned her, as she hoped to prosper, never to form a friendship or have any dealings with a Rae.

Eighteen—and the youngest representative of the Raes had come a-wooing to her!

During his lifetime Cuthbert Blackburn's own children, in obedience to his behest, had held aloof from the Raes. But his grandchildren had felt his interdict a hardship; since avoidance of the Raes meant (to the lads at least) exclusion from companionship and from such sports and games as called for numbers, and of which one or other of the two Raes was almost sure to be leader.

Certainly Hilda's brothers held out the right hand of fellowship to Stephen Rae almost over their grandfather's grave, but surreptitiously, and no one at home was the wiser.

Hilda, seeing the lads together, put in a protest in memory of her grandfather, and their cousin, Robert Blackburn, set his face against the new friendship; but all to no purpose. He himself had, in time, to go with the stream or be left in a minority. And even Hilda, when she grew old enough and strong enough to be sent to the beck for water, was not sorry to find a stronger arm ready to carry the full pail down the hill in her stead.

The Blackburns' cottage no longer looked down from an elevation on the village. It now stood with the Sandersons', almost in the front rank, with a sea-wall as a protection; at the edge of the rock on a higher level the Raes had built, and their footpath to the beach skirted the tumbling mountain stream; and so it came about that, without design, Stephen was so often at hand to do her a service.

That he proffered his services might be due to her pretty face; that she accepted them might be set down as much to the careless, matter-of-fact, yet masterful manner in which he had possessed himself of her pail in the first instance, as to his black eyes and curly head.

He was five years her senior, and the girl of fifteen, taken by surprise, submitted with something akin to fear in her breast, following him down the steep path with an eerie misgiving of evil to come, and answering his few brief remarks with mere monosyllables. She scarcely said "Thank you" as he set down the pail almost at her own door, and, without waiting even for those curt thanks, proceeded on his way to the beach with a net over his shoulder, whistling as he went.

His shadow darkened the cottage window as he stooped to set down the pail.

"Who was that?" asked Maggy Sanderson, looking up from her wash-tub.

"Stephen Rae, mother," she answered, half afraid of a rebuke.

"And what brought thee with Stephen Rae? Thy grondfeyther Blackburn would have given thee a word of a sort had he seen thee wi' one o' them folk, for a' they be better off than ourselves."

Hilda was conscious of this.

"I could not help it, mother. He took up the bucket, and was off with it down the hill before I could get out a word."

"Weel, lass, it was neighbourly; an' if thou didn't throw thyself in the lad's way, thou'rt noan to blame." And the energetic woman made the soapsuds fly as she rubbed away at a blue guernsey, and went on saying: "Will and Cuddy say we ha' no right to cast up to Peter and Steve what their great-grondfeyther was, an' that thy grondfeyther's tale was half superstition an' half prejudice, an' that it's time old animosities died out. May be it is. Me an' thy feyther have talked it over mony a time; as' though it did look like a judgment when old Peter was drowned, as his forebears were afore him, thy feyther said that, forbye a bit o' smuggling, nobody knew aught against him. An' it's noan Christian-like to turn a cold shoulder to the lads, seeing they're so good to the poor mother, though they do come of a bad stock. But surely, lass, thou needn't stand still while I talk. You might have had them potatoes peeled by this time, an' ready for the pot."

The bustling matron's reproof was not ill-timed. Hilda's knife went round the roots somewhat mechanically and slowly. She was thinking more of her mother's speech than of her occupation. It was a tolerant reversal of all preconceived notions and old beliefs—a doubt thrown on Grandfather Blackburn's theory of ill-luck as the White Woman's legacy to the Raes—a blow struck at the roots of prejudice and superstitious fear.

She hurried over the potatoes; set them to boil, and with them a dish of silvery fresh herrings, then carried the basket of newly-washed clothes to the beach, and spread them out on the shingle to dry, strewing pebbles over them to keep them down.

But all the while her mother's speech was in her mind, and consequently Stephen Rae: a conjunction Maggy Sanderson had scarcely contemplated.

When next she, on her way from the spring, in her pink half-gown and blue woollen petticoat, was overtaken by Stephen, much of her eerie dread had disappeared, and something of girlish shyness, which kept her tongue-tied, had taken its place.

Whatever her mood, if he chanced to overtake her on her way from the spring, he was certain to possess himself of her pail, and carry it down the hill, no matter what other burden he might have, and he was seldom empty-handed.

And he always stepped on briskly in advance, as if to show that, though willing to serve her, he had no desire to obtrude in the way of conversation. After a time she caught herself admiring the manliness of his bearing, the careless ease with which he bore the brimming pail down the rugged path, nor spilled a drop, though, it might be, a cable or a net was slung across his shoulder; and she was prone to contrast his black curls with her brothers' red locks. At such times she would take herself to task and resolve to avoid him as her dead grandfather had enjoined. But she could neither shut her eyes nor her ears, and she found herself looking and listening for his step, and when he was not there feeling a sense of disappointment which made her angry with herself.

Her brothers had long rallied her on her sweetheart, heedless of her angry disclaimer, and her cousin, Robert Blackburn, had provoked her even to tears with his taunts of barefaced impropriety in running after one of the Raes. But neither her brother nor Robert would accept her challenge to fetch water in her stead. Robert tried it for a week or ten days, but he soon found the task incompatible with his daily duty.

She was nearly seventeen before she would admit to herself that Stephen was more to her than a friend, and quite seventeen before he claimed a higher privilege.

He had watched her step by step on her way to womanhood, noted her modesty, her industry, and made himself sure of a place in her heart before he asked for it. Nay, he might have waited longer still had he not seen Robert Blackburn haunting her like a shadow, with all the facilities which cousinship and adjoining dwellings could give.

She had now to take her part with the women on the narrowed beach in unloading and preparing the fish for market and the curing-house: and as he saw red-haired Robert always at her side to lighten her labours, and was conscious she had avoided him of late, he had a salutary reminder that he might dally a little too long.

Accordingly he loitered on the path by the beck, and saw more than one damsel fill her pail and cast coquettish glances his way; but Hilda came not. He saw her busy on the beach, or leaning over the sea-wall in conversation with her brothers or Robert; but she scarcely looked towards him, and only nodded when he called to her.

In fact, she was avoiding him, fetching water when the boats were out or preparing to sail, having taken herself to task with a will.

Stephen was not easily baffled. He had gone down to the shore in his sea-boots and sailing gear, and was helping Peter to make all trim aboard the yawl, with an eye on Sanderson's cottage, when he suddenly professed to have left something at home, and set off in a hurry, leaving Peter, the two men, and the boy to get all right and tight without him.

He did not slacken his pace until he was fairly out of sight; then he stepped along at leisure and, where practicable, on the soft turf. Hilda was some paces in advance, toiling along in the hot sun with her empty pail as wearily as if it had been filled to the brim with lead.

The spring gushed cold and clear from the rock in a sheltered nook among heather and hart's-tongue fern, a few paces from the beck to which it was tributary, and here Hilda seated herself on a stone in a drooping attitude, sighed heavily, and clasped her knees with both hands as it forgetful of her errand.

A hand upon her shoulder made her start. She turned, and met the gaze of Stephen with eyes that sank before the new light in his.

"Where have you hid yourself, Hilda, the last fortnight? I had a fairing for you,[107] and had never a chance to offer it."

"I do not want a fairing. I—I would rather not have it," faltered she, going alternately cold and hot, as he pulled a gay silk kerchief from his pocket and proceeded to tie it under her chin, saying as he did so, "Yes, you do, and will give me a kiss for it." And holding her face between his two hands, as if to look how her new head-gear became her, he lifted it up to meet the kiss he had ready for her lips.

Her modesty took fright. Never before had he by act or word overstepped the bounds of propriety. She struggled to free herself.

His arm was around her, but the clasp was that of tenderness, not power.

"Nay, Hilda," said he, "I have brought you something more than a fairing. I have brought you a true heart and honest love, and I want yours in return. And now, my lass, how is it to be?"

---

107 Fairing: a gift, especially from a fair.

Hilda was not a fine lady to swoon in her lover's arms, but she had been caught in a melancholy mood, and she certainly grew sick and dizzy, half doubting her own happiness, half dreading the evils her grandsire had prognosticated. She was, however, too honest to keep him very long in doubt, and had coyly given him back his kiss, when a loud halloo farther down the beck reminded him that the tide was on the turn, and that Hilda's pail was still empty.

Home went Hilda in a sort of a dream, to be taken sharply to task for loitering; but Hilda's ears were impervious to sharp words since the magical sweetness of love had been breathed into them. It was not until the bright kerchief on her head attracted her mother's eye that she was awakened from her trance of new delight.

"Where did thee get that thing?"

There was not a colour in the silken square so brilliant as that which flushed her face as, with a sudden flash of recollection, her hand went up to her head. She had forgotten her adornment in thinking of the giver.

There was no longer hope of concealment.

"Steve Rae gave it to me for a fairing," she faltered.

"An' what business had thou to take fairings from Steve Rae?" Pull the thing off this minute. What would Robert say if he saw thee wearing aught that had come through Steve's fingers?"

"It's naught to Robert what I wear," jerked out Hilda, conscious that her cousin had assumed a right of dictatorship not conceded by herself; but she removed the offending head-gear nevertheless.

When the boats came in the next morning with a great take of fish, the goodwife was too busy to think of the "fairing." And by the time Maggy Sanderson bethought to broach the matter to her good man, as he smoked his long pipe in the nook, their two sons were in Steve's confidence and prepared to do battle in his behalf.

It was not so tough a contest as Hilda had expected. Her father puffed away, asked for a sight of the kerchief, turned it over, held it to the light, felt its texture, and with the air of a connoisseur decided "that were noan bought at a fair, and it's never been smuggled in thy time or mine, Maggy."

"I only hope he came by it honestly," suggested Maggy, with an expressive jerk of the head.

"That I'm sure he did!" put in Hilda promptly, resenting the impeachment of her sweetheart.

"So am I," supplemented Cuthbert. "Peter and Steve overhauled everything when their father was drowned, and they came across lots of queer things stowed away in a sort of cellar in the rock, that had never seen daylight in their memory, or their mother's either—a mouldy box of women's tackle amongst the rest. It fell to pieces as they moved it, the fastenings were so eaten away with rust. They thought it had been in the water. I'll be bound the kerchief came out o' that."

"Mebbe so, Cuddy. When I were a lad, folks told queer tales of the old Raes and what they had in hiding holes. But I've heard naught again the lads, though they do come of a bad crew. And as for Steve, if it were not for Robert——"

Here both Cuddy and Will launched out in praise of Steve; the end being tacit permission for Hilda to retain possession of her fairing, and to wear it openly with her best clothes on Sundays, greatly to the chagrin of Robert Blackburn, who counted over his savings with a rueful perception of their inadequacy to compete with Stephen Rae in the way of love-gifts.

Certainly a countess might have envied Hilda that Oriental kerchief worn by the fisher-maid in all simplicity, its value to her being only estimable as a token of Stephen's love.

Had she known whence it came, or by whom it had been worn, she would have cast it from her with a shudder. Blissfully ignorant, she walked from church, with Stephen by her side, in a flutter of pride and joy, damped—but only for a moment—by the sight of Robert Blackburn's mournful aspect as he leaned over the low parapet wall, looking drearily out to sea.

"Happy the wooing that's not long a doing! When's it to be, Hilda, lass? There's our Peter married, and Bet—it's quite time thee and me were spliced."

Steve was lying at full length, chest downwards, on the shingle, as he spoke; his elbows buried in the smooth pebbles; his upturned chin resting on his brown palms, his black eyes fixed on the face of Hilda as she—the week's work over—leaned against the stern of a boat turned keel uppermost.

"I don't know," answered Hilda, irresolutely. "Mother says there's no room under Peter's roof for me. Two sons' wives and their mother on one hearth would make it too hot for the men."

"Aye, aye, like enough. But there'd be room enough for thee and me on our own hearth, dearie. I know where there's a snug cottage to be had, so you've only to say the word, and by the time the banns are out, there shall be a home ready for us. What dost say? Shall I put up the banns next week?"

"Ask father. I don't mind," replied Hilda, shyly.

"Do you mind trying on these? You see, Hilda, when a fellow has made up his mind it's best to have everything ready," and he held up a massive wedding ring and keeper, the latter of curious workmanship, though neither was new.

He had her hand in his clasp, had slipped both rings upon her finger, and was raising himself to snatch a kiss, when she suddenly started to her feet, with her eyes fixed on the point of the Neb, and the startled cry, "What's that?"

The evening shades had been deepening unheeded whilst they lingered on the beach, but there on the summit of the bleak promontory she beheld a shadowy shape which thrilled her soul with fear. "What is that?" she repeated in a whisper, pointing with her finger as she spoke.

"What? Where?" questioned Stephen, in perplexity.

"That figure on the Neb?"

"I see nothing but the mist and spray. We'd best go in. The wind's rising, and we're like to have a rough night of it."

A rough night it was, but Stephen laughed at her belief that she had seen the White Woman, and said he knew the thing had never been more than mist and foam and fancy; he thought she had had more sense than to believe old women's tales.

His masterful manner kept her silent, but she could not conquer her impressions; and though she carried the two gold rings sewn in her bodice, and loved him, if possible, with a deeper and stronger affection, she put off the actual date of her marriage from time to time as if afraid to venture.

Robert Blackburn had something to do with this. Never a stormy night came but he protested he saw the White Woman hovering about the Neb, but as "nothing came of it," and no one else saw more than a wreath of mist, the village laughed him to scorn, until he held his peace and kept his previsions to himself. Yet neither Hilda Sanderson nor Hilda's mother joined the coarse mirth at his expense.

Steve had taken a pretty cottage, had fitted it up to receive his bride, not only with common appliances, but with one or two rare things brought from some secret hoard, a rarely carved coffer among the rest; had put up the banns and waited impatiently for her to fix the day. And as she put it off and put it off from time to time, for no earthly reason but that she "was afraid," he began to grow jealous of Robert Blackburn and his influence.

On Peter's marriage there had been some talk of having a new yawl built; and now it lay at its moorings on the beach; the finest and largest craft that had ever belonged to Slaith.

In proof of goodwill, and the better to bring Hilda to reason, the Rae brothers offered to take the Sanderson brothers into partnership, an offer Cuddy and Willy were only too glad to accept, having long aspired to something beyond their father's coble.

Their generosity overpowered Hilda; banished Maggy's last objection; the wedding-day was fixed; they were to be married on the Sunday.

On the previous Thursday the yawl, called the "United Brothers," was to make its trial trip, an extra man and boy completing the crew, with Peter as master.

That morning early Hilda wakened with a shiver. She had dreamed that Stephen placed the wedding-ring on its keeper on her finger, when the White Woman came between them and plucked it off. There was no more chance of sleep. The very moonlight streaming through her lattice seemed to mock her. For the first time the atmosphere of the narrow room seemed to stifle her.

To breathe more freely and shake off her fears she lifted the latch of the front door and stepped across the path to the sea wall.

Was she still dreaming, or had her fancy conjured up a ghost to haunt her? There, in the pale moonlight, the lofty, ethereal form of a woman robed in white, with a hood or shawl of misty grey was slowly making the circuit of the "United Brothers," one shadowy hand gliding over the smooth surface of the hull, the other touching mast and sails and rigging, one by one. Too much appalled to scream,

Hilda gasped for breath. Her head swam. She clutched the low wall for support. Another moment and the weird figure was gone.

Back to her bed she crept, stunned and terrified. A sort of stupor bound her senses. Then she slept so heavily, the shrill voice of her mother rebuking laziness could scarcely rouse her.

Once awake all the terrors of the night came back to her. Her first impulse was to seek her brothers and Steve, tell them all she had dreamed and seen, and implore them not to launch the new yawl that day.

Her brothers listened and looked one at another in doubt. Peter Rae frowned, and asked her how fishermen were to live and keep families if they stayed ashore when their wives had bad dreams. He scouted the idea that it was anything more than a dream.

Her appeal had more effect on Steve, to whom she clung in entreaty, though he too held that she was the dupe of her own fancy. Her pale face and tearful eyes unnerved him. He was half inclined to hold back, and induce the others to put off the trial of the new boat until after the wedding.

She saw her advantage, and to clinch her argument reminded him that Robert Blackburn had seen the White Woman, more than once.

Jealous Steve set his teeth sternly.

"Oh! Robert Blackburn! There, that's enough, my lass. I want none of Robert Blackburn's hand on our tiller, and shall not wait his breath for a fair wind. You'd best go up to our house and have all put to rights for the wedding; and remember you're mistress there till I come back, or, if I never come back." He said this with his ordinary lightness; drew from his pocket a curious necklet, with a heart-shaped locket, clasped it round her throat as a wedding gift, and with a hearty kiss said she was to wear it for his sake. But he would hear no more of keeping back the boat, either for Robert

Blackburn or the White Woman, whilst the sky was clear, and wind and tide in their favour.

Wind and tide in their favour. The "United Brothers" slipped her cable, set her helm, spread her brown sails to the breeze, and with all her nets in readiness, breasted the dancing waves as if proud that the antipathies of generations were at an end, and she bore the proof.

Wind and tide in their favour. A peaceful twilight. A promising nightfall. Only a low mist creeping over the waters. Women and children sleeping calmly as the waves.

What was that?

The invisible hand of a hurricane shaking the windows and doors of Slaith. Billows battering and breaking over the seawall in foam. A blacker midnight never roused a population to wait in fear and trembling for the morn.

And there, on the extreme point of the Neb, the only thing distinctly visible in the darkness, clearly outlined, stood the White Woman, slowly and majestically waving her arms as if in exultation.

Other eyes than Hilda's saw, other hearts than Hilda's sank with apprehension.

The swift storm was over; the turbulent wreck-strewn sea was at rest. One by one the fishing-boats came home, some laden, some empty; all in sorry plight, and all late.

All? No, not all. Robert Blackburn had piloted old Sanderson's coble safely mid the rocks and shallows. But what of the "United Brothers?"

There was never a wedding-day for Hilda. Brothers and betrothed had sailed together and sunk together, and with them had perished all her hopes.

Grey-haired as her own mother, she wept as she recalled too

late her grandfather Cuthbert's warning for all of his honest kith and kin to "steer clear of the Raes," and bitterly reiterated that her "dream had indeed come true—the White Woman *had* torn her wedding-ring from her finger!"

"Aye, and wrecked the last of the Raes and those who dared to claim brotherhood with them," cried Robert Blackburn remorselessly. "You knew the White Woman's silent curse lay on those who let her die unaided, and the good ship go down with every human soul for the sake of spoil. Yet you suffered Steve Rae to adorn you with finery from the wreck, and bind you to himself with rings his forebear Peter Rae cut from the dead woman's fingers. You did not know it? You knew they were never honest gains, and the Raes were a bad lot. You had better have been content with a poorer mate and a good name."

"I shall never mate. Poor or rich, good or bad, I shall take no man's name," said Hilda, with a shudder.

She kept her word, and, keeping it, has kept alive the dread of the White Woman of the Wreck among the fisher-folk of Slaith.

LARRY'S APPRENTICESHIP

AN IRISH FAIRY LEGEND

CHAPTER I

"AH, sure, an' did I ever tell ye how the M'Canns came to be carpenters?"

This query was put by Margaret M'Cann (an old, valuable, faithful, and warm-hearted Irish servant of my mother) to myself and my youngest brother, who were seated—myself on the kitchen fender, and he on a low stool—listening to her *true* stories of banshees and leprechauns, in both of which she was a stout believer.

She had just told us of the wailing banshee she had herself seen and heard on the river bank, and of a leprechaun in his red cap and miniature suit of green; and she had borne with perfect good humour our ridicule and banter over her credulity, when she put the sudden question, "Did ye know, then, how the M'Canns came to be carpenters?"

"I never knew they were carpenters," said I, with a light laugh.

"Why, Margaret, I thought all your family were farmers," cried Fred, with an assumption of prior information."

"Them's the Quins, Master Fred. They are all farmers, to this blessed day; an' the M'Canns were farmers too, an' had a fine holding amongst the Wicklow mountains, just a trifle beyant Enniskerry, till Larry M'Cann (my grandfather that was) met with an adventure amongst the Good People."

Here Margaret, being a devout Catholic, crossed herself.

"Good People! O, I suppose you mean fairies," was my amendment.

"Sure, miss, an' I do; but we never speak of them but as the

Good People. It's onlucky."

"O, that's only in Ireland," suggested Fred, with a droll wink at me. "In England, you may call them anything you lie, and they won't mind it one bit."

"Are ye sure now, Master Fred?"

"Certain. But, Margaret, what had the fairies to do with Larry M'Cann's carpentering?"

"Well, I'll tell ye, of course, as it wor towld to me, when I was a slip of a colleen no bigger than yez."[108]

And Margaret settled herself on her chair with all the importance of an old story-teller.

"Ye must know that Larry was as fine an' strappin' a lad as ever stepped over the daisies. It was he that could handle a flail or a plough, or dig the praties,[109] or stack the hay in the haggard.[110] And when he went to chapel on a Sunday in his best frieze coat, with the ends of his bright handkercher flying loose, an' his caubeen cocked rakishly on one side,[111] sure an' weren't all the girls in Enniskerry in love with his blue eyes an' yellow hair, an' weren't half of them dying to have him for a bachelor?"

I presume we listeners looked mystified with the word "bachelor" so applied, for Margaret explained. "That's what you call a sweetheart, miss."

"But Larry, though not consaited, laughed with one girl, an' joked with another; and' whenever he went to Dublin, or Phoenix

---

108 Colleen: girl.

109 Praties: potatoes.

110 Haggard: an enclosure on a farm for stacking hay, grain, etc.

111 Caubeen: Irish beret.

Park, or the Strawberry-beds, could take the flure with the best, an' have the purtiest girl for a partner—an' troth it's he that could dance a jig—but he never thought of takin' a partner for life, or of offerin' himself as a bachelor, till he met with Kitty Quin, an' her black eyes made a hole in his heart at wanst. He was nigh six-an'-twenty when he met her. It was at a pattern at the Seven Churches of Glendalough, an' sorra a bit could he mind his prayers for looking at her as she towld her beads so piously, without seemin' to think of the bachelors or her own pretty face at all.

"Well, I heard grandfather say that, though he was as bowld and impident in his way with the lasses as any lad in Enniskerry, his knees fairly knocked together, an' his heart went all in a flutter before he could bless himself, when Michael Quin tuk her by the hand, an' comin' towards him, said, 'Larry, here's our Kitty come back from Aunt Riley's;' an' when Larry was too dazed to speak, went on, 'Have yez got a dhrop in yer eye, man, that yez cannot see the colleen, or has Dublin made her so strange ye don't know her agin?'

"What Larry said he niver remembered, but he felt as if he hadn't a bit of heart left, and his words tumbled over each other like stones rolled downhill. He knew he had blundered out somethin', for Kitty's cheeks went red as the roses on her print gown. She put out her soft little hand with a smile that showed two rows of teeth as white an' fresh as hailstones; an' she said modestly as a nun, 'I'm glad to see any of my owld friends again, Misther M'Cann.'

He had sinse enough left to take howld of the hand she offered; an' sure he must have given to it a hearty grip, for the roses grew on her forehead to match her cheeks, an' she drew it back hastily.

"Larry, however, kept close to the brother an' sister; and when the prayers were over, an' the people began to enjoy themselves, an' the dudeens an' the whisky went round to warm the hearts an' the toes,[112] then Larry plucked up his courage an' asked Kitty to tak' the flure with him.

"Now Kitty was either shy, or her Dublin manners made her too proud to dance at a pattern, so she made excuses. Michael, who had kissed the whisky-jar very lovingly, would not have his friend said 'no' to; and so, to *keep Mike in a good humour*, she consinted to dance a jig with Larry.

"Sure, an' it was then he must have won her heart; for they all went back to Enniskerry together, an' she let Larry put his arm round her waist, jist to *hould her on the car*, bekase of the bad roads, an' stale a kiss when he lifted her down at Farmer Quin's garden gate. An' from that out Larry followed Kitty like her shadder.

"But Peter Quin farmed more than two hundred acres, an' Larry's father only held a hundred an' twenty, an' that's a good differ, Master Fred. Then Mike an' Kitty wor all the childer Peter had, whilst Larry's brothers—God be praised!—wer as thick on the flure as rabbits in a run: wheriver ye turned yez might tumble over a pig or a gossoon.[113]

"Troth, an' it wasn't long afore the neighbours began to look on Larry as Kitty's bachelor, an' one decaitful ould fellow, who had himself an eye to Kitty's bit of money, gave Peter a hint that Larry was coortin' the lass for the love of her fortin'; tho' sorra a bit had Larry M'Cann so dirty a thought as than same.

"Peter had a temper that was always on the simmer, an' it biled over at wanst. By some ill luck Larry showed his face at the Quins' door before it had time to cool, so Peter thrated him to a thrifle of

---

112 Dudeen: a short tobacco pipe made of clay.

113 Gossoon: a boy, lad.

his tongue, the mane blackguard.

" 'Div ye think Kitty, the illigant darlint, is for such a poor spalpeen as yez?' he shouted.[114] 'She that's been eddicated in Dublin, an' hez book-larnin', let alone manners, an' a fortin' to the fore! But it's the fortin', I'm thinkin', yez looking for wid one eye, an' the girl wid the other, Misther Lawrence M'Cann,' he said, with a sneer an' a turn up of his ugly nose.

" 'It's well for yez, Mr. Pether Quin, that yez Kitty's father, or, by jabers, an' it's showin' ye the taste of this blackthorn I'd be,' said Larry on the instant, kaping it down with an effort. 'Ye may kape your dirty money, bad cess to them as put the black thought of me into yer heart, if ye'll only put Kitty's sweet little hand into mine wid a blessin'.'

"You may be sure, miss, as they did not whisper; an' hearin' a row, Mike ran from the barn into the slip of garden fornent the house to join in the fun. He was jist in time to hear his father repate his insult, an' accuse Larry of wanting Kitty's hundred pounds; an' then Mike fired up, an' took his friend's part like a Trojan."

"And what's a Trojan, Margaret?" asked Fred demurely, with another sly blink at me.

"Whisht, Master Fred, an' don't be afther interruptin', or we'll never get to the Good People at all," said Margaret, ignoring the question.

Thus admonished, Master Fred allowed the story to proceed.

"But Mike could not bring his father to reason, even though he offered him a dhraw of his pipe. More by token, he himself was unwillin' to let his sister marry a man who had neither house nor furniture of his own.

---

[114] Spalpeen: rascal.

" 'It's not for the likes of her to lay her head undher a father-in-law's roof, an' have her childer runnin' over a flure that is not her own,' said Mike. 'I'd say nothin' agin the match, Larry, if ye had but a farm or a house of yer own, or even the bits of things to make a house dacent for the lass.'

"Larry went away with a very sore heart, miss, you may be sure, for he'd set his very sowl upon Kitty Quin.

"An' sure an' that was the black morning for Larry! Turnin' a corner of the quickset hedge on his way home, who should he come across but Kitty with a basket of ripe strawberries on her arm, an' she lookin' more temptin' than the fruit.

"Kitty had a tender drop in her heart, and seeing that he was sad, she set herself to discover what it was about; and didn't she regret her curiosity in another minit?—for he poured out all his love and his sorrow like a great gushin' stream, and held her hand as if he was drownin', an' only that could keep him from sinking quite.

"Taken by surprise, Kitty dropped her basket, an' would have fainted outright, had not Larry put out his arm an' caught her, and that brought her to her siven senses.

"Poor Larry *mistook* her faintness for a sign of her affection, an' in his joy kissed her sweet lips over an' over again. But Kitty soon told him the differ.

"She said she had only fainted from the heat. She was sorry he had mistaken her friendship for a warmer feeling; but though she was ashamed her father should have suspected him of a mercenary motive, she could not encourage his hopes. She should niver marry without her father's consint; an' besides, her bringin' up had made her unfit for a farmer's wife, an' so she had determined—yes, determined was the word—niver to marry any man who had not a good trade in his hands that would be a livin' either in country or town.

"Every word that Kitty said fell like ice on Larry's hot heart, and he reeled home as if he had had lashins of whisky; and when he got there, he took the whisky to drown his sorrow till he wor drunk in arnest.

"There was nobody to tell him of the battle in Kitty's breast between love and pride, nor how she had crept into the house by the back way, and shut herself up, all alone in her room, to shed tears like a February cloud over the very mischief she had done, and the pain in her own breast.

"Sure, all the fun and the frolic of Larry's nature were murthered that black mornin'. He went about the farm without a smile on his lip or a sunbeam in his eye, an' his mother would have it the boy was bewitched.

"Even Father Maguire noticed his altered looks, and his careless dress when he went to mass on the Sundays, and the good priest did his best to set matters straight, but all to no use, miss.

"Peter Quin was sorry when his temper was off, but—small blame to him!—he still thought she might do better than go to the M'Canns' to be undher a mother-in-law, and work like a slave for all Larry's younger brothers.

"As for Kitty, before the feel of Larry's kiss had gone from her lips, the colleen was angry that he had taken her at her word; but she fed her courage with pride, and put a calm face on, though her heart was all in a tempest of trouble. An' sure, miss, there's many and many a girl does that, although you are too young to know it, and I hope never will."

Here Margaret looked at me soberly, as if giving a leaf out of the book of her own experience.

"One fine June morning, when the roses were in full dhress, an' the air had the smell of flowers an' new-mown hay, Larry went to St. Patrick's Market to sell a cow that had gone dhry.

"Three weeks before, and that same Larry would have sung or whistled every foot of the road, barrin' he met a traveller and stopped to give him the time o' day, or exchange a joke. But now he kept his hands in his pockets, his chin on his chest, an' his mouth was as close as a miser's purse. He had a sup of whisky before he left the house, to keep his heart up, but for all that he looked as melancholy as the cow he wor drivin'.

"He had barely got a couple of miles beyant Peter Quin's farm, which lay in his way to Dublin, when he heard a thin weak voice callin' to him, like the wind through a key-hole.

" 'The top o' the morning to you, Larry!'

" 'The same to you, misther,' answered Larry, slowly lifting his eyes, an' then rubbin' them to clear the cobwebs away; for straight across the road was a gate where niver a gate had been before, an' sittin' cross-legged on the topmost bar was the queerest old man Larry had ever seen.

"He was no bigger than a two-year child, but his face was as wizen an' wrinkled as if he was four hundred. He was dressed in an old-fashioned coat an' breeches as green as the grass, had shining buckles in his shoes, and on his head a bright red cap. By all them tokens Larry knew that the little old man was a leprechaun, an' his mouth began to wather for some of the goold he knew the old gintleman must have hid in the ground somewhere about, an' his heart began to thump. But Larry was not the boy to be afraid, so he put a bould face on when the leprechaun, with his head cocked on one side and a knowing twinkle in his eye, said to him—

" 'That's a fine baste yez drivin', Larry.'

" 'Troth, yer honour, an' ye may say that same,' replied Larry, doffin' his caubeen an' scrapin' his foot, for he thought it best to be civil.

" 'An' so you are dhrivin' the cow to market bekase she's lost her milk; an' ye mane to ax sivin pound tin for her!' said the leprechaun with a comical chuckle.

" 'Bedad, an' I am!' exclaimed Larry, opening his eyes, and slapping his thigh in amazement, 'an' sure it's the knowin' old gintleman yer honour is!'

" 'Thrue for you,' said the leprechaun; 'an' may be I know, besides, that Larry M'Cann's goin' to the bad for love of the purtiest girl in Wicklow! But pluck up a speerit, Larry; don't be cast down. It's I that owe Pether Quin a grudge this many a long day, for his maneness in chatin' the fairies of their due. Niver a fairies' dhrop (milk left as a propitiatory offering to the Good People) is to be found in Pether's cow-house or dairy; and niver a turf or a pratie, or a cast-off coat has he for a poor shivering beggar or omadhaun (idiot), bad cess to him! An' so, Larry, I mane to befriend yez, for it's yez that have the warm heart and the open hand, an' we'll back thim against the cowld heart and the tight fist any day!' an' the leprechaun plucked off his red cap and swung it over his head, as if in high glee.

"Larry, with another scrape of his foot, thanked the green-coated old gentleman, an' asked him if he meant to show him where to find a pot of gold.

" 'Ay, an' that I do; but, Larry,' an' here he looked slyer than ever, 'the fortin's in your own right hand, man, an' it's I that mane to tache ye to find it there.'

"Larry opened his great brown hand, an' turned it over, an' looked in the broad palm.

" 'Divil a bit I see of a fortin' there,' says he.

" 'Whist!' says the leprechaun. 'Go on wid your baste, an' when ye meet a man wid his breeches knees untied, an' his coat tails down to his heels, an' a wisp ov straw in his shoes to kape his toes warm where they peep out ov his stockins, an' a caubeen without a brim, then ye'll know the man that'll bid for yer cow, an' give ye nine goolden guineas for her, not dirty notes.'

" 'Nine guineas! bedad, an' that's more than——' Larry stopped short.

"The leprechaun was gone, an' the gate gone, an' the poor cow walked on as if she had never been stayed."

"Perhaps she never had," suggested Fred.

"Now, Master Fred," said Margaret, "if ye interrupt me agin wid yer roguish doubts, *I* shall stop, an' ye'll never hear how it all ended."

"Go on, Margaret," urged I, and Margaret obeyed.

CHAPTER II

"Larry's surprise an' the leprechaun's promises drove the thoughts of Kitty out of his head, an' he stepped toward Dublin with something of his ould lightsomeness; when just as he crossed the canal bridge he saw Kitty Quin standin' on her aunt Riley's doorstep in Clanbrassil-street dressed as illigant as a lady, an' lookin' as grand an' as proud as a queen.

"Well, Kitty's face went crimson, an' Larry's heart gave a great leap; but she just made him a stiff kind of curtsey, an' the door bein' opened, went in without a word.

" 'Thim's Dublin manners, I suppose,' thought Larry, as he went on, with his heart aching worse than ever; while Kitty watchin' him from behind the window-blind as far as she could see, felt the tears rowl over her burnin' cheeks, an' then wiped them off angrily, as if ashamed of her natural feelin's, an' blamed herself for being silly.

"Larry hardly knew how to get to the market, but sure enough there he met that same identical man the leprechaun had towld him of. An' more by token, he made Larry a bid for the cow. He bid eight pound ten, but Larry heartened beforehand, stuck out for nine guineas; and sure he took Larry into a public-house that stood convanient, and took out of his breeches-pocket an owld rag tied round wid string to sarve as a purse, and there an' thin counted down the nine goolden guineas. Then he asked Larry to have a dhrop an' a dhraw to seal the bargain.

"Larry's customer called for the whisky, an' offered Larry his own pipe. So the boy had both the dhrop an' the dhraw, an' then they had another dhrop and a dhraw; an' Larry remembered no more till he found himself lyin' on the grass, wid the stars shinin' out in honour of Midsummer-eve, an' a rushin' in his ears as of a great sea.

"Then he heard a rustle as of leaves, an' a mighty whisperin', an' lifted himself on his elbow to look about him, an' there he saw hundreds of little people no more than a span high, dressed in all sorts of queer outlandish fashions. But all the little men had coats of green velvet, and leaves of green shamrock in their hats; whilst the ladies had scarves of green gauze as fine as cobwebs; an' shamrock was wreathed round their hair, which shone like goold in the moonlight.

"They were all in commotion, running hither an' thither, howlding long discoorses, an' appeared to be in some sort of trouble or difficulty.

"Presently he saw in their midst the loveliest little creature the light of his eyes ever flashed on. She was sittin' in a silver-lily of a car, an' drawn by seven-and-twenty grasshoppers, three abreast. She had a wand in her hand, on which a crystal dewdrop twinkled like a star, an' Larry knew at wanst they were all fairies, an' she was their queen.

"Then, miss, a they drew nigher to him, Larry heard that one of the old fairies lay dead, an' that they wanted a coffin for the berryin'. But sorra a coffin could they get, for fairy coffins must be made by mortals, or the dead fairies never lie at rest. An' that was what the council an' the confusion wor about.

"Soon Larry heard the fairy queen say in a voice for all the world like the chirp of a cricket, 'But who shall make the elf's coffin?'

"All of sudden at least fifty of the Good People laid howld of him an' cried out like so many bees humming, 'Here's Larry M'Cann, here's Larry M'Cann! it's he will make the coffin.'

" 'But he never handled a saw or a plane in his life; he cannot make a pig-trough, an' how will he finish a coffin fit for an elf?' said one of the Good People.

" 'Sure, thin, an' it's we that must tache him,' answered another.

"With that the fairy queen touched him on the forehead, as lightly as if a leaf had dhropped there, with her shining wand, an' it flashed before his eyes till they seemed to strike fire; an' before he could cry out, or ask a saint to purtect him, he felt himself goin' down, down into the very earth itself, an' it's lost he thought he was for evermore.

"Troth, an' Dublin Castle's but a mud cabin in comparishun with the palace Larry was in when he came to his sinses. The walls were brighter than sunshine or rainbows, an' goold, an' silver, an' prechus jewels were plentiful as praties. There was gardens with trees an' flowers, the likes of which were never in all Ireland, an' the birds were all crimson, an' green, an' laylock, an' sang sweeter than thrush or nightingale. He seemed to see all this at once, an' many a curious thing beside which I disremember, and amongst it all the Good People were as busy as bees in a hive.

"Almost the first thing he saw was the dead fairy lying on a bed of Indian moss, under a delicate silken quilt, with a tiny wreath of lilies-of-the-valley on his head, forget-me-nots all about him. There was a fine bird-of-paradise singin' over him so soft an' sweet, it charmed the very sowl of Larry. There were fairies watchin' the corpse, but sorra wan of them was sobbin' or cryin', an' sure that same bothered him; for ye must know, miss, when a pious body dies in owld Ireland the keening women come an' lament over the corpse, with wailin' and cryin'.

"It was not long he was left to stare about him. One of the Good People put an inch-rule into his hand, an' set him to measure the corpse, an' sure that same came as natural as hoeing the cabbages. Then he was taken to a fine fairy workshop, where everything was as nate an' orderly as if it had just been claned. There was piles of wood of all sorts, an' one owld brownie towld Larry their names; and there was lots of bright tools, an' another wee owld fellow towld him their names; an' then two or three showed him how to use them. Then they gave him the wood an' the tools, an' he made an illigant little coffin as aisily as if he had been at the thrade all his life.

"The dead corpse was lifted in by the moorners as never moorned, an' Larry fastened down the lid as cliverly as any undhertaker in Leinster.

"As the funeral percession, wid the coffin in the midst, moved away to the fairies' cimetry, the owld brownie who first took notice of Larry said, 'Very nately put togither, Larry M'Cann; sure an' ye're a credit to your taichers. Take your wages, man, an' go.' Larry put out his hand an' stooped for the glitterin' purse that wor held out to him, an'—whist!

"He was lyin' on his back, with his curly head on a hard stone, undher a big tree, wid the mornin' sun shinin' full in his face, Powerscourt Falls tumbling in foam down the great high rocks, that frowned above him, leapin' over big boulders, an' rushin' away wid a roar undher a little wooden bridge just beyant.

"Larry rubbed his eyes, sat up, an' rubbed them again, an' sure the more he looked about him the more he was bothered.

" 'Begorra, an' this is a quare thrick to be servin' a man,' says he, as he scrambled to his feet, wid his bones as stiff an' sore as if he had been beaten with a shillaly. 'Is it meself I am, or somebody else? an' whare have *I* bin? an by powers, how did I come here at all, at all? Is it dhrink, or dhraming, or aslape I am this blessed minnit? Be jabers, the Good People——'

"Larry stopped, an' crossed himself, an' bethought him of his wages, an' all that was in his grip was dead leaves!

"But he gave a great jump, and cried out, '*Plane laves*, bedad; an' it wur fairy goold, an' that iver turns to laves! An' it's a plane tree I'm lyin' undher! Musha, but that's a rare joke!'

"In another minute his heart sank, an' he thrimbled with fear lest he had been paid for the cow in fairy goold too, an' should find only yellow leaves in his pocket. But, faith, the nine bright goolden guineas—not dirty one-pound notes—were solid and safe.

"The sun was dancin' brightly on the waters as Larry hastened along the narrow footpath by the stream, an' turnin' sharp off before he reached the foaming waters of the Dargle, mounted the crooked an' dangerous way up the steep banks to the high road, wondering why the Good People couldn't have laid him down under a roadside hedge, or in a green field, instead of carrying him out of the way intirely to Powerscourt Falls. It was all a mystery an' a dhrame to him, an' as he went along he kept repeating, 'A fortin' in my hands, the owld leprechaun said he'd be afther showin' me. Sure, an' mightn't it be somethin' moore thin the *plane laves* he meant? Ah, Kitty, my darlint, if I'm sivin days owlder since ye saw me last, I've sarved an apprenticeship that's made me more than sivin years wiser.'

"From the day he saw Kitty at the pattern, Larry M'Cann had taken to savin' his money. It was kept in a crock hid under the thatch of the barn, an' there he went quietly before he put a foot on the kitchen floor. Takin' seven one-pound notes an' ten shillins out, he put the nine guineas in, an' took his father the price he had fixed on the cow.

" 'Where have ye been, ye vagabone, all this blessed night?' cried old M'Cann, as the broth of a boy put his bright curly head in at the door.

" 'All night, father, all night, did ye say?' cried Larry, bewildered; for ye see, Master Fred, he thought he had been a week with the Good People.

" 'Yis! all night; for isn't the sun shinin', an' this the blessed Midsummer-day, ye spalpeen? It is dhrunk ye are before the dew is off the daisies? Ah, Larry, me lad, it's the wrong way yez goin' ever since Kitty Quin showed ye the cowld shouldher; bad cess to the whole lot of them! But where's the price of the baste? If ye were dhrunk, sure ye'd sinse left to take care of that.'

"Aye, an' sure when he found he had not been more than a night with the fairies, he had sense enough left to keep his own saicret. His mother said a mighty change had come over Larry, but sorra a guess had she where it came from.

"He put the potheen aside when it came his way, an' took to the farm so kindly, he went about his work whistling, and did as much in one day as he had ever done in two. Then he went an arrand to Dublin with the car, an' brought back a lot of carpenter's tools, an' some dale boards. He put them in an old shed that was tumblin' down, unknownst to anyone but his brother Pat. Then he put a door on the pigstye to kape the pigs out of the house, an' persuaded his father to have the holes in the mud-floor of the kitchen filled up; an' conthrived somehow to make the farm dacent and comfortable, with odd bits of improvement here an' there.

"Amongst it all, he an' Pat got the crooked walls of the shed to stand upright, an' mended the thatch, an' put the door again on its two hinges, an' put a lock on the door, widout a word to father or mother. An' then, sure, he contrived to put up some sort of a carpenter's bench, after the pattern in the fairies' workshop. More wood was got, an' troth, one mornin', to her surprise, Mrs. M'Cann found a new dale table, an' a dresser, an' an aisy-chair in her kitchen, the like of which wasn't in all Enniskerry.

" 'Sure an' its illigant, it's fairy work!' said all the neighbours.

" 'True for you; it *is* the fairies work,' said Larry, with a sly wink at Pat; an' Pat, knowin' what he had seen, an' nothing of the fairies, burst into a loud laugh, an' let out that Larry was the workman.

"No neighbour was more astonished than Larry's own father an' mother. They knew nothing of Larry's friend the leprechaun, nor his fairy taichers; they said the blessed St. Joseph must have put the knowledge in his head, an' called the boy a rale born genius.

"Other farmers' wives envied Mrs. M'Cann her fine dresser, on which a set of new wooden platters an' bickers were ranged, with here and there a bright-coloured crock for show; an' they came beggin' of Larry to make the copy of it for thim. So, sure, an' it came about that soon Larry had so much of his new work he was forced to tache two of his brothers the trade, an' build a proper workshop; and Farmer M'Cann had to set the gossoons to work on the farm instead of lounging about an' propping up door-posts all the day.

"But niver a bit did Larry go near Kitty all this time, though many a longin' look did he cast that way when he passed Peter Quin's gate. If they met at mass, he just gave her the time o' day, as any other friend might do; but though his very heart was bursting with love, he kept it, like his other saicrets, to himself.

"As for Kitty, there were plenty of bachelors after her, either for herself or her fortin'; but she never got the feel of Larry's kisses off her lips, an' cared more for a glance of his blue eye than for all the bachelors in Wicklow.

"She knew she had sent him away with her proud words, but she would have given all her goold for a whisper of love from him now he had taken her at her word, and seemed to forget her intirely. She just went paler an' thinner, an' when the next Midsummer roses were red on the bushes, they were only white ones on Kitty's cheeks.

"Mike and Larry had been fast friends all the time, an' many a job of work Larry did for him on his own account, but sorra a nail would he drive for Peter Quin. It was Mike who let Larry into the saicret that owld Corcoran the agent was after Kitty, an' that she sent him about his business with a sharp word agen his desait in slandering a better man—meaning Larry.

"A smart young shopkaiper from Dublin had made her an offer besides, an' even set Molly Mulroony the Blackfoot to thry an' persuade her."

"What's a Blackfoot, Margaret?" we asked, in a breath.

"Sure, an' a Blackfoot's a match-maker, a woman as goes between shy lovers and helps the coortin'.

"Well, then, as Larry never went to the whisky shop, nor to Peter Quin's, Mike found his way to the busy carpenter's shop. He used to ask a power of questions about the work in hand; for I must tell ye, Larry had been so well taught by the Good People, he could turn his hand to cabinet-work as well as rough carpentry.

"About this time, Mike saw Larry and Pat workin' early an' late over furniture not meant for the farmers or gentry about; an', for a wondher, Larry never said a word who they were working for. But Pat, the sly rogue, let out as a great saicret that it was for Larry's own house, agin his weddin'.

" 'Whare is the house?' says Mike.

" 'At Bray,' says Pat.

" 'An' who's the sweetheart?' says Mike again.

" 'Arrah, now, an' that's jist what meself don't know,' says Pat, in reply.

"Mike went with his news straight to Kitty, who, with bare arms an' tucked-up gown, was makin' butter in the dairy, though she did despise a farmer's life.

"Down went butter an' butter-mould, an' Kitty into the bargain, an' Mike had much ado to bring her out of her faint.

" 'Kitty,' says Mike, when they were all by themselves, 'sure an' ye didn't care for Larry, did ye? I thought ye didn't, as ye trated him wid scorn and contimpt, and Larry tuk to the dhrink with the heart-break.'

" 'O, don't, Mike dear, don't! Troth, an' it was *my* own pride an' consait that druv Larry away, an' it's I that have had the heart-break ever since.'

" 'Be me sowl, an' it must be a new sweetheart, an' a cliver lass, that set him agin drink an' made him turn carpenter! Och, Kitty, I'd sooner ye'd had Larry M'Cann than the biggest lord in the land;' an'

Mike took out his pipe—his unfailing consoler—for a dhraw an' a think; an' Kitty, having no such consolation, he left her sobbin'.

"The next day was Sunday, but Kitty was not at mass. Mike, howiver, was there, an' Peter, an' Larry, as fine as a Dublin tailor could make him.

" 'How's Miss Quin?' asked Larry purlitely of Mike, as they walked home together.

" 'Troth, an' she might be better,' answered Mike; an' says he, quite abrupt, 'Whin's this weddin' of yours to come off, Larry?'

" 'It's not settled,' says he; 'I've not got the lady's consint yet.'

" 'Not settled, an' her a lady, an' your house taken, an' your furniture made! Bedad, this passes me intirely!' An' Mike looked hard at Larry, an' Larry looked at Mike, and whatever they saw they shook hands, an' Mike flung up his shillaly an' caught it again, and danced every foot of the way to their own gate.

" 'Mebbe ye wouldn't mind comin' in for a bit, as Pether's stayed behint for confession,' says Mike, with a grin. An' in they went together.

"Dinner wor bein' laid in the kitchen, but Kitty was in the parlour.

" 'As ye're not very well, Kitty, I thought I'd better bring a doctor to see yez,' says Mike, openin' the door, with aquare twinkle ov his eyes.

" 'A doctor!' says Kitty, starting to her feet, growing crimson an' then white as Larry stepped into the room, an' Mike discraitly shut the door upon them, an' being weak she might have fainted again, but Larry caught her in his arms—an' she got better.

"Dinner waited for Peter, and Peter waited for Kitty; but Mike towld him that Kitty was ill an' the doctor was wid her, an' they couldn't be disturbed. But Peter wanted his dinner, an' grew impatient; an' then Mike towld him that as he had been to confession, Kitty was at confession too, an' that Larry M'Cann was her confessor.

"Sure, Peter was thunderstruck; but he had sinse to see that Larry M'Cann, the thrivin' young carpenter, was another sort of a man from the Larry M'Cann who worked on his father's farm with scarce a thought of payment; an' Mike soon got his father to give consent with a blessin'.

"The praist followed the doctor in less than a month, but the praist this time was Father Maguire.

"The day before the weddin,' Larry took Kitty down to Powerscourt Falls, an' there sittin' with his arm round her slender waist, on the stone under the plant tree where his head had lain, he towld her all about the leprechaun, an' his own apprenticeship to the fairies.

"An' that was how the M'Canns became carpenters."

Fred and I tried to convince Margaret that the leprechaun was the result of her grandfather's morning dram, and that under the influence of further potations he had strayed in safety from the road down the precipitous path to the Dargle, and so on to the Falls; and there sleeping, had dreamt of the fairy funeral.

But Margaret was not convinced; and a few years later the faithful creature died, as firm a believer in fairies as when she told us the story of Larry's apprenticeship, and the fortune he found *in his own right hand.*

THE FATE OF THE FOSBROOKES

THOUGH possessed of no actual patent of nobility, the Fosbrookes of Fosbrooke Manor held heir heads high, and were as proud of their long pedigree, as any baronet in the county. And with good cause; so many intermarriages with right noble dames were emblazoned on that roll, so broad were the acres over which the Squire held manorial and territorial sway, so fine a specimen of Tudor architecture was his grand old mansion, that the lord of the manor it represented might well be pardoned if he boasted the blue blood which had come to him through successive maternal veins, and forgot that he held no other lordship.

The Fosbrookes of Fosbrooke, however, were not given to boasting. They had been squires of the land for so many generations that their position was assured, and needed no trumpet-tongue to proclaim it. I am myself a Fosbrooke, and perhaps inherit the old leaven, if I inherit nothing more.

For it happens, I am but the descendant of a degenerate and disowned Fosbrooke, who struck a deadly blow at the family pride, and my name—neither Rupert nor Reginald, but blunt, plain John, Barrister-at-Law—may be found on the lintels of a door in the Inner Temple; and three months ago Fosbrooke Manor was known to me only through tradition.

My grandfather's grandfather, so I have been told, was the Squire's second son, and destined for the army in accordance with established precedent. But he, Rupert, had no mind to gird a warrior's sword upon his thigh. He had watched the family portraits grow warn and life-like under the hand of Gainsborough; had gone with the artist into the woods and terraced gardens, in quest of fitting backgrounds; and, lingering by his side, the longing grew within himself to be a painter, and reproduce on the lifeless canvas the loveliness of life and nature. Unknown to Squire or Dame, their son sketched by Gainsborough's side; and he, proud of his art, fostered the youth's enthusiasm, all unwitting of mischief.

Thus it chanced that when the rising painter returned to the metropolis, after a prolonged stay in the ancient Manor House, he left behind a pupil longing to emulate his master, as well as a group of pictures in the oaken gallery.

Then it was discovered that Rupert dabbled in pigments; but so long as he only handled his brush for amusement, he might copy the old pictures on the walls, group together cottage children, or case a groom in armour from the staircase, and transfer to the panels of his chamber his crude imaginings of art, with no further token of disapprobation than the contemptuous laughter of his father and brother, who regarded a fox's brush as a trophy, but a painter's as the mere tool of a craftsman. Yet the very taunts and sarcasms which followed the young laggard in the hunting-field, the unsportsmanlike shot in woods or stubble, drove him for refuge to the solitude of his own chamber, and for solace to the art condemned by those around him.

But not until Rupert declined to be a soldier did opposition culminate, and wrath grow fierce. In vain did the good mother plead with son and sire; in vain did Reginald urge his brother to renounce his degrading pursuit as a slur on their ancient lineage and escutcheon, holding up the army as the only outlet for a Fosbrooke.

Rupert was as persistent as his elder brother, as resolute as his father was vehement; all argumentation ending with the same resolve, "I will *not* lay down my paint brush for a sword."

"Then, by heaven I'll make a bonfire of your painting rattletraps! No son of mine shall spend his days in daubing canvas to disgrace us all!" cried the old Squire in his wrath.

Presently there was a great blaze in the courtyard, that seemed to flame again in the dark eyes of Rupert, who stood in the doorway with knitted brows and folded arms, a fire kindling in his heart as all his treasures went to feed he holocaust.

His lip curled. "Ay, burn them, an' you will; I shall be a painter notwithstanding."

"You paint no more in Fosbrooke Manor, Master Rupert," replied his father, with decision. "There is your commission, take it or leave it. But if you leave it you quit Fosbrooke at once and for ever. See, then, if brush or sword be best to fight your way with."

"You may cast the commission among the burning rattletraps," retorted the young man proudly. "I'll none of it. You have kindled a fire to destroy, and it will die in ashes; but the fire of genius is unquenchable, and that creates."

"No weeping, madam," shouted the Squire, as Dame Fosbrooke's kerchief went to her tearful eyes. "Let him carry his genius elsewhere. He paints no more under this roof. And look you, sir," he called out to Rupert, who was following his distressed mother, "if ever you put a living foot on this threshold whilst I'm above ground, I'll have you pitched out neck and crop, you ungrateful whelp!"

Reginald stood apart, but made no sign of interposition. Rupert turned. "At your bidding, sir, I go. Fosbrooke Manor is now no place for me. But, living or dead, I shall come back to my home some day, and none shall say me nay when next I paint beneath its roof."

He sought his sorrowing mother, and clung to her embrace, but, proud and persistent as his kin, tore himself away. In half an hour he was on the road to London, with nought but what his steed could carry, and his mother's tearful blessing.

Squire Fosbrooke closed the chamber of his degenerate son, and the avenues of his heart. He made a will in which he utterly renounced him, and thenceforth woe betide the luckless wight who dared to speak of Rupert in his hearing.

He had been his favourite child, the son of his age—a posse of girls had come between Reginald and him—and the wrench made in a moment of anger set his heart-string quivering for ever. But a Fosbrooke of Fosbrooke was never known to yield where the family honour was concerned, and silence as of the grave closed over Rupert's name within the shadow of the Manor. If ever a whisper reached the mother's ear that he had found a welcome in Gainsborough's studio, the whisper never had an echo from her lips. The Squire, once bluff and hearty, grew stern—the blow he had dealt at his boy had fallen on himself.

Nothing was heard of Rupert for many years. His sisters married and went their several ways to distant homes. Reginald alone was left. Then he took to himself a wife, and grandchildren ran in and out of the tapestried rooms with a pleasant patter on the oaken floors, and climbed the old Squire's knee, and won smiles from the sad-eyed grandmother, who sighed so heavily as she watched their childish gambols.

The seasons came and went. It was the tenth anniversary of the day on which a prejudiced father drove forth his son (as stubborn as himself) to shape a future in an untried world. Ten years since Rupert, with the double fire of genius and obstinacy in his eye, rode away down the long beech avenue without one backward glance at battlements or mullioned window to stir the deeper emotions of his soul and change his purpose.

Squire Fosbrooke and his heir had been out with the hounds since dawn. The London carrier's waggon creaked slowly along a bye-lane to the back of the great house, and there surrendered a square, unwieldy, flat packing-case, over which conjecture wasted itself, until the white-haired dame, yielding less to the curiosity of her grandchildren, and their mother, Lady Annabel, than to some unconquerable impulse within herself, gave orders for the forcing of the lid. Whatever lay within was covered by a thick cloth, on which was inscribed in bold characters:

"RUPERT FOSBROOKE'S ADDITION TO THE FAMILY PORTRAITS."

The elder lady blanched to her very lips. With gesture rather than word she ordered the removal of the cover the while the children crowded round in wonderment, and Lady Annabel drew herself up disdainfully.

There, limned by no tyro, the discarded son of the house looked out from the canvas, older, manlier, nobler than of old, palette and brushes in hand, a fine boy's head before him on an easel; and by his side, with fingers lightly resting on his shoulder, a woman lovely as a painter's dream. No need the written legend to declare that Rupert's wife and son were also there portrayed, or that his had been the artist's hand.

"Rupert Fosbrooke, Maud his wife, and Rupert his son," read Reginald's eldest boy. "Why, grandmother, who are they?"

"Your uncle, and your aunt and cousin, child," sobbed the bereaved old lady in broken accents, whilst the servants drew respectfully apart and whispered beneath their breath. Lady Annabel plucked her children away, saying:

"Uncle and aunt, forsooth! They are neither kith not kin of mine, boy. No common painter's doll-faced wife claims affinity with me!"

"Lady Annabel," said the elder, gathering up her form, "Rupert Fosbrooke is my dear son. *I* never disowned him. I will not disown the fair mate he has chosen. He would never stoop to one unworthy."

"Stoop! He had sunk to the portrait-painter's level ere he wedded his master's niece. I heard so much, madam, when I was last in Town." So saying, Lady Annabel swept away to give her little ones a lesson in pride of birth, and obliterate, if possible, the pictured relatives from remembrance.

Lady Annabel was no favourite with the old servants, and dark-eyed Rupert had been.

Reverently they obeyed Dame Fosbrooke's behest, and carrying the picture into the long dining-room, set it upright against the tapestried wall by the side of the carved buffet.

As the Squire entered with a troop of hungry hunting friends, the picture caught his sight. For a few moments he stood gazing upon it with changing colour and breath that came and went; then, raising the whip he held, he struck at the figures fiercely, whilst he demanded hoarsely who dared to brave him thus; and bade the servants haul it forth and burn it.

There was a bonfire blazing in the yard whilst the Squire and his friends supped, and Lady Annabel looked on with stern satisfaction from an upper window. But the packing-case alone was burned. The picture itself had been quietly smuggled into the closed chamber of the artist, and the good dame's secret was well kept; not for fee or reward, but for love of Barbara Fosbrooke and her youngest born.

Four years Dame Barbara kept that secret, along with others, in her heart; and then, lying on her death-bed, she broke the long silence and prayed that Rupert might be summoned to close her dying eyes.

It may be that the Squire was likewise wearying for a sight of his discarded son, and only lacked a pretext for his recall, for he was no longer obdurate. No doubt in his hidden soul he had long repented his hasty orders anent the picture, and blamed the too obedient executants of his will. With barely a show of hesitation he consented, but Reginald and Lady Annabel, too crafty to demur, too proud to own a painter for a brother, threw obstacles in the way. "There was no clue to the vagabond's whereabouts."

From a locket worn concealed the feeble mother produced a tiny slip of paper. It held Rupert Fosbrooke's name and address. Here was an unlooked-for revelation. Annabel and Reginald exchanged glances.

"Ah! this implies correspondence. I presume, sir, you had no knowledge of any communication with my brother."

Once this would have been a spark on tow. It passed unheeded. All the Squire seemed to hear was his wife's appeal for haste; which his own voice seconded on her account, he said. Himself wrote a hurried letter of recall. At once Reginald became officiously active. He despatched a trusty messenger with the missive; so trusty, that he failed to return before the dame's ears were closed to any message he might bring.

Days went by. The white-haired Squire paced the corridors as anxiously expectant as the sick lady in the state bed. But the shifty or irritable answers of Reginald to her enquiries had aroused suspicion of treachery.

As the end drew night, she insisted on being carried to Rupert's chamber as the only chance of seeing the face of her lost son.

They thought her mind was wandering. Her meaning was

clear enough to them all when her chair was placed in front of Rupert's picture, which yet bore the mark of the Squire's whip across its surface.

Not more eagerly did Barbara Fosbrooke's filming eyes trace the well-remembered lineaments of her banished son than did those of the old Squire, in whom affection had seemed so long dead; whilst Reginald and Annabel looked lost in amazement.

Life's fire relit in Barbara's wan features as she gazed: strength came to her anew. She kissed the Squire's brown hand as the other dashed from his eyes the fast-gathering tears; and then marking the scowl on Reginald's swart face as he slunk behind her chair, she lifted up her withered right hand, and extending it towards the picture, said impressively, in a voice which seemed to have gathered preternatural strength for the effort: "Rupert, my son, I call and thou dost not answer; I have longed for thee and thou dost not come. But thou shalt come, and thou and thine be masters of Fosbrooke when treachery has done its worst. I cannot die in my bed for lack of thy presence. But if there be treachery, let those who kept thee back answer it, for never shall a Fosbrooke die in his bed till the lost be recalled, and younger and elder join hands in love and friendship under the old roof-tree.

"And mark you, Reginald! my curse shall cling to him who dares destroy or disturb the picture I have preserved and cherished, the solace of my old age."

The flickering flame was spent. Barbara Fosbrooke fell back in her chair; and there, with the painted eyes of son, grandson, and daughter-in-law fixedly set upon her, she closed her own for ever.

He "would never set living foot in Fosbrooke Manor again" was the verbal message said to come from Rupert: and the old man winced as he listened, for the words were his own—never forgotten, it seemed, by either. He had no doubts of the messenger's fidelity; no thought of duplicity in his eldest-born. He accepted the answer as final; made no second attempt at reconciliation; never again mentioned Rupert's name. But from that hour a change fell upon him. All his old sports were neglected. Reginald might hunt and shoot, and fill the manor-house with roystering squires: he kept himself aloof, and would pace the long corridor between his own chamber and Rupert's by the hour together, not seldom turning into the unused room and lingering there alone with his regretful memories.

The servants said he was bewitched; and Reginald threatened to burn Rupert's picture in earnest, since it seemed like to turn his father's brain. And no doubt he would have carried his threat into execution but for an appalling incident which made the very room and all within a terror to him.

The only sport to which the Squire had clung was angling. It was quiet, and all noise and bluster had, as it were, died out of his life. Reginald strode in and about with heavy tread and resonant tones; *he* came and went as silently as the silver hairs fell from his thinning scalp; and sat in the shade of the alders and willows by the moat side, heedless of the flight of time. At first his youngest grandson bore him constant company, and fished by his side with a willow-wand for a rod, prattling in boy fashion, with or without reply.

One memorable evening, as Lady Annabel was about to retire for the night, and the housekeeper bore a lamp before her along the corridor, they saw a pale light streaming under the closed door of Rupert's room: then there was a moan, and a fall.

Both women screamed; Reginald and a troop of servants rushed up the wide staircase. The latter hung back when told the cause of alarm, but Reginald dashed open the door and found, as he had expected, his father lying senseless on the floor.

But where was the light the pair had seen? There was only the lamp in the housekeeper's hand! And the servants whispered among themselves.

The Squire was raised and after a time revived. But he would give no explanation as to what had caused his swoon.

From that night, however, he would have no companion when he went to fish; sending his grandson back, kindly but peremptorily. He assigned no reason; and when the child cried, his lady mother encouraged him to disobey. His grandfather drove him back; but one day when so dismissed, he refused to depart, and then the Squire gave up his sport altogether, warning the boy not to go near the moat alone.

The warning was disregarded. Before many days had gone, a slimy and dripping form was drawn from the moat, and Lady Annabel, wringing her hands, accused the old man of having murdered her boy. And the Squire turned mournfully away—but answered he never a word.

A month or more elapsed. Squire Fosbrooke came not to the breakfast-board. House and grounds were searched. He was found at last, lifeless, before the painting of his banished son.

Reginald, now Lord of the manor, shut up the room once more, and kept the key. It was a needless precaution. From the time that Mistress Hope, the housekeeper, had confided to the steward that Rupert the painter had died in London the very night the old Squire was found senseless before his picture—from that time superstitious awe locked the door without a key. The old Squire, and he alone, would approach it night or day.

His death there confirmed the evil repute of the chamber, and Dame Fosbrooke's dying words were repeated under breath through house and village.

Mistress Hope having long rebelled against the rule of Lady Annabel, retired on the pension left by the Squire.

In less than a couple of years Reginald Fosbrooke was pitched clean over the neck of his hunter, and Lady Annabel was left a widow, to reign supreme at the Manor during the three years of the heir's minority.

Then the steward followed Mrs. Hope to London, and, though late in life, they made a match of it. They did more: they rescued Rupert Fosbrooke's wife and son from the poverty into which they were falling.

When the picture scheme of reconciliation had failed, Rupert grew bitter and angry with himself for having made the advance. But when, through Mrs. Hope, he heard of his mother's death, and the haughty answer Reginald's messenger had conveyed to the Manor as from him, grief and vengeance alternated in his breast, and in the turmoil he could not paint, and disappointed his patrons. A brain fever set in, and he died execrating his brother Reginald, and threatening to haunt him and his until the wrong was righted.

Maud, the unfortunate painter's widow, though too proud to appeal to her haughty sister-in-law, was not too proud to accept the home made for her and her son Rupert by the faithful steward and his wife; who, in their turn, felt it only an honour to devote to the service of a Fosbrooke the money they had saved in other Fosbrooke service. They lived to see the younger Rupert married, and impressed on him for his descendants this record of family history and estrangement, coupled with the doom hanging over the elder branch of the family; insisting that in some secret manner every fatality which befell a Fosbrooke had been mysteriously foretold or previsioned within the haunted chamber of the discarded son.

So the story was handed down to me, with an addition of casualties by flood and field which had carried off the Fosbrookes, either in infancy or age, and which were only to be averted when the elder Fosbrooke extended the right hand of fellowship to the younger, and Rupert's heirs became master of the Manor.

My grandfather believed this implicitly. As for myself, I was born in a sceptical and practical age, and have had to fight my own way so sturdily, I have had no leisure to waste on the ghostly traditions of bygone ancestors in a remote manor-house.

So it might have been to the end of the chapter but for a combination of fortuitous circumstances which, to say the least, were remarkable.

CHAPTER II

My friend Stretton, the solicitor, of Clement's Inn, to whom I owe whatever success I have made, came to my chambers in the Temple one summer day in unusual haste for him, and handed me a lengthy brief and a stiff retaining fee, saying: "There, run your eyes over that! If you can talk the jury over to give our clients a verdict, your fortune's made!" and he gave me a quick tap on the shoulder.

I had taken up the paper languidly. "Myers *v.* Fosbrooke."

With a quickening thrill I ran my eye rapidly over the brief and soon made myself master of the contents.

The client I was called upon to defend was Charles Fosbrooke, of Fosbrooke Manor: our opponent, the plaintiff, a neighbouring landowner. The cause simply this.

Three of the Squire's children had been drowned by the upsetting of a small skiff on the moat. He at once vowed no more lives should be given up to its greedy waters, and set about its drainage. In so doing he unavoidably diverted the current of a small watercourse known as the Fosse-brook, to the alleged detriment and damage of the plaintiff's property.

Had the plaintiff not been litigious the case might have been compromised at the outset, when the Squire offered compensation to Sir Joseph Myers.

By a strange coincidence, a letter lay open on my table before me containing overtures from the opposite side, wherein my supposed hereditary antagonism to the Fosbrookes of the Manor was openly relied on as a reason why they should retain me as counsel, and I rejoice to hold their brief.

It is possible to have too low an estimate of human nature. Why should I, John Fosbrooke, exercise such gifts as I possessed in order to oppose my own distant kin, who had never done me a personal wrong.

I had just declined the plaintiff's brief, when Mr. Stretton put his head in at the door. I showed him the letter and my reply.

It remained for me to prove black was white, or to suffer a non-suit. There is something in the old adage that "blood is thicker than water." I resolved to do my utmost for our client, in spite of dead-and-gone feuds. I threw myself into the case, ransacking legal records for points and precedents.

A day or two had elapsed. Leaving the Temple in the forenoon I encountered Stretton in the gateway, just as I was turning into Fleet Street. He caught me by the button-hole and invited me to luncheon with him. As I hesitated, a light basket-phaeton containing a gentleman and lady, with a small page in dark livery behind, drove under Temple Bar and stopped in front of us.

"By Jove!" exclaimed Mr. Stretton, and almost before the words left his lips the page was at the horse's head, and the gentleman, whose eyes and hair were black as my own, and who struck me as a disagreeable likeness of myself—but not a bad-looking fellow on the whole—had jumped out, throwing the reins to the lady, as lovely a young brunette as it had been my fate to meet, with eyes as soft and melancholy as her companion's were eager and fiery.

With barely a word of apology to me, he drew the solicitor aside and began in a hurried voice I could not choose but hear.

"What's this your clerk tells me, Mr. Stretton? Do you know into what hands you have committed our case? This Mr. John Fosbrooke——"

"Is a very rising young barrister—could not be in better hands," interrupted the lawyer imperturbably.

"He claims kinship with the Fosbrookes of Fosbrooke, sir. There is an old feud between his branch of the family and ours. You must withdraw the brief at any cost. He will ruin our cause. In my father's name I insist on the withdrawal of the brief!" This in answer to Mr. Stretton's visible protest.

I thought it quite time to interfere. As haughtily as himself I stepped forward. "Mr. Reginald Fosbrooke, I presume."

His brow said, "Ay, and who on earth are you?"

"Your brief, sir, and my retaining fee shall be in Mr. Stretton's office in less than twenty minutes. There is no need to withdraw the case—I throw it up." And I turned on my heel under the archway. I met my clerk on his way to dinner and sent him back flying for the offending brief and Stretton's cheque, which lay unchanged in my drawer. I had heard Stretton's remonstrance as I went, and the other's annoyed response.

I had barely taken three steps after my clerk, when a crash and a shriek called me back. Reginald Fosbrooke was lying stunned on the pavement, the page was scrambling to his feet, a bystander had caught the affrighted horse, the carriage-wheel was crashing in collision with a cab, and the lovely occupant was in imminent peril.

Darting forward, I managed to extricate the lady from the phaeton before plunging animal had made a total wreck of it.

She seemed as lifeless as the man on the ground. My clerk was back by this time. Shouting to him to bring a doctor to my chambers, and to Stretton to have his prostrate client conveyed thither, I hurried forward with the insensible girl in my strong arms, and placed her in my own chair. The couch had soon another occupant.

"This will be quieter than a shop," I whispered to Stretton, "and we can keep the crowd out *here*." He nodded a sort of dazed assent.

Before a doctor reached us my charge had revived. And then her distress over her "dear brother," her "dear Reggy," was pitiable to witness.

I did my best to console her, and to assure her that her brother was not dead, only stunned, and would doubtless recover shortly; and, as she turned her liquid eyes in thanks on mine, I felt there was *one* Fosbrooke who could never be my enemy.

A couple of hours went by before Reginald Fosbrooke gave a sign of returning animation. The doctor had muttered something of concussion of the brain, and internal injury from the horse's hoof; insisted on quiet, forbade removal, and, aside to Stretton and me, suggested telegraphing to friends.

Barbara—I could almost have guessed her name, had not the injured man murmured it, as she knelt beside him in sobbing agony—caught the suggestion and remarked simply—so simply that I am sure the doctor thought her wits were wandering—"There is no need: they will already now of this catastrophe at home."

They must have had a telegraph of their own, swifter than that of science! Surely enough, before the close of the afternoon Squire Fosbrooke—who must have been on the road before our message was despatched—stood by the side of his eldest son, and clasped my hand with grateful earnestness as that of a stranger, saying he was glad he had found him alive. He was a grave, dignified, but not haughty man, preternaturally old, and bent beneath the heavy burden of inexorable fate.

He and his daughter took possession of my chambers with many courteous apologies for turning them into a hospital; apparently unconscious that they were indebted to more than a chance namesake. Only the patient knew my antecedents; and when, at the close of the week, he recognized me as his involuntary entertainer he grew irritably impatient to be removed.

The doctor shrugged his shoulders, his gentle sister shed tears, his father, Mr. Stretton, and myself remonstrated. The heir of Fosbrooke was wilful.

He was borne thence with the tenderest care; but barely had he crossed the threshold than violent haemorrhage set in, and only a lifeless body was carried into the neighbouring hotel. A broken rib, displaced, had lacerated some internal organ.

Mourning did not arrest the law-suit. The Squire, ignorant of Reginald's prohibition, wrung my hand at parting, and said he was sure his cause was in good hands. I had gone with them to the station, possibly drawn thither by the grateful thanks in Barbara Fosbrooke's every tone and gesture. Then it occurred to the Squire that I might better understand how the case stood between him and Myers if I went over the grounds and tracked the Fosse-brook; and he asked me to follow them down in time for the poor boy's funeral.

I went to my chambers musing. Two strange events had come to pass. I, the descendant of Rupert the discarded, had been invited to the Manor. Moreover, I was in love with Barbara.

The Manor House was a magnificent pile with a background of waving woods. Perhaps it was the presence of undertakers, and a crowd of funeral guests with mourning robes and faces, made me feel the interior so gloomy in its grandeur, notwithstanding the faint smile of Barbara and the courteous reception of Barbara's mother.

Was it chance that assigned to me, the latest comer in the crowded mansion, the apartment at the end of the corridor? I had followed the servant mechanically, my mind filled with Barbara's greeting, and not his apologies; but my rapid survey of the hastily prepared chamber set me thinking.

A label outside the oaken door showed that it was set apart for "Lawyer Stretton's friend." The hurried and bewildered servants had no conception that they had shown Rupert Fosbrooke's representative into Rupert's room.

If I had had a doubt it was dispelled by the sight of a large picture reared against the wall, from which three faces seemed to look at me through a veil of dust.

I have not an atom of superstition in me—at least I had not then. It was rather with reverence than awe that I sacrificed my cambric handkerchief to the restoration of the picture. Then I was struck with the resemblance between my ancestor and myself; and wondered if any of the many assembled relatives would perceive it: never thinking how little was known of the faces I was scanning so minutely.

Yet I think my appearance at the dinner-table did excite some curiosity, if furtive glances and whisperings were any index. Sombre dresses and long faces spoiled the meal for me. I was glad when I found myself back in my room in front of a wood fire kindled at my request; and, taking advantage of the double doors, took out a cigar to make myself at home.

There was a suggestiveness of damp and rheumatism about the heavy velvet-hung four-post bed. I declined its invitation, preferring to wrap myself in my travelling rug and stretch my limbs on an antique couch at right angles with the hearth. A second cigar sent me to sleep, to dream of Barbara. I awoke shivering, with an uneasy impression of a hand laid on my shoulder to arouse me. The fire was almost out, the candles quite, but there was a light in the room, and—yes! in the very midst of that light stood Rupert the Painter, palette and brush in hand, painting away at a picture on his easel.

I rubbed my eyes and gave myself a shake. The artist was still at work, and I saw the picture growing under his brush. It was an Alpine scene familiar to myself. Now figures appeared upon the canvas toiling up the snowy ascent. The artist looks round at me, and back at his canvas. I see delineated a broken rope, a shivered alpenstock, and a figure slipping and falling headlong into a terrible crevasse.

Again the artist turns his head, and his dark eyes transfix me. The canvas is blank. Again the brush is plied. Judge, jury, counsel, take their places. I see a brother barrister of long standing addressing the court, see him painted out; and my very counterpart stands out in my very attitude in my most eloquent mood. I see the effect on the faces of judge and jury; it is cheering. The artist turns round and smiles. Picture, painter, easel, light are gone! I am shivering in the dark, with barely a ray of moonlight straggling in through the windows.

I give myself another shake, say I am an arrant fool, conclude I have been dreaming, and compose myself to sleep again.

Convinced, when I awaken in the morning, that I have been dreaming, I say nothing at the breakfast-table of my broken rest, not caring to excite either alarm or ridicule.

As Stretton and I return to town in the express the day after the funeral, I elicit from him that the Squire has another son, now travelling in Switzerland, to whom, of course, the heirship will descend. After that, I fear Stretton has but a stupid companion to the end of the journey.

My survey of the moat, converted into a shrubbery, and the track of the watercourse in dispute, did not tell in my client's interest. Nevertheless, I went into court with a conviction I should win, although I scouted the idea of being influenced by a dream.

And I was successful. The case was dismissed as litigious and vexatious, and when I shook hands with our client, he insisted on my returning with him to the Manor, and said I did honour to the name I bore.

Other cases kept me in town until the end of term. Then I, John Fosbrooke, availed myself of the Squire's invitation, and was welcomed; Mrs. Fosbrooke offering many apologies for my being thrust into an unused room on my former visit. I protested I was perfectly satisfied, and thought it a pity so commodious a chamber should be left to me and the spiders.

The Squire took to me amazingly, and Barbara's heart opened to me. I hesitated how best to disclose my ancestry and propose for the sweet girl, when the whole fabric of my future was shaken by a telegram from Switzerland.

Charles Edward Fosbrooke had perished in the ascent of the Simplon. I was staggered, and the whole family were overwhelmed. It was no time for love proposals.

I volunteered a journey for the recovery of the body; saying that I knew the precise spot in which he was lying. This involved explanation of what I called my dream.

"Dream! It was no dream," cried Barbara and her parents, simultaneously.

"But who are you?" demanded the Squire, rising to his feet, "who have seen the spectral painter of our house? Rupert Fosbrooke never reveals the future save to one of his own near kin."

My answer and its effect may be imagined. An avalanche could scarcely have overwhelmed them more completely. The old Squire, his eyes suffused with tears, held out his hand to me.

"This is no time to perpetuate feud," said he. "Fate is too strong for us."

Need I add that I went to Switzerland and recovered the remains of the last heir of the elder Fosbrookes.

But ere I took my departure, unknown to the family I spent a night in the haunted chamber, still inclined to be sceptical. I came out next morning converted. Once more the mountain scene was painted before me, but I saw myself and guides recovering the lost, and the means employed.

Another picture was painted before me, and then the artist seemed to fling brushes and palette aside, and vanish with a benediction.

I stood with my now acknowledged relatives by the grave of the Squire's last son, and saw his tears fall fast on the coffin-lid before he turned away, and grasping my hand, called me with a sigh, the heir of Fosbrooke Manor.

I could hardly realise it then. I can realise it now, as I stand amid a perfect bower of bloom and perfume, in a pretty country church, and clasp the hand of Barbara before the altar, in that bond which for ever reunites the severed branches, and averts the fate of the Fosbrookes.

And this was the last picture shown to me—now a Fosbrooke of Fosbrooke, a picture of love, and peace, and goodwill.

A NEW LEAF

CHAPTER I

THE NEW SECRETARY

THERE was a new inmate at the Hall. Squire Appleton, J. P., finding that increasing years did not add to the elasticity which once made business a pleasure, had engaged a young fellow from London to keep accounts, overlook matters on the estate, carry on business correspondence, and relieve him in many odd ways; in short, a kind of clerkly factotum, though his duties were by no means onerous, and he was by courtesy dubbed a secretary.

The servants' hall had, of course, somewhat to say on his appointment. What did the Squire want with a secretary? His father had done without one, and his grandfather before him. And if he must have a secretary, why not engage someone from Leigh or Manchester, instead of a fop of a fellow from London, whom nobody knew anything about?

From this it will be seen that Mr. Alfred Lawrence had not made a favourable impression in the lower domestic circle. Still, opinions were divided; and if heads grown grey in the Appleton service were shaken disparagingly, the maids one and all pronounced him "charming," and the "*bow-idol* of a fine gentleman."

Naturally these conflicting opinions drifted beyond the limits of the park railings, and if they reached the pretty cottage of the pensioned-off ex-housekeeper, no wonder. She had two fair granddaughters who, in their vocation as dressmakers, had many errands to the hall. Then, Mrs. Lane herself was on friendly terms with her successor, and, moreover, attended the same Dissenting chapel as did Mrs. Bridoake, the lodgekeeper's wife, and piety by no means precluded gossip, or closed Mrs. Lane's ears to the commentaries afloat.

Moreover, she had an interest in listening, for Mr. Lawrence had endeavoured to ingratiate himself in the good graces both of herself and her grandchildren whenever an opportunity occurred to render himself agreeable, or display his fascinating person in the vicinity of the cottage.

This was a rustic building, in a bye-lane leading to the high road between Leigh and Tyldesley, over which ivy clambered to the very chimney tops, curtained the transom windows against intrusive sunbeams, and in summer disputed possession of the trellised porch with the green fringes of the purple-blossomed tea plant. A strip of garden lay between the cottage and the road, effectually screened from observation by a tall privet hedge. From the low wooden gate a path of variegated pebbles, arranged in quaint devices, led to the broad step beneath the porch, and to the green door resplendent with a bright brass knocker. It was a knocker for ornament, not use, since it spoke but in whispers and fully one half the callers at the cottage ignored the knocker altogether, walking in *sans cérémonie.*

A narrow passage divided the seldom-used parlour from the "house"—a sort of compromise between a kitchen and a parlour; the stone floor and shining cookware range being suggestive of the former; the rug, the worn Turkey carpet, chimney ornaments, solid mahogany furniture (transfers from the Hall), and an air of spotless nicety, being equally suggestive of the latter.

In this room, one autumnal afternoon, when the new secretaryship was but a few weeks old, Mrs. Lane sat near the fire, a picture of primitive neatness. Her closely-fitting dress of dark merino had neither trimming nor ornament; a white spun silk kerchief was pinned closely down over the bodice, and her grey hair was banded down under a cap of plain white net, enlivened only by tiny loops of white satin ribbon interspersed within the close border.

At an ample work-table, placed close to the ivy-curtained window for the benefit of the light, sat Jessie (a bright pink bow at the throat relieving her dark merino dress), a wilful, wayward beauty, early spoiled by the foolish flatteries of a silly mother. Ruth, her plainer sister, sat there at work likewise, linen cuffs and bands her sole adornment. She had come at a more ductile age under her grandmother's care, and had grown up gentle and retiring, with a shade of gravity upon her face scarcely in consonance with her nineteen years. Indeed, there were people who spoke of her placidity as melancholy, but they must surely have been mistaken.

Mrs. Lane, fresh from meeting, and from Mrs. Bridoake (and surely with some mysterious prevision in her mind), had come to the conclusion of a homily on worldly-mindedness and sin in general, with a special application to the new secretary in particular, denouncing him as a specimen of typical "pitch," and warning the girls to shun all communication with him if they would escape contamination.

Ruth stitched and listened passively.

Jessie—who had formed her private estimate of Mr. Lawrence—contrasting him with her own sweetheart, much to the disadvantage of the latter—stuck the pins into the pattern she was adjusting with an impatient click, and handled her scissors as if longing to cut up her grandmother's sermon along with her work.

"Depend upon it, girls, he is a bad man: he went to church last Sunday for the *first* time, and then FELL ASLEEP!" The iniquity of this untimely nap was expressed more by look and tone than words.

"Well, if the stupid old rector preached, I scarcely wonder," said Jessie, apologetically.

Mrs. Lane raised her hands. "Jessie, you shock me! If a man wet to worship his Maker, or hear the gospel in a right spirit, no dull sermon would send him to sleep." Jessie was silent under the rebuke; and for a little while nothing was heard but the rustle of silk and lining, the sharp crunch of the scissors, the faint click of the needle.

"We have reason to be thankful all men are not like him! Look at Reuben Isherwood. *He* would not spend his money in cigars and perfumery, or waste his time in frizzling his whiskers and flirting with the girls!" burst triumphantly from the old lady as the result of long cogitation.

Ruth broke her needle, and rose to replace it.

"I wish he did," thought Jessie, with a sigh; *she* did not regard these delinquencies as very flagrant.

"Ah! Jessie, you have reason to be proud of Reuben; he will be a husband to esteem. Very unlike that scrapegrace at the Hall,"[115] continued the grandmother.

"Very!" murmured Jessie with another audible sigh, which somehow seemed to be faintly echoed by her sister Ruth.

With an innate consciousness that Mr. Lawrence was just the individual to catch a foolish girl's fancy, and with marvellous want of tact, Mrs. Lane thus held him up to constant reprobation, contrasting his vices, real or imaginary, with Reuben's known virtues. She hoped thereby to prevent Jessie from wavering in her

---

[115] Scrapegrace: an incorrigible rascal.

choice under the seductive influence of a plausible tongue and a handsome person: the very hope proving her fear. For Ruth, she knew her precaution was unnecessary. Her sister had long dubbed her "a little old maid;" she held all would-be suitors at such a distance, whilst at men of the Lawrence stamp she did not care to glance. Her heart was a mystery, as woman's heart so often is; yet, though no love-light was ever seen to sparkle in her eye or leave a bloom upon her pale cheek, there *might* be a "graven image" somewhere shrined for secret worship.

With Jessie, Mrs. Lane overshot the mark. She was fond of finery, and of admiration, so that when Reuben left Leigh to enter into a draper's shop in Fishergate, Preston, she pined for attentions he was no longer at hand to render. He was moreover a plain man, without dash or pretension, and in his absence the stylish secretary shone resplendent.

"I don't see why grandmother should say such dreadful things about Mr. Lawrence; he is quite a gentleman; and I'm sure half the girls in Tyldesley are in love with him. The new curate isn't half so handsome. I wish Reuben was more like him, and had such white teeth and such beautiful black curls. I hate brown hair!" (Reuben's hair was of the obnoxious colour.) Thus from day to day Jesse would talk to herself; and so from time to time, as she met this fascinating Mr. Lawrence, their intimacy grew closer.

This admiration became more outspoken, and was couched in language which cast honest unsophisticated Reuben's love-making into the shade. Gratified vanity more than affection had tied her to her country lover, and Mr. Lawrence was an adept at loosening such bonds. In spite of Reuben's weekly letters, Jessie gradually forgot her fealty to him, and Mr. Lawrence deliberately ignored *his* in another quarter.

Two months had passed since Mrs. Lane's antagonism to the foppish secretary had first broken out in words. It was mid-winter. The tea plant fringe upon the porch was worn to threads, and the tall privet hedge, now a mere network of fine stems from which the leaves had dropped, ceased to be a screen between road and cottage.

Possibly that was the reason why one of the young dressmakers, seated close by the window—of course for the benefit of the light—raised her head so frequently from the bodice she was stitching, and glanced across the strip of garden.

Was Jessie expecting someone? Most likely, for as one or two passing figures loomed dimly through the leafless hedge, a keen glance of scrutiny followed each.

The ground was soft with recent rain, and footsteps were inaudible; but presently a masculine shadow went by, and there was the sound as of a light switch whisking away the few lingering leaves.

The quick blood leaped to Jessie's very temples, tingled even within her silent thimble, as she looked out furtively; but, artful young damsel, she was as reticent as her thimble.

Giving herself time to still the tell-tale pulses ere she spoke, she observed, as if deliberating, "Ruth, I think now the rain is gone I had better step over to Leigh, and match Mrs. Heap's dress with velvet and buttons myself."

"I thought you gave Dixon a bit of the silk, with a message to Mrs. Arrowsmith."

"So I did, but if Dixon should stay too long as the Boar's Head, he may forget my message altogether. It will most likely rain again to-morrow, and if he *should* forget, and Mrs. Heap's dress not be finished in time——"

"We should certainly lose our best customer," said Ruth, completing the sentence.

"And half Tyldsley would follow her," added Jessie, as with a slight toss of her shapely head, she left the room and speedily re-appeared attired in a well-fitting mantle and most becoming bonnet.

"How pretty you always look!" exclaimed Ruth admiringly; "and what a colour you have got, to be sure!"

"We should both look prettier if grandmother would only let us dress like other girls. I'm sure we are always as prim as Quakers. It's a wonder anyone trusts us to make a dress tastily or fashionably!" and there was quite a grievance in her tone.

"Nay, Jessie, we only dress as befits our station, and I think grandmother is quite right in saying we had better be neat than flaunting."

"Now, don't you begin to preach too! I've quite enough of it from her!" exclaimed Jessie, petulantly; "You are as prim as she is."

Ruth had risen, and was moving towards the easy chair in which Mrs. Lane sat dozing by the fire. Jessie stopped her. "Now, don't disturb grandmother out of her sleep. You can tell her where I am gone when she wakens, just as well. Good afternoon."

Jessie was off. As the front door snapped in closing, Ruth snatched a scrap of silk from the large work-table, and ran hastily down the pebble-path, after her sister. The wooden gate had just closed behind her.

"Stop, Jessie!"

She turned angrily. "Why do you follow me? Cannot I leave the house without being watched like a child?"

"You were going without the pattern—here it is," said Ruth, apologetically, though not without marked surprise.

"Oh, so I was. Thank you. Now run in, or you will take cold." (Was that sisterly thought, Jessie, or only one more item in the sum of growing artifice?)

Ruth turned—but so did the lane into the Tyldesley road close by; and during that brief colloquy over the low gate she had caught a glimpse of a loitering figure just as the curve.

"Who is that?" she murmured, as she slowly retrod the short path to the porch. "Who is that? Surely not the Squire's new secretary! It was like his figure. Could he be waiting for Jessie? Oh, I hope not! Yet she seemed so unusually anxious to get out. And why was she afraid of being watched? Oh, if grandmother only suspected such a thing, how angry she would be! And what would Reuben say? She never met *him* clandestinely. Grandmother ought to know; but I hate mischief-making, and, after all, I may be mistaken. Our Jessie could never be so false to Reuben as to meet that man in secret after all grandmother's cautions. Poor Reuben!"

These and like ruminations occupied Ruth's mind long after her return to the window seat and her sewing. She stitched and thought, thought and stitched; and started like one from a dream, when Mrs. Lane, waking from her nap, asked—

"Where is Jessie?"

"Gone to Leigh for Mrs. Heap's trimmings." Ruth's voice hesitated; lurking doubt of her sister's real errand twitched at her truthful tongue.

"Gone to Leigh without my knowledge! Ruth, was not Dixon commissioned to bring those trimmings?"

Mrs. Lane was a strict disciplinarian, and her exclamation implied that Jessie's offence was of magnitude.

"Yes, grandmother; but she said he might get drunk and forget."

"Forget!"—(How much was comprised in that word!)—"Dixon has been a carrier for twenty years, but I never knew him drink enough to confuse his memory. Drunk or sober, he does his business. But, Ruth, have had my eye on the silly child for some time, and am truly uneasy about her. Have you not noticed how slight a pretext has served for a reason to call her out and neglect her work at home?"

Ruth acknowledged she had.

"Then she has grown restless and discontented, and is neither so frank nor good-tempered as she used to be. There is something the matter, I am sure. Mrs. Bridoake gave me a hint to look after her as we walked from chapel yesterday, and said that that man, Lawrence, had been seen hanging about the cottage. But I should not like to accuse Jessie of disobedience to me and inconstancy to Reuben on mere suspicion."

Now, Ruth, is your time! Ruth was silent—she could not make mischief.

The old dame lapsed into silence also, and took counsel with the ruddy fire.

The brief daylight gone, a lamp was lighted, tea prepared, and kept sputtering in its bright pot on the hob, whilst the toast on a brass footman, equally bright, frizzled and spoiled before the fire, waiting for the absentee.

When patience was exhausted, Mrs. Lane pronounced a tremulous grace, and the meal was partaken in very ominous silence, whilst the deepening shadows without were only equalled by the deepening shadows within.

As Ruth proceeded to clear away the cups and saucers wheels were heard outside: they stopped before the gate, and then a heavy foot blundered up to the door. Without the ceremony of knocking, Dixon, the red-faced carrier, presented himself, a huge bunch of holly, a small parcel, and an item of intelligence he had never been instructed to carry.

CHAPTER II
SOWING THE WIND

Ruth's eyes had not deceived her. The switch on the wintry hedge had been a signal to Jessie, and Mr. Lawrence himself waited her approach at the bend of the lane in not too amiable a mood. Profoundly impressed with his own superlative attractions, he was apt to bestow his favours on admiring maidens, not doubting their gracious acceptance. Fluttering here and there, displaying his elegant person to the best advantage, he had made many a silly girl's heart ache because he "meant nothing."

But now he did mean something; having resolved to take a desperate leap into matrimony, moved thereto by the double charms of Jessie's purse and person, he chafed at all delays.

"I wonder if that girl expects me to cool my heels under the dripping trees all the winter waiting for her? If her country bumpkin did it I shall not, pretty as she is. Unless she makes up her mind to-day I shall try my luck in another quarter. My face and figure should sell for a good round sum. Still, I think this is a safe card. Let me see."

The soliloquizing secretary flicked his boots with his cane, debating his own value as a marketable commodity.

"Let me see! I must *marry* her, that's clear; yet is it worth while running the risk—(what risk?)—on £190 and chances? Um—ah, she's deuced pretty. What if that swain of hers should turn up this Christmas? Well, I must cut him out, that's all. As luck would have it, he won't know me. Ah, she's coming at last!" muttered he, as the gate opened and the graceful figure presented itself. "What does that Methodistical sister of hers want now?" he cried with an impatient slash of his cane. "Always a spy at hand! Ah, my sweet Jessie, my winter rosebud, I was in despair. I feared the old dame was keeping your bloom to herself." And then the gallant gentleman raised her hand to his lips very impressively.

"Grandmother was asleep. I had to invent an excuse for coming. And oh! Alfred"—(it had got to that)—"I am so afraid Ruth saw you." He offered his arm, which she took unhesitatingly. They walked on towards Leigh.

"And what then, my charming Jessie?" he asked, with a pressure of her arm. "Why should you be afraid of her? Will you not be your own mistress immediately?"

"Yes; but——." And Jessie heaved a deep sigh—it may be of contrition.

"But what? She is not the arbiter of your destiny. Give yourself at once to me, and you will escape the tyranny you now endure."

Another sigh. He had talked of home tyranny until the girl fully believed herself a victim.

"Jessie, can you not trust the intensity of my love?"

"Yes, Alfred; but, then, I have been thinking I ought not to—to listen to you. You know I am already engaged to—to——"

"Oh, ah! to a country counter-jumper—so I have heard."

He dropped her arm, and pulled his perfumed black whiskers, in profound disparagement of his rival. Jessie blushed. The sneering epithet had somehow lessened her estimate of Reuben's calling. She hesitated, stammering out—

"I meant to say, Mr. Lawrence, that though—well, I have been promised to—to—Mr. Isherwood for a good many years, and cannot well run off my word. He would break his heart."

Mr. Lawrence laughed.

"Break his heart! A man who is content to see you twice a year!"

"But he has only two holidays, Mr. Lawrence," she said, deprecatingly.

"Then he's worse off than a schoolboy! But what are holidays to a man in love? *I* should take French leave, and the first train, if I had a governor without a conscience."

"But Mr. Lawson is a very kind master, Reuben says."

How Alfred Lawrence started!

"What is the matter?" asked Jessie.

"Oh, nothing, nothing; but if you prefer this draper's assistant, who has most likely forgotten you in his long absence, and may even now be making love to his master's daughter——"

"Mr. Lawson has no daughter," interrupted Jessie. "He had a son, who nearly ruined his father with his wickedness, and then ran away."

Her companion took several steps in silence.

"Miss lane, I have no desire to force your choice, or to enter into competition with this Mr. Isherwood. If he be likely to break his heart, Alfred Lawrence will not break *his*. There are other young ladies on whom my attentions will not be thrown away."

It was far from the speaker's intention to be taken at his word. Her hesitancy had taught him his advantage. He played with her vanity, her jealousy, her impatience of control, and urged the injustice of keeping an engagement made ere either of them knew their own minds, placing Reuben ever in a false light, until at length he argued her out of her better feelings. She became convinced that the perfumed being by her side, on whom she saw so many damsels, both in Leigh and Tyldesley, cast longing glances, must be infinitely superior to homely Reuben, for whom nobody cared but herself. So, finally, she promised her ardent admirer to place herself and her little fortune in his hands, with or without Mrs. Lane's consent, as soon as she could command it; but never a benignant star looked through the murky evening sky on the ratification of the compact.

She would be of age on New Year's Day, and her own mistress. She did not come to this decision readily. There were scruples to be overcome, qualms of conscience to be stifled; yet, when Dixon passed the pair on their lingering way homeward, his keen eyes, accustomed to pierce the darkness, saw the arm of Mr. Alfred's light overcoat crossing the shoulders of Jessie's black mantle in loving clasp. And *that* was his item of news!

A bombshell bursting on the hearth could scarcely have created greater consternation in Mrs. Lane's quiet home. She was a truly good woman, kind to all within her sphere, but, as I have said, was a strict disciplinarian, and intolerant of deception. Rigid in morals and manners, she held it a duty to be "instant in season" and out of season; and this caused her to be considered harsh by more persons than Jessie, whose awe of her aged relative had latterly somewhat abated—thanks to her new friend's training.

When Dixon was gone, Mrs. Lane and Ruth compared notes. Then the old lady posted herself on the window-seat, to wait the transgressor's return. The moon had risen when the offenders reached the gate; and if she did not hear the protestations, promises, and appointment for the next interview, she saw the close embrace at parting. Indignant, she confronted the flushed and excited girl, ere her excitement had time to cool down, in the shadow of the porch.

"What is the meaning of this?" Jessie's fluttering heart stood still for an instant, and her tongue was mute. "How is it, girl, that you, the promised wife of one man, thus meet in secret and suffer the caresses of another?"

"I could not help it, grandmother," she faltered. "He overtook me in the lane, and would kiss me when he went away."

"Do not add falsehood to disobedience, Jessie," remonstrated Mrs. Lane, leading the way into the house. "No man kisses a modest girl against her will. Modesty will awe even the profligate. Are you grown so shameless that you set my counsels at naught, and, in defiance of propriety, meet this man, and walk with him at nightfall, with his arm around your waist?—a man, too, of whom nothing is known!"

Jessie stood at bay.

"Nothing known! Then it is not for lack of tale-bearers." And her head went up with a toss.

Ruth's head was bent so closely over her work that she lost the glance which pointed this retort.

"Ill news flies fast," continued Jessie, advancing into the room, at the same time throwing back her loosened bonnet strings with a jerk; "and he cannot be a bad man of whom nothing evil is known. Besides, the Squire *must* know all about him; and what satisfies Squire Appleton might satisfy us."

"You simple girl! a man may be a good secretary (or clerk, for he is little more), yet be a worthless vagabond; and such I have an instinctive belief in this Lawrence. It would be a deep sorrow to me if you were entrapped in his meshes." And the good old woman resumed her seat by the fire, with a grave, sad face.

"I don't see——"

"No, child," interrupted the elder woman, "you do not see, but the people at the hall do. There is something mysterious about him. He has been three months there, and never once had either a letter or anyone to call on him, much as he brags of his London friends."

"Then he had no sweetheart anywhere else, that's clear," thought Jessie.

"And," put in Ruth, "it is thought that his name is not really Alfred, for all that his clothes are marked A. L."

"It does not take much to get gossips *thinking*. And pray what set that afloat? I suppose that meddlesome Mrs. Bridoake had a hand in it."

"It was noticed, no matter by whom, that whenever Tony the page was called sharply in his hearing, he started and turned as if to answer. Even the Squire remarked it, and his excuse was he 'had a brother named Tony.' "

"And quite a sufficient reason."

"But not a reason, miss, why you should defend him, allow his embraces, or meet him in secret. A maiden who is engaged should hold herself as sacred as a married woman. How can you answer this to Reuben?" demanded the grandmother.

Jessie hung her head, and muttered something inaudible.

"Reuben trusts you implicitly," said Ruth, sadly, "and it is a fearful thing to trifle with a true heart. I hope you are not deceiving him."

Jessie snapped her up sharply: "Mind your own business! What should a little old maid like you know of either true hearts of false ones?"

Mrs. Lane interposed: "Ruth is right. If you are playing Reuben false, he must be informed. It is evident this is not your first meeting with Mr. Lawrence, and flirtations of this kind are so discreditable, I cannot suffer a worthy man to be imposed upon."

"You can tell him what you please; fancy will supply the want of fact."

Mrs. Lane bethought herself she *knew* nothing beyond that evening's indiscretion.

"Jessie," said she, "you are bold and disrespectful to-night. We are all in an untoward frame of mind. Go to bed now. We may reason quietly to-morrow. If there be more in this than girlish imprudence, however painful the task, I shall acquaint Reuben

Isherwood when he comes on New Year's Eve, whatever be the result, and I will put up special prayers in your behalf."

And so the pious old lady did, little foreseeing how mysterious, how awful would be the answer.

All the following week Jessie thought proper to assume a fit of sulks as the best cover to her real feelings. She was not so heartless as her flippant tongue suggested, and did not brave the just indignation of her relatives, or conceal her treachery from Reuben, without many a sharp pang. But the tempter contrived to be often at her elbow, and kept her constant to him, regardless of Reuben. She assumed, too, an air of injured dignity; with or without pretext went out, leaving so much work on Ruth's hands that the Christmas festival proved no holiday to *her*. But for the evergreens and holly decorating the walls, and the good things sent in so abundantly from the Hall, she would scarcely have recognised the season. Not, however, being a gadabout at best of times, and now in no mood for visiting, she made no complaint, but stitched on, hoping to have her hands at liberty for the New Year—that New Year so full of presage for all.

CHAPTER III
"FROM THE DEAD"

The year drew to a close tearfully. Reuben was hourly expected. So was Mrs. Bridoake, for it was the Watch-night, and neither she nor Mrs. Lane would have thought of letting in the New Year outside the precincts of Ebenezer Chapel. Mrs. Bridoake was coming to take tea, and lend the old lady her arm afterwards, for it was a goodly distance.

Ruth had just completed her preparations for the birthday festival of the morrow—that New Year's Day to which Jessie looked for emancipation from one thraldom only to shackle herself with another. But Ruth, possibly depressed by the weather, her dread of Reuben's reception by her sister, and the threatened disclosures, moved about even more soberly than her wont. She had set the tray for an early tea, when Mrs. Bridoake came hurriedly up the path. As she was behind time her flurried aspect escaped Ruth's attention.

She was the bearer of strange tidings.

"Ruth, where's Jessie?" (Christian names come pat from country people.)

"In her room. She has only just come in."

"An' yo'r gran'mother?"

"Laying her things out ready for chapel. The rain will not keep *her* at home."

"Aw should think not! But what's a' this stir abeaut Jessie's weddin'?"

"Jessie's wedding!" echoed Ruth, turning pale, and dropping her hands on the tray, were the cups and saucers rattled like castanets. "Jessie's wedding!"

"Yo' didn't know? Th' banns wor axt in Leigh Church, for the first toime, yesterday."

"What is that?" asked Mrs. Lane, coming into the room.

Mrs. Bridoake repeated her news. The old lady looked displeased.

"Reuben ought to have let me know," said she, gravely.

"Reuben! It's noan Reuben," cried Mrs. Bridoake. "I wish it wur. It's that clooas-peg,[116] Lawrence—Squire's new *secatary*."

Mrs. Lane groaned, and stood aghast.

"Poor Reuben!" murmured Ruth, with a pitying sigh.

---

[116] Clothes-peg: a fashionably dressed person.

Jessie was hastily summoned downstairs. She came, singing, with an open letter in her hand.

"Jessie," said Mrs. Lane, sternly, "what is this I hear? Is it true that you intend to marry that coxcomb, Alfred Lawrence, without even asking my consent?"

"Yes," answered Jessie, faintly, nervously biting her nails the while. "It was no use asking your consent."

"And so, knowing my strong objections to this underhand stranger, you heartlessly break faith with an upright man who loves you well—who even now may be on his way hither, believing you true to him. Oh, Jessie!"

"Break faith, indeed! If Reuben loved me as well as you all seem to think, he would not stay away months at a stretch; nor is he on his way now. There is his letter." And she tossed it contemptuously into her grandmother's lap.

"Thank God! There will then be time to soften the dreadful blow to him. It will break his heart. Oh, Jessie! how could you serve poor Reuben so?" cried Ruth, with streaming eyes.

"Look you, Ruth, everyone seems to care more for Reuben's happiness than for mine. I don't think we should suit each other one bit; and, as you seem so much concerned about him, why not take him yourself, and try to piece his heart if it should break? But I want my tea!" So saying, she took her seat, as if dismissing the subject from her mind.

If that was more than a random shaft, it was a cruel one; it went home. The warm blood surged upwards, crimsoning throat and forehead with a sudden flush, leaving Ruth's fair face whiter than before. Fortunately, the deepening twilight shielded her from observation; and as she turned in silence to light the lamp and pour out the tea, both Mrs. Bridoake and her grandmother interposed.

In the strong emotions of the hour hospitality was all but lost sight of, though the meal was unusually prolonged. In vain Mrs. Lane reasoned and expostulated with her wilful grandchild. Both waxed warm, and words ran high. Twice Mrs. Brdoake reminded the incensed old lady that it was almost chapel-time before she essayed to move; and even then something seemed to fetter her movements, as if she had a reluctance to quit the house which she could not overcome. Going, she turned at the door, excited by Jessie's reiterated assertion—

"I shall be of age to-morrow, and have a right to please myself."

"Yes, to begin a New Year and a new life of sorrow together! And, mark me, girl, I shall alter my *will* with the New Year. Not one penny of my hard-earned savings shall that man have to squander in sinful vanities."

"We don't want your money; Alfred has plenty of his own, and there will be mine. He has a rich uncle in London.—(*Uncle*, indeed! Ah, simple Jessie!)—You can later *your will* to-morrow, if you like."

"I shall! We will all turn over a new leaf with the New Year. But, remember, Jessie, disobedience cannot prosper. You will live to rue your folly bitterly."

With a reproachful, sorrowing look both girls remembered throughout their lives, she took Mrs. Bridoake's proffered arm, and went out into the night and drizzling rain, as she told her companion, "to intercede at the Throne of Grace for the wilful child rushing headlong to her own destruction." Could she have pierced the shadows of that night, would she have gone on?

Silence fell on the house and on the sisters after her departure. Ruth had cleared away the tea-things during that long altercation, and now sat down by the fire. Jessie, after a while, went out into the porch, and there was presently a hum of voices. In about half-an-hour Jessie bolted the door and came back, looking very blue and cold.

"The rain is over and the moon shining; I think it is freezing," she remarked, as she stirred the fire, and seated herself opposite her sister.

"I hope not; it would make the roads so dangerous. I wish grandmother was back," said the other, anxiously.

"We need not expect her on this side of midnight; and I am sure I don't want her, if she comes in no better humour to let the New Year in. A nice birthday I am likely to have!"

Ruth made no response. She was gazing at the fire, thinking of the "might-have-been," and, perhaps—who knows?—of the man, and longing for power to assuage it. After a time she trimmed the lamp, brought forth her Bible, and sat down to read, with her back to the door and window. Jessie sat opposite, with her head thrown back, a mingled look of scorn and defiance gathering on her face. Hour by hour was told by the American clock on the wall. As its wiry pulses vibrated under the stroke of midnight came the sound of Tyldesley Church bells, with far-off echoes from Leigh, to welcome the new-born year.

"I wish you a happy New Year, Jessie," said Ruth, advancing to kiss her sister.

But Jessie was not conciliatory: she took the proffered kiss with an ill grace, saying, as Ruth resumed her seat—

"It won't be either you or grandmother who will make the New Year happy for me." And she looked sown on the hearthrug in sheer dissatisfaction with herself.

Something—she never knew what—after a long silence caused her to look up. *Behind her sister's chair, with her warm shawl pulled awry, her plain black satin bonnet crushed, its white lining and primly-quilled cap speckled with blood, stood her grandmother with pale face and finger up, as if she said, "Beware!"*

Jessie screamed, and started to her feet. The figure did not move.

"Oh, grandmother, what is the matter? How did you get in?"

Ruth, alarmed, rose, her eyes following the direction of her sister's. She saw *nothing*, and said so.

"Not grandmother, covered with blood?"

"Nothing!"

Jessie crossed the hearth hastily. The figure was *gone!*

"Oh, Ruth! Ruth! that was grandmother's *ghost!* I know it was. Something dreadful has happened."

"perhaps it was grandmother herself, trying to frighten you. It is almost time she was at home."

"She could not get in; I *bolted* the door."

Her alarm was infectious. Both girls ran screaming to the door; with trembling hands undid the bolt, and rushed out, only to fall over each other on a pavement like glass. Scrambling to their feet with equal haste, but more caution, they ran across the road to the lodge.

As they reached the gates Mrs. Bridoake came hurrying down the road, using her umbrella as a staff. She was *alone*. Descrying them in the moonlight, she cried out, "Oh, lasses, yo'r good, pious grandmother has fawn deawn th' chapel steps, an' hoo's killed!"

It was even so. That was a night of accidents, and as such remembered through a wide district for many years.

Freezing as it descended, the sleet had covered the ground with a treacherous glaze. Stepping out of chapel unprepared, Mrs. Lane, with several other persons, fell. They were bruised, no doubt, but she never rose again in this world. Fatally prophetic had been her own words. Whilst the echoes of her last prayerful "Amen" yet lingered in the little chapel, she had passed at once through its portals and the portal of Death, to "begin a new life with the New Year."

CHAPTER IV
NEW REVELATIONS

The sudden blow fell heavily on both girls—heaviest on Jessie, the violence of whose grief admitted of no consolation. Her last words to the dead had been those of ungrateful self-assertion. Her grandmother's parting words had been well-merited rebuke and auguries of evil. To her, and her only, had the phantom shape appeared, in the very instant of dissolution, even as she sat nourishing thoughts of disobedience and wrath. Ever before her seemed to stand the bleeding figure, with disordered dress, and warning finger up; and in her remorseful mood the conscience-stricken girl felt constrained to obey it. She refused to see Alfred Lawrence, and wrote kindly to Reuben Isherwood. Still she had not courage to confess her breach of faith, and the wrong was never righted. Of the apparition (which filled the gossips of the Hall and neighbourhood with consternation and amazement) he was informed later, and by another hand.

One ghastly circumstance, over which public comment was loud, must not be forgotten: neither inquest nor funeral had stopped the reading of the "banns" in due course; and though at the third reading a voice had been heard to cry, "I forbid!" no one had entered the vestry to record an objection. An unknown voice went for nothing in the ear of the law; but there were ears in the congregation on which it fell like a solemn protest from the dead.

No *new will* had been made. Jessie's moiety under the old one was just £200; so, besides being her own mistress, the new year had made her mistress also of nearly £400 in hard cash. It was not likely Mr. Lawrence would resign her now. Again and again he presented his speckless person at the cottage-door; but as the transparently leafless hedgerow betrayed his approach, and town manners taught him the use of a knocker, Jessie was warned from the window-seat, and Ruth was prepared to deny his entrance.

Could Reuben Isherwood have appeared at this juncture, I might have had a different story to relate. As it was, Mr. Lawson, his employer, continued seriously ill; and Reuben, being now manager, where he had formerly been only assistant, duty, as well as gratitude, kept the conscientious young man at his post. Jessie's demonstrative grief, as might have been expected, wore itself out. More powerful even than the memory of her grandmother's warning spectre was the spirit of vanity in her own breast. She became disgusted with her own red eyes and mottled face, and ceased her lamentations, since she found that tears destroyed her beauty. Every fresh consultation with her looking-glass made her long to air herself abroad, if only to show how well she looked in her new mourning.

"I cannot be expected to stay at home for ever," she argued, first with herself and then with her sister, who could only acquiesce in an observation so self-evident.

Going out, however, involved chances and mischances.

Besides his duties at the desk, Mr Lawrence had frequent business out of doors, and a not too curious master; so he contrived, by watching, to waylay Jessie in her walks, when he brought his subtle influence to bear on her instability and avowed affection for himself. Her resolution wavered, and before a month had flown, or the crispness gone from her crape, he had regained his old ascendancy over her. There was no secrecy in their intercourse now. He did not scruple to call at the cottage, although Ruth testified to her displeasure by carrying her work into another room whenever he came. The warning of her grandmother's ghost he "pooh-poohed," as the offspring of an excited imagination, treated the coincidence as accidental, and ridiculed the importance she attached to the "angry words of an old woman." She withstood Ruth's arguments better than his banter. In vain her sister strove to wean her from her infatuation, and pleaded the cause of the absent lover. Opposition only strengthened wilful Jessie's resolves.

Once more the wedding day was fixed. The announcement was made to Ruth one stormy day in March, when the wind moaned round the house, the tree tops bent their heads at every gust, and the loosened ivy beat like angry whips against the casement. It was not a choice season for such a communication, but the subject filled Jessie's mind, and a slight incident called it forth. The carrier's cart went by. As it passed, the flapping tilt-cover burst its bonds and showed a shivering woman seated amongst the boxes and parcels. It was no uncommon thing for the Dixon to give "a lift" to a tired child, or tramp, or market woman with her basket; but whilst the cart stopped, and one of two men walking with the sturdy carrier by the horse's head ran to help him in securing the rebellious tarpaulin, they saw that this present passenger was none of these. Only her head and shoulders were visible, but they belonged to a stranger, young, pale, with a miserable face, and a respectable bonnet.

Very trivial circumstances awaken interest and comment in remote country places. Curiosity and imagination were brought to bear on the carrier's unwonted passenger. The long discussion drifted to the night when he carried thither unwelcome news as well as Mrs. Heap's trimmings. With that, Alfred Lawrence came on the carpet, and, the subject, once broached, transition was easy. Ruth was deeply grieved.

"Going to be married! and *so soon*, too, after grandmother's shocking death!"

There was a long pause.

"Have you ever appraised Reuben of your changed sentiments and intentions?" she asked.

"No. I have left his letters unanswered; that is all. I have not opened the two last. There they are."

She took two letters from her work-basket, and threw them across the table to her sister.

"You can answer them if you like."

"*I* cannot answer them! But, Jessie, common honesty forbids that you should marry one man with your engagement to another uncancelled. Only write and tell him. Reuben is too much a man to maintain a claim to a woman's hand without her heart."

"Indeed, I shall not. You can write and tell him if you like. *I* think he will know quite soon enough."

"Quite too soon for his happiness. Poor Reuben! I wish his trusting heart could have been spared the pain you will inflict."

"I wish so too," replied Jessie, sobered—for the instant only. She resumed, carelessly: "But it can't be helped. We never did suit each other. And I say, Ruth, if you are so *very* anxious to spare his feelings, why not take pity on him yourself, as I said before? Your sober ways would just suit each other."

"Heartless!" exclaimed a voice from the doorway. The girls dropped their work, and started to their feet as if electrified. The crimson flush had not paled from Ruth's forehead, or from the tips of her round ears; and large drops stood in her eyes ready to fall.

There, in deep mourning, stood Reuben Isherwood, tall and erect—mingled pain and scorn visible in his expressive face. All that had once been homely in his gait was gone. He stood there, a man either sister might have been proud to love.

What had Reuben overheard?

He had overheard *all*—had seen his unopened letters tossed to Ruth like waste paper—had heard her plead for him—had heard the insidious taunt—seen the quick flush and swimming eyes, and was startled by the double revelation.

True, he did not come wholly unprepared. Mrs Bridoake—present on New Year's Eve—had, like a good wife, taken counsel with her husband, and the twain decided that Reuben Isherwood ought to know he was being jilted. They were no great scribes, however; and, before a letter was concocted to their satisfaction Jessie's penitence and seclusion disarmed their indignation. The proximity of the lodge to the cottage made it a post of observation; and, keeping a sharp look-out, Mrs. Bridoake saw signs of a reaction. The result was a long letter from Mrs. Bridoake, not too well spelled or indited. It told the story of Mrs. Lane's death—of the apparition (in which they thoroughly believed), and of Jessie's fickleness—a story which her prolonged silence confirmed. Had she but opened Reuben's letters she would have read—first, his demand for a refutation, and next, his bitter renunciation, and resolve to see her no more.

A strange errand had brought him to her presence now.

As Jessie stood before him, silent and abashed, he said coldly:—

"Miss Lane, I am not come to upbraid you—you have made your own choice—so be it! Whatever feelings of tenderness or pity I retained, you have yourself dispelled. You were queen of my heart—you have been deposed from your throne never to be reinstated."

Could this be Reuben—homely Reuben? And what did he mean by pity?

"As you have just said, we should *not suit* each other—Ruth." He gently took her trembling hand. "I came hither to save your sister from a great wrong. From my heart I am sorry for her!" he continued.

Jessie started. "A great wrong!—sorry for her!" What could he mean? She would not seem afraid—she would brave it out.

"Who called you to interfere with my affairs, Mr. Isherwood?"

"Who should interfere if not I? But that is past, Miss Lane," he added gravely. "I will trouble you to walk to Appleton Hall—there you will learn. You might incline to doubt my unsupported testimony."

Testimony! against what, or whom? Should she decline to go?

As she hesitated Reuben put in, "Do not keep the Squire waiting. It is for your own sake."

Shivering with sudden fear, she hastened to equip herself; but even then paused before her glass to re-adjust her crape bonnet more becomingly. Ruth was ready also. She knew from Reuben's manner something urgent and important called for their presence; indeed, he had said as much. A lad opened the gates. Grinning from ear to ear, he said, "Mother's oop at th' Ha'—there's foine doin's yond'." The wind blew keenly—the trees tossed wildly; but something keener than the wind smote Jessie's thoughtless heart with a sudden dread, as Tony, the page, met them at the open door, and, with a significant smirk and leer, ushered them into the Justice-room, and Reuben whispered, "I would gladly spare you *both* the pain, but duty is imperative."

There were assembled servants and tenants, whom swift-winged rumour and swifter-footed curiosity had brought together in a short space of time. There, too, was a strange, rough man, and half-fainting, on a chair by his side, sat the pale, lady-like woman they had seen in the carrier's cart. There, too, was Lawrence, shrinking, crestfallen—all his jauntiness gone. And there, too, sat Squire Appleton, no longer the easy master, but the *Justice*, stern and uncompromising.

"Jessie Lane," said he, "your grandmother was long a faithful servant of our house; I respected her highly, and for her sake I am sorry for the circumstances which render your presence here necessary."

Someone else *sorry!* But for her grandmother's sake, not hers. She felt faint, and grasped Ruth's arm.

"Mrs. Lawson," said the Justice, addressing the pale woman, "will you repeat to this young person that which you have deposed on oath to me? Tell her who that fine gentleman is." And he looked towards Alfred Lawrence.

"He is *my husband*, miss—Anthony Lawson.

Jessie put her hand to her side, and held her breath. Tony, close by the door, tittered audibly. The woman spoke with an effort.

"We were married five years ago. Here is the certificate,"—producing a paper. "He took me to London. He soon ran through my bit of money, and left me in ill health, with two children, chargeable to the parish. We were in Islington workhouse till we were passed on to Manchester, more than a year ago. Only last December the guardians ferreted out his father, and old Mr. Lawson, a better man than his son, has kept us ever since.

"An' a pretty hunt we've had to find the rascal, under his new neame," interrupted the warrant officer, by Mrs. Lawson's side. But thanks to that gentleman (nodding towards Reuben), we've got him safe now; an' I *rayther* think he's wanted i' Preston fur somethin' *more* than wife-desertion. He looks chap-fallen enough neaw—dunnot he, miss?"

Indeed he did. "An' would yo' believe it, miss, that them whiskers an' curls wer' red afore he dyed 'em?" A laugh, instantly suppressed by the Squire, went round the room. Jessie had fainted. When she recovered she was in the housekeeper's room with only Ruth and Mrs. Bridoake.

"Where is——where is——?"

"Reuben?" suggested Ruth.

"No—Alfred."

"On his way to prison—the villain!" blurted out Mrs. Bridoake, "and aw hope they'll keep him theer. Aw've had my suspicions o' eawr foine *secatary* for some toime, and reet glad aw am that I let 'em eawt to Mr. Isherwood, or a pratty mess you'd ha' been in. Why, who dun yo' think the chap is? Who, but that theer vagabon' lad o' Mr. Isherwood's measter, who robbed his feyther an' ran away from whoam nigh ten years sin'."

Jessie shuddered.

"Aye, yo' may weell shiver, Miss Jessie; but yo' may go deawn on yor bended knees an' thank God it's no waur. What if he hadno bin fun' eawt till a week further on?"

What, indeed? Well might her grandmother come back from the other world to warn her of peril! And to think she had despised that solemn warning! As the swift thought flashed through her mind, Jesse bowed still deeper her bent head, and covered her face with both hands, as if to hide her shame and suffering. Reuben came in with the housekeeper at this moment. He looked compassionately on the drooping girl, so long cherished as his future wife, and felt how keen must be her humiliation. He was a man of fairly developed intellect, and fully developed heart; and though his love had gone at one fell swoop, with his esteem, the bitterness of a broken trust remained.

"This is no season for reproaches, Jessie; your own sufferings will teach you to feel for mine," he said, with enforced calmness. "But an explanation is due to you and to Ruth also. You asked who called for my interference. I will tell you. It is too mysterious and remarkable an interposition to be passed over lightly." (He spoke to attentive listeners, though Jessie never raised her head.)

"The room I occupy in the house of my employer was once the chamber of his profligate son, Anthony Lawson. Over the fire-place still hangs a coloured portrait of him, which has never been removed. One night last week, as I sat ruminating on Mrs. Bridoake's story of your faithlessness, of the perfumed and be-whiskered fellow who had supplanted me, and cursing my own folly in yielding my heart to a pretty face without a sterling quality to ensure happiness—(Jessie sobbed aloud)—I must have fallen asleep and dreamed—I can account for it in no other way—your grandmother appeared before me, pale, very pale, bleeding from the temple, and very sorrowful. She raised her arm—pointed to the portrait—her lips moved—she said *'Lawrence'* distinctly and impressively; then melted slowly away, her finger still pointing to the picture. I suppose I wakened—for I *must* have been asleep—with the word 'Lawrence' in my ears and the vision fresh in my memory."

"It wur' no dream!" stoutly advanced Mrs. Bridoake.

"Oh, grandmother! dear grandmother!" broke from Ruth; while Jessie, choking with sobs, rocked on her chair in agony.

"Dream or no dream," continued the young man, much moved by Jessie's deep distress, "I was bewildered. All at once the character of Lawson flashed across my mind, coupled with the name of 'Lawrence' in the letters of your true friend, Mrs. Bridoake. The initials A. L. were identical. The clue once found was easily followed. His heartless desertion of a young and confiding wife and his two helpless children had exasperated his father beyond measure. I believe Mr. Lawson's illness arose from mental disquietude on that score."

"No doubt," said Ruth, quietly.

"With the consent of father and wife, the guardians were at once communicated with, and a warrant issued. Mrs. Lawson came hither for identification. She was too weak to walk, and we brought her on from Leigh in Dixon's cart. We have reason to be thankful the discovery was made before he added another to his many victims. Squire Appleton has not yet had time to look into his accounts."

Jessie Lane never held up her head in Tyldesley or Leigh again. Her story, and that of her grandmother's re-appearance from the other world, filled the mouths of gossips far and wide. She shrank alike from sneers and sympathy. Soon she went away amongst her mother's relatives in Bury, wiser, and, it is to be hoped, better for the sharp lesson she had had. She *did* rue her folly bitterly, as her grandmother had predicted.

Nor did Ruth remain very long at the old place—nor did she live to be a little old maid, stifling in her bosom a love she might not own. Mr. Lawson took his manager into partnership; and before twelve months were gone Ruth was in Preston, filling up the void in Reuben's heart and home—gentle and quiet as ever, but with no unnatural gravity shadowing her young face as heretofore. Her love had leapt from her heart to her eyes—they beamed with affection; and though many years have passed, neither she nor Reuben have yet regretted the "new leaf" which the Squire's secretary and Jessie's wilfulness had turned over for them.

THE PLAINBURY MYSTERY

CHAPTER I

PLAINBURY Castle had been long without a master. The earl, despairing of peace and rest in his life, had, it was said, sought both in the depths of a black pool in the recesses of his own woods. Yet there were not wanting hints and intangible rumours that rest in that watery bed was none of his own seeking; and from the day when he was carried thence, swollen, blue, and oozy, to be deposited on the table of the great hall, a fearful shadow of suspicion seemed to invest the countess as with a mantle. The dead earl's few aristocratic friends dropped from her like leaves from a decaying tree; even the ranks of her own less scrupulous set thinned.

How much she felt each defection could only be surmised. Oaths and curses were ready to her lip as to those of her lowest groom, and these fell in venomous showers at every rejected invitation, every deliberate cut in the hunting field. Her brow contracted with a perpetual scowl, and if her heart were only as wrinkled as her forehead, it must have been corrugated indeed.

She was a woman of strong bad passions, and every line of her wicked face showed it. Yet she had been a beauty in her time, a beauty with a haughty step and a dominant will, when her lord married her—or rather when the Lady Matilda Hanley married him; for never did eagle pounce on a devoted lamb more surely than she in her thirtieth year swooped down upon the Earl of Plainbury, and obtained from the infatuated nobleman unparalleled settlements. She was not without an ample dower, but every acre, every jewel of her own, was secured to herself most stringently.

He was a quiet man, of studious and retired habits, with a strong religious bias; and much society marvelled that he, of all men, had been caught by one whom more worldly men were content to dance, ride, boat, flirt, bet with, but did not care to marry.

The recluse life he had led was in her favour. There were no kind friends to enlighten him on the Welsh mountain where they met, and they were engaged and married before society awakened from its dream of astonishment.

And then his dream of astonishment began—a long, terrible nightmare, the culminating horror of which was a dark pool in a dense wood.

The earl was gentle as a woman; the countess bold, horsey, profane; in defiance of her lord filled the castle with strange guests, who drank and smoked in the drawing-rooms, played cards and dice through the night, and made the proud home of his ancestors a hot-bed of riot and sin.

Not all at once be it said; an oath hurled at a loitering postillion during the bridal tour was his first rude awakening. His next painful surprise was Lady Matilda's disregard of the Sabbath and all religious ordinances. Then followed his knowledge of her gambling and drinking propensities to fill his pious soul with horror, all the greater that her imperious will overrode his, and held him down as if with a spell.

Once, before his voice was utterly silenced in the household, he roused to the level of his own worth and duty. But then she had not reached the crowning-point of her assumption. This was when their only son and heir, Lionel, was old enough to observe and mimic the manners and language of the new guests who came in the train of Lady Matilda from the hunting-field and racecourse, or the new Brighton Pavilion.

Convinced that Plainbury Castle was no home for an innocent child, he resolved to sacrifice his own parental yearnings, and bear him away to a purer atmosphere. Perhaps had the lady's motherly instincts been stronger, her opposition might have borne down his. As it was, she gave a tacit consent to the little Lionel's removal; but all those preparations for her son's comfort or appearance which mothers of any rank love to superintend, she left to the forethought and affection of others. And much to the disgust of Anne Wilson, his nurse, when at mid-day the travelling chariot stood at the Norman entrance, and the old servants ranged in the ancient hall shed tears at losing their young master, as if heaven's purity went out with him, the boy had to be led to his lady-mother's bedside to say farewell, and to bear thence as strong an impression of her concern lest he should spill on the silken coverlet the chocolate she was sipping, as of the hasty parting kiss, in which irritability strove with lazy languor.

A college friend of Earl Plainbury's, the Rev. Lucas Woodward, held a living in one of the loveliest dales in Derbyshire. He was a man worthy of his high calling, and was as worthily mated. The good pair, full of pity for a babe so much worse than motherless, consented to receive the young viscount to rear and educate with their own children.

Lionel was a fair-haired, dark-eyed boy, with his father's sensitive tenderness and his mother's strong will. He had a broad open forehead, and there was a dimple in his chin, but there was a resolute set in his childish lip when, in his seventh year, he and his nurse Wilton took up their abode at the picturesque parsonage, and the little lord became one of the good clergyman's family.

These characteristics had only deepened when to the well-developed, well-trained youth of fifteen, still sharing the studies of the rector's sons, came the sad intelligence of his loving and estimable father's death. It was Lionel's first great sorrow, and he bowed beneath it. Not even the caresses of little Mabel Woodward, the sunbeam and darling of the household, could rouse him from his grief.

She came and stood by his side as he sat with his head buried in his arms on a table in the rector's study, and as heavy sobs broke from him all the sympathy of her nature was roused. She was an affectionate, auburn-haired maiden of twelve, with brown, loving eyes. They were full of sorrow for him who had been to her as a brother. Long she watched him in silence, then her soft arm stole round his neck, crushing unreproved his carefully-plaited cambric frill, and she whispered in his ear such consolation as her pitiful child-heart prompted. "Don't cry so, Lionel dear; you can stay here always now, and my papa and mamma can be your papa and mamma too; and I would like you for a brother better than Fred or Lucas. Don't fret so, Lionel dear, you make me cry too."

But his tears only fell the faster. He was old enough to know that the mother he had visited once a year was a very different being from the mamma of whom the Woodwards were so proud; and though he knew he was now Earl of Plainbury, what was the new honour to him, so dearly purchased? What cared he for dignity or title if the kind, sorrowful face he was wont to see every month would never smile upon him again; if the gentle voice, so eloquent in the cause of virtue and religion, should never more respond to his welcome, or bestow advice or blessing upon him again.

The Rev. Lucas Woodward had been summoned to the funeral as well as his young charge, and it was after the solemn obsequies, and prior to the reading of the late earl's will, that I, Thomas Skinner, of the Cathedral Close, Plainbury, made my first bow to the new earl in my official position as lawyer to her ladyship.

Why she had selected me I know not. Possibly because I had the chief practice of Plainbury. Still, I think she would have sought her business-man farther afield had she known how much I sympathized with her disappointed husband, and that I held it as a sacred duty to the dead, in the execution of her orders, to stand between her and any injustice her lawless inclinations might prompt.

No effort of memory is needed to recall a single incident of that day, or the library in which the will was read. Black cloth hid books and shelves, and draped the oriel window; the large oak table was dark almost as its sable cover; busts and statues were veiled and shrouded; the huge fireplace (from over which the painted semblance of the dead man was conspicuous in its black frame) seemed to lack a fire, though it was June; the mourning garments of the assembly gave a pallor to their faces, and added to the funereal aspect of the solemn scene. The countess herself, robed in a scant, short-waisted dress, so loaded with crape that the ostensible silk was a mere suggestion, sat (with little delicacy) in the late earl's chair by the table, her still magnificent black hair banded under the hideous cap, then the badge of widowhood.

Lionel, the young earl, with a face white as the broad-hemmed frill round his throat, was seated on the opposite side of the table, one hand holding fast that of his reverend protector. I myself, with sundry papers before me, occupied the side of the table between mother and son, and we thus confronted alike the noble friends of the deceased, seated in a broken semicircle, and the upper servants standing by order of the countess in two sombre and sorrowful groups on each side the door.

Mr. John Stiff, of Lincoln's Inn, being solicitor to the late earl, was, of course, present *pro forma.*

Knowing as I did that the will in my hand, which left the countess sole administratrix and executrix, and sole guardian of her son in his minority, had been drawn up by me that year under the dictation of her ladyship, and signed by her lord in a spirit of resignation which I had mistaken for cowardice, I shrank from the task imposed upon me. I fumbled among my papers, wiped my spectacles, lost them, coughed, and opened the parchment so deliberately that the impatient lady gave a smart tap on the table with her fingers as a reminder. Thus admonished, I cleared my throat, and went through my unpleasant duty as frigidly as though I had not been consigning the young earl and his estates into perilous keeping.

As I read, I noted that a smile of triumph crept over Lady Matilda's countenance. It flushed a deeper red, her eye kindled as she looked on the astonished listeners and their contracted brows, and her haughty head raised to its highest. I saw, too, with pain, how the young earl shrank closer to the Rev. Mr. Woodward, their clasped hands having a more convulsive grip, and as I completed the last folio I heard audible murmurs from servants and others disappointed of legacies.

There had been two enigmatical auditors in the room, whose demeanour had somewhat puzzled me. These were Sir James Tarleton, the late earl's bosom friend, and his lawyer, Mr. John Stiff. The former held a gold snuff-box jauntily in his left hand, from which he took long pinches at every pause I made. The latter crossed his knees, leaned back in his chair, his left elbow cradled in his right hand, his chin reposing on the left, the index-finger on his cheek-bone—a placid, stolid listener.

The puzzle was at an end when the triumphant countess, rising proudly to dismiss the assembly, was politely requested by Mr. Stiff to resume her seat.

She bridled, cast upon him a withering look of inquiry, and stood confronting him with a look which, plainly as words, questioned his right to interfere.

But she absolutely paled and sank into her chair, when he produced *another will*, dated one week later than that which I had just read.

An excited murmur ran through the assembly. Mr. Stiff raised one hand to impose silence, Sir James Tarleton closed his snuff-box with a snap, returned it to his waistcoat pocket, looked steadily at me, then glanced significantly from my lady to the boy, and thence at the pale portrait over the fireplace, as if *there* was a sentient witness.

And thither the boy's eyes followed his, to remain fixed in sadness until recalled by a sharp exclamation from Lady Matilda, who started from her chair only to reseat herself, with teeth set and hands folded tightly as if to hold her passion in.

Mr. Stiff had read in clear, impressive tones as strange a preamble as ever opened will. The last will and testament of Frederick, Earl of Plainbury, set forth that "having been coerced by his wife, Lady Matilda, to sign a will adverse to his own inclination, and the well-being of his dearly-loved son and heir, Lionel, he had submitted solely from motives of policy, that he might with more secrecy and security revoke that or any other former will, and do his duty alike to his son and his dependents."

Again a murmur like an electric thrill ran through the room.

The document went on to confirm Lady Plainbury's settlements, and to surrender Plainbury Castle to her sole use until her son's marriage or majority, provided always she left that son unmolested in the hands of his guardians, Sir James Tarleton and the Rev. Lucas Woodward, whom he also appointed his executors. With the exception of sundry legacies to friends and servants, all personal property whatever was secured to Lionel. Finally, the will provided that these faithful servants should be retained so long as it was their own wish and that of the executors.

As clause after clause fell distinctly on the ear, the baffled countess purpled with passion—her lips were closed, her hands clenched rigidly, her eyes blazed fiercely, she breathed alone through her panting nostrils; and when at its close the servants, who had expected instant dismissal, gave an involuntary shout, she strove to give utterance to her impotent rage, and in the effort fell forward in a fit.

For some months the good people of Plainbury had been troubled in their minds to penetrate the incognito of a certain mysterious Dr. Mendoza, who came—no one knew whence—and settled amongst us. He was a tall, dark, handsome, but not inviting man, whose age might be fifty—more or less. His skin was olive, his hair and piercing eyes black as midnight, his eyebrows, which almost met, grew upwards at a sharp angle, his lips had a sardonic curl, his form was lank but sinewy, and his long thin fingers terminated in long-pointed nails, like talons. He spoke broken English, interlarded with scraps of so many tongues that it was impossible to determine his own. Some said he was a Polish Jew, others an Italian, or a Spaniard, or what was then in worse odour—a Frenchman.

No matter; the Countess of Plainbury consulted him—her carriage was seen at his door, and curiosity brought him general practice. But no curiosity ever fathomed his secrets. He was close as he was skilful. He made no friendships, visited nowhere, save at the castle.

Instructed by the countess, he was present at the inquest on the drowned earl, and also at the funeral and the reading of the will.

It was he who raised the fallen woman, administered restoratives, bore her to her chamber, and remained in attendance during the fever which supervened. He introduced a dark gipsy-like woman as nurse, excluding Lionel and all others from the chamber on the plea of contagion, but not in time to prevent whispers floating through the household, concerning the fearful mutterings of Lady Plainbury in her delirium: whispers which hardly dared shape themselves into the ugly word they suggested.

On her recovery, an inventory was taken, certain cabinets and receptacles were sealed up in my presence, and the young earl was borne away by his guardians to spend a few weeks at Tarleton Court prior to his return to Derbyshire.

I cannot accredit the countess with a particle of maternal affection, yet their departure stirred her to fury, which she vented on all things animate or inanimate within her reach; and ere she sobered down, instructed me to institute proceedings to set aside the second will and obtain the custody of her son.

It was vain to argue with a woman inflamed alike by rage and brandy. I obtained the opinion of counsel. She refused to be guided, and threatened to employ another solicitor unless I proceeded at once.

I shrugged my shoulders, and let the mad woman have her way. Of course she lost.

Years passed, those years in which the castle was virtually without a master, and the Plainbury estate, through those unfortunate settlement deeds, was, in a measure, under the control of the countess.

The consequences soon became apparent. Neglect and misrule set their destructive claws on everything. Two or three of the old servants endeavoured to maintain order indoors and out "for the credit of the family" and for the sake of the young earl; but setting at naught superiors whom the countess barely tolerated, their underlings were seldom amenable to order. Oppression followed extravagance, and labourers and tenants grew alike discontented.

The executors and Mr. Stiff did what they could to keep matters straight; but they were distant powers, and Lady Matilda was a present and very evil one. Her widowhood seemed but an excuse for fresh licence. Blacklegs and courtezans were her only guests; stay—Doctor Mendoza came and went at will, and had rooms in the castle itself.

The young earl I saw at intervals. He visited his mother from time to time, and on these occasions generally strolled into my office, either for a chat, for information respecting tenants, or in hopes to correct current gossip. At first Sir James and Mr. Woodward bore him company; but as he neared manhood these visits became more frequent, and were often made alone. His school and college vacations were spent alternately at Tarleton Court and Darley-Dale Rectory, in society very different from that which polluted his natural home.

He was a fine-grown specimen of England's young nobility, with well-developed whiskers, light wavy hair, and a downy moustache above his firm lip; he had a feminine chin and quick dark eyes, which lit with fire or softened with shadows like a clear lake beneath a sunset sky, as indignation or pity moved him.

They were sad enough when he stepped into my well-warmed office in the quiet close, one March morning, when he was about twenty. Throwing aside his fur-collared cloak as he sat down, I saw that his left arm was in a sling, and his hand wrapped in a white kerchief, on which a spot of blood was visible.

"Has any accident befallen your lordship?" I asked hurriedly.

"No, Mr. Skinner, I thank you; not an accident by any means—a wanton injury!"

I echoed his words with amazement.

"Yes. It is, however, less serious than it might have been, but for timely attention." He saw I looked curious, and proceeded. "I arrived at the castle last night unexpectedly, and unattended, save by my valet and groom. I regret I cannot say to my surprise, but certainly to my sorrow, I found the house lit up as if for a carnival. Some time elapsed before I obtained admission. The man who opened the door was a stranger, and far from sober, and soon I found that his fellows were in little better condition. They had helped themselves freely to the wine and dessert, of which the remains yet strewed the table and floor of the dining-room."

"Shameful!" I ejaculated, not knowing what else to say—the case was, as I well knew, so common.

"You may well say so, Mr. Skinner; it *was* shameful. But I wish I had seen nothing worse," said the young nobleman sadly. "On inquiring for Ghrimes, I was told that the old butler had been dead and buried a fortnight. The housekeeper, I ascertained, was in her room. I found Mrs. Trowbridge sitting by her fire crying bitterly. She threw up her hands in lamentation: 'Ah, my dear young master, what a house is this for you to come home to!' and then assured me her authority over the domestics was at an end, and whispered that she had retired to her room like a fox run to earth, for safety, lest interference should place her by the side of Ghrimes. I was too much annoyed at the time to take in the full import of her words; but, Mr. Skinner"—he looked full at me—"of what did Robert Ghrimes die?"

The question took me unawares. It was an awkward question to answer, under all circumstances. The butler's death, though not sudden, had been, to say the least, mysterious.

"Well, it was generally considered he had taken something that disagreed with him."

"Disagreed with him?"

I think his lordship saw the *equivoque*; he literally looked me through.

"Why was I not informed? A faithful servant is not to pass to the grave unheeded."

"No instructions," was my excuse; but I saw that did not satisfy him, and not caring still further to disturb his peace with my own vague suspicions of foul play, I recalled attention to his own hand.

"Ah, to be sure!" he ejaculated, roused from a fit of perplexed musing. "That was done in my own mother's drawing-room," and he heaved a deep sigh. "I found her surrounded by eighteen or twenty people she had entertained to dinner. And such people, good heavens! I know that scant feminine robes are not yet banished from aristocratic circles; but there! what paucity of bodice, paucity of sleeve, paucity of skirt, and airiness of material! I felt as if so many nude statues would have been more delicate. True, one or two of these *ladies* had gauzy-looking scarfs floating over their bare shoulders, but the majority seemed to think paint and patches ample covering for their charms. I had just left a pure, modest girl and a chaste matron in the peaceful sanctuary of their tasteful home, and the contrast struck me painfully."

"Miss and Mrs. Woodward," thought I to myself, though I merely bent my head to show I was listening.

"Of the men, some wore scarlet coats, buckskins, top-boots and spurs, just as they had come from the hunting-field, in marked contrast to the pumps, pantaloons, dress coats, frilled shirts, and white cravats of others. The room was well lighted with lamps and candelabra, and dotted with tables of all sizes, devoted to sets or couples of card players. At one of these sat Lady Matilda" (he did not say "my mother") "in a purple velvet dress, with a pile of guineas, and, I blush to say it, a glass of brandy-and-water close beside her. All the players were drinking, and the fumes of spirits struck my nostrils not less painfully than the rattling of dice and the jargon of quarrelsome gamesters did my ears. It was not a scene, sir, for a nobleman's mansion, and I no doubt expressed my indignation in strong terms."

"And no wonder, my lord," said I, though I added no word to expose the orgies in which those gambling dinner parties were wont to terminate. I should have done no good, and only added to his sense of degradation.

"At my first word of protest the inebriated partner of the countess jumped to his feet with a face scarlet as his coat, and threatened with foul oaths to horsewhip me for my interference."

"And you?" I asked, bending forward.

"I called a couple of servants and ordered the expulsion of the brute."

"Quite right. And then?"

"The room was in an uproar. My mother, livid with passion, and, I fear, not in a state to control her own actions, snatched her glass from the table and dashed it at me. It shivered on the hand I raised to protect my face."

I could not suppress a shudder.

"A tall dark man in a loose black robe had interposed to quell the riot. He was one of the few sober men in that disgraceful company. Though too late to prevent the injury, he did efficient service. He dismissed the company, called a dark, handsome, foreign-looking girl from the fireside, and as one having authority, put the countess under her charge; and, to my surprise, Lady Plainbury, though still quivering with excitement, submitted to be led to her chamber without a word."

"So I suppose."

The earl darted a quick glance at me, but did not interrupt his narration.

"This tall, thin individual—this man in authority—promptly produced a case of instruments, summoned Mrs. Trowbridge, extracted the broken glass from my hand, bathed and bound it; and, seeing me faint from loss of blood, administered a restorative as potent as his influence over her ladyship, and, so far, I am his debtor," said the earl, haughtily; "but"—and here he paused—"my business here to-day is not to lay bare our domestic sore, but to ask you, as Lady Plainbury's man of business, *who is* this Doctor Mendoza who was present at the reading of my dear father's will, who assumed the right to attend the countess in her illness, and exclude all but his own creatures, whom I find domiciled with his niece in the castle, exercising a subtle and mysterious power over every member of the household, and of whom Mrs. Trowbridge, with many dark hints, bade me beware lest I should share the fate of my lamented father and poor Ghrimes? Who *is* this man, and what can be the nature of his influence on our hearth?"

"I am as ignorant as your lordship," was my answer.

Whatever were my own private theories respecting the doctor, I did not think it wise to foster in Lord Lionel's mind suspicions which I felt it would be impossible to verify, and the incautious airing of which might lead to disastrous results.

I therefore made light of the old housekeeper's fears and warnings. Lord Lionel's death would only serve to dispossess the doctor's patroness and induct a stranger, so I assured him his life was in no manner of danger from malpractices. Of his *heart*

I was not quite so sure.

He smiled and said "*that* was in safe keeping," shook hands with me, and departed.

That was on the Tuesday.

On the Friday I saw him again.

"I came out for a drive," said he, "to shake off the fascination of a pair of black eyes, which seem to follow my movements and haunt me everywhere."

"Ah, ah, my lord, your heart is not so secure as you thought," was my light rejoinder; "but is it fair to ask who owns the bewitching black eyes?"

"No fear for my heart, Mr. Skinner," he replied; "neither black eyes nor blue can bewitch me. Still, I must own the doctor's niece Mizpah has a pair of orbs which dazzle me. I feel almost spell-bound within their range."

"Much, I should think, as a mouse under the eye of a cat, or a bird for which a snake has opened its jaws," suggested I, drily, as a sort of hint.

"Possibly," assented he, and I thought I was understood.

That afternoon's post bore a private letter to Mr. Stiff and another to Sir James Tarleton, with an intimation that the atmosphere of Plainbury Castle was not good for Plainbury's Earl.

Posts were slow things in those non-railway days, and I had reason to congratulate myself on my prevision and forethought, when on the following Monday Mrs. Trowbridge's grandson (a deep little fellow that), watching his opportunity to find me alone, handed me an incoherent note from the good housekeeper. It ran thus:

"For God's sake, Mr. Skinner, get our young lord out of this wicked house. They are drugging him or something to make him stupid, and marry that awful doctor's awful niece. I just feel as if the doctor was a devil and she was a witch. As for my lady, she is just under the doctor's finger and thumb. I think *you* can guess *why*. Do save Lord Lionel. He is too good to be the prey of these wretches."

CHAPTER II

A pretext was never wanting for a visit to the castle, and ceremony had been buried with the late earl.

I found Lord Lionel, the present earl, lying on a sofa, languid, listless, heavy, with the black-eyed Mizpah by his side singing seductive songs, and showing off a graceful figure as she accompanied herself on a guitar. Her dress was foreign, picturesque, and sufficiently modest to meet his fastidious taste. Neither the countess nor any of her guests were present.

I saw the danger of the situation, and broke in upon it.

"My lord, can I trouble you to step with me to Farmer Wilton's? The old man is in some difficulty respecting his daughter, your sometime nurse, and is anxious—if you will so far condescend—to see you."

This was partly a fiction, but the *ruse* was successful. In the fresh air, out of sight of those intense eyes, out of reach of doctor or mother, his frame and mind recovered its electricity. His hand was still in the sling; but I did not share his belief that loss of blood had made him languid and inert.

Again he observed to me the strange influence Mizpah's eyes possessed over him, and plainly said he thought Dr. Mendoza and his mother had laid their heads together to entrap him into a marriage with the girl. She was by no means the sort of woman he should love; but, somehow, when with her he was not himself; and no sooner did her eyes rest upon him than he felt as though he were her slave. And yet—and yet, his heart was far away.

"In Derbyshire?" I presumed.

"In Derbyshire," he assented, and the subject dropped.

The first dinner-bell rang before we returned to the castle. The countess graciously invited me to remain. Before the second course was served, a post-chaise and pair drove Sir James Tarleton to the front entrance, and I knew the young earl was safe.

Sir James tapped his snuff-box significantly, but no stray glance betrayed any intervention of mine. He, however, professed to be in hot haste, declined refreshments, and in less than an hour bore his ward away.

Six weeks later Lord Lionel was hastily summoned to the sick-bed of his mother. The Augean Stable was cleansed. Doubtful women and more doubtful men were gone. The castle was quiet; servants went about their business in an orderly manner, and the young fellow remarked to Mrs. Trowbridge that the change was most satisfactory.

Five days elapsed before he saw me, and then he seemed perplexed with doubt. I had gone to the castle to inquire after the health of the countess.

Half way down the beech avenue, on my way home, I met the earl; he turned and strolled with me as far as the gate. The air was laden with the perfume of hawthorn and lilac, freshened by a light breeze which had sprung up after a slight shower.

I noticed that he drew his hand across his forehead more than once, as if he would throw off some oppressive feeling.

"Has your lordship experienced any return of the languor which attended your last visit to Plainbury?" I asked carelessly.

He smiled.

"You are as great a necromancer as the grim man who hovers round my mother's bedside, and occupies the suite of rooms adjoining; the very apartments"—and I saw his hands clench nervously—"of my honoured father. Yes," he added, after a brief pause, "I came out into the fresh air to see if I could throw off the inertia which is fast creeping over me again."

"Has the glamour of Miss Mendoza's presence aught to do with it?" and I cast a sidelong glance at him as I spoke.

He crimsoned to the very brow.

"I fear so. And yet, sir, I am not in love with the girl, and would avoid her were it practicable. But we seem perpetually thrown together. Her large dark eyes look into mine, or follow me with the pathetic devotion of a dog's. I am called upon for little acts of courtesy which bring us into continual contact. Her thanks are spoken in low and seductive tones, and I somehow seem to lack strength to resist her blandishments. I am half mad with myself at my own weakness. In her presence I seem as if under the influence of some intoxication."

I know I looked grave. I took off my spectacles, and wiped them fidgetily.

"My lord," said I, respectfully, "I am a man of mature age, in whom your lamented father placed confidence. I thank you for yours. It removes from my tongue the embargo of disparity in position, and leaves me free to caution and advise. Be on your guard. Miss Mendoza plays for a coronet, and is a most consummate actress."

"I feel assured of it," was his response. "Nay, more, the countess is lavish in her praise; and her malady, whatever it may be, is evidently heightened by the morbid desire that I should make this Mizpah my wife."

"And you?"

"Mr. Skinner, I am already engaged to one whose artless purity forbids a thought of Miss Mendoza."

"I am glad to hear it, my lord. Has the countess been informed of your engagement?"

"She has not. I feared to irritate her, having Dr. Mendoza's assurance that any excitement might prove fatal."

"H'm!"

We had reached the extremity of the avenue. The lodge-keeper opened the gate to let us pass. I kept silent until we were beyond earshot.

"May I ask the nature of her ladyship's illness?"

"Indeed, sir, I am not sufficiently informed to tell you. I hear of inflammatory action, of heart and nerves and brain in a critical state, yet not all the perfumed flowers and pastiles in her chamber can overpower the smell of brandy, and Mrs. Trowbridge assures me her dietary is not that of an invalid."

"Yet she is dangerously ill?"

"So I am to understand." But his tones were not those of conviction.

"Are you satisfied with Dr. Mendoza's treatment?"

There was a sharp contraction of brow as he gave involuntary expression to a secret thought.

"As much satisfied as if his Satanic majesty were in his place!"

"I am not sure but he would be as safe an inmate," was my significant addendum, which called forth one of those rapid searching glances which showed him on the alert. "Perhaps, my lord, you would like to have the additional opinion of Dr. Overton? He is a reliable authority."

"Thanks for the suggestion. I will walk with you into the city and see him myself."

I observed that as we walked on his step and bearing regained its firmness and elasticity, his voice became stronger, his eyes less heavy. He confessed himself invigorated by the exercise.

Remembering Mrs. Trowbridge's troubled note, without a seeming purpose I elicited from him that Dr. Mendoza and his niece had a kindred passion for rare perfumes—that his sleeping-room was odorous with flowers of Miss Mendoza's selection; that the coffee she poured out at breakfast was delicious, and singularly exhilarating; that the cup she insisted on handing to him after dinner, though equally pleasant, had quite another effect: he grew dreamy, melancholy, and sentimental. I advised him to breakfast in his own room, on any plea he liked, to decline coffee after dinner, and to drink no wine the doctor or his niece did not patronize.

"This is a terrible implication, Mr. Sinner," said he.

"No matter; caution can do no harm. Dr. Mendoza is not to be trusted. By-the-by, is Sir James Tarleton aware of your presence here, my lord?" I asked, as we were parting at Dr. Overton's gate.

"I should think so. I wrote to him the day following my hasty arrival; though, strange to say, I have not yet had an answer."

"Indeed. I suppose your lordship's letters go in the general bag from the castle?"

"Certainly. How else?"

"Well—a—you see lawyers are instinctively cautious," I said; adding, drily, "I think Mrs. Trowbridge could find you a much surer conveyance."

He took the hint. Jim, Mrs. Trowbridge's grandson (a lad seemingly hanging at her heels for the sake of stale pastry and confections), became his courier and mine. But letters to Sir James and to the Rev. L. Woodward were on their way before the Earl of Plainbury and Dr. Overton stepped out of the latter's gig at the great door of the castle.

Dr. Overton confirmed my suspicions: Lady Plainbury was simulating illness. No woman who drank brandy as she did could be in perfect health; but all beyond this was feigned, for some occult purpose. And he held that Dr. Mendoza was in the plot. Nevertheless he put on an air of grave profundity, and expressed his perfect faith in Dr. Mendoza's skill—whilst within Dr. Mendoza's hearing. But as the latter, with his long-flying foreign black robes and sardonic face, hovered about the English practitioner from the time he entered the patient's room until he closed the carriage door upon him with his own lank long-nailed hand (looking, for all the world, like an evil spirit or a big black bird of ill omen), no chance of private word or sign to the anxious young earl could he get.

He paid two more visits to be similarly baffled.

I met him after the last on one of our many bridges, and being old friends, he confided his doubts to me.

Meanwhile, Mrs. Trowbridge, in obedience to my secret instructions, removed Miss Mendoza's too odorous flowers from the earl's chamber and dressing-room; prepared his breakfast and carried it to him with her own hands, and saw that no food was tampered with on its way to the dining-room. Her love for her young master made her vigilant, regardless of self.

For a day or two the earl was on his guard, but, unfortunately, Dr. Overton's timidity lulled his vigilance to sleep. Then, as I afterwards learned, some misunderstanding had grown up between himself and his distant betrothed, widening almost to a breach; and laying him dangerously open to the seeming devotion of an accomplished beauty close at hand. His mother, too, who apparently lingered in an alarming state, artful as when she spread her lures for his unsuspicious father, cajoled him with professions of penitence and piety, with sad regrets for a wasted life, interlarding all with sly insinuations that Mizpah had been her good angel, and the blessing she would be to a husband she loved, and so on; not failing to wind up with a self-depreciatory remark: "If I had my choice of a wife for you; as it is—ah, well, dear, I fear I must die without that satisfaction. Yet, Mizpah adores you, I know."

There was a constant harping on the same string in that shadowy perfumed chamber where a seemingly-dying mother lay, and his filial instincts were strong as his duty. There were music, and perfume, and the witchery of thrilling eyes and love-subdued tones in the drawing-room; and the earl was impressionable. There was an irritating something in the letter-bag every morning, and he had a spice of his mother's spirit. And then everywhere and all over was the subtle doctor—whether as a pervading influence or a palpable presence, with his winged black robes, keen eyes, his slant brows, incomprehensible smile, and few but well-weighed words.

Many a man has married a woman for whom he cared little, piqued by a slight from one for whom he cared much; and there is no knowing how far these combined influences might have worked upon the earl to conquer his resistance, had I not met Dr. Overton on the bridge when I did.

I took my way to the castle, ostensibly anxious about the countess. Jim, my swift-footed messenger, had preceded me. Instead of going round by the carriage road, I took a short cut through the woods. To my surprise I found that the woodman's axe had been busy there, many fine trees had been felled, and the number marked for destruction was incredible.

"H'm!" said I to myself. "What does this mean? A gambling debt? This must be put a stop to, my lady."

The pool where the late earl's body had been found lay on one side of the path, and strangely enough, without any appointment beyond notification of my intended route, the earl and I met on its brink. On all other sides the reedy pool was shut in by copsewood, pendant willows, and larger trees, whose over-reaching branches cast their green shadows on it even at noon.

His lordship was standing in deep thought, gazing into the depths of the sullen water, as if to penetrate its unfathomable secrets. He wore a bottle-green coat, and as the path wound, I did not see him until close upon him.

"A fearful place this to be brought to by a friend at midday," was his salutation to me.

"A still more fearful to be brought to by an enemy at midnight," was the retort I would fain have unspoken soon as said, he was so swift to take my hidden meaning.

"Mr. Skinner, you speak in parables. You seem to hold the clue to a terrible secret," said he, in much agitation.

"My lord," I answered, with a solemnity which attested my truth, "I hold no clue. I hold theories, suspicions, which some day will be at your service—not now."

He was urgent; I was firm. I had another purpose before me now. It required some little tact to break to him Dr. Overton's conviction that his own mother was partner in a nefarious plot, and was no more in a dying state than he or I, and still more to induce him to wait quiescent the arrival of the legal guardians. At first he was incredulous. "Why should a lady of high birth plot to wed him to an adventuress?"

"It is not always easy to trace the secret springs of action, but here is duplex thought. By your marriage with Miss Mendoza, the countess hopes to retain power, influence, and income *here*, which she would surely lose by your marriage with any other lady."

"I see," said he, with contracted brow.

"Then," and I paused, "the scheme is Dr. Mendoza's, and the countess acts under pressure."

"Pressure! What pressure?" and two fiery sparks seemed kindled in his eyes.

"Ah, my lord, that is part of the mystery which has hung over Plainbury Castle so long."

I had given him food for thought. If he looked miserable as he stood over the pool, he looked still more wretched as we emerged from the wood, and took separate paths to the castle, and I was at a loss to account for his very haggard countenance. I was not then aware of his estrangement from Miss Woodward.

As I passed the Crown Hotel on my way home I saw an elderly clergyman and a young lady alight from the northern stage coach. She wore a gipsy hat, trimmed with pale blue, a soft grey dress and blue velvet spencer, and I thought she had the sweetest face I ever beheld.

In the clergyman I recognized the rector of Darley-Dale; and before I could approach to make myself known, Sir James Tarleton came down the steps of the hotel, raised his hat with graceful courtesy, took her little hand in his, and said:

"Miss Woodward, I salute you."

I stepped forward and was introduced. We entered the hotel together. After a little light chat a chambermaid conducted Miss Woodward to her room, and we three sat in solemn conclave, previously despatching Boots with a summons to the earl. We compared notes. I related all that I knew, with a running commentary; and they related that which I did not know.

It appeared that the earl had been engaged to Miss Woodward

with the full consent of both guardians more than a year, and were on the point of marriage when he was called so hurriedly to a "dying mother."

Of course, he left abruptly, promising with all a lover's ardour to write daily, and exacting the same promise from Mabel. She wrote and he wrote, their letters of course crossing on the road. But his were so strange, and grew so cold, and then so flippant, every post brought only torture to the troubled girl. Then came an anonymous letter from a "well-wisher," whom she took to be Anne Wilton, telling her that Lord Lionel was making fierce love to a beautiful lady staying in the castle, and was likely to marry her; and was not worthy of Miss Woodward's affection.

But for the change in his own epistles this had been innocuous.

It was shortly followed by my communication, and the next post bore a confused incoherent epistle from the earl, accusing his true little love of inconstancy, perfidy, and no one knows what.

I had suggested possible tampering with letters, and this missive of his (the first posted by Jim) almost confirmed the suspicion.

They heard also from Sir James Tarleton, and at his wish Mr. Woodward, with his daughter, had joined him here to bring matters to a crisis.

We were at dinner when Lord Plainbury was announced.

We rose.

"Mabel!"

"Lionel!"

There was an impulsive rush towards each other, a pause, a stop midway—the meeting was painfully embarrassing to both.

We old people, however, soon cleared away the mist, and dismissing them to an inner room to feast on love and kisses, resumed our dinner and laid out our plans.

At five o'clock I took Miss Mabel under my wing to show her our ancient city, whilst the three others whirled away to Plainbury Castle in Sir James's barouche, taking up Dr. Overton on their way, and avoiding the main entrance both to park and castle.

Lodge-keepers and porters opened their eyes wide as the gates and doors; but they alighted, and allowing no time for signals, hastened to the "sick chamber" swiftly but silently.

The earl was not expected home until nightfall. It was his habit to knock. Now he turned the handle and threw open the door.

My lady, jolly and comfortable, sat in a loose *negligé*, with wine and cards before her, at a small table. Dr. Mendoza was her partner. Her face was flushed and merry. She was winning. A laugh and an oath were arrested on her lips by the sudden opening of the door. Picture her consternation!

Miss Mendoza looked up from her tambour frame by the window, and a cloud, as of night, settled on her brow.

Even Dr. Mendoza was, for the once, disconcerted.

The interview was brief, stormy, but decisive.

Sir James, stepping forward, said, with a low brow of mock courtesy:

"Permit me to congratulate your ladyship on your speedy recovery."

She started to her feet in a fury, grasped a decanter by the neck, and would have hurled it at the baronet, but Dr. Mendoza clutched her wrist with one of his claws, and forcing it from her held her in her seat with a whispered "Be calm; you vill ruins all!"

But calm she was not; and her rage found vent in language not to be repeated. Dr. Mendoza simply watched, and glowered on the intruders.

At the first lull, the earl, with a face white with agony and shame (for the mother lost to shame), and a voice tremulous with agitation, said, with deliberation:

"Madam, you are anxious that I should marry. I am perfectly willing. My guardians are also agreeable."

Miss Mendoza flushed. The countess looked as if she felt she had been too precipitate.

He continued, and not a syllable was lost:

"This is Saturday. On Monday I propose to marry Miss Mabel Woodward, a young lady whose modest worth I know, and whose love I can trust. You can hand these forgeries to your protégée, at leisure;" and he laid a packet of letters on the table.

Again Sir James spoke.

"With our ward's marriage your ladyship's domain here ceases. He will wish to bring his bride home immediately. You will therefore retire to your dower house."

Her ladyship's eyes blazed with ferocity.

"Retire! Make way for that parson's brat! By——I will not, if a legion of devils come to drive me forth!"

But it is not pleasant to follow her ravings or her threats. It was not pleasant to look on the dark mocking faces at her elbows.

The next morning being Sunday, Miss Woodward and her father attended the cathedral service, sitting with the earl.

From my seat I saw them enter, her gipsy hat and muslin dress bringing a sense of freshness and purity with them long unknown to the Plainbury pew.

"From battle, and murder, and sudden death"——

The verger whispered me—

"Wanted, sir, outside."

A groom was in waiting with a led horse. He touched his cap.

"My lady wants you, sir, immediate."

I was ushered without ceremony into her ladyship's chamber, where I found her in bed, playing ecarté with Dr. Mendoza.

I had a thorough repugnance to this man, who always seemed to me like some foul bird of prey, and felt a shudder as I saw his claws on the cards and the counterpane.

Though it was barely noon, the countess was inflamed with wine. He was as ever—sober, wary, and watchful.

It was some time before I could ascertain wherefore I had been called; and on the Sabbath too. Her ladyship wished me to draught out her will; but between brandy and cards (in which she wanted me to join) hours elapsed before her instructions were complete. Dr. Mendoza, to my annoyance, sat with his eyes on her face as she dictated. She gave and devised all moneys of which she might die possessed to her dear friend Dr. Mendoza, all landed property or buildings not entailed to him, with reversion to his niece, to whom she also bequeathed her private jewels, plate, &c. I was to have the will ready for signature on the morrow.

The sun was setting as I shook hands with Mrs. Trowbridge at the hall door. Dusk was gathering as I passed the lodge gates at the end of the long avenue, deepening with every step I took. Shadowed by umbrageous trees, I went on absorbed in thought. As I turned a corner beyond the limits of the park, rapid hoof beats caused me to look up.

The sky was red, angrily red.

"The castle is on fire!"

It was Lord Plainbury who called to me through the gloom below, as he and Sir James rushed past at a gallop.

I hastened back, followed by eager crowds from the city, to render what aid I could; but the flames, which had broken out in the chamber of the countess, held their own, and rendered little back but blackened stone and charred timber.

Pictures and other valuables had been rescued; but the countess and Dr. Mendoza were both missing. One of the servants had seen him flying as with expanded wings along a burning corridor with a burden in his arms; and hence a rumour spread that he was the Evil One, to whom Lady Plainbury had sold her soul, and that he had carried her off at last. Miss Mendoza disappeared mysteriously the following day, and then, not unnaturally, she was set down by the vulgar as a witch.

How had the fire originated? The countess was still in bed when I left, half stupid with brandy. A servant who had borne candles to the room swore to a violent altercation between Mendoza and his lady, followed by a scream, only disregarded because so common. Had draperies or counterpane been set alight by accident, or had the man murdered her and set fire to the bed to hide the crime? The will I had draughted made that doubtful. In any case the bed was utterly consumed, and not even a charred cinder remained of the wicked beauty.

But there had been a depredator at work—half-consumed cabinets, locked and sealed, had been forced open: were empty, of course. And before news of the fire reached London, a tall, dark man, presented a cheque for many thousand pounds at her ladyship's bankers. Her gambling proclivities being known, it was cashed at once. The cheque was a forgery. The man gone.

Then I laid my theories before Sir James and the young earl, to remove the reproach of suicide from his father's memory. I maintained that after the signature of the late earl's first will, the countess and Mendoza had compassed his death to get possession and control; that the villain had stupefied him with narcotics, in that state plunged him in the pool, and so inquiry was baffled;

that he held some inculpatory agreement *in terrorem* over her; and that Ghrimes had overheard something which made *his* removal necessary to their safety.

Still, these were but theories, and they did not prevent the restoration of the castle, or a very happy bridal there in the autumn. But the Plainbury Mystery remains a mystery to this day.

APPENDIX

It has been hitherto a point of honour with me, wherever possible to indicate the source of my inspiration, as a matter of truth and justice; and though I have been met with the argument that "readers of fiction do not care a button for the underlying fact," I know there are readers who think as I do on this head, and for those few I adhere to the plan I laid down for this cheap edition, a plan for which I have the exemplary precedent of that great master of romance, Sir Walter Scott. And as I have in some cases laid history under contribution, I feel I have no right to appropriate others' property as my own.

A WORLD BETWEEN—Some few years since, my friend Mr. S. P—— was intimate with a young German student, who, on the emigration of his parents to Australia, went to reside with an aunt. Her house was so situated at the junction of two rivers (in Silesia) as to be cut off like an island from outer communications during any heavy flood. At one of these times, when he was utterly absorbed in his studies (carried on in an upper room overlooking a waste of waters), he was startled by the report of a pistol, and the whiz of a bullet past his ear. He rushed to the window, expecting to find it shattered. The window was intact, and neither boat nor human being was to be seen. His aunt below had heard nothing, seen no one; they were the only living creatures on the isolated premises. In due course a mournful letter reached them from Australia. His father had shot himself just as they reached the port, and at an hour coincident with the mysterious report the young man had heard. His name and address were communicated to me, but I unfortunately lost the note-book in which it was jotted down.

THE PRIDE OF THE CORBYNS—A West Indian friend who described to me the mausoleum said to be the scene of midnight disturbance and consequent terror such as I have portrayed, did so as a verity of which he had not the slightest doubt. The intrusion of alien dead is a motive the potency of which can scarcely be understood at this time, and in England. The two hurricanes which I attempt to describe are matters of Barbadian history. The family names those of early settlers.

WRAITH-HAUNTED—There may be persons yet living in Manchester who remember Mrs. Carson, my mother's sister. She was recalled from Bristol in the supernatural manner I recount, and with the same result. Where she met Mr. Carson I cannot say; he died suddenly, was married and buried in one week; but *his* wraith is *my* invention. In No. 13—or 18—Oldham-street, Manchester, occurred the other incident I have added, to which Mrs. Carson's sisters bore testimony. The person injured by the broken foil was a young foreigner visiting at the house. The little child who went upstairs with her mother, when the white figure passed them, became in due time my mother.

THE PIPER'S GHOST—There was a legend attached to the Old Gaol on Elvet Bridge, Durham, which was taken down in 1821, that the gaol and its precincts were haunted by the ghost of a Scotch piper, who had died within its walls after long confinement there. On this I based my story, pressing history into my service.

ST. CUTHBERT'S CUP—The vase which I have so designated was to be seen in the British Museum at the time this tale was written, and may be there still. The convulsion of nature which occurred in 1179, and resulted in the formation of the sulphurous pools known as Hell-kettles, has been put on record by Hutchinson and other local historians. I beg Sir William de Turp's pardon if he was a better man than I have shown him. Query: Was the "Jew of York," to whom Eustace-de-Eden stood indebted, the prototype of Sir Walter Scott's "Isaac of York?"

THE FAIRIES' CRADLE—In Surtees' "Hist. of Durham" may be found described "the remarkable tumulus, at the top of which is the small oblong hollow called the Fairies' Cradle," which "little green mound has always been sacred from the plough." We are there also told that the Hetton fairies "spoke with a voice remarkably small and shrill." In Lilly's "Life and Times" we are informed that "neatness and cleanliness in apparel, a strict diet, an upright life and fervent prayer, conduce much to the assistance of those curious in these ways," *id est*, to hold intercourse with fairies. Is it necessary to say respecting Lady Bell and her knightly brothers, "these things are an allegory," or that the Lady Bell typifies the verdant surface of the land, Sir Plumbius the lead of Weardale, Sir Ferris the iron of Cleveland, Sir Carbo the coal of Hetton and elsewhere? I may say that very sober Northern chroniclers tell how Mary, the daughter and heiress of Henry-le-Spring, married Rowland, son of Hervey Bellasyse, and became in her right Lord of Houghton. And how the Shevalds, headed by John de Weardale, came down on John-le-Spring, and murdered him in the arms of his leman in their bower, with other matter pertaining, even to the "sweating and groaning" of the buried Sir John's statue and armour. But the items are diverse and lie far apart, and those who are not "curious in these ways" may be content to take my piece of patchwork, stitched together by my thread of fiction, just for what it is worth.

MY WILL—The main features of this sketch, namely, the fraudulent will and the dream, with its warning refrain, through which the fraud was detected in time, reached me from the solicitor who had to take the case in hand.

JUDGMENT DEFERRED—Respecting this story, which is wholly imaginative, I have only to observe that a bite from an infuriated dog or cat may convey the virus hydrophobia without the animal being itself in a state of hydrophobia; and that the virus has been known to linger in the veins for many years before madness ensued.

A DOUR WEIRD—Amongst the "Annals of the Poor," published in "Chambers' Tracts" very many years ago, was given the succinct outline of "Auld Susan's" history, as that of "a poor widow." I have used it as a peg whereon to hang several old North-country superstitions, and for the introduction of Margery Grant, the Scottish spae-wife, who was during her lifetime well known on the borders. If I have made my Susan the recipient of a tardy pension, which the real Susan did not obtain, am I to blame her or George the Third's advisers?

THE WHITE WOMAN OF SLAITH—There is, on the North-east Coast, a belief still current amongst the fisher-folk in a misty white woman who touches the boats foredoomed to wreck. And on the Northumbrian Coast is a fishing station with a name similar to the one I have adopted, which is perched upon the rocks, and looks down on a sea-washed beach where the original village stood, until it was swept away in one night of terrible storm and devastation.

LARRY'S APPRENTICESHIP—Had Margaret's literary powers been equal to her belief in the leprechaun her grandfather saw sitting on a stile as he was taking a cow to market, or in the fairies for whom he manufactured a coffin, such might have been her vision of "how the McCanns became carpenters."

A NEW LEAF—A young person named L. J—— informed me that her mother and aunt, when young women, were sitting by the fire at night waiting the return of their grandmother, who had gone out after angry words with L. J——'s aunt, when she was suddenly startled by the appearance of her grandmother, with bonnet crushed, shawl awry, and face streaked with blood. She had slipped and been killed at that moment on a step glazed over with frozen rain. This, however, occurred in Essex, not Lancashire. But I remember a Sunday night, in either 1835 or 1836, when a number of serious accidents occurred to persons leaving places of worship in and around Manchester, who so stepped out on unseen and unexpected ice.

THE PLAINBURY MYSTERY—The Countess, her fate, and the rumours thereupon, are not wholly suppositious.

ISABELLA BANKS

www.ingramcontent.com/pod-product-compliance
Lightning Source LLC
Chambersburg PA
CBHW020931310726
48980CB00007B/727/J

* 9 7 8 1 7 3 9 3 9 2 1 3 0 *